© 2025 Kristy Pearson. All rights reserved.

This work is protected by the Australian Copyright Act 1968. Unauthorized reproduction or distribution is prohibited.

This book contains scenes of graphic violence, abuse, electrocution, bullying, torture, sexually explicit scenes, shifting, mutilation and death.

If you are sensitive to these subjects, please consider your personal mental health before continuing.

Part 1

A Land
Of
Moonlit Dreams

Written by Kristy Pearson

For Tyler Posey and Tyler Hoechlin.

Thank you for getting my young heart racing, and for helping me dream up my very own sexy werewolf.

For Cody Saintgnue. Thank you for being my visual embodiment of Gunner.

Chapter

One

Zelena

I lifted my head slightly as the cool breeze brushed against my neck. My long raven hair waved gently with the breeze. It was a glorious morning, the air was still fresh and there wasn't a cloud in the sky. The sun felt warm on my face as it struggled to shine through the trees. There is something about being outside alone that I have always loved. Most people around here are afraid of the forest, they don't go near it. Me on the other hand, I love the forest. The sound of the wind in the trees, the feel of fresh air on my skin, and the faint smell of salt water. It makes me feel like, I don't know, free, I guess. I relish the time I get to spend outdoors, however short it is.

I live in a little fishing town in the far north of Cape Breton Island, Nova Scotia, population of around two thousand people. The town's inhabitants are spread roughly twenty kilometres along the coast, there's the sea on one side, and a thick forest on the other. We're a little isolated, but that's how the locals like it. People in this town have lived here for generations, they never leave, and the ones who are lucky enough to get out, they don't come back. The little town has all the basic necessities and people can usually find what they need in one of the few small stores. For what they can't get, they make the trip to one of the bigger cities, if you can even call them that. Not that I have ever been, I have never left the island.

This short walk through the trees each day on my way to school was my only solace in my otherwise hellish existence. I would take short steps, slow, delayed steps, as if to make each passing second in the open air last longer. There are only a few weeks left of my last year of school and although every second of the last twelve years has been hell on earth, I shudder to think what will happen when it's all over.

As I got to the black cast iron gates of the school, my small sense of freedom withered away. I looked at the dark brick walls and small windows and sighed, it was a prison. I pulled my hood up over my face, put my head down, and made my way to the entrance. I pushed the heavy door open and puffed out a breath of relief, at least the hall was still empty. The majority of the other students were still in the car park, standing around and chatting with their friends until the bell rings. But not me, I prefer to go straight to my locker, shove my bag inside, and wait at the door of my first class. If I get there before the halls fill up, I can usually avoid most of the morning abuse. Watching the kids marching through the hallways, I often let my mind wander a little, thinking about what it could be like to have friends to stand around and chat with. It would probably be nice to have at least one friend in this shithole.

I lingered at my locker this morning, recounting the events of last night's beating. I closed my eyes and listened to my body. The parts of my shirt that stuck to the raw lashes on my back stung with each slight movement. The broken skin felt hot and tight under my clothes. The gash on my forehead was still throbbing, causing a headache to spread from my hairline and down to behind my ear. I did my best to cover it with makeup, but the foundation burned when I tried to rub it into the open wound. So, I stuck a band-aid over it instead. The band-aid was plain skin colour anyway, so it should blend in with my face okay. My dark, messy hair could sit across most of my face and my hoodie would cover the rest.

I suddenly became aware of the increased noise in the hallway behind me. The other kids had started coming in. Damn it. I quickly closed my locker, bowed my head, and started down the hallway to my first class. I quickly turned the corner and smashed face first into something hard. I fell backward into the middle of the hallway, dropping my books as I tried to catch myself. The hall fell silent as I lay on my aching back, sprawled out on the floor. I clenched my eyes together, the pain spewing from my wounds was almost enough to make me gag.

"What a loser" I heard Demi snicker as she burst out laughing. the rest of the people in the hallway quickly joined in. I scurried onto my hands and knees, trying to gather my belongings in order to make my escape.

I reached for my notebook, but it wasn't on the ground anymore. As I looked around for it, I froze. He was crouched down in front of me, his knees showing through his dark ripped jeans. I felt like I could feel the warmth radiating off him. He was not two feet away from me. I could smell him, his sweet sweat smelled like the air on a hot summer day. I breathed him in. Who is this?

"Sorry, is this yours?" he asked as he held out his arm with my book in his hand. His voice was soothing and velvety, smooth with a low rumble to it.

I snatched my book from his grip and began to stand up. I felt his big hands grab my shoulders and pull me upwards. The shock of his touch sent me falling back to the ground. I closed my eyes tight, turned my head into my arm, and waited for him to hit me. The laughter in the hallway erupted again.

"Whoa" the mystery boy gasped as I cowered from him.

"She's such a fucking freak" Demi cackled.

The pain I expected never came, he didn't hit me, no one did. I peered out from under my hoodie as a tear rolled down my cheek. He had taken a step back, holding out his arms to pull with him the other kids who had gathered around to laugh at me.

I sat there for a moment on the cold floor, taking in this boy. I had never seen him at school before. His dark brown boots were unlaced and very worn in, his ripped jeans hugged his hips. He had on a faded grey t-shirt with a red W printed on it. It hung loosely over his belt but clung to his muscular chest. He was tall. Very tall. He stood high above all of the other students behind him. I examined his arms which were still outstretched beside him. His sleeves hugged his bulging biceps. I looked at his face, his jaw was smooth and strong, his pink lips pursed together. His dark sandy blonde hair sat perfectly atop his head, short on the sides and long on the top. His bright blue eyes were staring at me with a frightening intensity. He was mesmerising, something of an ancient Greek God. Butterflies burst into my stomach and danced around. I began to feel hot and nervous as I looked at this beautiful being. Wow. He tilted his head slightly to the side and examined me. Shit! He could tell I was looking at him. I jumped up from the ground and ran, ducking my way through the crowd of laughing teens.

I got to my English class and hurried to my seat in the back corner of the room. I put my books on the desk and then curled myself into my seat. Wiping the tears from my cheek, I whispered to myself 'I hate this place'. I rested my head on my folded arms and replayed the event in the hallway. I've never been interested in boyfriends or dating, but something about this new boy had my stomach doing backflips.

"Class" the teacher called out as she stepped into the room,

"These are two of our new students, Cole and Peter".

I lifted my head, just enough to see the new kids, and I reared back slightly. Holy heck, they were gods too. The first one, the taller one, had dark brown hair, smooth cream skin, with slim toned muscles. His dark eyes were staring in my direction from across the class. The second one was a little shorter with dark red hair, tanned skin, and glowing green eyes, eyes that were also staring in my direction. I lowered my head again and huffed. Why on earth would these gorgeous specimens be looking at me? I'm just a dirty and broken rag doll.

"Boys, take a seat please" the teacher cooed.

The two boys made their way to the back of the class. I could feel the shift in the atmosphere of the room, and I had no doubt that each set of female eyes followed them as they walked. The tall one sat at the desk next to me, the other sat in front of me. The boy in front turned to face me, his head angled down, trying to see my face from under my hoodie. Probably just want to get a look at the hideous beast that caused all that drama in the hall this morning.

"Hey, I'm Cole" whispered the boy beside me. His voice had a somewhat calming but sceptical tone. He pointed to the desk in front of me,

"That's Peter, but everyone calls him Smith" the boy, Cole, said. The boy sitting there gave a crooked grin and wiggled his fingers at me. At first glance, he at least looks nice, but they usually all start out that way.

I awkwardly nodded at them and lowered my head again, keeping my eyes on them the best I could. I don't like this, I don't trust this show of friendliness. They both looked at each other and shrugged, turning their bodies to the front of the class. I could feel my panic building, what did they want? Why were they talking to me? It's just a joke, it has to be. They are going to be like every other asshole in this place and bully me, just like everyone else does. There is no reason for them to be nice to me, so it must be a trick.

As class continued, the presence of the two new boys made me uncomfortable. I squirmed in my seat as their closeness to me began to feel like it was shrinking by the second. Finally, the first morning bell rang, and the students started getting up and walking out the door. Cole and Smith both stood in front of my desk, blocking my exit. I was cornered and alone, everyone else had left the room already. Right away I knew this had to mean trouble, and I sank myself lower into my seat, preparing myself for their incoming attack.

"Do you think me and my friends can sit with you at lunch?" Cole asked, peering down at me with his head tilted to the side. I lifted my head slightly to gauge his facial expression. He didn't seem malicious, it didn't look like he was joking. But I shook my head anyway, I don't trust them. I don't trust anyone.

"Well, okay, I guess we'll see you later then" said Cole overly cheerfully, then he turned and headed for the door with Smith on his heels.

"Hey, what's your name anyway?" Smith called back to me from the front of the class, I lifted my head to look at him, surprised. Both he and Cole were standing by the door looking at me, waiting.

Why would he care what my name is? It's not like we're going to be friends or anything, why would boys like that be interested in being friends with a beast like me? I was confused and unsure, was this just another trick, some sort of mind game to gather information? I paused, considering all the thoughts swirling through my head. But I figured they have been nice to me so far. Nicer than anyone else has ever been. What's the harm in letting them know my name? I got up out of my chair and stood next to my desk, with my head still lowered and my arms crossed in front of my body clutching my books.

"It's Zelena" I whispered with a croak.

The two boys looked at each other wide eyed. They looked back at me and smiled.

"Nice to meet you, Zelena" said Cole as he nodded his head and walked out the door.

Smith continued to smile as he lifted his hand and wiggled his fingers at me again, then turned and walked out the door after Cole.

Once I was alone, I puffed out a breath that I didn't realise I was holding. I stood there for a moment, placing my hand on my desk to steady myself. What the heck was that about? My head was pounding and my breath was shaky. I put my other hand to my chest, my heart was thumping hard and fast. I felt dizzy and nauseous. I'm just hungry, I thought, I didn't eat this morning. I rushed off to my next class, zipping through the other kids in the hall. I got to the door and went straight in and to my seat, everyone else was already seated. I put my arms up on the desk and rested my head in my hands and started to daydream about the beautiful man in the hallway.

The lunch bell rang, snapping me out of my daze. Once all the other kids had left and the hallway seemed quieter, I headed out of the classroom towards the cafeteria. I walked through the doors and went to grab my tray, thank God for meal vouchers. The rest of the school was already seated at their tables, talking and catching up on the happenings of the weekend. I took my food and slowly made my way to my usual seat by the rubbish bins. I bit into my apple, keeping my head down. The room was full of noise and laughter amongst the few groups of friends.

Demi and her minions sat at the table next to the footballers. Demi was your typical mean girl. She was beautiful and stylish, with long wavy blonde hair that bounced down her back and flawless bright skin. She was the kind of girl that all the guys wanted, and all the girls wanted to be. She would prance down the hall with her short skirts and high heels, as everyone else stepped out of her way. You would never catch me in clothes so short and tight, no one would want to see that anyway.

My little daydream was broken when my orange juice suddenly tipped all over me, spilling down my stomach and over my lap. I looked at my tray and saw that someone had thrown a half-eaten slice of pizza at me. Lifting my head, I saw Demi flick her hair over her shoulder laughing and high-fiving her followers. One of the jocks, Brian, was standing on the table pointing at me and laughing.

"What happened, Snow White, did someone have an accident?" he laughed as he jumped off the table and onto the back of one of his bros, his face turning red from his laughter. I felt the eyes of the entire school on me as I sat alone at my table with orange juice dripping onto my legs. I looked down at my clothes and my plate of mushy food. I turned my head to look at the exit and saw at the table by the door were the new boys, Cole and Smith, sitting with the mystery Greek God from the hallway. None of them were laughing. Cole was glaring at Demi with hatred in his eyes. Smith was looking between Demi's table and his tray of food, furiously stabbing at his plate with his fork. The mystery man was looking at me. A look of deep hurt and sadness covered his face. His gaze followed me as I got up from my table and walked to the exit.

"Bye Bitch" I heard Demi call as I pushed the doors open and walked through. I went to my locker to get my spare clothes. I know now from experience to keep a change of clothes at school, for those times that Demi is feeling extra cruel. I was pulling my jumper out of my bag when I heard a voice.

"Are you okay?" It was that same smooth and velvety voice that I had been daydreaming about all day. It was deep and demanding and left me with a warmth that spread through my chest.

I peered out from behind my locker door. Oh my God, it was him. I took a deep breath and that smell hit me. Hot air on a summer day, delicious. A lump grew in my throat, and I thought I might faint. I quickly dropped my head, I didn't want him to see my horrendous face. I nodded softly. He lifted his hand and placed it over the top of my own, the one that was gripping the locker door. Feeling terrified, I quickly dropped my hand, sliding it out from under his, slicing my palm open on the corner of the door as I did. I hissed and scrunched my nose at the small pinching pain.

"Sorry, sorry I didn't mean to scare you" he quickly spluttered as he took a small step back.

I grabbed my hand and lifted it to my face to investigate the damage.

"Oh shit, your hand" he said as he stepped forward grabbing both my hands in his, forcing me to drop my jumper.

I looked at him with terror at the thought of what he might do. He must think I'm such an idiot for cutting myself, surely it made him mad too. My eyes were wide with anticipation, waiting for my punishment. I froze, and my body stiffened, waiting expectedly. He looked at my face and must have seen the terror in my expression. He gently and slowly let go of my hands, a move that surprised me.

"Sorry" he said as he slowly raised his hands in surrender.

"I didn't mean to hurt you".

Hurt me? He didn't mean to hurt me. I did that to myself, it was all my fault, why would he be sorry. I looked at him curiously as I held my hurt hand to my chest.

"Will you let me help you?" he asked me softly, still holding his hands out.

I didn't understand. I am a monster compared to this beautiful being. Why would he care, why would he want to help me? I nodded again slowly. He held out his hand toward me, gesturing for me to take it. I pulled away turning my body away from him. He dropped his hand and looked at me with sadness and confusion. My own confusion was ebbing its way into my brain, why the heck would this boy care anyway?

"That's okay" he said softly, bending over to pick up my spare jumper.

"Follow me" he turned around and started walking slowly down the hall. He paused and looked back at me to see if I was following. He smiled. A big toothy grin that covered the bottom half of his face. Oh my goodness, that smile. Everything inside me melted. My fear and panic just slipped away. I felt warm and fuzzy inside. I felt safe. I nodded again and closed my locker. I trailed off behind him as he led me to his locker in the next hall. He looked at me again and smiled. I dropped my head letting my hair fall over my face. He opened his locker and pulled out a greyish blue bandanna, holding it up for me to see.

"May I?" he asked, gesturing to my hand that I was still holding up to my chest. I looked down at my hand and looked at the bandanna. I glanced up at his face, he was still smiling. So, I nodded and held out my hand. He slowly placed my jumper over my shoulder and I resisted the urge to flinch at his movements, then he carefully began to wrap his bandanna around the cut on my hand.

If only he knew how insignificant this tiny cut is. If only he knew the thrashings and lashings that I get at home. This small little cut is nothing. I have scars and slashes all over my back and stomach from beatings way worse than this tiny little scratch. If only he knew. But I have never had someone offer to help me before, I've never had someone even be remotely nice to me before. Why do I feel so comfortable with his hands on mine? I've never liked being touched, though I've never had someone touch me so soft and gently, not like this.

He tied the ends of the bandanna together to keep it from coming off. I let my hand rest in the palm of his hand. It looked so tiny sitting there like that. I looked so tiny standing next to him. I've always been small framed, but that could just come down to being malnourished. I like to think that I'm a little like my mother, but I don't remember what she looks like, so I wouldn't know for sure. I could feel his eyes on me as I stared at our hands together. He gently rubbed his thumb on the back of my hand. It all felt so intimate. My body relaxed and that same warmth I felt before spread through my arms and legs. I still didn't completely understand it. Why would anyone who looks like him, care about someone like me?

The surprise of the bell ringing made me jump. I pulled my hand from his and crossed my arms in front of my body. The hallway got louder as people started making their way to their next class. "Gunner, we gotta go" I heard Cole say behind the big, beautiful man. I glanced around his massive frame and saw both Cole and Smith were standing there. I hadn't even noticed them there before. Were they there the whole time, did they see my stupid clumsy accident? Oh, how embarrassing. The beautiful boy crouched down slightly to be closer to my face and whispered loud enough for me to hear over the noise of the hallway,

"My name's Gunner" he said. I leaned back a little, scared of his sudden closeness to me. He stood up straight again and tilted his head to the side slightly.

"Can I see you after school?"

No. This is just a dream, surely it is. Maybe that beating last night was worse than I thought. Maybe I'm unconscious on the basement floor and this is all just happening in my head. There is no way on earth that this person wants to spend time with me. Not me. No way. I shook my head a little, not looking at his face.

"Hmph" he groaned unmoving,
"I'll see you later" he said confidently and then he turned and walked away.

I leaned back on the locker behind me and tried to catch a breath. As he disappeared from view, I could feel the same lonely darkness creep back into my chest. I quickly changed out my jumpers, shoving the sticky juice soaked one back into my locker, then I put my head down and shuffled off to my next class.

The rest of the day dragged on and on. After what felt like days, the final bell rang at last. As usual, I very slowly gathered my things, waiting for the majority of the kids to clear out before I made my way to my locker. The longer I wait the fewer people I have to see. And I like it that way.

I walked out the doors and there he was. Gunner. Leaning against the fence, arms crossed in front of him, and one knee bent up with his foot resting on the fence. Ugh, he is perfection. He was laughing and talking with Cole and Smith. Jeez, they were inseparable. What were they still doing here anyway? Everyone else had gone already. So, what were they waiting for?

Gunner turned his head and saw me at the door. He quickly stood up off the fence and turned to face me with a half-smile across his face. Cole and Smith were looking at me as well. Smith was again doing his wiggle finger wave. I bowed my head and headed for the gate.

"Hey Zelena" Smith called out in a sing-song voice. I glanced up and saw Cole elbow him in the ribs, Smith looked at him and mouthed 'what'.

I put my head back down and continued for the gate.

"Hey there" smirked Gunner,
"I thought we might walk you home" he said nodding to his friends behind him.

Why would they want to walk me home? Are they just trying to get me alone so they can attack me? I started to feel a little scared and confused. Why were they showing me so much attention? The three boys stood by the gate looking at me intently, waiting for me to respond.

"W-why?" I questioned quietly.

"Well, because it would be a good chance for us to talk" Gunner responded without hesitation. What would we have to talk about, we are nothing alike and I doubt we have anything in common.

"Why would you want to talk to me?" I asked assertively.

Gunner tilted his head to the side, a confused look spread across his face.

"You're beautiful, Zelena, why wouldn't I want to talk to a beautiful girl?".

I scoffed quietly at his remark. What on earth is he talking about? I'm not beautiful, I'm broken. He is either playing some kind of game, or he's blind.

"I'm not beautiful, I'm an ugly swamp monster" I whispered with a hint of disdain in my tone. I dropped my head, letting my hair cover my face and I crossed my arms with a slouch to my shoulders.

Smith let out a giggle and Gunner snapped his head around and growled a deep ferocious growl, the kind an animal would make. I've never heard a human growl like that before, it was strange, to say the least.

"What?" Smith squeaked, throwing his hands in the air,

"She's funny" he chuckled. Cole hit him over the back of the head and Gunner huffed at him, turning his gaze back to me.

"Don't ever say that about yourself again" Gunner said as he leaned forward, crouching down so that his face was in line with mine.

"You, Zelena, are breathtaking".

My insides melted, and my knees felt weak under my tiny frame. I stumbled back a bit as I was caught off guard by his intensity and warmth. He quickly stood up straight and stepped back away from me. I looked up at him, his brilliant blue eyes still set on mine. I must be out of my damn mind.

"Okay" I said as I zigzagged through the giant boys and out the gate. The three boys followed closely behind me.

We were walking through the forest, taking my usual route home. Gunner was walking next to me, Cole and Smith were just behind us.

"So, tell me about yourself" Gunner said with a smile. I shook my head a little, not looking up at him.

"Not a big talker, are you?" he asked, and I shook my head again.

"This is going great so far" I heard Smith whisper to Cole,

"Shut up" Cole whispered back. I don't think they knew I could hear them. Gunner growled out of the corner of his mouth at them. I looked up at him and he quickly smiled back at me. I glanced behind me, and Cole and Smith were behind us, close but definitely not close enough to hear them whisper. Weird.

"You lived here long?" Gunner asked,

"As long as I can remember"

"Wow ay, you've never lived anywhere else then?"

"No" I shrugged

"So why are you so quiet at school?" he looked down at me, waiting for me to answer.

"I, I um, I-I just don't fit in there" I mumbled. He was quiet for a minute as we kept walking slowly.

"That Demi sure is a piece of work".

I huffed at him, of course he thinks she's gorgeous, why wouldn't he. So that's why he is talking to me, he thinks that messing with me is going to somehow impress Demi.

"Yeah, a right piece of shit" Cole yelled out from behind us. He and Smith laughed and nudged each other. I looked up at Gunner, he was laughing too. Wait, so he doesn't like Demi then? He looked down at me and our eyes met for a second. I felt butterflies in my stomach and a burning in my chest. I've never had a crush before, is this what a crush feels like? He smiled at me and his blue eyes sparkled. I felt a tingle run through my body. From my toes to my fingers, up and down my arms and legs. It was like hot needles were poking into my spine and a pang of fiery pain hit me in the chest, knocking the wind out of me. I stopped walking and grabbed at my chest leaning forward. What was happening to me?

"Whoa, Zee, are you okay?" Gunner had knelt down in front of me, his hands were on my shoulders. Did he call me Zee? Did he just give me a nickname? Holy shit the pain!

"Zelena, what's wrong?" he asked again, his voice was shaking, like he was scared or something. He couldn't possibly be worried about me, he doesn't even know me.

"What's going on" I heard Cole next to me, I felt his hands grab around my waist and I winced from the contact. Gunner lifted his head and growled at him, what's with this guy and growling? It worked though, because Cole let me go.

"Is she alright?" he asked Gunner,

"I don't know, she just kind of stopped" Gunner responded,

"What do you mean she just stopped?" demanded Smith,

"I don't know" growled Gunner,

"I felt her pain and then she shuddered and just stopped".

Did Gunner just say that he felt my pain? How could he feel my pain, what does that even mean? He put his hand under my chin and lifted my head to look at him. With his other hand, he gently pulled the hood off my head. I opened my eyes, and his face was right there in front of me. I could feel his warm breath on my cheeks. His hand on my chin was sending electric sparks down my neck. His eyes stared into my soul. He placed his other hand on my cheek and took a deep breath. Oh God, what was he going to do? Was he trying to kiss me? Of course he wasn't going to kiss me, don't be ridiculous. I was scared, I didn't know what was happening to me. I closed my eyes tightly and listened to my body. The lashes on my back were still stinging but it was my bones that were aching. My ribs felt like they were being pulled and pushed every which way. My spine felt like it was twisting and turning.

"Zelena, open your eyes" Gunner's voice was soft and calming.

"Zelena, I want you to open your eyes and look at me".

I obeyed, I opened my eyes and looked at him. His face still directly in front of mine. I could feel his breath on my face, I could smell his skin. His hand on my cheek felt warm and safe. I looked deep into his eyes. His beautiful blue eyes. But that wasn't all I could see. There was something else in his eyes, it was like a feeling, like a wave of calm washing over me.

"Take a breath Zee. Take a long breath and try to relax" he whispered calmly, so I did. Keeping my eyes on his, I breathed in deep and very slowly breathed out. As I released the air from my lungs, with it went the aching in my arms and legs, the twisting pain in my back and chest. The heat I could feel running through my body, all of it went out of me with that one deep breath.

"Duuuude" Smith exclaimed. I heard Cole smack him over the head again.

"That's better" Gunner sighed.

I slowly stood up straight as Gunner got up from the dirt. His hand was still firmly placed on my left cheek, his gaze still locked with mine.

"I'm s-sorry" I mumbled,

"I don't know what just happened". I lowered my head and pulled away from his hand.

"It's all good Zee, but we gotta go" he said, stepping back from me and standing in line with Cole and Smith. I've ruined everything now, they think I'm an absolute nutcase. My stupid little freakout moment has them running for the hills.

"Will you be okay to get home from here?" Gunner asked with a tilt of his head. I pulled my hood back over my head and nodded. He grabbed my hand and gave it a little squeeze.

"See you tomorrow" he sang. And with that, they were gone.

What did I just do, what was that back there? I was hating myself the rest of the walk home. I'm such a freak. What kind of eighteen-year-old has a semi heart attack in the middle of a forest. I got to my front door and paused, I just needed one more minute before I went inside. I know that I'm late and he isn't going to be happy. I just hope that he hasn't had too much to drink already. I opened the door and walked through. Straight away a bottle came flying at my head. I fell to the ground to avoid it, slamming the door closed as I fell. The bottle smashed on the door frame and I was showered in glass. A shard cut my cheek and a bit of blood trickled down my face.

"Where the fuck have you been, you worthless cunt?" he screamed as he stomped over to me. I curled myself up against the closed door.

"I'M SORRY" I shouted.

"Don't you fucking shout at me you gutter slut" he yelled as he grabbed hold of my hair, pulling me to my feet. He was drunk, I could smell it on him. He was sweaty and dirty, the stench of him made me feel nauseous.

"You were supposed to be here half an hour ago to cook dinner and clean the fucking kitchen" he screamed in my face, his saliva spitting on my cheeks as he screamed. I had my eyes closed tight but there were still tears running down my face.

"I know, I'm sorry" I sobbed as I held onto the base of my hair. The pain coursing through my head was profound. He threw me against the wall, my back slamming into the plaster. I felt some of my half-healed wounds open up again and start to bleed. I fell to the floor on my hands and knees with my head down. I wanted to get up and run, I wanted to fight back, but I couldn't. I was frozen in fear. I am always frozen in fear in the face of this man.

"Go and fucking cook something before I lose my temper" he spat. I hurried up off the floor and half ran, half stumbled, into the kitchen. Once away from the stench of my father, I grabbed a tea towel and wiped at the blood dripping down my cheek. I can feel the blood pooling under my shirt on my back. I reached behind me and very gently ran my fingers over my ripped skin. As I lifted my hand to my face, I could see the fresh blood covering my fingertips. There's not much I can do about that right now. It will have to wait until later. The kitchen is a mess, he's been in here again today, pulling everything out of the cupboards in his terrible attempt to feed himself. I tossed the tea towel on the bench and stood in front of the fridge. I rested my forehead against the fridge door and wiped away the tears that threatened to fall.

Why? Why is this my life?

Chapter Two

Zelena

The piercing sound of my high pitched beeping alarm clock woke me up early, well before Hank wakes up anyway. Quickly hitting the button on the top to silence the sound, I looked to my closed bedroom door for any signs of movement on the other side. Nothing. I laid there for a minute, contemplating, did I really need to go to school today? I scrunched up my nose at the thought of having to spend 8 hours at home with my dad. I sat upright and perched on the edge of my bed. Yesterday seemed like a distant memory. The three Greek Gods and their odd kindness, were they real, or was that a concussion induced hallucination? I don't know which theory I'm more hopeful for. Doesn't matter, I'm sure today will be the same old boring, lonely life. I rubbed my temple, remembering my little freak out in the forest. Oh God, now I really hope it was all a hallucination. How embarrassing, as if I'm not enough of a freak already. Oh well, it's not like I'll see him again anyway. Surely not.

I grabbed my towel and went for a shower. I turned the tap and let the water heat up. I like my shower water scolding hot, always have, even with the seeping wounds constantly littering my body. Once the steam filled most of the room, I climbed in and let the hot water run over my bruised and battered body. I poured the soap in my hands and scrubbed my hair, the water running off my body had that familiar tinge of red to it. I didn't dare touch my back, instead, I let the hot water rinse the wounds clean. I tipped my head back and let the steaming water run over my face. Hot showers are so relaxing.

Holding my towel loosely at my hips, I stood in front of my mirror and examined my broken body. My wet hair, long and knotted, hung down just past my shoulders, so black it looked to have a purple hue to it. My pale clammy skin was spotted with new pinkish purple bruises and old yellowing bruises. Some are the size of a small coin, others inches across. My gold lifeless eyes sat above dark purple circles, with bushy dark brows that spread all the way out to my temples. My small and perky breasts hung slightly to the sides. My thin waist and stomach accentuated my ribcage, with my hip and collar bones protruding out. The pale skin was splattered with dark pink scars. My body, used as the canvas to exhibit my father's abusive art project. I pulled my towel up and turned away as a tear fell. I don't want to see it anymore. I'm disgusting, everything about me is grotesque.

I threw on some baggy jeans and a loose green t-shirt. I ran a brush through my wet hair and threw it over my shoulders. I inspected the gash on my forehead. It had scabbed over a bit now but still looked horrible and red. I got my trusty foundation bottle, which I stole on one of my grocery runs, and tipped it onto my fingers. I spread it over my face, covering my dark eyes and the new cut on my cheek. It disguised the small cut well enough, but it wasn't going to do any good for the scabby mess on my forehead though. So, I pulled out another band-aid and strategically placed it over the red gash. Picking up my grey hoodie, backpack, and ratty old shoes, I quietly walked out of my bedroom. I tiptoed to the front door, passing the lounge room. Hank was in there passed out in his armchair with beer cans scattered around his feet.

I went through the door and closed it as quietly as possible behind me, running down the driveway and onto the street, I let out a sigh of relief. I walked a fair distance away from the house before sitting down and pulling my shoes on. Looking up to the light blue morning sky I took a deep breath. Another clear and beautiful day. After a few more deep breaths, I picked myself up and took off into the forest, still gazing up at the sky as I went. Walking slowly, enjoying the fresh air and cool spring breeze, I could easily lose myself.

"Good morning". I jumped, startled at the sound of a voice from behind me.

"Whoa, sorry" he giggled, as I spun around to face him.

"I didn't mean to scare you" Gunner said putting his arms up with a smile.

"You didn't" I whispered. I dropped my head and went to pull my hood up over my face.

"Stop" he pleaded, grabbing my wrist and forcing me to let go of the hood. My heart rate sped up and a cold shiver went through me. The hood fell and slid down the back of my head.

"Please don't cover your face". He moved to stand right in front of me, still holding my hand by my face. My entire body tensed up. I was frozen with panic, staring at his hold on my wrist. He stared at me with confusion and followed my gaze to our hands. He let me go and took a step back dropping his head.

"I'm sorry, I shouldn't have grabbed you like that" he mumbled, sliding his hands into his jean pockets.

"Just don't cover your face, please, you don't have to hide from me".

His eyes were sad and longing as they stared me down. I didn't mean to upset him, I just panicked for a second there. All my life being grabbed usually means pain is coming. But something about Gunner was different. I don't know what. But it's like I could feel that he didn't mean me any harm. Why do I have to be like this? Why do I have to be scared of everything? I had this strong urge to want to make him feel better, but I didn't know how to, or why I needed to.

"I'm, I'm sorry, it's just um" I mumbled as I dropped my head letting my hair fall over my face. He stepped forward and put his hand under my chin to lift my head. I complied and allowed him to slowly lift my face to his. I closed my eyes as he tucked the hair from my face behind my ear. He gasped and let go of my chin.

"Zee, what happened to your face?" he asked with a stern tone. I turned my head away, ashamed, and pulled my hair back out.

"Zelena, who did that to you?" he growled at me.

I stepped back from him, scared of the growl in his tone and the idea of having to answer his question. I couldn't tell him about my dad. If I did Hank would kill me, and he'd kill Gunner. I felt my face pale, I wouldn't let that happen. Gunner stepped forward with a snarl on his beautiful face,

"Whoa, easy mate".

Cole was suddenly there with his arm around Gunner's chest. Where he came from, I have no idea. I looked around and Smith was behind him too. He held up his arm and wiggled his fingers at me. I smiled awkwardly back at him. Gunner threw Cole's arm off him and stepped towards me grabbing my hands in his, he leaned down and looked into my eyes. There it was again, that warm and soothing feeling. How does he do that to me?

"Zee. I didn't mean to scare you, I'm sorry" he said softly. He smiled at me with a half-smile, but he didn't mean it, his eyes were full of worry and hurt. I smiled at him and nodded. He stood up straight and went to let go of my hands, but I held on to one of them. Gripping his huge hand with mine, I admired our interlocking fingers. Small pins and needles slithered their way through my fingers and up my arm. I looked up at him and smiled. His eyes sparkled and his whole face smiled back at me.

"Wow" he breathed,

"You are beautiful". My cheeks burned as I blushed under his adoring gaze.

"Okay you two" coughed Smith,

"Let's go or we'll be late for school".

Smith and Cole walked off ahead of us. Gunner entwined his fingers with mine, making sure that I didn't let go. He nodded with his head gesturing down the path and raised his eyebrows. Still blushing, I smiled and nodded. We began walking together with my hand still in his. A small and simple gesture, and yet it meant everything to me.

When we reached the school, the lot was empty, meaning everyone was already inside. We followed Cole and Smith through the doors of the school, still hand in hand. As we entered the hallway an eerie silence befell the halls, they all turned and stared at Gunner and me. My eyes darted around the hallway, seeing everyone whispering to each other and looking at me with disgust. It's the most visible that I have ever felt, and I hated it. I dropped my head and pulled my hoodie back up. Letting go of Gunner's hand, I made a beeline for my classroom, leaving the three boys behind me.

"Zee wait!" he called after me, but I didn't stop.

I passed whispering faces and dirty looks as I made my way down the hall.

"There's no way"
"She's dreaming"
"Is this a prank?"
I kept my head down and avoided eye contact. The looks and the snide comments were nothing new, I got them every day. But I was so stupid to think that Gunner and I could actually be together. He was high class royalty, I was dumpster smut, and everyone knew it. I reached my class and hurried to my usual seat, in the back corner of the room. I sat down and leaned over to put my bag on the floor, when I sat up again, Smith was sitting next to me. He smiled and pulled his calculus book out.
"I hope you're good at this crap, because I suck" he said with a crooked smile. I half smiled back at him with a shrug of my shoulders.
The tiresome Mr Phillips was our math teacher. He is a middle-aged balding man who always dressed in beige khaki shorts with colourful tartan socks pulled up to his knees. He was boring at most, but with the wit and sarcasm that could floor most of his students. In the middle of class Smith plopped a folded-up piece of paper on my desk, he looked at me with anticipation. His cheeks were red and bursting with his barely held in giggles. I unfolded the note and studied it. A smile crept across my face as I started to understand what I was seeing. It was a terribly drawn picture of who I assume to be Mr Phillips, wearing a bikini, with pigtails in his hair, and riding on, what I think is a dolphin. I glanced at Smith, and he was nearly crying from his silent laughter. He had his hand over his mouth to muffle the sounds. He then pretends to push up his boobs, flick his hair over his shoulder, and gallop away on his dolphin. It was funny, and I couldn't help but giggle with him. I gave him back the drawing and looked back down at my book, still smiling to myself. Is this what having a friend feels like? Joking and giggling, having a reason to smile. I like this feeling, this blissful comfort. I like having a friend.
The lunch bell rang, and the students all got up and left, except for Smith, he waited for me to put my books in my bag. He stood by the door with a smile.
"Ready for some grub?" he asked with his hand rubbing his stomach. I smiled and nodded,
"Just got to drop my bag off" I squeaked.

"Want me to come, or shall I meet you there?" he asked with his thumb pointing down the hallway towards the cafeteria.

"I'll be okay" I said pulling my bag onto my shoulder and sliding through the door around him. He smiled and wiggled his fingers at me and took off down the hall.

I walked to my locker with a smile on my face. This is turning out to be a good day, for a change. I got to my locker and started to put in my combination when I was violently yanked around by my shoulder. I put my hands up to cover my face, ready for whoever it was that was about to hit me.

"You don't actually think that he likes you, do you?" Demi's high-pitched voice snickered at me. I dropped my hands to my side, bowed my head, and said nothing. It's always best to just let her get it out, when I speak or try to fight back, it's worse.

She slammed her palm into the door beside my head, which made me flinch and turn away.

"Oh my god" she huffed,

"You're seriously so pathetic, why do you think everyone is out to fight you?" she snarled at me leaning closer to my face. My face was turned away from her and my eyes closed tight, just waiting for her to hit me, kick me, pull my hair, do something. I could smell her perfume, the overbearing floral scent burned my nose. But I could smell something else as well, it was a cold bland smell. Something I would relate to fear or anger. That couldn't be right, how could I smell fear, emotions don't have a scent. She grabbed my shoulders and shoved me hard against the locker, my tender back burned from the sudden burst of pain.

"Gunner doesn't want you, why would he want a pig like you?" she spat at me, only inches from my face. I whimpered at the feel of her hot breath on my cheek.

"Stay away from Gunner, okay bitch, he's mine now".

I nodded my head quickly. The sharpness of her words sliced through me. Of course she and Gunner would get together, they're both ridiculously beautiful, and beautiful people tend to stick together. She let go of my shoulders and took a small step back. I didn't dare lift my head to look at her, but I could picture her evil smirk in my mind, I could basically feel her heated glare burning my flesh.

"What a useless waste of space" she laughed turning to her minions and the crowd that had gathered beside her.

Even after she turned away, I could still feel the burning from her glare. It was like a wave of heat burned through me, engulfing my arms. I clenched my fists, digging my nails into the palms of my hands. Those hot pins, the same from yesterday in the forest, I could feel them running up my legs and into my chest. Without a second thought, I stepped forward and slapped Demi clean across her face. I hit her so hard that her head snapped to the side and the sound echoed through the hallway. Everyone fell silent, surprised to see such an outburst from me. For years I have sat quietly and taken their abuse without a word or any show of retaliation. Demi grasped at her face and turned to look at me. Her upper lips curled up into a snarl and fiery hatred filled her eyes. She lunged at me grabbing my wrist with one hand and the other hand around my throat. She shoved me against the locker, slamming my head into the door. I let out a small squeal of pain. "Who the fuck do you think you are? You filthy slut!" she screamed at me whilst slamming me against the locker again. I tried to take a breath but her grip around my neck was too tight. I could feel her fingers tightening around my throat and I closed my eyes to prepare myself for more pain. Desperate for air, I pulled at her hand around my neck, to no avail. I could feel my head starting to spin and a fogginess clouded my vision. Demi's grip suddenly released, and I fell to the floor coughing and struggling to breathe. I stayed crouched on the floor on my hands and knees, frantically trying to catch my breath. My throat burned and the air felt like knives as it began to fill my lungs.

When I was finally able to breathe again, I managed to register the sounds of yelling and screaming in front of me. Hesitantly, I looked up. Cole and Smith were both struggling to hold back a violent looking Gunner, who was desperately trying to lunge at Demi. Demi was clutching onto Brian's arm trying to shield herself from Gunner. Brian, Demi, her minions, and everyone else in the hall were staring at Gunner with shock and terror on their faces.

"LET ME GO!" Gunner screamed, thrashing his body while trying to get free of Cole and Smith's grip.

"I'll fucking kill you if you ever touch her again" he screamed at her, still fighting to get free of Cole and Smith's hold. Demi was sobbing as she buried her face into Brian's jacket, Brian was standing back with his hands up in surrender just shaking his head.

"Come on mate. Enough" Cole pleaded with Gunner.

I slowly started to stand up, gripping the locker for support when I felt fresh blood running down my back. Oh no! I have to get out of here before anyone sees it. Getting into a fight at school is one thing, but if anyone found out about my back and the beatings I get at home, my dad would kill me. I coughed and I stumbled on my feet as I tried to take a step. Gunner turned around, locking eyes with me. He pushed past Cole and Smith and grabbed me around my waist. I flinched at his hands holding me.

"She's a fucking psycho, Gunner" Demi screamed. Gunner looked over at her and growled a deep bellowing growl that echoed through the halls. The crowd went silent, the aura of fear was thick in the air.

Gunner lifted me up with ease and began to carry me away. My toes were touching the ground, but I was barely able to walk with Gunner holding me. We burst through the front doors and out into the parking lot. He was so quick, I don't know how we got out here so fast. I must be more out of it than I realised. He put me down and stood in front of me, his eyes looking me up and down, running his hands over my face and arms.

"Are you okay?" he demanded urgently,

"Are you hurt?"

Looking into his frantic eyes it dawned on me, what Demi said in the hall. Why would he care, why did he bring me out here and why is he asking if I'm okay? I hit Demi, and they're together now, so shouldn't he be with her? She told me that they are together now. But he still threatened her. Didn't he, that did actually happen, right? I could feel that burning sensation running through my body again. Only this time, it was ten times more intense. I covered my face with my hands to muffle my cry of pain. I felt like my ribs were pulling apart and my spine was twisting under my skin. The hot needles were stabbing me all over my body.

"Zeleeeeena" Gunner said slowly with concern. But I couldn't listen to him right now, I didn't want to. The burning feeling was too much, my bones felt like they were breaking inside me. I threw myself to the ground, my body writhing in the dirt, trying desperately to ease the pain. My aching body shook and squirmed.

If Gunner was still there, I couldn't tell. I screamed out, begging for some kind of release from this torture. My body flung up from the ground until I was perched on my hands and knees. It felt like the ground under my hands was shaking, my whole body was on fire and the pain was excruciating. I tossed my head back, and a truly harrowing scream burst from my lungs. The sound pierced my ears and echoed through the forest in front of me until it melted away to silence.

Everything stopped. The pain was gone, the burning was gone, the aching in my bones was gone. I was okay. I turned around to see if Gunner was still there. He was. He was standing with his hands up in front of him, slowly backing away from me. Cole and Smith were behind him. They all looked at me like I had grown a second head. I get it, they should be scared of me. They see me now for the head case that I am. The way I snapped like that and hit Demi, she's right, I am a psycho.

I turned on my heels and ran off away from school away from Gunner and into the forest. Holy shit, I'm fast. I could never run this fast before, could I? I kept running and running, darting through the trees, bounding over boulders and logs. Where did this come from, this energy, this endurance? I love it! The wind brushing through my hair as I ran, the dirt under my feet. This feeling of freedom, it was amazing.

I skidded to a stop as I came upon a small stream. With the thought of cooling off in the water, I walked over to it. I sat down at the edge and peered into the water. I jerked back in fright, it wasn't my reflection I saw, it was a wolf. I snapped my head around to see the wolf behind me but there was nothing there. I looked back at the stream and there it was again. I turned my head to the side and so did the wolf. I leaned in close to the water, and so did the wolf. Then, like a brick to the face, it hit me. I 'am' the wolf, the wolf is me.

I looked at my reflection in the water, taking in every inch of myself. I am beautiful. My eyes were what caught my attention the most. They glowed a bright yellow that twinkled in the light. My coat is just like my hair, it's so dark that it looks almost purple. I looked down at my furry paws and my claws that scratched at the dirt. I drew my eyes up and traced them down the side of my smooth and silky fur, to my long fluffy tail. At the tip of my tail is a pure white patch. I huffed happily and looked back at my reflection in the water. At long last I finally believe that I can be truly beautiful, well at least my wolf is. A calming resolve took route in my mind, this is how my life was meant to be. I was born to be a wolf, to be wild and free.

I looked around the forest, everything was so clear and in focus. I couldn't stand still anymore, so I started to run. Not going anywhere, just running, dashing through the trees of the forest. I passed fields of flowers and large boulders and I even jumped over a little waterfall that I didn't know existed. I suppose no one ever comes this deep into the forest, so there would be lots of undiscovered sights.

As I was running, I caught the scent of something strange and somewhat unpleasant. I slowed my run to a trot. Lifting my snout to the air, I took a deep whiff. I immediately recoiled and scrunched my nose. It smells like burnt metal and coal, but there's another scent that I don't like. It's a hot garbage like smell, mixed with a rotting animal and burning chemicals. I stopped walking and stood silently, looking slowly around the forest. I couldn't see anything, but the scent was starting to burn my nose. I don't like this, it's time to go. I turned on my paws, heading back the way I came, and the smell soon disappeared behind me. I came up to one of the flower fields I passed earlier and laid down in the grass for a quick rest. I feel a little tired, that running took a lot out of me. I rested my head on my paws and closed my eyes as I panted softly.

~

My eyes flew open and I sat upright, I had fallen asleep in the grass. I held my arm out and examined my hand, turning it around in front of my face. Human again. I looked around me at the forest. The sun had already begun to set, and it was getting dark. Oh no, I'm late, Dad will kill me. I stood up and looked down at myself. Crap! I'm naked. Do I really have to go back, couldn't I just live in the forest now? You know, survive off the land and all that? I shivered as the last bit of sun left me and wrapped my arms around myself. Who am I kidding. I don't know the first thing about surviving in the wild. I'd barely last the night. No, I have to go back, I will freeze out here.

I ran back to the house as fast as I could, staying on the edge of the forest, sticking behind the trees. How was I going to explain my clothing situation, well lack of clothing situation? He will definitely kill me this time. He can't catch me without clothes on.

I snuck around the back of the house to the clothesline, I'm sure I did some washing the other day. That small sliver of hope died when I saw the line. All that was left was one of Hank's shirts and a couple of socks. I snatched down the shirt and threw it on, it was just long enough to cover my backside. I opened the back door to the kitchen and tiptoed through, closing it gently behind me. I turned back around and there he was. Eyes black and glaring right at me, his face screwed up in anger. He grabbed me by the face and slammed my head into the door behind me. A dull ache ran through the back of my head where it connected with the door.

"Where the fuck have you been, girl?" he screamed at me. He pulled my head forward and again slammed it back into the door. The dull ache intensified.

"And what's this?" he pulls on the shirt,

"You're wearing my fucking clothes now?" He threw me across the room onto the kitchen floor. The shirt rode up my stomach as I rolled.

"And no fucking panties ay, you filthy little slut". I curled myself into a ball in the furthest corner of the kitchen, tucking my head and face into my knees.

"I'll show what I do to little whores" he snarled as he stomped over to my shaking body, grabbing me by the hair and pulling me up onto my knees. The back of my head and now the top of my head were throbbing.

"NOOO" I sobbed as I struggled to break free of his hold.

He dragged me across the floor by my hair, stopping at the basement door. Terror instantly flooded my body. Please not the basement. He kicked open the door and pushed me through, throwing my small body down the stairs. My elbow smashed into the first step, my back and head hitting the next. I rolled and rolled down the stairs hitting every part of my body. When I finally landed on the cold concrete floor, I felt like a truck had hit me. I lay sprawled across the floor trying to distinguish the sorest part of my body. I heard Hank coming down the stairs, his heavy feet stomping on each step. I feebly attempted to push my weak body away from the stairs, away from him, sliding myself along the floor on my hands and knees.

"You think I'm going to let 'my' daughter sleep around with whoever the fuck she wants?" he spat. He reached the last step and continued his stomping towards my quivering body. He kicked me in the ribs and sent me flying back across the floor. I landed hard on my side and quickly tried to move away again.

"I didn't" I coughed, gasping for air.

I felt as though my chest had caved in, I couldn't breathe. I thought I was about to vomit when Hank grabbed my hair and lifted my head. CRACK! It felt like my eye had exploded inside my skull when he punched me in the face. I landed on the cold concrete and pressed my face onto the floor. He used his foot to roll me over so that I was on my back.

"Look at you, you disgusting cunt" he huffed as he crouched down beside me. He wiped the hair from my face and smiled, a terrifying evil smile.

"I have something extra special for you tonight" he whispered. He stood up and walked away but I could still hear him moving around in the basement. I fought hard to keep my eyes open, well one eye, the other eye had fused shut from the force of his punch. I was fighting hard not to pass out, no matter what, I can't pass out. I don't know what he might do to me if I did. He came back over to me and grabbed my shoulders, lifting me upright to sit up against the wall. He put his hand around the back of my neck, I thought he was about to choke me, but he didn't. There was a loud click sound and then he stood up and stepped back. I felt something heavy drop onto my collarbone, I reached up to feel for it. There was a strap like thing around the base of my neck with a small box attached to it. I could feel spikes on the inside of the strap, stabbing into my skin. I tried to look at Hank to see what he was doing but I couldn't, my eyes were blurry, and my head felt heavy.

Something was tapping on the side of my face, and it wasn't exactly gentle.

"Wake up now little slut, it's time for some fun".

I shuddered awake and tried to lift myself up. I couldn't. I was too weak. I wasn't chained up either, I don't know if that is a good thing or a bad thing. I peered at him with my one good eye. He was standing up in front of me, holding something, like a little phone. He put his chin down and smiled a crooked smile, his eyes glaring at me from under his brows. He held out his hand as if to show me the little phone he was holding. Only it wasn't a phone, it looked more like a walkie-talkie. Confusion and fear flooded my mind, I have no idea where he was going with this. His usual beatings are bad but when he decides to get creative, it's always worse. He snickered and pressed his thumb down on the button on the side.

Everything went black, my body stiffened from the pain shooting through it. I fell to the floor, my entire body shaking in agony. I couldn't breathe, I couldn't scream, I couldn't move my arms or legs. The feeling was indescribable, it was like I no longer had any control over my own body. My body stopped convulsing and feeling rushed back in. I could feel every morsel of pain as I lay panting, unable to move. I could hear him cackling at the top of his lungs.

"Oh my God" he laughed,

"You should see how stupid you look".

It happened again. My eyes rolled back in my head, I tried to scream but nothing came out. I wanted desperately for the pain to stop. I would do anything to make it stop. Perhaps if I was strong enough, or if I had enough willpower, then maybe I could die right here and now, then it would all stop. My body relaxed again, and I tried to catch a breath. My father was laughing uncontrollably. His sick and twisted laughter echoed in the stale air of the basement. With all the strength I could muster, I lifted my arm to my neck. What the fuck is this thing. I tugged at the strap around my neck trying to get it off. I began to frantically feel for a buckle or a clip, or something to release it.

Hank's foot slammed down onto my stomach and I immediately vomited.

"No you fucking don't" he yelled.

Choking on my blood and vomit, and gasping for air, I rolled to the side and spat out the bile in my mouth. I couldn't breathe, my ribs were for sure broken. Sharp pains shot through my chest with each strained breath I took.

"Please" I coughed with more blood coming out of my mouth,

"Stop" I gagged as my head fell back to the floor.

"Now why would I do that?" he taunted me,

"We're having so much fun".

He pressed the button again and my body convulsed. Everything hurt. I could feel everything, but at the same time, I felt nothing. I was in agony, but I couldn't pinpoint the source. The pain was coursing through my entire body, every cell, every fibre, it was all torturous. I just wanted it to stop. I tried again to beg him but all I could do was make a horrible gagging sound. He released me, and my body melted into the floor. My eyes twitched and went dark. Let this be death I prayed, and then I was out.

~

A blinding white light surrounded me. A tall, thin figure stood before me with its hands outstretched towards me. I felt nothing, no pain, no cold. Nothing. Nothing but stillness.

"It's time to get up now, sweet girl" the angelic figure sang.

"I can't" I whispered.

"You can, my child. Your journey does not end here" the gentle voice cooed. The figure slowly backed away, taking with it the bright light, until I was once again alone in the darkness.

~

I started to come too. My legs and arms felt like they were floating, my muscles were sore and numb, and there was an awful burning sensation around my neck. I took a deep breath and winced at the stabbing pain that shot through my chest. Was I dying? Or was I dead? Please let this be death, I can't live through another night of this torture. I tried to open my eyes, but they felt so heavy. I blinked a little trying to detect something I could recognise. There were tiny lights above me. They almost looked like stars in the sky. Oh, I am dead. As I slowly became more conscious it was apparent that I was moving. No, I was being carried. There was an arm under my head and my legs flopped over another arm. My head was rested against a warm bare chest. I don't understand, Hank would never carry me so gently, he would just drag my lifeless body along the ground by my wrist or ankle.

This was not right. I stirred and thrashed in a panic. Where was I, what was going on? I tried again to focus my good eye, but it was no use, my surroundings were too dark. I tried to scream for him to let me go, but nothing came out but a little squeak.

"It's okay Zelena, I've got you now".

That voice. I know that voice, that ever so smooth and calming voice. I nuzzled my nose into the chest that my face was resting on and sniffed. Mm... warm sunshine. It's him. It's Gunner. I must be dead, this is heaven.

"She doesn't look so good mate". I heard another voice, I think it was Cole. Why would Cole be in heaven too?

"No, she'll be fine" the deliciously intoxicating voice of Gunner rumbled.

"I really think we should go to the hospital" this voice was shaking and ever so quiet.

"No" Gunner responded, so stern and demanding. It's okay. I can die now. If being dead means seeing Gunner in heaven, then I will gladly go. Everything began to spin, my eyes went fuzzy, and my head felt dull.

"Gunner" I whispered. My head fell back and I thought 'Heaven here I come'. And I lost consciousness again.

Chapter Three

Gunner

I can't believe Dad agreed to let me go to an actual human high school. The pack kids have always been home schooled, it's kind of an unwritten law. With Mum's help and the use of my puppy dog eyes, he couldn't say no. There are only four weeks left in the school year but hey, who's complaining? At least I can get out of this house for a bit. Of course, I would have to take Cole and Smith with me, which is fine, mostly. Smith can be a bit immature at times but he's good to have around when you need something to lighten the mood, plus he's my Delta and I know he's got my back. Cole, on the other hand, he's like my brother. He is a bit on the serious side and not exactly a social butterfly, but he's been my best friend since we were crib mates. We grew up together, trained together and we changed together. His father, Spartan, has always been loyal to my dad. He has been Dad's Beta for as long as I can remember. And Cole, he'll be my Beta when the time comes.

"Fuck yeah man" Smith said jumping onto my back with his arm wrapped around my neck,

"We're going to school" he laughed loudly.

I pushed him off and smiled. I usually hate academics, they're so boring. I'd rather be out in the forest running or training or goofing off with these two idiots.

"There's going to be so many new fine little females for me to taste" Smith said rubbing his hands together and licking his lips.

"We're going for our Alpha-son" said Cole, smacking Smith across the back of his head,

"Not to hook up with random high school girls. 'Human' high school girls"

"I know, I know. But hey, no harm no foul, right? A little play time never hurt anyone" Smith smiled with a shrug of his shoulders.

"Smith you're deplorable. Now go to bed you two, we gotta go early and register before class" I scolded as I pushed them out the front door, and quickly closed it behind them. I walked up the stairs to my room, passing the portraits of the previous alphas. One day my picture will be hung next to my father's. I've been training for the role since my wolf was born.

I went for a shower before bed, so I didn't have to bother in the morning. I let the water warm up first, Weres run hot, so the hotter the water, the better. I stood under the water contemplating my future obligations and responsibilities. I really don't know if I'm ready for this. Granted, I still have a few years, but I don't know if I'll ever be ready. It's a huge honour to be an Alpha, but lately, it's been seeming more like a burden. If I had a Mate, she could at least help me out, and keep me grounded. Ugh forget it. I haven't felt the right one yet and who knows, maybe I never will.

I got out of the shower, patted myself dry, and slid on my boxers. I perched on the edge of my bed and picked up the medallion from the bedside table. I studied the symbol on its face, three crescent moons intertwined and connected. The symbol of our pack. The Tri-Moon pack. I twisted the large round coin like piece in my hands, feeling its smooth edges. My bloodline has run this pack for generations, we settled this land over three hundred years ago. I don't know what would happen if I didn't take up the mantle after my father. I just can't help but feel like something has been missing. I sighed heavily and put the medallion back on the table.

Jumping into the bed and under the covers, I rolled over and buried my face into my pillow. That's a problem for another day I figured. I closed my eyes and drifted easily off to sleep.

~

"Cry you filthy bitch. Come on and cry, louder" a faceless man holding a whip was screaming. A little obsidian wolf lay on the ground, bleeding, its back slashed open. The man hit the wolf with the whip again and again, but it didn't howl or bark or whimper, not once.

"Stop" I yelled, but no sound came out of my mouth.

"STOP" I was screaming at the top of my lungs, but it wasn't loud enough. The man couldn't hear me, and he didn't stop, he didn't even hesitate. His onslaught continued to rain down on the broken creature.

I wanted to run at him, tackle the man to the ground, but my feet wouldn't move. They were planted deep into the ground. He just kept hitting it and hitting it. Blood splattered over his face and body, and his sadistic laughter echoed around my ears. The little wolf looked over at me, and a single tear fell from its glowing yellow eyes. I reached out for it but was still barred from moving. Its head slumped to the ground and the glow of its eyes dissipated. It was dead.

~

I flew up in my bed, sitting upright. A cold sweat coated my body, and I was panting harshly. I hit the light beside me and looked around the room. Thank fuck, it was a dream. What even was that? What kind of messed up TV have I been watching. I grabbed my phone and pressed the home key, the dim light lit up the room. 5:58 am. Well, there's no point going back to sleep now. I tossed myself back on the bed and tried to picture the little wolf from my dream. The details have already started to fade away from memory, all I can see are those yellow eyes, and the pain and torment within them.

I got up, pulled on some sweats, and walked down to the kitchen. Mum was there already, getting breakfast ready for Dad and the pack.

"Good morning sweetheart" she cooed as she grabbed the back of my neck and pulled me down so that she could kiss my cheek.

At eighteen I'm already about two feet taller than my mum, I get my height from my father. She's a smaller woman with chocolate brown hair that sits in curls on her shoulders. Mum and Dad got married not long after my dad turned twenty, Mum's a year younger. She's almost always wearing an apron over a brightly coloured dress. She's the sweetest lady anyone could meet, but mess with her pack kids and she'll tear your throat out with no hesitation.

"You want some breakfast, Darling?" she asked walking over to the fridge.

"Just toast Ma" I said as I sat down at the counter and rested my head in my arms.

"Gunner, my baby, you look so tired" she fussed.

"Yeah Mum, I had this weird dream last night"

"Well, you know what I say about dreams?" her voice got higher in a snooty kind of way.

"I know Mum" I groaned,

"Every dream has a purpose, my Darling".

Mum has always been superstitious. She's a Were equivalent of a highly religious human. She gives thanks to the Moon Goddess and believes all the legends and stories, even about True Mates, blessed wolves, and all that stuff. She teaches a class for the young pups about our histories and legends. I adore my mum, she's the greatest one there is.

I was just done eating my toast when Cole and Smith came walking into the kitchen, both already dressed and ready to go.

"What's this oh fearless leader?" Smith mocked,

"You're not even ready yet".

I gave him a little growl and shoved up from my seat.

"Here you go boys, have some eggs" Mum said, sliding each of them a plate with a mountain of scrambled eggs and a huge side of bacon. Cole and Smith smiled at each other and sat down to eat.

Leaving them to stuff their faces, I dashed upstairs to change. I pulled on my jeans and grabbed the shirt on top of the pile. I ran my hands through my hair and quickly checked the mirror. Eh, that'll do for now. I picked up my bag and took off back down the stairs. Cole and Smith were waiting for me on the porch.

"Bye Mum" I yelled closing the door before she could make a fuss. I ran at the wooden railing using one hand to lift myself up, I jumped up and over, landing perfectly on the grass. I turned back to Cole and Smith and smirked.

"Come on boys" I teased.

Cole and Smith shoved and pushed each other as they ran down the steps. We all jogged off together through the forest towards the school, Cole and Smith flanking me on both sides. Our village is not too far from the human town. Deep enough in the forest that we remain concealed, but close enough that we can access their facilities. The humans have no idea we're out here, nor how many of us are living out here. We aim to keep it that way. Humans are easily scared and unpredictable creatures, especially with things that they don't understand. It's best that the supernatural world remains just something from a storybook or a TV show in their minds.

We reached the edge of the forest where it opens onto the school car park and slowed to a walk. We were making our way through the lot when people started to notice our presence. The girls gasped and whispered and giggled, the boys stuck out their chests and looked us up and down.

Look at all these little ladies ripe for the picking

I smiled at Smith's comment, I could hear a girl to my left whisper to her friend,

"Oh my gosh they're gorgeous, I want the dark haired one".

See Cole, mate they love ya

Cut it out Smith

I do love our Were telepathy thing, so useful. I smiled and lowered my head as we walked. We got to the door and I pushed it open walking through with Cole and Smith on my heels. Something smells spectacular, like fresh fruit, do all human schools smell this good? I stopped and surveyed the hallway, it was mostly empty, but the people from the car park were all following us in now. I followed the sign that said 'Office' and turned down the left hallway. I opened the door and walked in with Cole and Smith still following behind me. An older lady in a red sweater with lipstick to match sat behind the desk, her short greying hair sat in tight curls on top of her head, and they bounced slightly as she lifted her gaze.

"Hello ma'am" I said stepping forward,

"We're here to register for classes" The woman grinned with a slight blush gracing her cheeks.

"Of course dear, I've been expecting you" she put three booklets up on the desk and slid them forward. I took them down and handed one to Cole and one to Smith.

"Just sign here and you're free to go".

I stepped forward and signed the form on the clipboard and then handed the pen to Cole. The office was small and overcrowded with cabinets and boxes. With the three of us boys in there as well, it was too much. I stepped out of the door and into the hallway and turned around. A little kid in a hoodie ran straight into me, flying back on the floor. A weird smell filled my nose, like fresh citrus and cherry blossoms. One of his books landed at my feet, I crouched down to pass it to him.

"Sorry, is this yours?" I asked him. He snatched the book and tried standing up, but the fall must have hurt him because he was wobbly on his feet. I grabbed his shoulders to give him a lift, but as soon as I touched him, he jumped and fell back down again. There was a tingle in my hands, a spark that travelled from my fingers and all the way into my chest. I never felt something like that before. The kid was scared, I could smell that, but something about him smelt different, something I couldn't make out.

A crowd of nosy kids started to gather to laugh at the poor guy, so I held out my arms and pulled them back from him. I watched as his head slowly lifted from my feet up my torso and to my face. Was this dude checking me out? I tilted my head to try and see his face. Holy shit. It's not a boy, she's a girl. I took in her appearance, her small frame cowered on the ground against the wall. Her long and messy raven hair covered most of her face, but I got a quick glimpse at her striking golden eyes. She immediately reminded me of the little wolf from my dream. I was about to help her back up but just like that, she flew off the ground and ran into the crowd of people to my left, she was tiny and able to zip through them with ease. There was something about her, something I couldn't let go. I needed to know more.

"What's going on?" asked Cole as he stepped up behind me.

"There was a girl" I said still looking down the hall after her,

"Woooo" sang Smith,

"Shut up" I growled,

"It wasn't like that, there was something about her"

"Okay, and what? What do you want us to do?" asked Cole with his serious Beta voice coming through his question,

"I want to find her" I answered him bluntly.

"The bell, man, we gotta go to class" said Smith. I flashed them an image of her sitting against the wall with her hair over her face.

Find her

They both nodded and walked off to their class and I headed down the hall to my locker to drop off my bag. When I got to my first class, I entered the room and dropped my registration form on the teacher's desk. Everyone was staring as I made my way to the back of the room. I had just sat down when Cole flashed me.

Gunner, she's here

She's where?

She's in class with Smith and me

Ask her to sit with us at lunch, I want to talk to her

Got it

The first class went by quickly thankfully. After the first bell, I walked over to my next lesson. I scanned the hallway for the mystery girl, but she was nowhere to be seen. I went in and sat down again towards the back of the room. As the class dragged on, I was unconsciously bouncing my knee and tapping my desk, each minute felt like an hour. I don't know what has come over me. I don't even know this girl, why am I so desperate to see her again? I was feeling anxious and nervous, like I had butterflies in my stomach. I racked my brain trying to recall the last time I was nervous enough to get butterflies. It hasn't been since I knew I was about to go through my first change. The lunch bell rang, and I was out the door before it had stopped. I met Cole and Smith at the cafeteria. Noticing that they were alone, a swift wave of anger flew over me.

"Well?" I demanded gruffly,

"Where is she?"

"I asked her man, but she said no" Cole answered with a shrug of his shoulders. I growled and turned away walking into the cafeteria. I grabbed a tray and some food and sat at the table closest to the door. I'll be able to see her come in from here. I waited impatiently, sitting up a little as each person walked through the door.

"What's wrong with you Gunner?" whispered Cole,

"I can smell your anxiety"

"I don't know" I snapped,

"Why isn't she here yet?" I hissed.

"There she is" whispered Smith.

We all turned and watched her walk. She was so small, but her feet moved fast. She never lifted her head and her hair never moved from in front of her face. It's like she was hiding or trying to hide. You can't hide from me, little one. She sat alone in the corner of the cafeteria, by the rubbish bins. Why does she sit alone, where are her friends? I watched her curiously play with the apple in her hand. It was hard to see her features from under her hood and through her dark hair, I wanted desperately to move the hair from her face and gaze into her eyes. Oh Goddess, what am I even thinking. Since when do I get this way about random girls. But still, something about her was pulling at me.

What is it with this one, Gunner?

I'm not sure, I feel drawn to her

I dunno mate, she seems, damaged

I jerked up straight when she suddenly threw her hands up, I noticed her drink had tipped down the front of her.

"Did you see her face?" a blond girl giggled from across the cafeteria as she flicked her hair behind her shoulder. Everyone in the room began to laugh at her, the blonde girl who threw her food and the guys she was sitting with mocked and teased the girl.

"What happened Snow White, did someone have an accident?" the bigger guy was jumping around his friends pointing at the girl and laughing. A growl worked its way up and was bubbling out of my gritted teeth, a deep hatred burned through my chest. I wanted nothing more than to rip that idiot's arms from his body.

Don't Gunner, let it go

Cole flashed me. My anger was affecting Cole and Smith, I could smell it on them. They were both glaring at the table of asshole kids. I looked back at the girl, and a heavy sadness fell over me. I wanted to make her feel better, I wanted to protect her. She got up from her seat and walked quickly towards the door. I watched her as she went, drenched in juice.

I'm gonna go check on her

I stood up abruptly and left the cafeteria. I caught sight of her turning at the end of the hallway and I hightailed it after her. I rounded the corner and there she was, standing in front of a locker. She looks so small and frail. I felt like I needed to hold her, to tell her everything was going to be okay. What is going on with me! I walked over to her as she was reaching in her locker.

"Are you okay?" I asked her softly. She didn't reply.

I took a deep breath through my nose and I nearly moaned out loud. Fresh citrus and cherry blossoms, this girl smells heavenly. Without fully realising what I was doing, I reached out for her, I needed to hold her. I put my hand over her hand that was holding the locker door. Whoa! Sparks again. Little tingles danced across my fingers where our skin was touching. She pulled her hand away so quickly. I stepped back from her, giving her a little extra space to try and clear my own thoughts. The poor girl must think I'm a total creep.

"Sorry, sorry I didn't mean to scare you" I rushed out.

I'm such a weirdo. The girl grabbed the hand that I touched and held it to her face. Maybe she felt the sparks and tingles too. Then I smelt it, blood. Nope, she didn't feel it, she just cut herself. A drop of blood fell from her hand to the floor. Fuck, I scared this girl so much that she sliced her damn hand open. I immediately began to worry and felt a deep need to fix it, to fix her. The overwhelming feeling of protectiveness washed over me and I stepped up to her, I grabbed both her hands and gasped at the sparks tickling my skin.

"Oh shit, your hand" I exclaimed.

I looked at her hand closely, it wasn't a bad cut but there was a lot of blood, probably more than what is normal. I need to wrap it up for her. The scent of terror suddenly filled my nose. Is it coming from her? I looked at her face, it was the clearest that I'd been able to see her. She wore a lot of makeup, not that she needed to, I could tell she was beautiful. She was petrified of me. Her whole body was frozen, the fear coming off her was intense. I very slowly released her hands and lifted mine up to show her I wasn't going to hurt her.

"Sorry, I didn't mean to hurt you" I felt defeated. Had I really scared her this much, just by standing near her?

"Will you let me help you?" I asked her softly.

She didn't say a word, why wouldn't she speak to me? She was just staring at me through her hair. Very slowly, she nodded, so I held out my hand to walk her to my locker. She pulled away, turning her whole body away from me. This can't all be about me, there is something else going on here. I looked at her face trying to figure out what was going on in her head.

"It's okay, follow me".

I didn't take her hand or get too close to her, I wanted her to trust me. So, I started to walk off towards my locker. I stopped a few steps away and turned to see if she was following. She wasn't, she was just watching me. I smiled at her, the biggest, friendliest smile I could muster. She nodded her head, closed her locker, and started walking towards me. I got her to follow me all the way to my locker and I smiled at her again. I opened it up and pulled my old bandanna out of the front pocket of my bag. This will do to wrap her hand up. I turned around and showed her the bandanna, still smiling, trying to keep her from running away. She nodded again and held out her hand. She doesn't say much, this one. I began to tie the bandanna around her hand, being as gentle as I possibly could.

As I was working on her hand, I couldn't help but to take deep inhales of her scent. She is intoxicating, the most delicious thing

I have ever smelled. I finished up with tying the ends together and opened my fingers, keeping her hand in the palm of mine. This time she didn't pull away, she rested her hand there. What is it about her, how can she make me feel like this, like she is the only woman on this planet? It's like I've known her my whole life, like she has forever been a part of me. Using my thumb, I softly rubbed the back of her hand. Fireworks. I could feel her, she was relaxing and releasing her fear. She was starting to trust me.

Could this be her, I wondered? The woman my mother used to tell me about when I was a little boy. My Mate. I never actually believed that True Mates existed. I just thought they were a nice story to tell your pups at bedtime. But this girl, she felt different, she felt like…. Mine. I breathed in deeply, taking in her sweet scent. She smelled like the leaves in the forest mixed with the petals of cherry blossoms, all wrapped up in fresh orange peel.

The bell rang and it made her jump and pull away from me again. That damn bell. The hallway filled up with people and very quickly began to burst with noise. Cole and Smith, who had been watching us from down the hall, were now right behind me.

"Gunner, we gotta go" Cole said to me. She looked over at them and then put her head down. She's adorable, so small and shy. I don't even know her name, I haven't even told her 'my' name yet. I crouched down so that she could hear me.

"My name's Gunner" I smirked. She leaned away from me again, so I stood up to give her back her space.

"Can I see you after school?" I asked a little too excitedly. She didn't say anything, just shook her head a little.

"Hmph" I huffed, this is going to be harder than I thought.

Gunner, come on man let her go

Cole was getting impatient, and he was about to piss me off. I leaned down to her again and whispered,

"I'll see you later".

I turned and took off with Cole and Smith. I wasn't giving up, she was going to see me again if she knew it or not. This girl was special.

My next class was with Cole, we sat together at the back of the room flashing about my interaction with the mystery girl.

Do you want to tell me what all that was? I've never seen you so interested in a girl before
There's something different about this girl, I just haven't figured out what it is yet
She just doesn't seem right, she feels broken, you can find better
She's been hurt but she's not broken, shit I didn't even ask her name
It's Zelena, I asked her this morning
I looked at Cole and smiled. Zelena, I said to myself, how beautiful.
You can't be serious about this one, Gunner. You deserve better, the pack deserves better
I don't think there is anyone better. I feel like she could be my Mate
You can just pick another Mate
No, you don't get it, I think she could be my real Mate, like my True Mate
Cole turned his head and looked at me confused. He knows that my mum believes, and is all about searching for your True Mate, but I've never really believed. Not until today.
Gunner, the whole True Mate thing is just a myth. They aren't real
You don't get it. This is different. I'll prove it
Cole kept watching me out of the corner of his eye. He probably thinks I'm going crazy, but I'm dead serious. This could be her, I feel it. At the end of the day, as the bell rang, I flashed Smith,
Meet us out by the gate
Sure thing boss
Cole and I walked slowly through the hallway. We were both taller and bigger than all the other guys, it was hard to push through the hoard of horny teenagers. I felt eyes on us and heard whispers from all around us. We got through the doors and hung around waiting for Smith. The bitchy Blonde from the cafeteria came out and headed right for me. She walked with a sway to her hips and a seductive smirk on her over pouty lips. She stopped directly in front of me, popped out her hip, lifted her chest, and started playing with the end of her hair.
"Hey, I'm Demi". Her voice was too high pitched and held a whiney tone. Her overly confident sneer made my blood run hot. I forced a half smile and nodded, trying not to growl.

"I've not seen you around before" she said with a flutter of her eyelashes,

"We're home schooled" I scoffed.

I didn't want to talk to her. Her perfume was burning my nose and there was something about her face that made me want to rip her throat out. Cole must have felt my anger growing, he grabbed her hand and pulled her to the side.

"It ain't going to happen, Sweetheart" he told her with a shit eating smile.

She dropped her hair, glared and me, and huffed, turning on her heels and storming off towards the car park. Cole turned back and winked, I just shook my head and smiled. My man, always the bodyguard. The untapped adolescent hormones running through these kids was straight up nauseating. I could smell their desires and feel the sexual tensions in the air. I leaned against the fence and crossed my arms as we waited for Smith. He came bursting out the doors with a big smile on his face.

"Pulled my first number" he grinned holding up a small torn piece of paper. I can't deny it, the boy has game. He's just turned eighteen and he's hooked up with almost all the passing through Omega girls, dating back since he was maybe fourteen. I looked down at my boots and laughed shaking my head. The kid has some serious stamina.

"Don't be jealous" he laughed throwing his arm around Cole's neck and smacking his cheek. They both laughed and wrestled around a bit, hitting and shoving each other before Cole pushed him off still laughing. They each turned to me with a smile.

"So, what are we waiting for?" puffed Cole.

"We're making a new friend" I grinned at them both.

They glanced at each other confused. I caught a scent and turned my head. There she was. I quickly stood up straight and smiled at her, Goddess I hope she doesn't get mad or scared again. Cole and Smith both snapped their heads to see what caught my attention. Smith smiled and waved at her.

Oh Gunner, come on

Cole whined. She dropped her head down and her hair fell over her cheeks. She started walking for the gate.

"Hey Zelena" Smith sang. Cole hit him in the ribs and growled,
Don't encourage him
"Hey there" I said stepping forward,
"I thought we might walk you home". She didn't answer me right
away, which is good, means she's thinking about it.
"Why?" she squeaked.
It was the first time I heard her voice. Although she was nervous
and quiet, her voice still rang like celestial bells in my ears.
"Well because it would be a good chance for us to talk" I told her.
"Why would you want to talk to me?"
She surprised me, she has a bit of fire behind that shy exterior.
My chest burned a little as my desire for her touch grew. I tilted
my head trying to decipher her tone.
"You're beautiful Zelena, why wouldn't I want to talk to a
beautiful girl?"
Again, she was quiet, she dropped her head and crossed her arms.
"I'm not beautiful, I'm an ugly swamp monster" she whispered
with a hint of disgust in her voice.
I was taken aback. Why on earth would this girl think that she is
ugly? I heard Smith giggle at her, and it infuriated me, I turned
to look at him, bared my teeth, and growled.
"What, she's funny" he squeaked with a cautious smile.
I huffed at him and Cole hit him across the head. I looked back at
Zelena and crouched down to get a better look at her face. Her
brilliant golden eyes were shiny through her hair.
"Don't ever say that about yourself again... You, Zelena, are
breathtaking".
I wanted to kiss her right there, I burned for her. But I controlled
myself, I quickly stood up and took a step back. I didn't want to
scare her again, I was already starting to scare myself.
"Okay" she squeaked as she zipped past me and through the gate,
I smiled and followed closely behind her.
Well, that was intense. Flashed Smith.
Let me talk with her, you two hang back a bit
I ordered the boys and quickly caught up to Zelena. I let her lead
the way and she went straight for the forest. I thought the humans

around here feared the forest. My little Mate must be fearless, I thought, smiling to myself.

"So, tell me about yourself".

She didn't look up at me just shook her head.

"Not a big talker, are you?"

Again, she didn't answer. Okay, I'll have to go easy with her. She's so damn shy and quiet. Cole and Smith were whispering behind us, I could hear them of course. I growled a little to shut them up. Through my peripherals, I saw her turn her head to look at me. Oh shit, she heard me. I looked down at her and smiled.

"You lived here long?" I asked her, surely this is an easy enough question to answer.

"As long as I can remember" she responded.

Holy heck she's talking to me. Okay just don't push her, keep it simple, she's starting to open up.

"Wow ay, you've never lived anywhere else then?" I said cheerfully. She replied with a shrug of her shoulders,

"No".

"So why are you so quiet at school?"

I was watching her waiting for a response, was this pushing it?

"I um, I just don't fit in there" she mumbled quietly.

I wanted to grab her hand or take off her hood or something. I wanted more from her, I needed more from her. My stomach was doing flips and my heart was pounding in my chest. Just keep talking to her.

"That Demi sure is a piece of work" I joked sarcastically. She just huffed at me. Wow okay, she really doesn't like Demi does she.

"Yeah, a right piece of shit" I heard Cole call out.

He and Smith were laughing and shoving each other. He was right though, I smiled to myself, she came across as a cocky asshat. I saw Zelena was looking at me, I glanced down at her and smiled. Our eyes connected, unlike any other time before. It was as if our gazes clicked together like puzzle pieces. I felt a flash of heat and saw sparks shoot across my vision. A wave of electricity coursed through my arms and legs. What the fuck was this. Suddenly it stopped and all I felt was pain. An aching in my bones similar to the first time I changed. Zelena stopped and suddenly arched over grasping at her chest. It was her pain I could feel. I knelt down in front of her and felt the panic kick in.

"Whoa, Zee, are you okay?"

I grabbed her shoulders trying to get her to answer me.

"Zelena, what's wrong?" I demanded but she didn't answer.

Boys get over here

"What's going on?" Cole grabbed her hips to hold her up, but she flinched, she didn't like his touch. I growled at him.

Remove your hands!

He did so with a raised eyebrow,

"Is she alright?" he asked me,

"I don't know, she just kind of stopped"

"What do you mean she just stopped?" said Smith with an urgency in his voice,

"I don't know" I growled. I was frustrated and felt helpless, I don't know what was wrong with her, or how to fix it.

"I felt her pain and then she shuddered and just stopped".

I tried to lift her chin to get her to look at me. I slid her hood off so that I could see her better. She opened her eyes and stared right into me. I placed my hand on her cheek and started to siphon off some of her pain. As soon as I felt it enter me, I knew what was happening. I flashed the boys,

She's changing

She's changing? questioned Smith.

Changing into what? Cole sneered.

She's a Were

That's impossible, we would have scented her. Cole snapped angrily.

She's a Were I'm telling you

I turned my attention back to Zelena, trying to be as calming as possible. I couldn't let her change, at least not right here.

"Zelena, open your eyes" I said softly,

"Zelena, I want you to open your eyes and look at me". After a second she complied, her eyes blinked open, and looked right at me. I tried to take more of her pain, but she wasn't hurting anymore. It was just fear and confusion she felt now.

"Take a breath Zee. Take a long breath and try to relax" I told her. She did, not taking her eyes off mine the whole time. Her breathing slowed and her pain was long gone.

"That's better" I breathed a sigh of relief.

She stood up straight, still staring into my eyes.

"Sorry" she mumbled, pulling her head away from my hand,

"I don't know what just happened".

A wave of excitement came over me. She's a wolf. She's 'my' wolf. I stepped back with Cole and Smith to give her some air. I gotta get back to my mum, I have to talk to her about this. Maybe she will confirm my suspicion and tell me that Zelena is my True Mate.

"It's all good Zee, but we gotta go. Will you be okay to get home from here?"

She looked sad and embarrassed. I tilted my head to try and see her eyes again. She dropped her head, pulled her hood up, and nodded. I didn't want to upset her, but I couldn't wait, I needed to see my mum. I stepped closer to her and grabbed her hand, giving it a small squeeze.

"See you tomorrow" I told her happily.

I let go of her hand and turned to run with the boys, I gave them each a quick nod and we took off. Thanks to the speed at which we ran, we got home super-fast. Partly because Weres already have additional speed, but mainly because I was in a rush.

"Later fellas" I yelled as I ran for the main house.

I burst through the front door and started searching for Mum.

"Mum" I screamed running to the kitchen,

"Mum, where are you?"

"Gunner?" she called from the staircase in the foyer.

I ran out of the kitchen and saw her, her eyes went wide and her face flushed with worry.

"Baby, what's wrong?"

She ran down the last few steps and grabbed my hands. I was huffing with excitement.

"Mum" I breathed heavily,

"We need to talk".

She looked at me with concern and nodded her head. She led me to the loungeroom, and we sat down together on the sofa.

"What's got you all riled up, dear?" she asked as she shuffled closer to me and held my hands in her lap.

"Mum, I need you to tell me more about True Mates" I said with a smile.

She sat up a little straighter and squeezed my hands a little tighter. A look of excitement flashed across her face and then she smiled brightly.

~

I lay in bed later that night, thinking about everything Mum had told me. Everything made sense now. From just the first look the True Mate bond begins. For me with Zee, that's all it took. With a True Mate bond, wolves can share thoughts and feelings on a scale way deeper than an Alpha does with his pack. True Mates can even share powers. Mum said that once you first sense your True Mate the bond will only grow stronger and more uncontrollable until you seal the bond. To seal the bond, you have sex. But apparently, a bond can turn, you either become more powerful together and flourish, or you destroy each other with jealousy and rage.

So much is running through my mind. I want to see her again, I want to hold her and touch her. My desire for her is stronger than anything else I have ever felt. I could feel my sweatpants tightening the more I thought about her. I pictured her eyes, her glowing golden eyes staring into mine. I pulled down my pants a little, releasing my already throbbing cock and I wrapped my fingers around it. I remembered her scent, cherry blossoms, and citrus. I squeezed my hand a little tighter rubbing up and down slowly. I could feel the sparks running through my arms and legs when our skin touched, it felt so good. I tilted my head back and moaned. The thought of my lips on hers, tasting her and kissing her, it was driving me mad. I rubbed my rock hard member faster, I was close, already. I imagined the feel of her soft skin under my hands, and her breasts pressed against me. I pictured again her eyes staring intensely into mine. My muscles tensed and my balls began to throb, I could feel it crawling up from my knees into my thighs. I pumped my hand a little faster, my insides were going off like pleasurable fireworks. The sensation hit my cock and I exploded. A calm relaxation waved over my body. I cleaned myself off with a towel from the floor, pulled up my pants, and slowly drifted off to sleep.

Chapter Four

Gunner

I woke up feeling refreshed and excited for the day. I couldn't wait to get to school and see Zelena. Actually, I didn't want to wait until school. If I go to the path in the forest where we left her yesterday, she'd be bound to come past there this morning. I went for a quick shower, barely able to contain my excitement. I got out and brushed my teeth and combed my hair. I got dressed and headed downstairs. As I opened the kitchen door, I saw Cole and Smith both with their mouths stuffed full.

"Ahh, there he is" Mum said with a smile.

She was standing at the counter with her hand on her hip, facing the boys.

"Morning Mum" I said as I walked over to her and kissed her on the cheek.

"Aren't you in a happy mood?" she cooed excitedly,

"Well, I haven't been able to get anything out of these two about this mystery girl, that has you all spun out" she said expectedly.

"See, I told you Mrs M" Smith mumbled with a mouth half full of food,

"He's proper whipped".

I smiled at them all and grabbed a muffin.

"Come on boys. Later Mum".

The boys mumbled farewell to my mum and followed me out the door.

"Why do we need to be early today?" Cole asked, even though I guessed he already knew the answer.

"We're going to the forest to meet Zee on the way to school"

"Of course we are" Cole groaned.

We took off into the forest, but it wasn't far until we reached the path from yesterday. I stopped by a tree just off the path and then we waited. It wasn't five minutes until I caught her scent through the trees. She was walking slowly with her head facing up to the sky. Goddess, she is beautiful.

Wait here you two

I took a deep breath to calm my nerves and then I walked up behind her,

"Good morning" I said softly. She jumped and spun around with wide eyes and a surprised expression, which made me giggle at her reaction.

"Whoa sorry, I didn't mean to startle you" I said raising my arms with a smirk on my face,

"You didn't" she whispered as she reached for her hood.

I didn't want her to cover her face, I wanted to see her in the morning light. I jumped forward and grabbed her wrist before she could pull it all the way up.

"Please" I pleaded with her as she dropped the hood. I stepped around in front of her to see her more clearly.

"Please don't cover your face" I begged.

She froze, I could smell the fear coming from her. Why was she still afraid of me? I looked at her face. Her lips were parted slightly and her eyes were wide, she was pale and looked scared. I followed her line of sight to my hand holding her wrist. I hadn't realised I was still holding her. I released my grip and stepped slightly back.

"I'm sorry, I shouldn't have grabbed you like that. Just don't cover your face, you don't have to hide from me".

I just wish she knew what I knew. I don't want her to be scared of me, I just want to make her feel happy and safe.

"I'm, I'm sorry, it's just um" she mumbled quietly dropping her head.

Her hair fell over her face. Oh man, I didn't mean to upset her. I need to make it right. I quickly stepped forward and lifted her chin so that I could see her more clearly. I tucked her hair behind her ear and examined her beautiful face. Her eyes were closed tightly, which made me feel a little rejected. I wanted to feel that same spark, that connection I felt with her yesterday. As I roamed my eyes over the beautiful creature before me, I noticed that there was a small fresh cut on her cheek. That definitely wasn't there yesterday. I kept studying her face when I saw the band-aid on her forehead. There was an older looking wound poking out of the bottom of the band-aid. This was much bigger than the scratch on her cheek. She would have had to hit her head on something really hard for a gash like that to happen. Then it dawned on me. She didn't hit her head, someone else hit her on the head. Someone was hurting her. I let out a shocked gasp and let go of her chin. I went straight from zero to a hundred. My blood burst into flames and I could feel the beginning of my change coming on.

"Zee, what happened to your face?" I asked her gruffly, trying and failing to control my anger.

She pulled away from me and turned her head pulling her hair back out to cover the band-aid. My rage filled every inch of my body and I could feel my ribs starting to spread and twist. I clenched my fists in an attempt to ease my anger, pressing the tip of my claws into my palm. I needed to know, who was hurting my Mate?

"Zelena, who did that to you?"

A growl erupted from my chest and I instantly swallowed it down again. I want to hurt them like they hurt her. I want to make them suffer for putting these marks on my little wolf's face. She took a step away from me, she's frightened of me. I went to jump forward to grab her, to shake some sense into her, to make her tell me who was hurting her. I need to protect her. I will do anything to protect her. Cole wrapped his arms around my chest, pulling me back, and held me in place.

"Whoa, easy mate" he said calmly.

Like a bucket of ice water had been thrown over my head, I snapped back to reality. Zee was standing in front of me, fear written all over her face. My anger subsided instantly. Oh, thank the Goddess Cole was there. I don't know what I was doing, I just got so angry. I can't believe I nearly lost it at her, I could have ruined everything. Somehow, I need to show her that it's okay, that she can trust me to take care of her.

I'm okay I swear

I flashed Cole as I threw his arm off me and stepped forward taking Zelena's hands in mine. And there they were, tingles. Like little electrical sparks dancing through my veins. I crouched down so I was close to her face.

"Zee. I didn't mean to scare you, I'm sorry" I summoned up a smile, but it felt fake.

She smiled at me with a closed mouth and nodded. I stood up straight and released her hands, but she didn't let go of mine. She was still holding one of my hands gently rubbing the back of my hand with her fingers. She did feel it too. I knew it. A warmth filled my chest and my cheeks. She looked up at me and smiled, her whole face smiled with her. She had the most spectacular smile that made her eyes glitter in the sunlight. Like I'd been kicked in the chest, I was breathless.

"Wow. You are beautiful" I stared at her struggling to control myself again.

It took everything I had in me not to pick her up in my arms and crash my lips to hers.

"Okay you two" coughed Smith,

"Let's go or we'll be late for school".

I let Smith and Cole walk off ahead of us, I wanted a moment with her. I wrapped my fingers around her tiny hand and smiled. I nodded my head in the direction of the school and raised my eyebrows. No words were needed and she understood what I meant anyway. She smiled with a blush gracing her pale cheeks. She nodded her head, and we began walking together.

I didn't even notice when we got to the school, I was too focused on Zelena, on her hand in mine and the tiny sparks and warmth that the contact expelled. Cole and Smith opened the doors and we followed them in. I couldn't stop staring at her. Her relaxed mood quickly changed, and I could feel her growing anxious. There were a lot of people in the hallway, and they were all staring at us. It's pretty clear to me now that Zelena doesn't like attention. She pulled up her hood, dropped my hand, and took off before I could do anything.

"Zee wait!" I called for her, but she didn't stop. I frowned at the people in the hallway, why can't they leave her alone. Smith hit me on the shoulder and smiled,

"It's all good dude, my first class is with her. I'll keep her company" he said with a large smile. I nodded and he left. I walked slowly to my first class, listening to the whispers in the hall as I went.

"Is he blind?"

"What's he doing with her?"

Each comment and accusation made me angrier and angrier. It shouldn't matter what these idiots think anyway, I'm only here for a couple of months. Then after that, Zee and I never have to see them again. I got to my classroom and slumped down at my desk. I managed to wait an hour into class when caved and finally flashed Smith,

How's it going, is she okay?

Dude she's fine, I even made her laugh

Thanks Smith. Walk with her to lunch okay

Whatever you say boss

When lunch came, I went straight to the cafeteria to wait for Smith and Zelena. Cole got there before us, so he stood with me and waited. When Smith came running down the hall alone, I looked for her, but I couldn't see her behind him.

"Where's Zelena?" I asked raising my eyebrows at him,

"She wanted to drop her bag off at her locker first, said to meet her here"

"I told you to walk with her" I growled leaning closer to Smith.

"Gunner, she'll be fine" Cole said putting his hand on my shoulder. I wasn't happy, but I let it go. We stood and waited for another minute, but she still didn't show. I felt uneasy in my stomach, like something was wrong. I remember what my mum said about sharing feelings on a deeper scale. Is that what's happening here? I closed my eyes and listened. I could hear something happening in a few hallways over. Something wasn't right.

"I'm gonna go find her" I said to the boys over my shoulder as I began speed walking towards the lockers.

I didn't need to look back, I knew they were right behind me. As we got to the hall there was a crowd of kids all piled in, trying to see around the corner. I pushed my way through them easily enough, and as I got around the corner my entire body blistered with rage. Demi had Zelena by the throat up against the locker. I threw kids to the side as I forced my way through the crowd. I got to the front of people and grabbed Demi by the back of the head. With inhuman like strength, I threw her across the floor. She landed at the feet of the ape from the cafeteria yesterday. I stood glaring at her as she picked herself up off the floor. I could feel my bones starting to twist and break and the heat run through my body. I was going to tear this bitch apart with my teeth. I advanced towards her baring my teeth when Cole and Smith pounced on me, holding down my arms. I shoved them off and took a few more steps closer to her before they pounced on me again. I struggled and fought to get free, managing to only get one arm loose. Throwing my arm out towards the repugnant bitch, I clipped her shoulder with my protruding claws. Nowhere near deep enough, but enough to get a squeal of pain from her.

"LET ME GO!" I screamed, fighting to break free.

I want her dead. I want to taste her blood in my mouth as her life leaves her body.

Calm down Gunner, you're starting to change

Cole begged me silently, but I ignored him.

"I'll fucking kill you if you ever touch her again" I howled at her. The little bitch was now hiding behind her big jock friend.

"Come on mate, enough" Cole said out loud.

I was still trying to shake Cole and Smith off me when I smelt the blood. I turned around and saw Zelena struggling to stand.

Let me go now

I pushed through them and ran to Zelena's side. I grabbed her waist to help her up and she flinched, which made my blood boil even more. Couldn't she see I was the one protecting her, I was helping her. Why does she shudder from my touch, if we're truly destined then she should crave it, not fear it.

"She's a fucking psycho Gunner!" Demi screeched at me.

I turned to look at her and growled, if she says just one more thing, I will tear her to pieces. The crowd fell silent, and I quickly glanced around the hall at some of them. They were all scared of me, all of them looking at me with terror on their faces.

I lifted Zelena's feet off the ground and began to run for the exit, once we were through the doors and outside, I used my speed and got her away from those parasites. I stopped on the edge of the car park by the forest. I put her back down and stood in front of her. I looked at her arms, her face, her neck, everywhere, but I couldn't see any blood.

"Are you okay? Are you hurt?"

I could still smell the fresh blood on her, but I couldn't see where it was coming from. I put my hands on her cheeks, she was burning hot. She was about to change. I could feel her pain and I could hear the bones cracking inside her. Cole and Smith ran up behind me and I waved to them to get back.

Stay back, she's changing

"Zeleeeeena" I said slowly backing away from her.

On the birth of a Weres wolf, the change can make them very unpredictable and lash out at whoever is closest to them. This is why the pups in the pack are always closely monitored around changing age. Then when the symptoms start showing more regularly, they're taken out of the village to ease into the transition, without a pack full of bystanders in the crossfire. We're shit out of luck here though, I definitely didn't get her far enough away from the school.

Zelena threw herself on the ground tossing and floundering around. I would give anything to ease her pain, but there is nothing I can do now, she's too far into the change. She was up on her hands, her back end already in the form of a wolf. The deep obsidian fur was slowly crawling its way over her neck. Arching her back and twisting her neck out to the side, she lifted her head and screamed. As the last of her change took over, her face morphed and elongated into the shape of a wolf's muzzle. Her scream melted into a howl and the change was done. She was magnificent. A smaller than average werewolf, with a shining coat, so deep dark black that it had a purple hue to it. She is the most beautiful wolf I have ever come across. She jumped around and stared at me. Her eyes were glowing a bright yellow, she was truly breathtaking. I had my hands up to show her that I meant her no harm. I was taking very small slow steps back from her. I held her gaze hoping she would still recognise me. She quickly turned on her back legs and took off into the forest, faster than I've ever seen a new wolf run.

"Okay, I believe you now" breathed Cole.

I turned and grinned at them with a sense of pride washing over me.

"Wasn't she spectacular?" I gushed,

"Did you see that coat, it was beautiful"

"I've never seen a wolf that dark in colour before" said Smith scratching his head.

"I know. me either" I smiled,

"Come on, let's go after her" I said as I started to turn to the forest.

"No Gunner, we're meant to let them run, you know that" Cole said firmly.

"I know, but this is different she's my Mate"

"Mate or not, let her be".

I didn't like it, but I knew he was right. We took off into the forest and headed for home, probably best not to go back to school again after all that. We got to the village not long after lunch. Dad and Spartan were sitting with two other pack members by the smoking hut. He spotted us as we ran in.

"Gunner, get over here" he bellowed from across the clearing.

We shuffled over to them slowly, preparing ourselves for the tongue lashing we were about to get. My dad was a very strict man. That's how Grandpa raised him. And that's how he's kept the pack safe for so many years. He was a tall man with big broad shoulders and bulging muscles. His hair was a dark sandy blonde, like mine and my sister's. I don't remember the last time I saw my dad without a big bushy beard. Smith's worried voice filled my head as we neared them,

Oh shit we are in so much trouble

Yep

Are you going to tell him about Demi?

No, just follow my lead

"Hey Dad, what's up?" I asked trying to play it cool,

"Why aren't you at school, boy?"

"Free period this afternoon, so we came home to study"

"Really, all three of you?"

He didn't look up from the deer he was skinning. I gulped, I was nervous. I had to fight so hard for him to let me go to an actual school, if he found out what just happened in the hallway, he won't let us go back.

"Yep, all three of us" I said with a cheerful tone.

He was quiet for a minute, still not looking up from his deer.

"Go on inside the house, your mother has chores for you to do" he grumbled and I sighed with relief.

"Yes sir" I said as we turned and walked away, walking a lot faster this time.

Phew that was close

I turned and gave them both a crooked grin as we walked into the main house.

When it came time for dinner, I was relieved. I hadn't stopped thinking about Zee all afternoon. I was worried for her, I didn't even know if she had a pack. As far as I know, we are the only pack in this region. The closest pack wasn't even on the island, it was nearly three hours away. I couldn't let it go and kept telling myself over and over again, that I should have followed her, I should have gone to check on her. The worry was stewing in my mind.

I was helping Nat set the table for dinner when I suddenly felt this weird headache come on. It was probably from being in the sun all afternoon. I shook my head and went to get some water. I went to the fridge and pulled out a bottle of cold water. As I was drinking, I felt as though someone had just kicked me in the ribs. I spat the water out across the kitchen floor and curled over clutching my stomach. Mum walked in and dropped the cutlery on the counter. She rushed over to me putting her arms around me.

"What's wrong, Gunner?" she questioned. I couldn't talk though, the hit to my ribs had knocked the wind out of me.

"Baby, what's going on?" Mum demanded.

I coughed and spluttered trying to catch my breath.

"I don't know" I croaked,

"It felt like I got kicked in the ribs"

"Come on, come and sit down".

Mum ushered me over to the breakfast nook. I sat leaning over trying to breathe again.

"Lupus" She called out to my dad.

"Lupus, get down here now!".

I started to catch my breath when Dad walked into the room.

"What's the screaming for?" he groaned,

"Something's wrong with Gunner" she hissed,

"What's the matter boy?" he asked,

"I'm not sure" I croaked,

"Come on son spit it out" he demanded,

"I got a sudden headache, so I came in here to get a drink, as I was drinking my water, I felt a kick to my ribs. That's it" I rushed out taking a big breath.

He knelt in front of me and grabbed my chin turning my head from side to side.

"He looks okay now" he said, standing up again.

At that moment a series of jolts hot through my body. It felt like I was being electrocuted, the pain was immeasurable. I fell to the ground convulsing, my body tensed, and the room went dark. As the pain coursed through my body, I could see something familiar. I tried to block out the pain and focus. It was the man with the whip from my dream the other night. He was standing over something laughing. I tried to see what it was, I was straining to focus but the pain was overwhelming. Then I saw it, the little black wolf. It was Zelena and he was torturing her.

I burst out of my convulsion and sat up on the floor. Mum, Dad, Nat, Spartan, Cole, Smith, and Smith's mum Deena were all standing around me yelling at each other.

"It's Zelena!" I screamed jumping up off the floor,

"He's gonna kill her".

I took off out the door and jumped down the porch steps. As I was running through the clearing, I ripped off my shirt and threw myself onto my hands and knees in the dirt. I let the fire run through me as I broke my bones. Once I was changed, I flew out of the clearing and into the forest. I got to the path where I met Zelena and started sniffing the air. Cole and Smith ran up on me in their wolf form, I growled and snapped at them. I caught the scent, it was faint, but I have a direction.

This way

I ran off following her scent with Cole and Smith flanking me.

Gunner, what's going on?

There's a man and he's killing her

How do you know this?

I just do. I barked.

We came to a house at the edge of the forest. Her scent was all over it. I could smell her pain, her fear, her sorrow, but mostly I could smell her blood. Not wasting another second, I rammed into the front door, sending it flying off its hinges and across the room. Cole and Smith followed me inside. I quickly looked around the room. The place was a disgrace. Dirty, messy, and very worn down, but empty. The scent was fresh, but no one was in here. I put my nose down and pricked up my ears.

"Please... stop" I heard her faint voice coming from under the floorboards. I growled,

The basement

I found the basement door, Zelena's scent was strongest here. So was the smell of her blood. I crashed in the door and jumped down the stairs, landing on the ground below. I looked around and saw her half naked body lying on the floor, unconscious and covered in blood. The man was standing over her, sweat and Zelena's blood coated his stained singlet shirt.

"What the fuck!" the man exclaimed.

I lowered my head and bared my teeth, growling and snapping at the man. I slowly stalked towards him as he took steps back. Cole and Smith jumped down the stairs and stood behind me on either side. The man turned around and rustled around on the workbench, he quickly whipped back around, holding a small crowbar in his hands. He held it out in front of him waving it at me. Interesting, he doesn't seem overly shocked to see three giant wolves in his house.

"Get back" he yelled.

Gunner, you can't kill him

I snapped at Cole over my shoulder

Look at what he's done to her

He will pay I promise but we don't kill humans

I growled louder at the man, stalking closer to him. He swung the crowbar at me, but I caught it in my jaw. I ripped it from his hands and tossed it across the room. I want to taste his blood. I want to rip him to pieces and then scatter them across the town. I was past angry now, I was enraged.

Stop now Gunner

Gunner, please

I lunged at the man pinning him to the ground under my paw. I leaned down to his face so that he could feel my hot breath and let my drool drip onto his fearful face. I continued to growl and snap at the man. He started to cry and beg.

"Please god help me" he pleaded.

I extended my claws and dug them into his chest, ripping at his flesh. He screamed out in pain, his hand coming to grip my paw.

GUNNER STOP!

Cole was growling at me. I was about to snap my jaw around his neck when I heard a moan from across the room. It was Zelena, I looked over at her and saw her head tip to the side. She was still alive. I snapped again at the man under my paw, just brushing my teeth across his cheek. I got off him and ran to Zelena. I cracked my neck backward and changed back into my human form.

"You're a fucking werewolf" the man cried at me.

Cole growled and snapped at him. He curled himself into a ball next to an old mattress that was leaning against the wall.

"Oh Zelena" I whispered helplessly.

I gently removed the shock collar from around her neck. Her skin was scorched and raw from the top of her neck down to her chest. Her eye was swollen shut and her face was covered in blood from the gash on her brow, and more from cuts on her lip and cheek. The shirt she was wearing was covered in blood and torn in places, she wore no pants and no underwear. I pulled a raggedy towel down from the bench beside her and covered her up. My blood boiled at the thought of what that monster did to her. I looked over at him and growled, letting my canines extend. He was cowering beside the mattress, trying to dig himself in behind it.

Pick her up Gunner she needs a hospital

"No!" I growled.

I scooped her up into my arms being as gentle as I could. I walked toward the stairs and stopped at the bottom, I glared at the man one last time,

"Never again" I snarled at him.

As I made my way up the stairs Smith followed behind me, still in his wolf form. I heard Cole snap at the man one last time and then he ran up the stairs, as he reached the top he was back in his human form. I left the house and walked to the forest in the direction of home. Zelena stirred a little in my arms, regaining some semblance of consciousness. Her head lifted slightly, and she let out a small, grunted squeak like sound.

"It's okay Zelena, I've got you now" I said to her, and I meant it.

I will never let another human harm my little wolf. She turned her head into my chest, and I held her a little closer, my heart breaking at the sight of her battered body. Cole came up beside me and peered at Zelena over my shoulder. I growled a warning at him to back up, and he did. I don't want him near her, I don't want anyone near her.

"She doesn't look so good mate" he said quietly.

"No, she'll be fine"

"I really think we should go to the hospital" he pleaded, I could smell his anxiety and fear, it's not what I need from him right now. "No" I snarled back angrily, and we continued to walk through the forest towards home.

"Gunner" she whispered as her head tipped back and she lost consciousness again.

Smith was still in his wolf form, he's a young wolf and still learning so he can't change back as easily as Cole and me.

"Smith, run ahead and get Artemis and send him to my room" I barked.

Smith whined softly and took off into the trees ahead.

"I think this may be beyond Artemis' skills, mate" Cole said quietly, still beside me but not as close to Zelena now.

"She can do it, she's strong enough" I walked on in silence, not daring to look at her anymore.

Her beaten little body was tearing my insides apart and I thought I would break at any moment. I walked as fast as I could without disturbing the precious cargo in my arms. We reached the clearing and went straight for the main house. I didn't care a lick about my nakedness, as a Were it's a common occurrence. Everyone that was here earlier, was now waiting on the porch. My mother ran over to me and gasped loudly, putting her hands over her mouth.

"Oh, the poor dear" she cried.

Dad came up beside her and wrapped his arms around her.

"She'll be alright, love" he whispered into her neck.

They both followed closely behind me. I reached the porch and walked up the steps. I could hear the shocked reactions from the pack members waiting there. I went straight to my room and was relieved to see Artemis waiting by the bed. I gently placed Zelena down and wiped the hair from her face.

"Out!" Artemis yelled waving us away,

"No, I'm staying" I insisted,

"I not work with you here" he snapped at me.

I leaned forward and growled at him. Mum grabbed my shoulders and pulled me back.

"Come on dear, best do as he asks" she said gently, as she led me out the door.

I turned around trying to see Zee one more time before the door closed. Her lifeless body lay on my bed, her skin was red from dried blood and her raven black hair was knotted and sticky. She looked so small and helpless lying there alone. Mum closed the door, and I could feel my heart break. My knees were weak and giving out and I thought I might pass out. I stumbled on my feet backward until I hit the wall behind me. I slid down the wall and tucked my head into my knees.

"Who is she?" whispered Nat.

I lifted my head and looked at them, they were all staring at me waiting for some kind of explanation or indication as to who the mystery girl was.

"She's my True Mate" I said matter-of-factly.

Chapter

Five

Zelena

Roses, I can smell roses and it's making my nose itch. I tried to lift my hand to scratch but I couldn't move it. I tried the other hand, and I can't lift that one either. I started to panic. Oh God, what has he done to me now? I want out, please let me free. I tried to open my eyes. They are very heavy and dry. I blink my eyes open and try to focus on something around me. Oh, that hurts, I blinked my eyes a few times to get the moisture on them. I can start to make out a few objects. I turned my head to the side and there's a window with blue curtains, and a small brown leather armchair sat in front of it. Where the heck am I? Next to the window is a bookshelf with a lot of books piled on top of each other. I've never seen this place before. I look to the end of the bed and there's an open door leading to a bathroom. I turned my head to the other side and there was a head lying on the bed. I blink a few more times to focus better. A man is sitting on a chair next to the bed, he is leaning forward with his arms and head resting on the edge of the bed. But who is it? I tried to move my arms some more, but they were tied down at my sides. Why am I tied to the bed? I kick my legs and try to pull my arms free.
"Zee, Zee, Zee, calm down you're alright".

I snap my head to the side and Gunner is now standing by the bed. I close my eyes tight and open them again, he's still there. I look down to where the head was lying, and it's gone. This can't be right, why is he here? This must be some messed up kinky sex dream, tied to a bed with this ravishing man standing over me. I close my eyes again and shake my head a little. Nope, not a dream, he's still there.

"It's me. You're okay" he soothed.

He sat down on the edge of the bed putting his hand on my knee. I don't understand what is happening, why is Gunner here and whose room is this? Where is Hank? I opened my mouth to talk but nothing came out. My throat burns and itches, I want to rub it with my hand but the restraint bites at my wrist when I pull. Gunner noticed me struggling to talk and grabbed the water bottle on the table by the bed. He held it to my face and bends the straw to my lips. I stare at him, feeling very uneasy but my throat is on fire. I take the straw into my mouth and gulp down some water. Oh, that's good. He started to pull it away, but I shook my head and he put the straw back between my lips. Ah, that's so much better. I lick my lips, pleased with the newfound saliva. I look at Gunner and he has sat back down on the chair staring at me.

"I thought I'd lost you there for a little while" he said shakily.

A single tear rolled down his cheek and he quickly wiped it away, placing a half assed smile on his gorgeous face.

"But you're okay now".

He took hold of my hand and squeezed it gently. I lifted my hand and pulled on the restraints while staring at him, the question of 'why' written all over my face.

"Oh right" he says jumping up and started unbuckling my first wrist.

"You were thrashing around a lot while you were out, and we didn't want you to hurt yourself anymore, so we thought it best to, you know, tie you up".

Who's 'we'? He was talking as he moved around to the other arm and untied that one. I grabbed my wrists and rubbed them. As I tried to lift myself up on the bed a little, pain shot through my chest and stomach.

"Whoa, whoa, slow down and I'll help you" he blurted out, he walked quickly back over to the chair and grabbed the pillow he had been leaning on. With so much care and tenderness, he helped me sit forward and placed the pillow behind my back.

"There you go".

He smiled and sat on the edge of the bed, he seemed happy. But I'm still confused, and I still don't know where I am or how I got here.

"Where?" I coughed and cleared my throat a little.

"Just take it easy, try not to talk too much" he said patting his hand on my knee again.

I stared at his hand, it made me feel a little uncomfortable. Not that I don't like his touch, but any kind of human contact is not something that I'm overly fond of. It's different with Gunner though, I remembered, with him it feels different, it feels safe. I figured if he wanted to hurt me, he would have done that while I was sleeping, right?

"Where am I?" I croaked out.

"This is my room" he said stretching out his arms in the air and looking around the room.

"How long?" I muttered.

"You've been here for five days now. What's the last thing that you remember?" he asked softly.

I rested my head back on the pillow, closed my eyes, and tried to think. I remember running through the forest and turning into a wolf, I smiled at the memory. I'm a fucking wolfwoman! Then, I remember getting a shirt off the clothesline and sneaking into the house. Hank was there and he threw me into the basement. I scrunched my eyes and I felt Gunner squeeze my leg. I remember him punching me in the face. And then I remembered the pain and the convulsions. Fear and panic coiled into my memory. I opened my eyes and sprung up on the bed. Ow, my chest. I felt around my neck, but the strap was gone, my neck was now covered in bandages. I lifted the baggy grey top I was wearing, and my abdomen was wrapped in bandages as well. I looked at Gunner and he was watching me. He looked both angry and sad at the same time. What did Hank do to me, what was that thing he put on my neck? He nearly killed me. I thought I died. I wanted to die. I started to hyperventilate, and my chest ached with each sharp intake of breath.

"It's okay, you're safe now" Gunner's soothing voice said as he slid forward on the bed and gently wrapped his arms around me, pulling my head into his chest.

Wow, this is different. I don't think I've ever been hugged before. This feels so nice, so warm, and safe. I don't know the last time I felt safe, truly unequivocally safe and secure. But here it is, wrapped in the arms of a boy I've known for two days. I threw my arms around his waist and pressed my face into the heat of his chest. Before I understood what my body was doing, I began to sob into his shirt. Why did this happen to me, why does that man have to be my father? I want my mum. I don't even remember her, but still, I yearn for her. The patch on his shirt was soaked in my tears, but he didn't relent, he held me tight and tried to soothe me. I buried my face further into his chest and continued to cry.

"Shh, it's okay" he whispered stroking my hair,

"I won't let him hurt you anymore".

After a few minutes of mournful sobs and a few more of silent crying, he gently laid me back down on the bed and pulled himself in next to me. My head was resting on his arm and my face was nuzzled into the crook of his shoulder and chest. He made me feel better, like I didn't hurt anymore. I felt somewhat protected in his arms. And something else that I'd never felt before. Home. I squirmed further into him, wrapping my leg around his leg and my arm around his back. I held him tightly and he let me. Right here on this bed, wrapped in his arms, everything that's wrong in the world just disappears. After another few minutes, I was fast asleep again.

When I woke up it was dark, with nothing but the light from the moon outside lighting the bedroom. Gunner's arms were still around me, he was spooning me from behind. I could feel his soft warm breath on the back of my neck. I shuffled myself back a little so that my whole body was pressed up against his. He was so warm, I could feel the heat radiating off him. I breathed in deeply, oh my, he smells so good. There was something about just being close to him that made all my fear and anxiety slip away. He nuzzled his face into my hair, I think he's awake. I felt something start to poke into my backside. Oh yes, he is definitely awake. At least a part of him is. I felt my cheeks get hot with blush as I smiled to myself. He lifted his hip forward a little, grinding his hard dick on my ass. Holy heck, what do I do? I'd never even kissed a boy before, and now here I am with the most beautiful creature I had ever seen, and he's grinding his erection between my ass cheeks. He growled and squeezed me a bit tighter. Pain shot through my chest and I let out a painful squeak. He very quickly rolled himself off the bed, jumped up, and stood by the door.

"I'm sorry" he said with a panicked tone.

I carefully turned over on the bed to look at him. Unsure of what I was meant to say.

"I didn't mean to" he said rubbing his face.

He was holding a pillow over his crotch. I couldn't help it, the sight made me giggle. He looked over at me, his eyes glowed silver in the moonlight coming through the window.

"Did I hurt you?" he asked still standing by the door,

"No, I'm okay" I smiled and patted the bed in front of me

"I'm sorry, I should have controlled myself better"

"Gunner I'm okay, please come and sit back down".

He walked awkwardly back over to the bed and sat on the edge, keeping the pillow firmly in his lap. We sat silently for a minute, both of us a little embarrassed about what just happened. "Are you hungry? I can go and get you some food" he said as he turned to me and smiled,

"I'm starved".

I hadn't noticed how hungry I was until he mentioned food. I don't remember the last time I ate. It's normal for me to long periods of time without food, but I am positively ravenous right now.

"I'll run downstairs and grab you something" he said standing up and putting his pillow back on the bed.

"Actually, if it's okay I'd really like to walk a little" I said sitting up,
"Can I come with you?"
He tilted his head and looked at me, contemplating, I imagine.
"Are you sure you're up for it?" he asked,
"I'm sure".
I tried to lift myself up off the bed but struggled. Gunner jumped to my side holding my waist and my hand for support. I blushed again at his touch, recollecting the other part of his anatomy that I was sort of touching just moments ago. He led me out of the bedroom door, down a short hallway, and to a massive open staircase. There was a giant chandelier hanging from the roof. He helped me down the stairs slowly as I gazed at the beautiful site. I had never seen anything so shiny and extravagant. I bet it looks magical in the daylight. We walked through the big foyer and into the kitchen. Gunner turned on the light, it was huge in here too. There was a big black marble counter and a breakfast nook under a window. I looked up at Gunner and smiled enviously, he's really been living the life, hasn't he? He carefully placed me down at the breakfast nook and walked over to a tall kitchen cupboard, he grabbed out a floral apron, put it on, and curtsied with a big toothy grin.
"How can I serve you madame?" he asked in a terrible French accent.
I giggled blushing again. He was so sexy, even wearing a floral apron. I put my elbow on the table and rested my head in my hand.
"What are my options, kind sir?" I laughed, ignoring the pain in my chest.
He walked around the kitchen going through the cupboards and the fridge, rattling off a bunch of words in his bad French accent. I kind of zoned out and forgot to listen to him, I was too busy drooling over his sexiness. He was wearing a grey shirt with a deep v in the front, his bare chest showing through. He had dark grey sweatpants on and when he turned around, I could see how they stuck to his perfectly toned ass cheeks. His hair was a mess flopping from side to side as he turned his head. Everything about

him is positively delicious and I want a taste. Whoa, where did that come from? 'Down girl' I scolded myself, I need to get a grip. "And that's all there is".

He turned around to face me, I lifted my head snapping back to reality. I have no idea what he just said...

"Cereal sounds nice" I guessed.

"Huh, huh, huh, that is a very good choice" he chuckled, still going with the accent. I smiled and shook my head. He grabbed the coco pops and milk and put them on the table in front of me, he then took off the apron and hung it back in the cupboard. He grabbed two bowls and two spoons. He brought them over and squeezed into the booth next to me. I watched him as he poured in the cereal and then the milk. His biceps bulging a little as he lifted his arm. I breathed in through my nose smelling his sweet odour. Warm sunshine. A hot flash ran through my cheeks and down to my stomach where it danced around. I sniffed him again and my legs felt numb. My crotch tingled with a fiery longing. I squeezed my thighs together as I felt my heart begin to race. What the heck is going on with me. I nearly died and am still in pain, but all I can think of is ripping his clothes off and licking his body from head to toe. Get a grip girl.

"Are you okay?" he asked looking down at me.

I felt the blush in my cheeks burn again. I smiled with my lips closed and nodded, worried about what I might say if I spoke aloud. He slid the bowl to me and held out the spoon.

"Bon appétit" he said with a smile.

I dipped the spoon in my bowl and lifted it to my lips, as I opened my mouth and felt the cold wet spoon against my tongue, the kitchen door flew open. I peered under Gunner's arm toward the door and saw a small lady in a baby pink fluffy dressing gown. She had her chocolate brown hair tied up in a messy bun on top of her head. She looked over at Gunner and her body visibly relaxed.

"It's late, Gunner baby, why are you up?" she whispered from across the room, crossing her arms in front of her.

Gunner didn't say anything, he only leaned back in the chair so that the woman could see me.

"Oh" she gasped, taking a small step towards us.

"Zelena, Darling, you're out of bed".

She looked at Gunner, then at me, and back at Gunner again.

"Zee, this is my Mum, Romeá" he smiled looking down at me and then back at his mum.

His mum, holy shit he just introduced me to his mother. I swallowed my cereal coughed a little and smiled at her.

"Nice to meet you ma'am"

"Oh, hush now, you can call me Roe" she said flicking her hand in the air.

"I'm surprised to see you down here though".

I don't think she was talking to me as she was looking at Gunner as she spoke.

"We were a little hungry" said Gunner watching his mum and sitting forward a little, blocking my view of her.

I leaned forward so that I could see her, and Gunner turned and looked at me with a frown dancing on his forehead. We were quiet for a second, gazing back and forward at each other, it felt very awkward, there was a strange tension in the air.

"Zelena, my sweet, I'd love to have a talk with you when you're ready" she said with a smile,

"Not now Mum" Gunner snapped,

"Well of course not now Gunner, but maybe in the morning"

"Maybe" Gunner said as he looked back at his bowl.

I don't understand why he is being so short with her. She seems lovely, and she's being so nice, was I missing something?

"I'd love to Roe" I said smiling at her.

Gunner looked at me and frowned a little. Roe looked happy and smiled brightly back at me.

"Okay my loves, just don't stay up too late and keep the noise down or you'll wake your father"

"Sure thing Mum" Gunner said watching her as she left the kitchen.

Once she was gone, he looked back down at his bowl and kept eating. I stared at him trying to understand the mood he was in all of a sudden. He was so blunt with his mum and a little rude. I hope she didn't think it was because of me, like I'm a bad influence on him or something. I turned back to my bowl and kept eating slowly. My throat burned with each swallow, which made me wince a little, but the food hitting my stomach was instant pain relief. Gunner finished before me and sat back in the chair and watched me eat. When I finished, I looked up at him and smiled, and he smiled back,

"Come on, let's get you back to bed, it's still early" he said as he stood up holding out his hand for me.

I looked at his outstretched hand and hesitated for a moment, I'm still not used to this kind of human contact. Everything up until this point in my life has been hurt and pain. But with Gunner, it was loving and caring and gentle, it made my head spin. I took his hand and struggled to my feet. He then bent down and scooped me up into his arms, kissing me on the forehead. He just actually kissed me. I blushed bright red. He carried me bridal style to the kitchen door where he motioned for me to get the light. I hit the light switch and then we made our way up the stairs, I again got to see the beautiful chandelier. As we got to his room, he gently placed me down on the edge of the bed and went to the other side.

"I'd like to use the bathroom" I said standing up slowly. He grabbed my hand and started to walk with me. I stopped and looked up at him and smiled,

"I think I can manage on my own"

"Oh yeah, sorry" he laughed letting my hands go and sitting on the end of the bed.

I walked in, hit the light, and closed the door. I sat down on the toilet and looked around at the little bathroom. Two dark green towels hung on the hooks behind the door. The shower was pretty big and had a glass door, there was a mix of shampoos and body washes on the floor. Next to me was the basin with a big mirror over it. I finished my business and went to wash my hands. As I looked up at the mirror, I saw my face and my heart dropped.

The old cut on my forehead was almost healed, however, there was a new cut below that on my eyebrow. It was dark red with a little white strip over it, holding the skin closed. My entire right eye was purple, from the bridge of my nose to my eyelid and halfway down my cheek. My actual eye was bloodshot and slightly swollen. A cut on my bottom lip made it swollen and dark red, and another cut lay on my cheekbone. Poking out of the bandages around my neck were blistered burns. I pulled the bandage down a little to see more of what was under it. My skin is dark red with small raw looking splotches. Parts of the skin was curling back and peeling. I was monstrous. How has Gunner been able to look at me without vomiting? I lifted my shirt and inspected the skin under the bandages there too. The skin of my torso was now a ruby reddish colour, littered with dark purple patches. I could still feel the slashes on my back when I twisted, so I didn't need to see those to know they were still there. Dropping the hem of my shirt, I slumped down on the floor and hid my head in my hands. Sorrowful sobs echoed through the small bathroom. How could anyone be this cruel, why would Hank do this to me? My own father. He's a monster. Parents are supposed to love and protect their children, aren't they? How could he so callously inflict so much pain and torment onto his own child? A light knock on the door, followed by a cautious voice, broke my sobbing.

"Zee, are you alright?" Gunner asked softly,

"No" I whimpered,

"I'm hideous".

I pulled my knees in closer to my chest and a sharp pain shot through my ribs. Gunner slowly opened the door and came to sit down beside me.

"Please don't cry" he whispered putting his hand on my leg.

"Don't look at me" I cried pushing his hand away,

"You'll heal Zee, it just takes a little longer for young wolves".

For young wolves? What does he mean by that? Then I remembered the school parking lot, he saw me change. He knows I'm a wolf. Why would he know stuff about wolves though? I lifted my head and gazed at him curiously.

"What do you mean young wolves?" I asked him bluntly.

No point in dancing around the subject, I want answers and I want them now.

"You're a newborn wolf. You've only had one change, right? Well, the healing ability gets quicker the more you change" he answered nonchalantly.

"But how do you know?" I asked wiping the tears from my cheek. He couldn't possibly know any of this, I'm the only wolfwoman out there, aren't I? A total freak of nature.

"I just do, we got taught this stuff as pups" he shrugged his shoulders.

What does he mean by 'we get taught this' and why would he say pup?

"Pups?" I questioned, tilting my head at him.

He didn't answer right away, he just smiled at me. I stared at him intently, waiting for him to speak.

"Come and sit on the bed and I'll explain".

He stood up holding out his hands for me. I put my hands in his and he gently pulled me up. We went out of the bathroom and sat down on the bed facing each other. I looked at him again waiting for him to explain.

"What do you want to know?" he asked crossing his legs.

"Pups?" I said looking at his face.

"Pups are wolf kids, little kids before they have had their first change. Once they change, they are young wolves or just Weres, until they are named otherwise"

"What does that mean?" I asked confused. Is he some kind of mythical creature research buff or something?

"Like the head of the pack is the Alpha, he is called the Alpha Wolf, and his wife is the Luna. Their children will be called either Alpha-son or Alpha-daughter"

"What's the pack?"

"The pack are the other wolves that live under the Alpha. An Alpha will have his Beta, a Were he trusts to help him with the welfare of the other pack members. Besides the Luna, the Beta is next in charge. And then there's the Delta, they act as the pack representative, so to speak. The rest of the members in the pack are just wolves, unless they hold a title".

I nodded slowly as I took in what he was saying. Then it hit me, like a grand piano falling from the sky, I wasn't the only wolf, I'm not a freak of nature. There's more of us, apparently a lot more, and they all live together like a family. And Gunner, I think he is one too.

"Are you a wolf too?" I asked looking at him wide eyed,

"Yes" he chuckled,

"Though we call ourselves Weres. I'm the first-born son of the Alpha".

I tilted my head to the side and stared at him full of questions, I just didn't know how to ask them.

"Meaning I will be the Alpha one day" he continued after picking up that I wasn't asking more questions.

"This is the pack house, or the main house. It's where the Alpha family lives and we hold pack meetings and ceremonies and all that".

I gulped as I looked around the room. Holy cow, he 'is' a wolf or a Were, whatever. But he's not just any wolf, he'll be an Alpha one day. A leader, the top of the pyramid, the man in charge. But what does that make me? I don't have a pack or an Alpha or any of that, what am I then? I looked at Gunner a little puzzled,

"What does that make me?"

"You're a newborn wolf, having just had your first change. Some would say that you're an Omega"

"What's an Omega?" I asked loudly.

"Shh..." he said putting his finger over his lips, with a slight chuckle.

"An Omega is a lone wolf that isn't part of a pack"

"How do you find a pack?" I whispered,

"An Omega has to be accepted into the pack by the Alpha"

"But what if they don't get accepted?" I was worried about his response having just been told of my loner status.

"If an Omega is rejected then they have to move on out of the region that that pack controls".

I lowered my head in shame. Is that what I will have to do, leave? I couldn't leave, where would I go. My father is all that I have ever known, this damn island is all that I've ever seen. I don't think I would survive on my own. Hank, I survived, but facing the whole world alone, no way. Gunner put his hand under my chin and lifted my head up.

"You won't be an Omega for long, I promise".

A smile grew across his face and his eyes were staring deep into mine, I smiled at him, a weak half smile. He leaned forward close to my face,

"You're not going anywhere" he whispered.

His words filled my heart with joy. The thought of being accepted and taken in, of one day being part of a real-life family, it gave me hope. But to stay here in this place, with him, is more than I could have ever dreamed of. I was completely overcome with happiness. I jumped into his lap straddling him and wrapping my arms around his neck. He was shocked by my sudden movement and paused holding his arms up. After a beat, his body then relaxed and he wrapped his arms around me, laying his cheek on the top of my head.

The butterflies came back to my stomach, and I could feel my heart rate rising. Being close to him like this was sending my hormones into overdrive. The heat from his skin and his smell, the way my skin prickled where it touched his, it set loose a frightening desire that I didn't know I had in me. I turned my face into his chest and planted small kisses leading up to his collarbone. His body tensed again and his arms around me tightened slightly. I continued my little kisses up to his neck. He moaned softly as I reached his earlobe, biting it. He growled at me, but not the kind of growl I'd heard from him before, this was somewhat seductive. It set fireworks off in my crotch, I could feel my clit pulsating. As I nibbled on his ear, I grabbed the bottom of his shirt and tugged on it pulling it up. He lifted his arms and I pulled it over his head, he then threw it across the room. His hand gripped my thighs squeezing them. He angled his neck back and I continued to kiss down his neck to his chest biting him harder, which made him moan.

I sat up on my knees and he slid his hands higher up my thighs digging his fingertips into my legs, the pressure felt good. I bent my head back and he began to kiss the top of my neck, biting and kissing from behind my ear and over the side of my jaw and back again. He moved his hand up my thighs and onto my ass, gripping the cheeks and squeezing. I dug my fingers into his back, I'm sure the wetness between my thighs was soaking through the boxer shorts I was wearing. I wanted him and that was all I knew at this point. He carefully moved his hands up my back over the bandages and to the top of my shoulders. He pulled me downward making me sit down on his lap. I could feel his full hard dick between my legs. I moved my hips forward very slowly grinding myself along his shaft and back again. I grind forward again pressing myself down harder on his dick. He then quickly grabbed the sides of my shoulders, lifting me off his lap and standing up. He was panting and I could see his huge member pushing forward under his sweatpants.

"Stop. We can't" he breathed heavily. I was reeling. What the fuck just happened. I've never acted like this before, so why now? I don't even recognise myself anymore.

"What?" I whispered blown away with embarrassment.

"I want to, I REALLY want to. But not now, you still need to heal" he said, his voice shaky but firm.

Goddammit, why did he have to be so good to me. No, don't think like that, he's just trying not to hurt you. He is good, be thankful. Besides, I can't do 'that' sort of stuff. I never have before, in fact, I've never done anything remotely close to sexual with another person. I wouldn't even know what to do, even if I did want to. It's so unbelievably frustrating, but he's right.

"Okay, I'm sorry" I whispered, the weight of what could have happened hitting me all at once.

"Will you still lay with me?" I pleaded, gesturing to the bed. Gunner smiled and nodded.

We got in under the covers and he pulled me into his arms wrapping his leg around me. He kissed me on the forehead and I nuzzled into his chest. I closed my eyes and drifted off to sleep.

Chapter Six

Zelena

I opened my eyes slowly. The sun was already shining brightly through the window. I reached my arm behind me and felt around the bed. I sat up quickly and looked around the room. Gunner wasn't there. I took a deep breath and yawned, stretching my arms out above me. Wait, my chest didn't hurt. I twisted my back from side to side waving my arms in the air, my ribs didn't hurt at all. I got up from the bed and walked around the room, still no pain, how weird.

I noticed the bookshelf and decided to take a look. There were so many books, some with older worn covers and others a bit more newer looking. I picked up a small red book and read the cover 'A Lycanthropy Reader; WEREWOLVES IN WESTERN CULTURE'. I flicked through the pages and put it back on the shelf, a little too intense for some early morning reading. I picked up another one and read the cover, 'The Garden of Eden' by Ernest Hemingway. Not what I expected from a teenage werewolf soon-to-be-Alpha. I put it back and my eyes fell on a really older looking book. I pulled it out and it was big and very heavy. It looked very worn down and must be hundreds of years old. It was bound in leather with a brass buckle. I turned it over and on the back are three crescent moons all twisted together, branded into the leather.

"Careful with that one, it's older than my great-great-grandpa" Gunner's voice came from the doorway. He was leaning against the door frame with his arms crossed in front of him. He was wearing a tight plain black t-shirt and jeans. I looked him up and down and smirked, good God he is handsome. I carefully put the book back on the shelf and crawled back onto the bed sitting up and smiling at him.

"How'd you sleep gorgeous?" he asked walking over to me,

"Pretty good actually"

"That's good" he leaned down and kissed me on the forehead. I frowned, a little disappointed. I am still yet to taste those lips.

"Get dressed, Artemis is here" he said standing up again,

"Who's Artemis?"

"He's our healer, he's the one that bandaged you up when I brought you here". I figured that he had brought me here, the how part though, I haven't worked out yet. I haven't had the stomach to ask him about what happened that night.

"Okay, but I don't have any clothes" I said with a shrug of my shoulders. He smiled and nodded to three plastic bags sitting by the bathroom door.

"I sent my sister out shopping for you. She was more than happy to spend my money" he huffed. Did he buy me clothes? I'm not sure I like that, but I won't lie, I'm a little excited. I don't get new stuff very often. My dad used to bring back op-shop clothes once or twice a year. But never anything new or pretty. I was itching to see what was in the bags.

"I've gotta go help Dad out with some things. Once Artemis has seen you Mum will have some food ready"

"Okay boss" I smiled,

"Mm... boss ay? I could get used to that" he smirked leaning forward again. I lifted my chin ready for a kiss but instead, he growled playfully and snapped his teeth at my nose, he quickly stood up straight and walked to the door.

"Don't take too long, he's waiting downstairs" he winked and blew a kiss at me and left. I jumped up and sat on the floor and proceeded to spill the contents of the bags over my lap. 'Woo pretty' I thought lifting up a black singlet top with lace sleeves. There were a few other tops and some jeans and denim shorts, even some boots and sandals and thankfully, some underwear. I sniffed at myself, I could use a shower. Badly. But Gunner said that the healer was waiting. Shit. I suppose I will have to shower after then, gross.

I got changed into the jeans and a loose bright blue top, they were a little big on my small gaunt frame, but I appreciated the gesture. After slipping on the sandals, I walked quickly out the door and down the stairs. Waiting in the foyer near the front door, was a short older man with a grey beard and long thick hair with streaks of dark brown and grey. He was wearing a big long brown coat that hung past his knees. Weird, seeing as it isn't even a cold day. As I got closer to him, I could make out his features more, he was very exotic looking with tanned skin and dark eyes with wrinkles on the corners. I got to the bottom of the stairs and he nodded at me, then walked to a room on the left. I followed him in, and he pointed to a cream-coloured armchair. I sat down and put my hands in my lap. He knelt down in front of me and began to lift my shirt,

"Whoa!" I said pushing his hands away. What in the hell is this creeper doing? He looked at me and frowned.

"I need to check the ribs" he grumbled in a thick foreign accent, that I couldn't place.

"Oh, okay" Hesitantly, I lifted my shirt to show the bandages around my abdomen. Wearing a permanent scowl and not saying anything further, he started to unwrap the bandages, not sparing me a single glance. He dropped the pieces of fabric on the table and started to press and feel around my ribs and torso. His touch made me very uncomfortable, but surprisingly not pained. Having a stranger laying his hands on my body made me feel very uneasy. I don't know this man. I know that Gunner said he helped me, but I don't remember that.

"Does this hurt?" he grumbled,

"No" I answered,

"How about this?"

"No"

"And here?"

"Nope"

"Hmm..." he groaned pulling my shirt back down.

"Ribs are healed" he mumbled. He turned away and fiddled with his medical case. Wow, that was quick. Hank has broken a rib before, but they've never healed this fast. Must be my new wolfy powers.

"Now the neck, pull down sleeves" he demanded, then paused, "Please" he added with a frown.

This Artemis guy is a little rough around the edges but efficient, I guess. I pulled my arms out of the sleeves and pulled down the shirt to the top of my breasts. He started unwrapping the bandage from around my neck and chest. I felt so exposed and uncomfortable. I wish Gunner was here. He dropped the last of the bandages on the table and began to inspect the burns. He used his hand to lift my chin but other than that, he didn't touch me, much to my gratification. He looked over my neck from the front to the back. I was waiting for me to comment on the slashes on my back, but he didn't speak to me directly. I could hear him huffing and mumbling inaudibly to himself, yet he made no comment about the markings. Surely they haven't healed yet. After a minute he turned away and rummaged through his bag.

"The neck is okay" he said while not facing me,

"No more bandage, just cream now".

He kept digging through his bag and then turned around holding a glass jar with mossy green goo looking stuff inside.

"After shower" he said tapping the lid of the jar. He stood up, put the bandages and the rest of the things in his bag, and turned to walk out.

"Thank you" I called to him. He stopped and nodded at me from over his shoulder and walked out the door leaving it slightly open. I held the jar up and inspected its contents. It's an awful green booger looking glob and smells like mouldy tree moss. Whispering in the foyer caught my attention, so I put the jar down and leaned forward, trying to listen.

"Too quickly" was Artemis' voice,

"What do you mean it was too quick, how is that possible?" it sounded like Roe, Gunner's mum,

"Not possible"

"Could it be the bond, is it making her stronger?"

"Is possible"

"What do we do with them now?"

"Need to be careful, give too much to one and other get weak"

"Thank you, Artemis, your help is always greatly appreciated".

There were footsteps, and a door opened and closed again. What was too quick, were they talking about my healing? What did she mean by bond and how is it making me strong? I need to find out what's going on. The door was pushed open all the way and Roe stepped in.

"Hello Darling" she said with a smile,

"I've got some lunch for you"

"Perfect" I said standing up. I followed her to the kitchen where there was an extravagant slew of sandwiches and wraps spread out on the counter. Wow, I thought. This lady really has the housewife thing down, doesn't she?

"Help yourself dear, take as much as you like".

I grabbed two quarter sandwiches and one small wrap and sat down at the breakfast nook with my food. Roe came over with a glass of juice, she put it down next to my plate and sat across from me in the booth. I lifted my sandwich and took a bite. Mm… it's good, like really good. Roe didn't have any food, she just sat and watched me eat. It was a little weird and uncomfortable. She didn't say anything, just watched me. When I was done, she picked up my plate and took it to the sink. I watched her glide effortlessly across the floor and I took a sip of my juice. She walked back over and sat down again, this time with a determined look on her soft and delicate face.

"I was hoping we could have a little chat" she said. She was smiling, but the way she said it made me really nervous.

"Sure" I croaked back,

"First of all, what has my son told you about our world?" She rested her hands on the table and interlocked her fingers.

"Not much, just about Alpha's and Omega's"

"Has he said anything about Mate's?"

"Uh, I don't know what you mean"

"I mean, soul mates, lovers, partners in life"

"Oh, well he told me the Alpha's wife is called the Luna".

She huffed, looking down and shook her head softly. There was something going on, she was anxious, and I could smell it on her. When did I start smelling feelings? Or when did I learn what emotions even smelled like?

"Have I missed something?" I asked getting a little annoyed.

"My Darling, it's time you hear about some of our legends. Particularly about the True Mate bond". The True Mate bond sounds interesting, maybe that was what she meant earlier when she was talking to Artemis.

"O-okay" I stuttered. My stomach was in knots, something about her energy was making me feel queasy.

"Try to listen and stay calm, I'm not telling you this to frighten you, you just need to understand some things before this goes too far". I nodded my head, indicating for her to begin, and then sat back and crossed my arms.

"In our world, you don't just choose a husband or a wife, you choose a Mate. For one of us, a Were, the connection with your Mate is very strong. You can talk to each other using your minds, like telepathy, though we Weres call it flashing. An Alpha or Alpha-son can also do this with a small selection of his pack members. You can also feel what the other is feeling. If one is sad then the other becomes sad, if one is angry the other becomes angry. Having a Mate puts your senses into overdrive, because of this, there is a strong urge to protect what is yours. And when I say that, I mean your Mate. Weres are a very jealous and possessive folk" she paused, looking at me.

"How do you choose a Mate?" I asked curiously,

"Once you feel a connection with another Were, you share your blood" she answered. My eyes bulged and a lump formed in my throat. Share blood? Are Weres like vampires, do they drink each other's blood?

"I'm sorry, what?" I sputtered,

"It's nothing like what I think you're thinking, Darling. It's as simple as a pinprick on each Weres finger and pressing them together, or consuming just a single drop. Nothing gory" she said with a slight chuckle.

"Oh" I breathed out with relief.

"May I go on?" Roe asked. I nodded my head and she continued.

"There is a legend among our people about something called the True Mate. It is a very uncommon occurrence that only happens once every three or four generations. It is so rare in fact that most Weres believe it to be nothing more than a myth. It is somewhat similar to the bond between Mates only everything is heightened. You cannot choose your True Mate, they are chosen for you by our Holy Goddess. The legends say that the pair that share the bond can also share their powers, making them faster and stronger than any normal werewolf. Just like with a normal Mate, the True Mate can feel the other's feelings, though it is said that the feelings are intensified. Anger becomes rage, sadness becomes sorrow and lust becomes insatiable passion. In one of the stories passed down from our ancestors, the True Mate bond shared between two Weres made them very powerful. It also made them very volatile. The story says that the she-wolf had grown up with the pack Alpha, they were very close friends and were able to flash with each other. This connection made the male very jealous, and in a single fit of rage, he killed the Alpha. When the pack retaliated for the murder of their Alpha, the male tore them all apart, in doing so he also fatally wounded his True Mate. When she died, he became weak and sickly. Since he had killed his pack and was left alone, he was easily killed by hunters when he was in his wolf form". She stopped talking and looked at me. I was processing the story trying to figure out the relevance. I had so many questions, but I didn't know how to word them.

"How do you know the difference between a Mate and a True Mate?" I asked quietly.

"Well even though they are similar they are also vastly different. A Were can share many Mate bonds with different wolves, never at the same time, but there can be more than one. For a True Mate, there is only ever one. And as the bond is chosen for you, the blood sharing is not required. Once the two Weres sense each other, the True Mate bond begins and then they will never share another bond with any other wolf. To lose one's True Mate is to lose a piece of themselves. The history says that one does not live long without the other".

This is intense stuff. Soul mates and dying without each other. It's like something out of a fairy tale. The night of the... incident, with my father, I was beaten pretty badly. I imagine that I would have been bleeding a lot. Gunner said that he brought me here, so if he was bleeding when he saved me, and our blood mixed together somehow, does that mean we could be Mates now? Is that what she is trying to tell me, I have accidentally been Mated to her son?

"Is Gunner my Mate now?" I asked her. She tilted her head to the side and gazed at me with a puzzled look on her face. I didn't really think it was that hard of a question to answer. A simple yes or no would suffice.

"Is he your Mate?" she asked again, like she didn't hear me the first time,

"Yeah, like is that why we have gotten close so quickly? We shared blood accidentally, right?"

"Zelena, honey, I don't think you understand what I am telling you this for. Gunner isn't your chosen Mate. He is your True Mate. You have the bond". She leaned forward staring at me. Wait, he is my what now? Is she for real? I felt nauseous and dizzy. This can't be real. Is that what has been going on with me? I'm not just a horny teenager, I'm Mated. This mythical Goddess has given me a person and deemed that I am to stay with that person for the rest of my life, or I die. What the actual fuck.

"Wait what? How do you know that?" I snapped.

"He has spoken to me about the connection he feels with you. It started to bloom well before the night he saved you. When you were being hurt, he could feel it, that's why he went to rescue you. And your injuries are all but healed, a newborn wolf like you can't usually heal this fast. Especially from injuries as severe as yours were. That was Gunner. He shared his healing powers with you.

He is making you strong, just as you are making him strong" she said while staring at me intently.

Wow! This is all so much. I need time to think. I need water. I picked up my juice and chugged it down. Of all people or werewolves, whatever, to be paired with, Gunner isn't exactly a bad pick. I mean just look at him. It's not just that he is exquisite to look at, but he is also kind and caring, really sweet, and he makes me feel safe. I like Gunner. But I never expected to find love, I didn't think I'd live long enough to experience it if I'm being honest. Now I'm being told that I have been given to someone who is to be my soul mate, and I am his. What if I'm not enough for him? What if he doesn't want me? This would be a lot for anyone to hear, but does Gunner even want to be stuck with me for the rest of his life? I'm nothing special. Most would say that I am a burden. What would happen if he decided he wanted more? Something better? What would become of me then?

"Can I ask you, Sweetheart, have the two of you been intimate?" Roe asked softly, interrupting my crazy thought train. I nearly choked on my own tongue and made a bizarre gagging sound. Roe lowered her head and chuckled quietly, I think she was just as embarrassed, asking about my relationship with her son. I thought about last night and the steamy dry humping, I tried to hide my smile and blushed and I shook my head.

"No, I haven't even kissed him" I whispered,

"Ah, that makes sense" she said leaning back in her seat,

"I can see that you already like him a lot" she said with a small giggle. My cheeks burned with embarrassment. I leaned forward putting my elbows on the table and hiding my face in my hands.

"You don't need to be shy dear. I still remember making my first bond with Lupus. Oh, how that man could drive me wild. He still does" she moaned with a little growl. Oh my god, I could just die of shame right now. She leaned forward holding my arm from across the table. I lifted my eyes and looked at her through my fingers.

"Once you share your first kiss you will understand" she smiled, and a light blush flushed her cheeks.

"Now there is one other thing" she said letting go of my arm and sitting up straight. I dropped my arms crossing them on the table and looked at her.

"I can't believe I'm about to say this to my eighteen-year-old son's girlfriend". The sound of her calling me Gunner's girlfriend, sent a flurry of butterflies swarming around my stomach. Roe wiped her brow with the back of her hand. I could sense her nervousness.

"You will need to seal the bond and you will need to do it soon" she sighed, dropping her head and blurting out a small laugh. Seal the bond, what in the heck does that mean? Do we need to sign some sort of contract, or make a blood oath or some shit?

"Uh, how do we do that exactly?" I asked slowly. I'm a little unsure if I want to hear the answer. My mind was swimming with gruesome and gross possibilities. Everything from drinking each other's blood to getting married. Roe's cheeks blushed a deep crimson and a bead of sweat rolled down her forehead.

"Through intercourse" she blinked as her blush spread down her neck as well. Intercourse, as in sex. Did my supposed Mate's mother just tell me to sleep with her son? What the flipping fuck kind of backwards life am I living right now. I could feel a giggle bubbling just under the surface.

"You want me to sleep with your son?" I asked her while trying not to laugh at the absurd irony of it all. She smiled with her mouth closed and jaw tensed and nodded slowly. Oh my goodness, I think I am in love with this woman. I mean this is super embarrassing, I can't actually believe what is happening right now, but still. Yes Miss, I would gladly climb your son like a tree and ride him into next week. I could no longer compress the laugh, and I let it out in a rather abrupt roar. Thankfully, Roe smiled wide and joined in on my somewhat inappropriate laughter.

"I know this is a very strange conversation to have with the mother of the boy whose bed you have been sharing" she choked out between chuckles.

"Nothing is surprising me at this point" I breathed heavily.

"Okay, well I'm glad that is over and done with" she said putting her hand on the table and standing up. She walked over to the sink and turned on the tap. She began clanging dishes together while still giggling to herself. I got up and headed for the door.

"Thank you for lunch" I cooed at her,

"You're most welcome dear".

I headed up the stairs and back to Gunner's room. I plopped myself on the bed and stared at the ceiling. Wow, how crazy was that. I thought back to the first day that I saw him, bumping into him in the hall. He made me feel so nervous even then. It makes sense now why I couldn't get him out of my head, why I felt so drawn to him. And in the hallway when he bandaged my hand, he is the first person that has ever made me feel safe. It's all so clear now, this weird crazy world that I've been plunged into, it's where I'm meant to be. With him. I sat up on the bed and decided to go and find him. I need to know if he feels the same way. I walked back downstairs and as I got to the door, Roe called out,

"Zelena, Darling where are you off to?" she asked peering at me through the door of what looked like a small library.

"Just wanted a little fresh air" I smiled opening the front door,

"Okay, just don't leave the clearing"

"No problem". I walked through the door and pulled it closed behind me. I stood on the porch and checked out my surroundings. The deck I was on was huge. There was a big wooden porch swing to the left and some wicker chairs to the right. I walked over to the railing and looked out over the clearing. There was a big fire pit in the middle, surrounded by huge logs lying on the ground. A few small cabin-like houses were lined up on either side and more lining up behind them. How many people, or werewolves, live out here, I wonder. A few people were walking around the clearing. Two big men were chopping firewood at the tree line to the right and a group of men were sitting together under an open wooden hut. I was a little far away, but I swear one of the men in the hut looked exactly like Gunner, only older and with a beard. There was a smell of roasting meat wafting through the air, I lifted my nose and breathed it in. Smells good. I looked around the clearing, but I couldn't see Gunner, I went down the porch steps and headed toward the fire pit.

A strong surge of unease settled in my bones, and I could suddenly feel eyes on me from all directions. I turned my head and realised that the men sitting under the hut were all watching me. I heard whispers off to my left, I snapped my head and saw two women watching me and whispering to each other. They looked unsure, like they were sizing me up. I could feel the anxiety growing in me as I began to panic. I started walking faster heading to the back of the clearing, away from the scrutinizing eyes. The whispers grew louder in my head, but I couldn't make out the words. I started to jog towards the trees, wanting to escape the glaring eyes and inaudible whispers. As I picked up speed towards the edge of the clearing, I ran into someone, smashing my face into their body. The person grabbed the top of my arms and kept me from falling over. I looked up and saw that it was Smith, I felt a wave of relief wash over me, finally a familiar face. In a move still foreign to me and completely out of character, I threw my arms around his shoulders and hugged him. His body tensed and he held his arms up not hugging me back. I let him go and stepped back, looking up at his face I realised, he was actually not that much taller than me, only by about a head.

"Well hello to you too" he smiled leaning back from me,

"Hi" I breathed smiling back at him,

"I'm glad to see you're up and about, Gunner mentioned that you were doing better"

"Gunner? Do you know where he is?" I looked around behind him, but there was no one else with him.

"He uh, he had to do something with Cole" he stuttered,

"He shouldn't be too much longer I reckon". Smith crossed his arms and looked over his shoulder, he was clearly very edgy. What have I missed?

"Is something wrong?" I asked,

"Nah nothing, don't fret it"

"Seriously Smith what's up?"

"Since when do you talk this much?" he scoffed,

"Don't do that, don't deflect. What's going on? Is it Gunner?" Feeling a little annoyed and anxious about his apparent mood change, I poked him hard in the chest. He turned his head from side to side, bouncing his foot. He stank of nervousness.

"Look you ahh... you can't grab people like that. Especially males". He was biting his lip and not looking me in the face. What does that mean, 'grabbing people' I didn't grab anyone.

"Huh?" I said screwing up my nose.

"Gunner, he'll be able to smell my scent on you now, and he'll be pissed" he whispered leaning down a bit.

"What, why?" I was so confused, why would Gunner be mad? I just hugged him, do werewolves not hug each other or something?

"You're his now, and if another man tries to claim you, he'll kill 'em. And it doesn't matter who either"

"Okay, whoa. And also, I wasn't trying to seduce you, it was just a hug. I didn't mean anything by it, I was just relieved to see a familiar face"

"Yeah, I know that, but he doesn't". I still didn't understand but I could see how worried he was. Whatever I guess, I'll just let it go.

"Okay sorry, I'll keep my distance" I said as I took another step back. He sighed, dropping his arms,

"I didn't mean it like that, we're still friends, just no touching" he smiled as he shrugged his shoulders. Friends, I smiled. I have friends.

"Okay" I grinned with a big toothy smile,

"What are you doing out here anyway?" he asked walking forward, away from the forest edge.

"I was looking for Gunner" I said as I walked beside him.

"Well, Gunner's not here. But I am" he smiled with a little jump in his step.

"So, you are"

"Well, what do you want to do?"

"I don't know, what can we do?" I asked. He thought for a moment looking around the village, then he snapped his fingers and smiled jumping forward in front of me and walking backwards.

"I've got it, follow me".

He turned around and started jogging off to the left. I followed behind him. This was the most I've exercised since getting here. It felt good to run, to be outside, and to feel the fresh air on my face. I closed my eyes and took a deep breath. Freedom. We ran between two of the cabins and through some trees until we came to another small clearing. Smith slowed down and turned to look at me over his shoulder,

"We're here". He stepped to the side so I could see the full field.

"Wow" I gasped. It was beautiful. The field was covered in flowers, there were patches of pink, purple, and yellow. The smell of sweet wildflowers filled my nose. I walked forward into the field, brushing my hands along the flower bushes as I went. I turned to look at Smith. He was standing with his arms crossed watching me with a huge, satisfied smile on his face.

"This is amazing" I gleamed at him,

"Thought you might like it" he huffed proudly. I ran to the middle of the field and spun in circles, it was the most glorious place that I'd ever seen and I never want to leave again.

"I love it here, I want to stay forever" I called out with a widespread smile. Smith laughed and walked slowly into the field towards me,

"That's what all the girls say" he chuckled. I snapped my neck and looked over at him. What did he just say?

"How many girls have you brought here?" I questioned. He chuckled again with a blush of his cheeks, and rubbed at the back of his neck,

"Three or four" he said, as his smile got bigger.

"And here I thought I was special" I faked scoffed and giggled. I sat down in a patch of yellow flowers, grabbed a large bunch, and buried my face into the petals. The scent was so good, so fresh and wild. I laid back on the ground and looked up at the blue sky. This is what I imagine heaven would feel like. Smith walked over and laid down in the flowers a few metres away from me.

We lay there quietly, just looking at the sky, for what felt like hours. We talked a little about the other girls that Smith had brought out here and the trouble he had caused with them. He told me jokes and funny stories about Gunner when they were kids. I've never met someone like Smith. So laid back and unapologetically themself. It's refreshing. It's honestly the kind of person I want to be. But I don't see that ever happening. Not any time soon at least.

The sun was moving away, and I was starting to doze off when Smith jumped up with a sudden burst of energy.

"We gotta go" he said quickly,

"Why?" I asked sitting up,

"Gunner's looking for you" he said waving his hand at me.

"How do you know that?" I started standing up slowly, hesitant to leave the beautiful field.

"He's flashing me". Wait they can flash with each other, why didn't I know this?

"You guys can do that?"

"Of course we can, now let's go" he said waving his arm again. I started to jog in the direction of the village. Smith was beside me but started inching in front. We ran through the trees and came out into the clearing, slowing to a walk. I smiled at Smith, and he nodded towards the fire pit. I looked over just as Gunner spun around. My heart exploded as I saw him, I felt an urgency to run to him, to be in his arms. I walked quickly towards him, not wanting to look desperate. He took a step forward, and in a blink, he was right there with me wrapping his arms around me and picking me up. I wrapped my legs around his waist locking my ankles together and squeezed my arms around his neck. He had his hands on my backside holding me up. He nuzzled his face into the crook of my neck and sniffed at my hair. His body tensed a little as he sniffed harder into my hair and around my neck. That's when he lifted his head and growled. His skin started to burn hot, and his heart was racing. He very slowly put me down and stepped around me as he continued to growl ferociously. I turned to see what he was growling at and saw Smith raising his hands and walking backwards, staring at Gunner with fear on his face. Gunner walked towards him leaning forward, growling, and baring his teeth. I remembered what Smith said about me hugging him and his scent on me. A flash of heat waved over me, and I began to feel a deep rage running through my body. I jumped in front of Gunner and shouted,

"STOP NOW!" Gunner glared at me, growled, and tried to step around me. His growl enraged me and I felt the fire burn in my chest and the needles run up and down my arms. Without a thought, I smacked him across the face. One huge hard slap, right on his cheek. I didn't give myself a moment to question my own sanity. I just stood up on my toes to get close to his face and growled at him. I could feel the growl grumble through my body as it roared in the back of my throat. My first ever growl. Gunner stopped looking at Smith and stood up straight looking down at me. He was shocked. To be fair, so was I. I'd never felt so bold before. But now that Gunner was staring at me with a look of shock and a hint of amusement, my bravado quickly died. I can't believe I just hit him, what the heck is wrong with me? Gunner blinked his eyes quickly as a smirk started to spread across his face.

"Did you just growl at me?" he snickered,

"Yes" I said as strongly as I could, though I faltered, and it ended up sounding more like a question than an answer.

"Fuck you're sexy" he smiled picking me up and spinning me through the air. I have no idea what the shit is going on. Is he, is he happy that I hit him? He put me down and pulled me into his chest hugging me tightly.

"I'm sorry Smith, I didn't mean it" Gunner said with his cheek pressed to the top of my head. I could feel his body start to cool down, as did my own. The anger I felt a second ago was nowhere to be found, and neither was the confidence I showed when standing up for Smith. I don't even recognise myself.

"All good, man" Smith sighed loudly. Cole and a few other men had gathered behind us watching on. Gunner then lifted me up, throwing my body over his shoulder, I squealed with shock and excitement.

"Come on you" he laughed smacking me on the ass,

"We've got business to discuss". He started walking towards the main house and I looked up as we passed the group of men. They were all smiling and laughing, grabbing Smith on the shoulder and shaking him, patting him on the back, and ruffling his hair. He looked scared but relieved. Smith looked over at us and I lifted my hand and wiggled my fingers at him, he smiled at me and did the same.

Chapter

Seven

Gunner

I sat slumped on the floor, the tears rolled freely down my cheeks. Cole, Smith, Nat, Deena, Mum, and Dad, all stood in the hallway whispering to each other.

"Your what?" Nat asked, stunned.

I didn't respond, all I could think of was Zee. I couldn't lose her, not now, not ever. I have only just found her, and I know in my heart what we have together, I know the bond is real, I can feel it.

"Did he say True Mate?" Nat whispered again.

"Just get out" I said dejectedly. They didn't move. I jumped to my feet, my canines extended and my eyes holding all the fury in the world,

"LEAVE!" I roared. They all quickly turned and shuffled down the stairs. I fell back to the floor, feeling my insides breaking all over again. My self-control was weaning, I could feel the surge of emotions boiling to the surface. I just can't lose her. Please Goddess don't take her away from me. I felt Mum's arms slowly wrap around my shoulders as she sat next to me on the floor. I collapsed into her arms and sobbed. She gently patted my head and tried to calm me.

"It's okay" she whispered,

"She'll be okay". We sat together like that for what felt like hours, with Mum still stroking my hair. When Artemis came out of the door, closing it slowly behind him, I jumped to my feet, as did

Mum. She held on to my arm tightly and we both waited for Artemis to speak. Artemis stood silently before us, his face not giving away any emotion.

"Well?" I snapped,

"She okay now but very weak, hard to tell" said Artemis quietly. I dropped my head into my hands as the tears started welling up again.

"Will she survive?" asked my mum softly,

"Tonight, I don't know. If still breathing in morning we look again"

"What else can we do? You have to try something else" I yelled looking at Artemis.

"No more to do. Up to her now" he grumbled pushing past me and off down the stairs. That's it? That's all our great and magical healer has to offer. There has to be more, something more, I'll try anything. I looked at my mother as my lips trembled. I felt like my legs were about to give out from under me,

"Mum" I cried as she hugged me tight,

"Come now dear, it'll be okay" she soothed me. I hunched over, crying into her hair,

"Come on, you need to rest" she said as she tried to lead me away,

"No" I snapped, ripping my hand from her grip,

"I'm staying here".

"Gunner, Baby there's nothing more you can do for her now"

"I can sit with her at least. I can make sure that she isn't alone". Mum looked at me with pity. Her eyes were red, and her face looked droopy and sad, not her usual cheerful self.

"Okay my boy" she said caressing my cheek. She stared at me for a minute, breathed out deeply, and left. I watched her walk down the hall and to the stairs until she disappeared from view. I turned and put my hand on the doorknob, then froze. I rested my forehead on the door and took a deep breath. 'Keep it together Gunner' I told myself. I opened the door slowly and walked into the room. The bedroom was dark, apart from the light from the bathroom shining through the partially open door. The room smelled of blood, sweat, and whatever medicine Artemis had been using. I walked over to the bed and stood next to it and stared down at my broken little wolf. Artemis had cleaned most of the blood from her face, revealing a large swollen eye with a visible slice through the eyebrow. Another slit in her skin sat on her cheekbone, just below the swollen eye. Her lip was busted and swollen, and her face was scattered with quickly bruising skin. There were still small remnants of the brown cream that Artemis rubbed over her face, some in her hairline and blobs on her cheeks. She had bandages wrapped around her neck and chest. The blood-soaked t-shirt she had been wearing, was discarded on the floor beside the bed. Her arms lay motionless at her sides and her legs were under the blanket. I had never seen her without a hoodie on before. Now that her arms were bare, with only the bandages covering her, I could see the extent of her horrific life. Laid bare across her skin like a painting, showing me that she had endured more than just this one night of torture. No, she'd been living with it for years.

Her pale skin was spotted with bruises and scars. Some are still fresh, some aging, and some very old. The entire length of her arms were covered in scars, I could barely run my finger down her arm without hitting a mark. How could anyone do this to such a sweet girl? If all this was what her arms held, I feared to think what secrets the rest of her body would tell. My heart wrenched looking at how broken and beaten she looked. That sick fucking bastard. That human scum. I will kill him for this. She looks so small and frail lying in my king size bed. How can I be feeling so strongly for her already? It's only been two days. This isn't just the bond, it's more than that. I know it is. Zelena is special. She may be quiet and a little shy, but there is a fire in her soul, I can sense it. Her strength and tenacity is unmatched by any other she-wolf. If... No, when, she lives through what that monster did to her, I will cherish her until my last breath. I swear it to the Goddess.

I took the chair from my desk, pulled it close to the bed, and sat down. Gently and carefully, I lifted her hand and held it in mine. As I watched her in the unconscious sleep, I stroked the back of her hand. The sound of her heart beating slowly, and her breaths staggered and weak, filled my ears. It only made me that much more determined. I gripped her hand a little tighter and started to siphon her pain. She moaned a little, turning her head to the side. It was a small movement, but I'll take what I can get. It was working, that's all that mattered. I closed my eyes, lowered my head, and focused hard, taking more of her pain. After a while, I lifted my head to look at her, but I felt weak and tired. I rested my head on the edge of the bed and passed out.

When I started to wake it was still dark, though I could sense the sun was rising. I could still smell blood on Zelena, so I went to the bathroom, got a wet cloth, and filled a bowl with warm water. I sat on the edge of the bed near her head and began to wipe the blood and medicine from her hair. She was so still and so lifeless. I listened to her heart, still slow but beating a little stronger now. I rinsed the cloth in the bowl and gently turned her head to the side to wipe behind her ear and the back of her neck, being careful not to touch the burns. As I cleaned her neck, I could see a portion of a very pale pink birthmark at the edge of her hairline. It looks like a crescent moon. Huh, that's cute. I went to rinse the bowl out in the bathroom and heard a knock on the door. I didn't want anyone to see her like this, so I ran to the door holding it closed. They knocked again. I opened the door slightly and peered out, it was Artemis with my mother. I nodded at him to come in and opened the door wider. He stepped through and Mum was about to follow, I shook my head at her,

"Just him, Mum" I said and closed the door before she could argue. He walked to the bed and looked down at her, he then slowly hovered his hands over her body. Starting at her feet and finishing at her head, not touching her, just feeling her energy. He then bent down turning his head to the side and hovered over her chest. He looked at me and frowned,

"She is strong" he grumbled,

"You heal her?" he asked me while pointing to her. I didn't quite know what he meant, werewolves can take pain away, up to a limit, but we can't heal other Weres. I tilted my head and stared at him without answering his question. He huffed and started rummaging through his bag. He pulled out the brown healing cream and started to unwrap the bandages on her neck. I didn't want anyone else to touch her, I especially don't want to watch someone else touching her. I growled at him and he growled back. "To heal" he snapped,

"I'll do that" I said walking forward and snatching the jar of cream from his hand. He huffed with annoyance at me again, picked up his bag, and walked out. Shit. I'm acting like a total dick. I didn't mean to be rude to Artemis, I just have this need, this urge to protect Zelena. I can't help it.

I dipped my fingers in the jar pulling out a dollop of the sticky brown goo. It smelt like mouldy tree bark and honey. I carefully smeared it over her eyebrow and cheekbone, being sure not to get it in her eye. After applying it to her face, I then rolled the rest of the bandages from her neck and smeared more there, spreading it over her chest as well. I placed the bandages back into place and then very gently rolled her onto her side, so that I could get to the marks at the back of her neck. I moved her hair out of the way and started to move the bandages covering her neck, but Artemis had placed bandages further down than I thought was necessary. They covered her entire back. I slowly untangled the fabric, and with each piece I removed, I could see more and more of the large slash marks marring her skin. They shared similarities to the marks that Scottish fella from Outlander had on him. Multiple huge red gashes, already closing over, but clearly only days old. The sight made me want to vomit from pure fury. That son of a bitch. He whipped her. He whipped her so fucking hard that her skin split open. Yet she was walking around the school like nothing had happened. Like she wasn't in agony the whole time. How can that be? I slowly rolled her back over on the bed and stared at her bruised and battered face. My hands were shaking, and I could feel my claws starting to sprout through. My skin began to burn and the blood in my veins bubbled with rage. That monster beat her bloody, he whipped her, and has done Goddess knows what else to her. Seeing as she was half naked when I found her, the monster probably raped her as well. I want him dead. My bones started cracking and breaking and I quickly ran out of the room. I got to the bottom of the stairs when I snapped my head back and screamed into my change. I stood in

the foyer on all four paws and threw my head back and howled.
I'm going to tear that beast apart. I started to run for the door,
when my father ran in from the kitchen and stood in front of me,
blocking my path.
I'm going to kill him!
"No, son, you're not"
*Yes, I am. I'm going to tear his arms and legs off and then I will eat
his fucking heart*
"Gunner, cool down"
GET OUT OF MY WAY!
"NO! Gunner. Go back to your Mate, she needs you here now"
She needs that barbarian dead, that's what she needs
"I said ENOUGH" he roared. The chandelier above us shook and
the windowpanes rattled at the sheer force of my father's voice. I
tilted my head as I felt his command start to bend my will, I shook
out my fur and my body changed back. I sat on the floor of the
foyer naked, panting hard with the anger still flowing through me.
Dad stood above me breathing heavily, his Alpha command was
still weighing over me.
"Go back up to your Mate, son". I looked up at him and felt a tear
escape my eye. I wiped it away and got up off the floor and
stomped back up the stairs. I would never say it to his face, but he
was right. She needs me here, at least for now. I pulled on a pair
of sweats that were discarded on the floor and sat down in the
chair by the bed and watched her sleep. Right now, I'm here, I'm
with her. But soon, as soon as she's better, I will kill him. I swear
it.
Hours have passed and I'm still watching Zelena. My eyes were
starting to feel heavy again when I heard her heart rate rise. I
leaned forward to look at her face. Her eyes were moving around
behind her eyelids. She started to toss her head from side to side
and mumble and groan. She began kicking her legs and twisting
her body, thrashing her head around.
"MUM!" I screamed standing up and holding down Zee's arms. I
was worried she was going to hurt herself. With all the injuries
she has, it's amazing that she could even move about this much.
Zelena started yelling and screaming in her unconsciousness,

"Stop, please stop" she begged. Her body was thrashing around as she pulled at her arms from my grip. I have to do something to stop her,

"MUUUM!" I screamed again.

"Let me go" Zelena cried out, still not awake. Mum then burst through the door and ran to the side of the bed,

"What's going on?" she yelled,

"It's a nightmare! Get the cuffs, bottom drawer" I nodded at my dresser. She opened the drawer and pulled out the training cuffs from when I was a kid.

"Why do you still have these? You haven't needed them for years" Mum asked as she looked at the cuffs in her hands.

"Here, help me put them on her". Mum ran over and buckled on the first cuff and clipped it to the bed base, she then did the same to Zee's other hand.

"No, no!" Zelena called as her thrashing started to slow. Her crying stopped but her eyes and head still moved around. I sat back on the chair and sighed. Mum was standing beside me looking at Zelena, I heard her start huffing and looked up to see her crying. I stood up and hugged her.

"I'm sorry Darling, you don't need me being all emotional" she sobbed,

"It's okay Mum, will you sit with me for a bit?" I pulled her down to sit on the edge of the bed. She wiped her tears and smiled at me sadly. I sat back in my chair and watched Zelena sleep while Mum was watching me. After a while of silence, she finally spoke,

"Baby, you said you think she is your True Mate?" she whispered,

"Yes" I replied without hesitation,

"I'd like to think that I have taught you enough to know just how rare that kind of bond is?"

"I know Mum"

"And you still believe?"

"I don't just believe it, I can feel it". She glanced at Zelena and then back at me,

"Will you tell me about it?" she smiled leaning forward. I paused for a moment and looked at my mother's face, was she just trying to indulge me or did she really believe me. Her face was calm, and her eyebrows were bent up with curiosity. I think she believes me, or at least she wants to. So, I told her.

"On the very first day I saw her, I could tell right then that she was different. Then, when I looked into her eyes, something in me snapped and I had this kind of urgency to know who she was. Kids at the school were bullying her and they infuriated me, like I wanted to hurt them and protect her. When our skin touches, I feel tingles, like tiny vaults of electricity shooting through me. One smile, just one dazzling smile, and I was hooked. I don't know Mum. It was like I could feel what she felt, I needed to be where she was, and to know what she was doing and if she was okay. I knew from the start that she was going to be my Mate, but it wasn't until I knew that she was a Were that I started to understand it was more than that". I looked at my mum and she was smiling proudly at me.

"Do you know what I'm saying?" I asked her. She leaned forward and put her hand on my cheek,

"Yes, Darling, I know exactly what you're saying, and I think you may be right". I smiled excitedly at her. She got up and kissed the top of my head and left the room. Zelena had calmed and faded back into a deep sleep, I sat watching her all day, until the sun had set again. There was a quick knock on the door, I got up and stretched my arms, and walked slowly to the door. I opened it and sitting on the ground was a huge plate of spaghetti and a vase with red roses. I picked them up and placed them on the table next to the bed.

~

The next few days all blurred together. I spent most of my time in the chair next to the bed. I slept there, ate there, and sat there for hours on end watching over Zelena. Zee had good days and rough days, some episodes were worse than others. She would lay motionless for hours and then have a sudden burst of panic, thrashing about and screaming, but she never fully woke up and never opened her eyes. I found myself feeling very grateful for holding onto the training cuffs all these years. They kept her reasonably still through most of her episodes. Which is what they were built for. Restraining a new wolf through their uncontrollable outbursts.

A few times a day a tray of food was left by the door with fresh flowers, which was Mum's way of taking care of us. Nat came by at one point asking to come in and see Zelena, the only way I could get rid of her was with my Visa card and the opportunity to go shopping to buy Zee some necessities. Both Cole and Smith flashed me a couple of times to check in, but I didn't feel like talking to them, or seeing them, or anyone else really. Artemis dropped off another jar of cream, but seeing how I barked at him the last time he tried to help, he just left it by the door. The whole time Zelena's heartbeat got stronger and her breathing steadied. With me siphoning what pain I could, her wounds were healing really fast. Now I was just waiting for her to wake up.

It was a little while after midday, and still no sign of life from Zelena. I put my laptop away and rested my head on the end of the bed. I had just dozed off when I was disrupted by another of Zee's thrashings. But when I sat up, I realised that her eyes were open. Holy crap she's finally awake. I jumped to my feet and stood over her.

"Zee, Zee, Zee, calm down! You're alright" I said trying to get her to stop. She looked at me with confusion, blinking her eyes a few times.

"It's me, you're okay". I sat down on the edge of the bed and put my hand on her leg to stop her from kicking. She was looking at me like she didn't know who I was. Oh Goddess, I hope she doesn't have amnesia. She tried to talk, but instead, she croaked and choked a little, so I grabbed a water bottle to let her have a drink. I sat back down on the bed and breathed a sigh of relief.

"I thought I'd lost you there for a little while". I was overcome with joy as a tear fell from my eye. I quickly wiped it away, hoping she didn't see that. I slipped my hand into hers and held it there, any skin-to-skin contact to help me stay calm.

"But you're okay now" I said with a smile. She pulled at her arm, and I realised she was still strapped down,

"Oh right". I quickly jumped up and started undoing the buckles, jeez I hope she doesn't think I'm some kind of kinky freak for tying her up like this.

"You were thrashing around a lot while you were out and we didn't want you to hurt yourself anymore, so we thought it best to you know, tie you up". She didn't say anything, just stared at me. She started to lift herself up and winced, and of course, I freaked out again.

"Whoa, whoa, slow down and I'll help you". I ran and got my pillow and put it behind her back as gently as I could.

"There you go" I said with a smile and sat down on the edge of the bed. I was damn happy she was finally awake; I knew she was strong, but I'm still impressed.

"Where?" she coughed, her voice sounded terrible,

"Just take it easy, try not to talk too much". I wanted to make her feel better and I wanted to comfort her. Her golden intense eyes staring right at me, made it difficult not to just pick her up and hold her. I put my hand on her leg, any contact with her was better than no contact.

"Where am I?" she asked hoarsely,

"This is my room" I said,

"How long?" she croaked,

"You've been here for five days now. What's the last thing that you remember?" I asked her softly. Once I know where she is at with her memory, I can fill her in on the rest. She leaned back on the pillow and closed her eyes. Goddess, she is beautiful, even with all the bruises. With my hand on her knee, I could feel her going through the motions. I leaned closer to her and concentrated on what I could feel from her. She was a little happy but that quickly disappeared, and it turned into anxiety and fear. I squeezed her leg to let her know I was still here. Her fear turned to pain and sorrow. I felt such sadness for her. I wanted to make her forget. She quickly flew upright and grabbed at her neck. I could smell the anxiety coming off her so strongly now. She lifted her shirt and inspected her ribs, then turned to look at me, she started to panic, and her breathing fastened.

"It's okay, you're safe now" I assured her. Moving forward on the bed, I wrapped her in my arms as she began to cry. Her tears were soaking into my shirt, but I just squeezed her tighter and gently stroked her hair.

"Shh, it's okay, I won't let him hurt you anymore" I whispered. I held her close to me, wanting so badly to make everything better. I began to siphon her pain and after a minute it made me feel weak, so I laid down and pulled her down with me, still holding her close. She squirmed her body closer, wrapping her arms and legs around me. I felt her energy seep into my skin, and it instantly made me feel stronger. Being close to her was revitalising my own energy. It made me remember what Mum had said about True Mates and how they shared their powers. I've only been taking her pain, but maybe I could actually heal her. I closed my eyes and tried to concentrate on healing her wounds. I pictured my own energy entering her body and working on her injuries. I pictured the wounds closing and the skin healing over, leaving nothing behind. I began to feel fuzzy, like a hairy blanket had been wrapped around me. It was working. Zelena fell asleep in my arms, and I along with her.

~

We were lying together in the grass, she was happy and smiling. It was sunny and warm and there were wildflowers all around us. She sat on top of me with my shoulders pinned to the ground. She is perfect in every way. She is everything I always wanted, and more. She leaned forward and licked from my chin over my lips and nose and growled at me seductively. Oh Goddess, I want her, more than I've ever wanted anything. She kissed me passionately, rolling her tongue in my mouth and biting on my lip. I felt my erection growing as she sat on my lap. She started to kiss my neck as her hair fell over my face. Mm… she smells so good. She reached down and began to stroke my hard cock so I thrusted my hips into her hand. She started to rub my cock harder. Fuck yes, that feels so good. I squeezed her thighs, and she squeaked.

~

I opened my eyes, shit, it was a dream, and I'm hurting her. I threw myself off the bed, grabbing a pillow as I rolled. I stood in the corner by the door covering my huge erection with the pillow. Holy Goddess, I'm an idiot. I rubbed my face trying to wake myself up,
"I'm sorry, I didn't mean to". My cheeks blushed red after I realised what I had just done. She giggled from where she lay on the bed. Actually giggled, and I've never heard anything so beautiful. I pressed the pillow against myself harder. I guess she's

not mad then. I looked over at her. She is heavenly, just lying there looking at me innocently.

"Did I hurt you?" I asked. The sight of her lying like that wasn't helping to ease the situation in my pants.

"No, I'm okay" she said patting the bed for me to come back. I couldn't, not yet. I don't know if I have full control of myself, the moonlight is making me a little wild. I've been able to control the effects of the full moon for years, but now with her in the scene, I'm nothing more than a horny and undisciplined kid again.

"I'm sorry, I shouldn't... I mean, I should have controlled myself better" I whispered.

"Gunner, I'm okay, please come and sit back down". I walked slowly back to the bed, keeping my pillow where it was. I am so embarrassed with myself, grabbing her and grinding on her like that, after everything she's been through. I need to change the subject, and get my mind off it. I bet she's hungry, she hasn't eaten in days.

"Are you hungry? I can go and get you some food" I asked her with a smile,

"I'm starved" she moaned,

"I'll run down and grab you something" I said standing up,

"Actually, if it's okay I'd really like to walk a little. Can I come with you?" I looked at her and tilted my head. She couldn't be ready to get out of bed yet, could she? How much could she have actually healed already.

"Are you sure you're up for it?" I asked, feeling unsure. She tried to lift herself up but couldn't. Okay, so there hasn't been too much healing then. The exterior may look a whole lot better, but the interior still has a lot more healing needed.

"I'm sure" she said adamantly.

~

The entire time we were in the kitchen, Zelena was letting off some serious pheromones, and it was making my boy bounce. Her scent is addictive, and I could spend the rest of my life with my nose pressed to her skin. I want her, all of her, but I know that I have to wait. She has been through too much for me to just stake my claim over her. Even though I so badly want to. Even though everything in me is begging me to claim her.

When Mum interrupted us, I was only seconds away from stealing a kiss. I'm both glad and furious for the disturbance. Zelena isn't ready for me to claim her, and I was letting my instincts take control instead of being a damned gentleman. When I do finally taste those pouty lips of hers, I don't want anything to interrupt us.

Zelena closed the bathroom door and I waited for her impatiently to finish her thing. I don't want to be away from her again, even if it's just a door between us. After a minute, when she didn't come out again, I could hear her sniffling. I walked to the door and pressed my ear against it. She was crying, I could feel her pain and sadness radiating through the door. I knocked.

"Zee, are you alright?" I called through, she paused for a second and then answered,

"No, I'm hideous" she sobbed out. I opened the door and found her curled into a ball hugging her knees. I sat down beside her and placed my hand on her leg.

"Please don't cry" I begged her, but she pushed my hand away. I curled my fists and resisted the urge to force her into my arms.

"Don't look at me" she mumbled through her sobs. She doesn't want me to touch her, that's fine, hurts like a knife, but completely understandable given everything. However, she needs to learn that I don't give up that easily.

"You'll heal Zee, it just takes a little longer for young wolves" I cooed, trying to calm her down. She stopped sobbing and lifted her head to look at me, her eyes were red and puffy, and her cheeks were wet from tears.

"What do you mean young wolves?" she snapped. A little taken aback by the question, I almost tilted my head to study her.

"You're a newborn wolf. You've only had one change, right? Well, the healing ability gets quicker the more you change" I answered like it was obvious. She looked at me confused, like I was losing my mind or something.

"But how do you know?" she asked wiping the tears from her cheek,

"I just do, we got taught this stuff as pups". Where was she going with this? Why wouldn't she just know this, it's basic information. "Pups?" she questioned, tilting her head to the side. Oh. Oh, I see. Of course. She's not in the pack and there are no other packs nearby. So, unless she comes from a family of recluses, which seems unlikely, she was living in our land and there's no way my father wouldn't know about another family of Weres. If she was truly alone, I guess she probably had no idea that werewolves existed. Her father didn't smell like a Were, and he was beating the living crap out of her, so why would he bother to teach her about what she is… Unless he didn't know himself. I am about to blow her mind. I stood up and reached for her hand.

"Come sit on the bed and I'll explain" I said smiling down at her. She grabbed my hand and I pulled her up off the floor. We sat on the bed and I looked at her, she was staring at me anxiously.

"What do you want to know?" I asked getting comfy on the bed.

"Pups?" she demanded. And so, I began to explain the simplest way I could, answering her questions as I went. I told her about the Alpha and Luna, about the pack. She even asked if I was a wolf, which made me laugh internally. As we moved on to Omegas, I could feel her starting to grow anxious. I confirmed that at this very moment, she is technically an Omega. But I didn't want to scare her with the whole True Mate thing, at least not yet. She just got a whole brick to the face worth of information. Best to take it slow with the whole destined to be together forever thing, I think. I calmed her nerves the best I could. Though her scent seemed permanently stained with fear and anxiety. I lifted her face and looked into her eyes,

"You won't be an Omega for long, I promise". She is mine. Those eyes, those lips, that little twitch her eye gives when she's thinking really hard. Every scar, every bump and dimple. This girl was my everything, and I was never letting her go again. I leaned in close ready to kiss her,

"You're not going anywhere" I declared. I stared at her, ready to feel her lips. Just as I was about to kiss her, she surprised me by jumping across the bed and into my lap, tightening her arms around my neck. She was hugging me. She initiated contact. Her sudden show of affection made me feel happy and validated, like I knew now that she wanted me to. I took a relaxed breath and hugged her back, resting my cheek on top of her head. I held her close, simply enjoying the fact that she was letting me hold her like this, after everything that her dad had done to her.

She nuzzled her face into my chest and placed soft peppered kisses on my exposed flesh. Her lips on my skin sent shivers up my spine and I froze. Heat slid its way up my spine and I felt my canines push against my gums. Zelena continued kissing my chest, up and over my collarbone. Her scent had completely changed, I could smell her heat and desire and it was messing with my self-control. She bit down on my earlobe and I moaned, unable to hold it in anymore. My vision clouded over and all I could think about was sinking my teeth into her supple flesh. A growl bubbled up from deep within me. I want her, I need her. She tugged at my shirt and I lifted my arms tossing it away as she pulled it over my head. I gripped her thighs, pressing my fingers into her, anything to stop myself from tearing off her clothes. She kissed down my bare chest, biting into my skin. I lifted my head back, my canines were extending, my body knowing what it needed to do next. I tried to resist the overwhelming urge to dig my teeth in, but her pheromones were strong, and I could feel myself giving over to them. The full moon is definitely not helping, the silver light poking through the slit in the curtain was all it took to stir the animal inside me.

Zelena sat up higher, still straddling me, her neck now right in front of my mouth. My claws were starting to extend, I could feel them pressing into the skin of her thigh. I kissed her neck gently, imagining the feel of my teeth pressing into her flesh. I grabbed hold of her perfect tight ass, wanting so bad to be inside her. I lifted my hands to her shoulders and pulled her down onto my lap. I could feel the heat from between her legs pressed against my throbbing cock. She moved her hips forward, sliding her crotch along my dick. I can feel my wolf taking over from inside me. I wanted to sink my teeth into her, taste her blood, and bury myself deep inside her. She moved her hips again, pressing herself harder onto my cock. I shook my head to clear it of the lust filled haze, I need to stop this before I hurt her. I pulled together every ounce of strength I had left and grabbed her shoulders, lifting her off my lap. I placed her gently back on the bed and stood up, taking slow backward steps away from her.

"Stop. We can't" I panted. I tried not to breathe through my nose, knowing that if I smelt her beautiful juices, I wouldn't be able to hold back again.

"What?" she whispered. I took a deep breath to steady myself.

"I want to, I really want to. But not now, you still need to heal". How could I have been so reckless, nearly taking advantage of her like that, even after her father had raped her. She's just a young wolf and would have no control over her emotional actions yet. Especially under the control of a full moon. I can't believe my own selfishness.

"I'm sorry" she whispered.

"Will you still lay with me?" she asked softly. Avoiding my gaze, she lifted the covers and slid underneath. Oh, Goddess, I love her so much. I nodded and got into the bed, I pulled her in close and wrapped myself around her, then kissed her on the head. Wow, I do, I actually really love her. She was asleep in seconds breathing softly into my chest. I couldn't risk this again, I couldn't risk hurting her in a burst of passion. I closed my eyes and relaxed, letting my power seep into her. I'll give her all that I can and hopefully soon, she'll be healed.

Time ticked by and I felt the tingle of where our skin connected. I was hazy and everything felt heavy. I was pushing as hard as I could, forcing my strength into her, but I didn't have anything left to give. I managed to lift my head, just enough to see her black eye, or what was left of it. My head started to spin, and my body was weak and tired. I let my head drop back into the pillow and I passed out.

Chapter Eight

Gunner

The light shone through the window on my face, waking me up. Zelena was still asleep holding onto my arm. I brushed the hair from her face. She is gorgeous. She has a small purple mark still on her eyelid and the cut has healed over with only a tiny scab left. Her lip was back to normal as are the other cuts and bruises on her face. The healing worked. I lay there admiring her beauty, she is perfect. I leaned forward and sniffed at her hair, she smells so sweet, it's hard not to nuzzle into her. I want to pull her into my arms and hold her, but I don't want to wake her. I reached out to stroke the soft skin of her cheek but snapped my hand back. I'd better go before I wake her up. I carefully slid my arm out of her grip and very quietly crawled out of bed, being extra careful not to disturb her. I grabbed some clothes from the basket on the floor and ducked out the door. I changed in the hallway leaving my sweats by the bedroom door. I went downstairs and walked into the kitchen, Dad was already seated at the bench eating some eggs. Without saying anything I made myself a bowl of cereal and sat down beside him. It was quiet for a few minutes, he was waiting for me to break the silence. I gulped and finally spoke,
"I'm sorry, for the other day" I said shoving a spoonful of coco pops into my mouth.
"It's okay son, you were in a heightened state" he said with a grumble. We sat and ate together quietly for a while, and then

Dad put down his fork and rested his hands up on the counter. Great, here it comes, the scolding.

"So, your mother has been talking to me" he said without looking at me,

"Uh ha" I mumbled through a mouth full of cereal.

"She believes that this girl is your True Mate and Artemis agrees with her"

"Yep"

"You think so too then?"

"I do, yes" I answered without hesitating. He paused for a minute, fidgeting with his fingers.

"Tell me" he said not turning his head but looking at me out of the corner of his eye. This is not the direction I thought this conversation was going. But I do think that he wants to believe. I know he thinks of the Mate bond as sacred and something to be respected, and like Mum, he gives his thanks to the Moon Goddess. He has never been one to speak about his belief or nonbelief in the legends. But he did ask me, so the door is open right? Eh, whatever, I'll just tell him the same thing I told Mum. I took a deep breath and spilled.

"It started the very first day I saw her, I knew right away that she was different. But when I looked into her eyes, I had a need to know her, and I felt like I had to protect her. Plus, she is beautiful, Dad. The most beautiful girl I have ever set my eyes on. The first time I heard her voice my heart felt full, I knew from then on that she was meant to be my Mate. And she's strong, so strong and really powerful. And her wolf, wow, her wolf is magnificent. Completely different from any other wolf I have ever seen. She's special Dad, I can feel it. I know deep in my soul that this is more than just an ordinary bond. It's something more, way more". I looked at him as I poured my heart out, but he didn't turn his head. He sat quietly and listened without interrupting. After a minute of uncomfortable silence, he stood up and placed his hand on my shoulder.

"Well okay then" he grumbled. I looked at him confused, I had no idea what he was thinking. Did he believe me or not, is he going to accept her?

"I would need to meet her" he said raising an eyebrow,

"Yes of course" I mumbled, my hopefulness increasing slightly.

"Tonight" he said firmly,

"T-Tonight?" I gulped, so soon,

"Yes, dinner, with the others". And just like that, that hopefulness just crashed into the ground in a fiery explosion. Shit, now I'm a little scared. It's going to be so much to throw on her at once. Not just meeting my dad, her potential Alpha, but his senior pack as well. And what if she is rejected in front of everyone, it will destroy her. Not a lot I can do about it though. I can't refuse him, he's my dad but he's still my Alpha, and what the Alpha says goes.

"O-Okay" I stuttered,

"I will tell your mother". With that, he walked out of the kitchen. I slumped my head into my hands, this could be bad. Should I tell her now or just surprise her later I wondered. She'll probably panic. How would I even tell her? 'Hey Zee, tonight you're meeting the Alpha and the pack and may or may not be rejected and forced from our territory' I don't think so. Oh Goddess, what if she tries to leave me? I got up and put my bowl in the sink and left the kitchen. I was about to head upstairs again when I heard Dad talking to Artemis on the porch. I listened to a bit of their conversation. He was back to check on Zee, apparently Mum told him that she was up and about. I better go and get her. I ran up the stairs and slowly opened the door. She was standing in front of the bookshelf looking at my books. She took down the pack histories and legends journal and turned it over in her hands brushing her fingers over the pack symbol.

"Careful with that one, it's older than my great-great-grandpa" I said with a smile. She put the book back on the shelf and sat down on the bed grinning up at me. I walked to the edge of the bed and grinned down at her,

"How'd you sleep gorgeous?"

"Pretty good actually" she said with a small stretch of her arms.

"That's good" I said leaning down to kiss her on the head,

"Get dressed, Artemis is here".

"Who is Artemis?" she asked tilting her head,

"He's our healer, he's the one that bandaged you up when I brought you here". She was quiet for a minute, looking down at the bed.

"Okay, but I don't have any clothes" she said shrugging her shoulders. I nodded at the bags of clothes that Nat dropped off earlier.

"I sent my sister out shopping for you. She was more than happy to spend my money". Zee's face lit up with excitement, smiling brightly. I got that urge to pounce on her again. How does she manage to get me riled up so easily. I really need to let off some steam and go for a run. I flashed Cole

Cole, meet me by the pit, we gotta go running
Right now?
I'll be there in five
Okay

"I've gotta go help dad out with some things. Once Artemis has seen you. Mum will have some food ready" I lied clenching my fists.

"Okay boss" she said with a smile. Grr. Everything that comes out of her mouth feels like a tease. I leaned down to her lifting her chin with my hand and pulling her close to my face.

"Mm... boss ay? I could get used to that" I growled and snapped my teeth at her. Holy fuck, I've really got to go. I walked quickly to the door and turned back to her,

"Don't take too long, he's waiting downstairs". I gave her a wink, blew her a kiss, and ran down the stairs. What the fuck is happening. I think Mum may be right and we need to seal the bond. Every time that I'm near her I'm basically rock hard. Her scent is intoxicating, and I'm drinking it in like it's my very own life force. I got out to the fire pit at the same time that Cole strolled over.

"What's going on?" he asked,

"I gotta let the wolf out for a bit before I go mad"

"Aw, what's happening? Isn't the old ball and chain playing with the crown jewels?" he smirked and chuckled. I lowered my head and growled. How dare he talk about her like that. Without realising I snapped my hand up and grasped it around his neck,

"Watch your mouth" I growled. He threw his hands up with his eyes open wide.

"Okay, my bad. Shit mate, you really do need a run" he squeaked. I huffed at him with a frown and released my grip. Leaning down to take off my boots, regret quickly filled my stomach, it's just Cole. He didn't mean anything by it.

"Alright let's go" he said pulling his shirt off with a smile. I guess he was letting it slide then.

We got undressed leaving our clothes by the fire pit and headed for the trees. By the time we reached the tree line, we were both on all four paws. It felt so good to run, to feel the wild freedom of being a wolf. I let out a howl as I ran, and Cole howled along too. I ran through the forest at top wolf speed, the trees were flying past me, but I could still see every detail so clearly, every leaf, every branch, and every piece of bark. I was jumping and pouncing through the shrubs and over rocks, looking at the flowers and berry bushes along the way. With every stride all my anger and my built-up lust, all of the energy that was overflowing inside me, it all just melted away into the wind. Cole stayed close on my right flank the whole time, keeping pace. Eventually, we burst through the trees and were on the sandy coast. I looked down along the beach, good, no people today. I scratched my claws into the sand as I walked to the water's edge. I lay down in the damp sand and rolled onto my back, wiggling myself from side to side, burying my back and nose into the sand.

Feeling better yet?

Yeah I am, thank you brother, for coming out with me

Any time

We sat quietly side by side looking out across the ocean, breathing in the salty air. Our territory is beautiful, both forest area and coastal area. And one day it will all be mine to rule over. Something was wrong with Cole, I could sense it. He smelled of frustration and anger.

Now that my mind is clear again, shall we talk about yours?

There's nothing wrong with my mind

I'm your Alpha-son and your best friend, don't you think I can tell when something is weighing on you?

Don't worry about it, it's nothing

Cole, you are my brother and I love you

I know, I love you as well

Cole stood up and shook off the sand turning away from me.

I'm hungry, let's go for a hunt

Yeah alright

He wasn't ready to talk to me, but I'll get it out of him soon, I always do. We took off back into the forest, running side by side. We got to the stream and paused, I lifted my nose into the air and sniffed. I can smell wet moss on the dirt and wild mushrooms, I can smell berries and tree sap. The smell of the ocean wafting faintly through the trees was mixing with leaves. I caught a fading scent upwind, it's elk.

There's elk upwind

Yeah, I smell it too

We ran off towards the scent following the stream. As the scent got stronger, we slowed, staying downwind and treading carefully. The elk was ahead, I stalked forward behind a tree, keeping my body low to the ground. I scanned the tree line in front of me, there it is, just a single young male.

Take the right

Cole growled softly and nodded tracking off quietly behind some trees. I stalked up on the elk, crouching down into the shrub, and crawled forward.

On my mark

Ready

NOW

I propelled myself forward, jumping onto a fallen tree and then pushing myself onto the young bull. I landed on its neck and shoulders, Cole landed at the same time on its hindquarters. I dug in my claws as it reared up trying to shake us. I bit down hard into its neck, feeling my teeth rip into the flesh and tearing the carotid artery. Blood began to spill out, covering my jaw and mane. We managed to drag the deer down to the ground and held it steady as its life faded away.

Nice kill

Got him good

Let's dig in

I chomped into the small elk's shoulder and ripped the skin from its body, revealing the juicy meat underneath. Cole was happily eating away at the rump. I never used to care for raw eating in my wolf form. When I was a young wolf, the blood and the kill used to frighten me. It felt so murderous. But as I grew up and understood more about my nature and the way of my wolf, I learned to like it and even enjoy it. It became natural, like instinct. When we had our fill, we were both covered in blood. Cole was lying beside the half-eaten elk licking his paws. He lifted his head to look at me and huffed.

Best wash off before heading back

Yep, ocean swim?

Definitely

I stood up and shook out my fur, then we headed off back the way we came, towards the coast. As we came up to the sand I looked down along the water's edge, still no people. I ran for the water, prancing over the small waves and diving under them as they got bigger. The blood of the elk washed off with each hit of a new wave. I was swimming in a circle around Cole when he jumped onto my back, playfully pushing me down. I turned my neck and nipped at his hind legs causing him to fall off, splashing into the water. I swam around and hit him in the face with my tail and then slowly made my way back to shore. Walking up onto the sand, I shook off the excess water and laid down further up on the dry sand. The sky was blue and cloudless, the sun was getting low but was still warm. Cole shook off and dropped down next to me. He rested his head on his front legs and looked out across the water.

Are you ready to tell me what's bothering you?

There isn't anything bothering me

That's a lie

It doesn't matter anyway

So, there is something then?

It's nothing just forget it

Cole you're my best friend, we've told each other everything since we were pups, just talk to me, please

I can't

Of course you can, you always can

Not about this

What does that mean?

It means I can't talk to you about this. You wouldn't understand

Try me

Cole was quiet for a minute, not looking at me, but I could smell his anxiety and his sadness. He lifted his head and turned to look at me, dropping his ears down.

Please don't be angry with me

I couldn't ever be angry at you

This time you might be

Cole, what is it?

It's Zelena

What about Zelena?

I, I'm jealous of her

You're jealous?

Yes

Why?

Because you are hers now, she's taken you from me

I don't quite understand what he meant by that. She hasn't taken me anywhere, we are still here, still together. All that's changed is I have a Mate now.

Don't think of it like that Cole, she is my True Mate, yes, but you are my Beta, my best friend, my brother. I will always love you

You don't get it

What don't I get?

I love you

I know brother, I love you too

No, I'm in love with you, idiot

He is in love with me. Is that what he said?

You're what?

Gunner… I think I'm gay

Oh

We sat quietly as I processed Cole's revelation. Okay, so your best friend is gay, that's fine. But he just told you that he loves you. A little less fine but nothing you can't work through. Is this why he was against Zee, telling me she wasn't good enough, whinging and moaning every time I brought her name up? I mean of course it was, right. His behaviour makes a bit more sense now. He didn't want me to fall for Zee because he wanted me for himself. I did start to feel a little angry, not about his declaration of love but because we have been together every day of our lives and he is only just telling me this now. No, stop it, don't be self-centred. This isn't about you and your feelings, this is about Cole, your closest friend. This must have been so hard for him.

I looked over at my best friend as he looked out at the water. A wave of pride washed over me. He is so strong and brave. I'm happy that he could finally confide in me. I'm worried for him though, I don't know of any same-sex mated Weres. What would that mean for him, will he be alone all his life? I don't want that for him. I will do everything I can to make sure he doesn't feel alone, not ever. I love him, and I always will. It doesn't matter if he's gay, I won't abandon him.

He turned his head and gazed at my contemplative face. His eyes were sad and droopy.

Do you hate me now?

Never
Are we okay then?
Cole, you being gay doesn't change anything. You're still my brother and I still love you, nothing could change that. I may have Zee now too, but there will always be a place for you in my life
I stood up and pressed my head against his, he rubbed his head into my neck and licked the side of my face.
Nothing has to change between us, as long as you are loyal to me and support me, I will do the same for you
Thank you, brother
Come on, let's get back, the sun is setting
Cole stood up and shook out his fur, then we walked for the trees. We got to the tree line and began to run. The wind dried my coat as I went. Using our wolf speed, we made it back to the village in minutes, the clearing was mostly empty. We walked to the fire pit shoulder to shoulder, I cracked my head back changing back to human. I grabbed my jeans from a log and pulled them on. I turned around and Mum was walking over to us, Zee wasn't with her though. I pulled on my shirt as she reached us,
"Where's Zelena?" I asked her. She had an uneasy worried look across her face.
"She went for a walk a few hours ago and hasn't come back yet" she said quietly playing with the corner of her apron. Fear filled my stomach, what if something has happened to her, what if she was hurt. She wouldn't have just left me without warning, would she? I spun around on the spot searching the clearing. I couldn't see her anywhere. I lifted my nose to the air and sniffed. I could smell her scent towards the tree line. I ran to it sniffing the air some more, Smith's scent was here too.
Smith, is Zee with you?
Yes, we're at the flower field
Bring her back, now
On the way
I walked back to the fire pit where Mum was waiting, still looking worried.
"She's with Smith at the flower field" I told her, and she sighed with relief.
"Okay Darling, don't forget dinner is in an hour"
"I didn't forget". Mum smiled and turned on her heels and went back to the house.

"There they are" Cole nodded behind me. I spun around as they came through the trees. She smiled from across the clearing and my heart jumped, I ran to her picking her up into my arms. I missed her so much, only half a day apart and yet it felt like a lifetime. I smelled at her hair, she is so sweet. What's that, there's another scent on her. I breathed her in more, a male, what man has touched her. My skin shivered and my canines stared to extend. I sniffed around her neck, taking in the scent that should not be anywhere near her. Smith. A burning rage set in, it spread through my body at the realisation that she had been in the arms of another man. It was Smith all right, I could smell him all over her. He dares try to take my woman. I looked over Zee's shoulders at Smith, a growl rumbled out of my mouth.

You tried to claim my Mate!

I didn't I swear, she hugged me out of nowhere, I didn't do anything

I put Zelena on the ground and walked towards Smith baring my teeth.

Your stink is all over her, don't lie to me

I'm not lying I promise, she was running for the trees and I stopped her, that's all

Then why can I smell you all over her?

She was scared and just grabbed me, I told her not to, I swear it

I growled at him ready to tear at his throat, and then, Zelena jumped in front of me.

"STOP NOW!" she screamed. Of course, she would try to protect him, her new lover. I growled at her and tried to step around her, but she didn't let me. Then, without warning, she hit me, a clean slap across the face. Goddess is she strong because it fucking stung too, enough to pull me out of my rage spiral. My body cooled instantly, and the rage was replaced with shock. She stood up on her toes and growled right up in my face. I haven't heard her growl before. It was fucking hot. It was ice water was tipped over me, dissipating my rage. Instead, I now burned for another reason, I burned for her. Tingles ran down my spine and my dick jerked a little, so much for that run.

"Did you just growl at me?" I smirked at her,

"Yes" she barked, a little quiver shook her tone.

"Fuck you're sexy". I grabbed her under the arms and spun her around. Wow, this woman is something else. I put her down and pulled her into my arms. Shit Smith, I just raged out on Smith.

"I'm sorry Smith, I didn't mean it" I said looking up at him, his face was pale and his eyes wide, he was terrified of me.

"All good man" he said letting out a breath. I needed to take this girl back to the house and now. We need a little privacy, especially if even just one of the very, very, many things I want to do to her happen. I grabbed her legs and threw her over my shoulder making her squeal. I smacked her ass and laughed. She's in for it now.

"Come on you, we've got business to discuss" I winked at Smith and turned for the house.

Chapter Nine

Zelena

We got to Gunner's room with me still hanging over his shoulder, using his foot he flicked the door closed behind us. My heart was racing, and my stomach was doing excited backflips. He threw me down on the bed and climbed on top of me, grabbing my hands and pinning them above my head. A flash of fear tore through me at my inability to move. Being tied down to endure a punishment has been a reoccurring thing in my life, so it's safe to say a little bit of claustrophobia has set in.

Gunner held my wrists with one hand and using the other he gripped the back of my knee lifting it up so that my leg was around his waist. His face was so close to mine, I could feel his breath. If I just lifted my head a little bit, I could feel those lips. He squeezed my thigh, pressing his fingertips in hard. He nuzzled his face into my neck using his head to push my head back, he kissed my neck gently.

"Are you going to growl at me again?" he asked, I could hear the smirk in his tone. He's teasing me, deliberately. He pulled my earlobe between his teeth, eliciting a moan from me. The sound startled me slightly.

"I may" I groaned harshly. I don't know what was happening to me, or where this desire came from so suddenly. The weight of him pressed against me was turning me on. I could feel the tingling start in my crotch, a feeling I'm beginning to accept is standard when this close to Gunner. Feeling emboldened, I pulled my other leg out from under him and lifted it over his waist and hooked my ankles together, trapping him between my thighs. He slipped his hand down my thigh and under my top, slowly sliding his hand up over my belly, he cupped his fingers around my breast. I should be embarrassed, or ashamed, but my mind and body were at war with each other. My skin was crawling. But not from being constrained or restricted, from need. I needed to feel more of him. It was like an insatiable hunger, and I was ravenous. I tried to pull my hands free, but he wouldn't let go. I lifted my hips and squeezed my thighs together, pressing my crotch into his. I could feel his dick throbbing against my jeans. I want friction, I want to rub myself against him like a cat. I've never had this kind of reaction before, it's surprising, yet totally welcome. Gunner withdrew his hand from around my breast and pushed my hips down away from his, taking away that contact between us. Feeling unnaturally angry at his retraction, I growled softly. He lifted his head from my neck and looked at my face.

"Ah, there it is" he whispered smirking at me. I lifted my head and snapped my teeth at him. My god, I'm acting like a crazy woman, but I love it. Gunner let go of my hands and I tucked them under his arms and around his shoulders. He gently grabbed the back of my neck, stroking my cheek with his thumb. I was breathing heavily looking into his bright blue eyes. I want him, I want him bad. I want to taste him and to bite him, I want to feel his lips against mine. I lifted my head a little reaching for his mouth. He stared into my eyes, I could feel his breathing get faster and the skin under my touch started to burn. He pressed his face into mine as our lips locked. I closed my eyes tight as I felt electricity shoot through my body. I dug my nails into his back and dragged them down. He pushed his tongue into my mouth and massaged my tongue with his. Our lips moved together in perfect synchrony. My skin prickled with a thousand hot needles. I saw rainbow stars swirling around like a whirlpool. I could hear the blood pumping through his veins, and I could smell the desire seeping out of his skin. He tasted like honey mixed with something salty, his lips had now become my all-time favourite flavour. I could feel myself in his arms and he in mine, it's like we were now one entity. He was my person, my everything, my True Mate. I knew now that I would go where he goes, do as he does. I would travel the world to protect him and kill anyone and anything that tried to bring him harm. He was mine, and I was his.

I could kiss him like this for hours, but much to my disapproval, he peeled his lips away from mine and lifted his body up, holding himself above me. Everything was different now. I was different. We were different. It's like all the puzzle pieces of my life snapped together. All the tiny pieces of myself that I could never quite understand, they now fit perfectly with the pieces of Gunner's life.

"Wow" I breathed heavily. My view of him changed. He wasn't just handsome anymore, he was heavenly. He was the sun and I would eternally be in his orbit.

"I know right". He rolled over and plopped himself on the bed next to me. Holding my hand in his. We lay like that for a moment cooling down and catching our breath. I felt as though I had just run a marathon, all that from just one kiss, our first kiss. I can only imagine what making love to him would be like. I rolled onto my side to admire him. I lifted my hand and gently touched his lips, trailing my finger down his chin and over his chest to his stomach. He turned his head and looked at me placing his hand on my cheek.

"You are so beautiful" he whispered. He leaned forward kissing me softly, letting his lips linger on mine for a moment. I will never get enough of the feel of his lips on mine. He pulled away too quickly and sat up. Outside the sun was setting and the room was getting dark. Gunner sat up and patted my knee.

"Well, I think it's time I show you off a little" he smiled.

"What?" I asked shocked, sitting up as well.

"Since you're staying here now, it's probably best that you meet the Alpha"

"You mean your father, you want me to meet your dad?" I started to feel very anxious.

"Yes, Zee my dad" he chuckled. I felt my mouth drop open and my eyes haze over. Holy shit I'm meeting the Alpha, what if he doesn't like me, what if he doesn't accept me into the pack. So many things could go wrong here, I could be sent away, I could be sent back to Hank. My stomach knotted over, and I started to feel sick and dizzy. Gunner put his arm around me and pulled my head to his chest.

"It'll be fine little wolf, don't worry" he said, his voice so smooth and velvety. It's hard not to feel calm and relaxed at the sound of his voice and the feel of his strong arms.

"Can I shower first?" I asked, realising it had been days since my last shower. I must smell horrid, I breathed in through my nose but all I can smell is Gunner's natural perfume.

"Of course you can, there's a towel in there for you already". He let my head go and I stood up and walked into the bathroom. I turned on the hot tap and let it warm up. I pulled off my shirt and giggled to myself, I have an idea. A naughty, cheeky idea. I tossed my top through the open door into the bedroom and then did the same with my jeans. I tried to focus my hearing and listened, I caught the sound of his heartbeat, and it was racing ever so slightly. I took off my bra and held it up in the doorway, swinging it around before throwing it.

"I know what you're doing" he growled from the bed. I slipped off my underpants and popped my head out the door, covering the rest of my body with the door frame.

"I'm not doing anything" I smiled and flung my panties at him. He caught them and looked up at me with a devilish gleam in his eye. I winked and quickly ducked into the shower.

The hot water felt incredible, I breathed in the steam and felt my body relax. I lifted the blue loofah ball off the tap and picked up one of the body washes that was lying on the floor. I scrubbed the loofah over my skin, it felt so good to wash the dirt and grime away. Like I was washing away the last remnants of my father and his abuse. I bent down to wash my legs and heard a rumbling growl from inside the bathroom. I stood up and wiped my hand over the shower door to clear away the condensation. Gunner was leaning against the door frame staring into the shower, staring at me. Naked. For a split second, I felt exposed and vulnerable, ashamed of my small and abused body. As I looked into his eyes through the steam, I found nothing but lust and pure adoration, making me remember again how calm and safe I felt in his presence.

"Well, are you just going to stare, or are you going to help me wash my back?" I asked him with a sly smile. He stepped closer to the shower but stopped, looking down he shook his head.

"As inviting as that sounds, if I get in there with you, we both know what will happen" he sounded angry with himself.

"Is that so bad?" I asked, wanting badly to persuade him.

"It's not bad, but we have time, there's no rush" he half smiled and left the bathroom.

Ugh, what is wrong with me! Asking him to join me in the shower, could I be any more slutty. It's like all logic and morals are out the door when he is around. He just drives me so damn crazy. I got out of the shower, dried myself off, and wrapped the towel around me. I looked at myself in the mirror. My eye was basically back to the right colour, with just a small dark pink patch remaining on my eyelid. The burns on my neck were nearly gone. There were still some patches of discolouration and some spots that looked like small round scars, but the skin itself was healed. I turned slightly to look at the slashes on my back, they were all gone too, not even a scar. Wow, I huffed at myself. I held out my arms and looked them up and down, there were no bruises and no scars. The same with my legs and stomach, all my old scars, even the ones I have had for years, are all gone. This is impossible right, how could I heal permanent scars? Is this what being a Were is all about?

I walked back into the bedroom and saw Gunner standing by the dresser in just boxer shorts. My heart dropped and my stomach tightened. I could right away feel the moisture between my legs. Holy shit, this bond thing is turning me into a sex craving, hormone driven, wack job. God, how I want to jump his bones.

"Hot damn" I exclaimed fanning myself with my hand. He looked over at me and smiled, a pale pink blush settling on his cheeks.

"I could say the same about you" he chuckled.

"What, this old thing?" I held out the bottom of my towel and twirled. He laughed and put his hand over his eyes,

"Stop it" he cried still laughing. I skipped over to him and wrapped my arms around his waist, snuggling my face into his chest. He put his arms around my shoulders and gently tickled my bare back.

"I'm so happy" I whispered. He squeezed me a little tighter.

"Me too" he said back. It wasn't a lie. I have never felt so much blissful happiness before in my life. Sure, I've had a few huge bombs dropped on my reality over the past few days. With my dad nearly killing me and knowing that I can never go home again. Finding out that I can transform into a wolf and discovering that I have a soul mate. My life has legitimately done a full one-eighty. But I couldn't be happier about it. Gunner let me go and pointed at the bed where a purple dress was laid flat,

"Put that on"

"Woo pretty" I said holding it up.

"I'm glad you think so, now get dressed and stop teasing me"

"But you're so easy to tease" I said sticking my tongue out at him. He stepped forward and grabbed my chin, lifting my face up to his, then leaned down close to my face. He growled, snapped his teeth, and kissed me. Well, that was both frightening and incredibly hot at the same time. I stood staring at him with my mouth open. He pulled on a pair of pants and smiled at me, pointing to the dress and snapping his fingers. I shook my head and grabbed the dress along with a bra and panties from one of my plastic bags. I thought about going into the bathroom to change, but he's already seen me naked in the shower, so what the heck. I turned my back to him and dropped my towel, standing butt naked in plain sight. I'm actually surprised with myself, I have never been so bold or unashamed before. I pulled on a pair of black cheeky panties and a matching black bra, I then slipped on the dress and turned around. Gunner was sitting on the edge of the bed biting his lip. He was gripping the covers so tight that his hands were turning red, and the veins were bulging.

"What?" I said with a shrug of my shoulders. He jumped off the bed and picked me up, I squealed as he spun me around. I gripped his shoulders and wrapped my legs around his waist. He held me in his arms and kissed me softly.

"You're going to be the death of me" he said with a smile.

"And what a wonderful death it will be" he whispered, placing one more feather light kiss to my lips.

Gunner carefully put me down and took my hand, leading me downstairs. He led me to a door I hadn't seen yet, he pushed it open and ushered me in. The room was long and narrow and had a huge wooden table in it, the table could easily seat like twenty people. There were no windows and just one other door at the end of the room. Over the table were a row of three hanging lights, similar to the chandelier in the foyer. There were eleven place settings already set out with silver cutlery and big white plates.

"I thought we were just meeting your dad?" I whispered as I clutched his arm.

"We are, plus two or three others" he chuckled rubbing my hand. He directed me to the seat nearest to the end of the table and pulled the chair out for me. What a gentleman he is. I sat down and he sat in the chair next to me.

"Where is everyone else?"

"They're on the way". He put his hand on my knee and squeezed it gently. Just then, Cole walked through the door followed by a very tall and very muscular dark-haired man. He had a bit of short stubble covering his chin and very bushy eyebrows. The mere sight of him was intimidating. Gunner stood up and embraced Cole, and then the big man. I stood up as well and smiled at Cole.

"Glad to see you're doing better Zelena" He nodded at me with a forced half smile.

"This is my father, Spartan. He is the pack Beta" he pointed to the man beside him.

"Hello sir" I squeaked.

"Nice to meet you" he nodded in response. I looked over the giant man in front of me. I swallowed down the ball of nerves that had lodged itself in my throat. If a man as huge and intimidating as Spartan is only the second in command of the pack, I dread to think what Gunner's father will be like.

Next through the door was a tall and ridiculously beautiful girl, with straight silky dark blonde hair in a short bob cut, she looked like a model. Her skin was flawless and tanned. I immediately felt self-conscious. She walked straight over to me, pulling me in for a hug. I was a little surprised by her friendliness, but I hugged her back. She let me go and stepped back holding my hands in hers.

"I am so glad to finally meet you" she said with a beaming smile that instantly put me at ease,

"My overprotective brother has kept you locked away in that room for days. Not letting anyone but Artemis in" she frowned at Gunner.

"But now you're here and I can finally get to know my future Luna" she squealed with a small jump.

"Natalia" Gunner hissed at her,

"What, isn't she though?" she snapped back at him.

"Ease up" he hissed again,

"Ugh, whatever" she groaned with a roll of her eyes.

"You can call me Nat by the way" she pulled me in for another hug and Gunner growled quietly at her.

"We'll talk later" she whispered with a wink. I watched her as she went and sat down, trying to digest all the information I was just given. 'Overprotective brother' that means she's Gunner's sister. She is stunning, just like her brother. I felt a little inadequate in her presence, but her disposition was nothing short of friendly and inviting. Makes me feel a little giddy and hopeful.

Gunner gestured to my chair, so I sat back down.

"You boys sort out your business today?" Spartan's voice rumbled across the table.

"We did, everything is taken care of" Gunner said as he smiled warmly at Cole.

Spartan nodded and huffed. The door opened again and a short lady with pale skin and bright red hair walked through, behind her was Smith. I smiled at him, glad that he was going to be here too. Gunner stood up and kissed the lady on the cheek and then embraced Smith, he held his arms around him for what felt like a long time. I started to worry, considering their altercation this afternoon. When they let go Gunner grabbed his face and kissed him on the top of the head. What! Is that normal? Hank never showed affection, to anyone or anything. Plus, he always cussed out people on the TV, saying that boys were getting soft and weak, in his time real men fought, they didn't hug and talk and all that bullshit. This was new. But at least all was well between them, apparently. I didn't dare stand or say anything, I just put up my hand and wiggled my fingers at him. He smiled back and did the same.

"Zelena, this is my Mum, Deena" Smith said grabbing his mum around the shoulders and kissing her temple. A small pang of jealousy hit me at the sight of their affection.

"Hello, sweet thing" she said with a smile as she pushed Smith off her.

They sat down and we waited for the others to come. The door opened and two more men walked in, one very short with a bald head, and the other, tall and skinny with long grey hair tied in a ponytail at the base of his neck. Gunner stood up and shook their hands, he reached for me, so I stood up and took his hand,

"Zelena, this is Mazz and Julian, they're senior pack members and close friends of my father"

"Hello, nice to meet you" I smiled at them. They both nodded back and took their seats.

I realised now that none of the men offered to shake my hand, hug me, or anything like that. The only person who did was Gunner's Sister. Is that normal? Smith said I wasn't meant to touch other males, that's what caused all the drama this afternoon. But the feeling that I was getting the brush off was potent in my thoughts. Was this their subtle way of showing that they disapprove of my presence? They don't actually want me to join the pack at all. Anxiety settled in the pit of my stomach.

We sat down again and just as my ass hit the seat, Roe walked in with a man behind her. I remember seeing him today, he was sitting under the open hut in the village. My god, he looks just like Gunner only hairier. Same blue eyes, same coloured hair, and same height and build, it was uncanny.

"Zelena dear, this is my husband, Lupus" Roe said stepping to the side to let her husband pass her.

Gunner stood up and stepped forward, I followed close behind him. He hugged his dad and then stepped beside me. Lupus walked right up to me standing very close. He picked up both my hands and held them tightly between his. He was a giant compared to me, and very intimidating. Definitely worthy of a name like 'Alpha'. I could feel Gunner's hand on my lower back shaking a little. His nervous energy made me feel nervous. I gulped and smiled weakly up at Lupus.

"Hello sir" I choked.

"Zelena, my wife and son have both told me a lot about you. I'm happy to see that my son didn't over exaggerate when telling me how beautiful you are. He was right, you are indeed stunning" his voice was loud and frightening, although he was saying nice things, I felt like I needed to cower from him.

"I am very honoured that the Moon Goddess has blessed our pack with a True Mate bond. Though a Were that has shown as much courage, heart, and determination as you have, would have been welcomed into our pack regardless, True Mate bond or not" he smiled through his bread and looked at Gunner.

"She will make an exceptional Luna one day" he proclaimed.

I felt Gunner let out a deep breath beside me, and the whole room suddenly felt ten times lighter. Lupus let go of my hands and threw his arms in the air,

"Let's fucking feast" he shouted.

Everyone at the table clapped and Woo Hoo'd and two ladies walked in through the other door carrying huge trays of food. Gunner grabbed me around the waist pulling me close to him.

"I'm so proud of you" he whispered resting his forehead on mine. I'm not one hundred percent sure what just happened. I've also never heard someone say such nice things to me before.

"Did I just get accepted into the pack?" I asked shyly,

"You sure did, Baby" he kissed me hard.

I could feel the tears welling up in my eyes. I have a pack now, I have a family. This is all I have ever wanted. I wrapped my arms around his neck and kissed him back.

"Come on you two" shouted Lupus.

"There's time for that later" he roared with laughter.

I blushed bright red as we sat back down. There were more trays of food on the table now, all filled with vegetables and meats and bread, and so much of it, I've never seen so much food. Before now, I would only have whatever Hank didn't eat, and that usually wasn't a lot. Gunner started filling my plate with food until it was nearly overflowing.

Everyone was eating, laughing, and having a good time. They all looked so happy and so comfortable with each other. There were too many conversations happening at once, it was hard to follow. Mazz, Julian, and Spartan were on the other side of the table down from me, they were all talking together. Cole and Smith were across from us and a seat down, Nat was next to Gunner, and they were all talking and laughing. Roe and Deena were deep in conversation. Lupus was at the head of the table right next to me, he ate quietly observing everyone else. I was slowly eating as I gazed at each person at the table.

"They can be a lot to handle" Lupus said leaning over a little.

"This lot, and the pack" he nodded down the table.

"I kind of like it, I've never had a family before" I said with a shy smile.

He frowned a little, putting a piece of meat in his mouth.

"Where's your mother?" he asked mid chew.

"She died when I was a baby, I don't remember her"

"And your father, he's just a human, right?"

"Yes. As far as I know"

"So, your mum was a Were then?"

"Uh, I guess so"

"Your father never told you?"

"Nah, he wasn't big on talking with me"

"Uh yes, I'm very sorry you had to go through that"

"It's okay, I was used to it"

"Hmm" Lupus huffed as he placed his hand on top of my hand squeezing it softly.

"That is not the life a little girl should have to be used to".

I looked up at him, his light blue eyes were full of pity and pain as he stared into my eyes. I could tell he was genuinely sorry for the way I lived and for all I had to endure. A tear rolled down my cheek and I quickly wiped it away. He let go of my hand and cleared his throat and went back to eating quietly. Gunner put his hand around my waist and pulled me close to him, kissing me on the cheek softly.

"Are you okay?" he whispered.

I looked at him and smiled with a closed mouth.

"I'm better than okay".

I leaned forward pressing my forehead against his. He grabbed my neck and kissed me. I turned back to my plate and noticed Roe and Deena looking at us and smiling. Roe had one hand on her chest and the other fanning her face. She was smiling and crying at the same time.

"They are just so perfect" she blubbered to Deena. I put my head down and smiled to myself. Yes, the mother and the father like me, winning!

Everyone slowly stopped eating, I didn't even get halfway through my plate, but I thought I might burst if I ate any more. The same two women who brought the trays in came back and cleared the table. Lupus stood up.

"Let's go sit by the fire" he announced.

Everyone stood up and started making their way out the door. Gunner grabbed my hand as I was about to stand.

"The rest of the pack will be out there, are you sure you're ready for this?" he asked with concern.

"Of course I am. I'll be fine" I said kissing his nose and standing up. I was on too much of an endorphin high to call it quits now. The whole evening had been magical, and my body was vibrating with happiness.

We followed everyone outside. There was a raging fire burning in the fire pit and a lot of people sitting and standing around it. The night air was cool, but I could feel the heat of the fire all the way from up here on the porch. We walked down and headed for the fire. People looked at us and said their 'hello's' and 'nice to meet you's'. Three young boys who were sitting on one of the logs got up to let Gunner and I sit down. He put his arms around me and kissed my cheek. There were so many people out here, all of them looked happy and content.

"Where's the music?" Lupus bellowed through the large clearing. Some thumping rock music began to play loudly from the closest cabin. Lupus grabbed Roe's hand and twirled her around dancing. They were beautiful together and anyone could see how much love they shared. I felt happy as I watched them dance and laugh together. Another pang of jealousy hit me as I wondered what my own mother was like, if she was a Were like Lupus said, and what really happened to her. As I looked around at everyone dancing and enjoying the night, one girl on the other side of the fire caught my attention. She was tall and thin, with dark brown hair tied up on top of her head. She wore very tight blue jeans and a small white singlet top that accentuated her large chest. As she caught my eye, her top lip curled into a snarl.

"Who's that?" I asked Gunner nodding my head in her direction. Gunner looked over at her and his body tensed. He was quiet for a moment, then he tightened his arms around me and kissed my cheek.

"No one important" he snarled.

She threw her drink into the fire and stormed off in a huff. I watched her walk away into one of the cabins. She was definitely someone, important or not. Why else would she react like that? Gunner stood up and held his hand out to me.

"Come on kid, let's dance" he said smiling down at me.

"Kid?" I mocked, and he chuckled at me.

"Just get up off your sweet little ass and come dance with your Mate".

I stood up and reluctantly took his hand. I've never danced before, I don't know how to dance. Gunner twirled me around and then pulled my body into his, and then began moving his hips from side to side. I blushed as we twisted and twirled together laughing. The song slowed and he pulled me in again, I wrapped my arms around his waist as he rested his head on the top of mine. We swayed slowly from side to side holding each other.

"I love you" he breathed heavily.

Wait, what did he just say? I pulled my head away and looked up at his face. Did I actually just hear that or was I imagining it? He looked and me and bit his bottom lip, he was shocked. I don't think he meant to say it, at least not out loud.

"What did you say?" I asked up at him.

He closed his eyes and gulped. He then leaned down and looked me directly in the eyes.

"I love you, my little wolf" he said strongly and with a straight and certain face.

My heart exploded with happiness. I had never felt such warmth and acceptance before. What an odd feeling it is. I wanted to dance and shout and sing. He loves me. He loves ME. I grabbed his face and kissed his lips.

"I... I think I love you too" I said with a shy smile.

"You think?" he asked with a quirked brow.

"I don't have a lot of experience with love" I admitted. Gunner picked my chin up and forced my eyes to his.

"I'll teach you" he smiled. My own smile spread across my face, so big that my cheeks hurt.

Gunner gleamed at me happily. He picked me up and I wrapped my legs around his hips. He kissed me on the mouth and then again on the nose and cheek and back to my mouth again. He kissed my face all over, mumbling 'I love you' as he went. I have never felt something like this, it was like the sun was shining inside my chest. I thought my heart might break through my ribs and start dancing on the dirt. I grabbed his face and pressed my lips against his. He licked my lips softly and I opened my mouth. He flicked my tongue with his and I rubbed the tip of his tongue with mine. I moaned quietly at how good he tasted. I bit down softly on his bottom lip and he growled at me. I opened my mouth again and our tongues continued to dance together. I could kiss him like this forever, I didn't want to stop. I wrapped my arms around his neck, pressing my body flush against his, and grabbed a handful of his hair in my hand. He withdrew his tongue and kissed my lips softly a few more times. He pulled his head back and smiled.

"You're going to get me all excited" he said resting his forehead on mine.

"I'm okay with that" I whispered, giving his lips a quick lick. He smiled and huffed.

"I don't think the rest of the pack want to see that though".

I completely forgot that we weren't alone. Looking out of the corner of my eye, I saw that there were eyes on us from all directions. My cheeks burned with embarrassment.

"Later" I whispered. I gave him one last kiss as I jumped out of his arms, and went and sat back down by the fire next to Nat. She put her arm through mine and snuggled in close to me with a big smile on her beautiful face. Her warmth and friendliness was a little alarming. I've never had a girl treat me nicely before, besides Roe of course. But I welcomed her affection.

"So" she smiled enthusiastically

"Tell me everything".

Chapter

Ten

Gunner

Spending time with Zelena is so easy, natural. It's been such a short time, but I already feel so connected to her. She's the first person I seek out in a room, it's her scent that I first search for, it's her face I see when I close my eyes. Every time she isn't in my arms, there's an undeniable tug in my chest, pulling me to wherever she is. She's It for me. I know it.

As I held her in my arms, her chest pressed to my chest, the taste of her still on my tongue, and the strain of my pants definitely not easing in the slightest, I knew it was the right thing to tell her my true feelings. I do love her, it's as simple as that.

"Later" Zelena whispered. She kissed me quickly and jumped out of my arms. Maybe she doesn't need a few weeks, maybe she is ready for more now. I growled quietly as she turned and walked away back to the fire. Watching her perfect perky ass sway from side to side as she walks, it took a lot of strength not to jump her. She sat down next to Nat and dived right into conversation.

I took a few deep breaths to calm myself. I groaned internally, realising how badly I need to release this pressure. I want to, no, I need to be inside her. To fully claim her as my own. I carefully adjusted the bulge in my jeans, which seemed to be sticking around from here on. When I turned around I spotted Cole and Smith standing together with a couple of other pack kids our age. I picked up a beer from the cooler and walked over to them.

If fucking Zoe does anything to fuck with Zelena's night, I may just kill the bitch. When Zee pointed her out across the fire, and I saw her snarling back at Zee, it took a lot of strength not to choke her out right then and there. Zee was curious and confused, I could smell it coming from her. Fucking Zoe. The slightly older girl who tried to convince me that she was my Mate. She didn't actually love me or even care about me remotely. She was only interested in getting a step closer to being Luna, to having more power and authority in the pack. I was young and dumb. Thinking back on it now, she doesn't even come close to being on Zelena's level. I looked back at Zelena as I walked, she was smiling brightly at my sister. Her pale skin glowed in the firelight. This life, doing this with Zelena, this would be perfection. I want so much to give her happiness and protection, a life that she deserves.

"Heeyyyy, Casanova" Smith sang and slapped me on the back as I reached them. I chuckled and took a drink from my bottle. He's such a dork. Not like he can talk, he's shagged more she-wolves than I can count.

"Here I thought you were the one with all the moves, Smithy boy" Daniel, one of the guys, teased Smith.

"Well, I've taught him well obviously" Smith laughed along with the others.

"In all seriousness, Gunner, she seems like a great Were. You made a good choice in a Mate" said Ari.

"Thanks man, though I think my choice was made for me"

"I know what you mean man, those she-wolves have a way of pulling you in" they all laughed.

"Yeah, something like that" I smirked taking another drink. If you only knew, I thought to myself.

The news of our True Mate bond hasn't exactly been told to the other pack members, for now that's the best way to go. It's possible that not everyone will be so thrilled about it. At least until we seal the bond, and until Zee has had a chance to get to know the pack a bit more, it'll stay a secret. All they need to know is that their Alpha-Son has chosen a Mate. The rest will come out eventually.

The boys all chatted and laughed, joking about fighting and humans, and of course the she-wolves. I listened and joined in as much as I could, especially when Smith was insinuating that he was the strongest fighter for our age group. Granted, he has skills, but he is no pack fighter, not yet anyway. I found myself continuously zoning out of the conversation, my focus was fixed on Zelena. Watching her laugh and smile with the other she-wolves, she was fitting in perfectly. The way the light of the fire made her skin glow and her golden eyes light up like pieces of the sun itself, took my breath away. She laughed and tossed her hair back over her shoulder. The effortlessness of her grace and beauty made my dick jerk with lust and excitement. I cleared my throat and rubbed the back of my neck.

"I'm gonna grab another beer" I said to the guys before I made my way over to the cabin. The cooler was sitting open at the bottom of the stairs, I picked up a bottle, twisted off the cap, and took a swig. I was suddenly yanked back by the shoulder forcefully, making the beer spit from my mouth. I was pulled backwards behind the cabin out of view from the rest of the pack, and then pushed against the wall. A body was pressed up against me and wet lips smashed against my face. At first, I thought it was Zee, but the feeling of the lips and the taste of alcohol was repulsive. I had to force myself not to gag. I breathed in through my nose taking in their scent. Zoe. I shoved her off me and growled.

"What the fuck are you doing?" I snarled.

"What's wrong, Gunner, Baby, you know you want me?" she snickered and tried to lunge at me again. I pushed her back and she hit the cabin wall behind her.

"You wanna get rough, Baby, I can play rough".

She launched herself forward and jumped onto me, wrapping her legs around my waist and biting down on my ear. I hissed at the feeling and grabbed her arm, pulling her down and off me. I tossed her to the ground and bared my teeth. I wiped my fingers over my ear and looked at my hand, she drew blood.

"You're drunk" I huffed, looking down at her sitting in the dirt.

"Go and dry off" I snapped. I was about to walk away when she screamed at me.

"What happened to you, huh? One day at your little school and you just forget all about me?" Zoe blubbered, brushing the dirt off her hands.

"Don't kid yourself, Zoe, we were done well before then".

I tried to stay calm, but my anger and disgust was rising. She wasn't helping herself either.

"What we had was great" she spat, standing up and brushing the dirt from her too tight jeans.

"What we had was bullshit. Nothing but lies and manipulation. All you cared about was getting power, you never actually wanted me, you only wanted an ego boost" I clapped back.

She walked towards me, swaying her hips and slowly sliding her hands up my chest. I turned up my nose and retreated, stepping backward until my back was against the wall. I turned my face away from her as she got close enough for me to feel her sticky breath on my cheek.

"Of course I want you baby, I never stopped wanting you" she whined.

I don't want to deal with this, with her. It's just pathetic, her attempts to cling to our stupid past mistakes. I'm done with this. I have to get away from her before I snap her neck. I grabbed her wrists and lifted them off my chest, standing up straight, I was now towering over her.

"Let it go Zoe. We're done. I have my True Mate now, and you could never compare to her. So will you please, just stay the fuck away from me".

I threw her hands away and walked off, leaving her behind me.

"Gunner" she cried out as I turned to the front of the cabin.

I found Cole waiting for me with his usual serious face. He knows about Zoe, and our attempted relationship, if you can even call it that.

"Everything good here?" he asked.

He had been listening to Zoe's lame attempt at a seduction. Cole was the one who helped me see through her lies and manipulation. Thank Goddess he was able to smack some sense into my young and horny mind.

"Is now" I said grabbing him around the shoulders.

We headed back over to the fire and stood behind Zee and Nat. Keeping one arm around Cole, I put my other hand on Zee's shoulder. She pressed her cheek into my hand and lifted her head back to give me a smile. I leaned down and kissed her forehead. Nothing and no one could ever compare to her.

"How's about a nice campfire story?" Dad called out to the pack.

Excited murmurs and calls of agreement rang out, and they all began to move in close to gather around the fire.

"My love, will you do the honours?" he smiled, reaching for my mother who was sitting on a log. She smiled and stood up, taking my father's hand.

"What would we like to hear?" she turned in a circle asking the gathered pack members.

"I think in honour of our newest wolf and pack member, the sweet Zelena" Dad spoke looking over at Zee with a soft smile. She squeezed my hand and shifted nervously in her seat as the eyes from the other pack members looked over at her.

"And of course, the new pairing between her and your Alpha-Son. Tonight, we should hear the story of Selene and her human lover" he continued.

He turned in a slow circle looking at the waiting faces of the pack.

"Any objections?" Mum asked.

No one refused, and instead, they all cheered and called for her to begin the story.

"Okay, now remember, no interruptions" Mum smiled looking around the fire at her pack.

Dad sat down on the log that Mum had been sitting on, everyone began to get comfortable and settled in for the story.

The night was quiet, all attention on Mum as she began the story. "A long time ago, before the time of the wolf, the world was quiet and peaceful. During the day the human folk worked hard to farm their land and sow their crop. The children would run and play in the sunlight and humankind thrived. Though, alone in the sky sat the beautiful Selene, the Goddess of the moon. Every night she would ride her dragon chariot across the sky to bring the moon to the people. But as the sun fell and the night sky spread across the land, she became lonely, as the humans would sleep through her glorious night sky. Night after night she searched the land for signs of any human that would splendour in her nighttime hours, but none did. Until one night she came across a lonely shepherd, sitting on the top of a hill with his flock, gazing at the night stars. His name was Endymion. Selene became overjoyed by the sight of this lone human man enjoying her creation. Selene searched for Endymion night after night, and without fail she would find him, gazing up at the stars. Selene began to long for the mortal man, she found comfort in his peaceful gaze and wanted to know why he found such solace in her stars. After many nights of torturous desire and having to watch him from afar, Selene made the decision to visit Endymion on his hilltop. She appeared to him in her long white robes with the bright light of the moon, shining all around her. At first, Endymion was frightened, but he quickly became captivated by her beauty. Each night after their first meeting, he would wait for her visit. The two fell madly in love and wanted to spend every moment together. But Endymion was becoming distracted by their love, and his flock began to fall prey to foxes and other predators. Endymion was saddened by his inability to take care of his flock and spend his nights with Selene. As a way to end her human lover's conflict and to assist him with his shepherd duties, Selene blessed the mortal man with many gifts. One such gift was the ability to transform his human shape into that of a wolf, becoming stronger and faster. The ultimate predator. In doing so he was able to fend for his flock against the creatures they had fallen prey to. After many, many nights together Selene bore Endymion a son, Lycaon. The first werewolf. He was a beautiful and happy child, but he grew cold and angry at his mother Selene. Lycaon resented the fact that his mother had to leave him at the rising of the sun. As he grew into a man, Lycaon's anger turned sour. One night in a fit of rage, whilst in his wolf form, he fatally wounded his father. Selene was heartbroken by the actions of her son, and so she took Endymion to a hidden cave. There she laid him to rest in an ageless sleep for all eternity, so that she might still visit and look upon her beloved's peaceful body. In a bid to warm the cold heart of her son, Selene blessed him with a lover, a Mate made just for him. Lycaon's heart was thawed by the love of his Mate, and his cold anger melted away by her touch. They were happy together for a great many years and their union spawned many children. It is said that one of those children was a young daughter, given the name Selena. The daughter Selena shared a great likeness to that of her grandmother the Goddess. Therefore, Selene favoured the young girl and blessed her with great power. The other children of Lycaon spread across the globe far and wide, and the lines of their children now make up the packs you know today. But Selene's namesake and favourite grandchild forever remained close to her heart. Those daughters are still blessed by the touch of the Goddess today. And so you see, the wolf was born of a great love, full of heartache and happiness. It is because of that love that Were-kind are emotionally driven creatures. Without the sacrifice of the Goddess's true love, and the gift of a Mate for her son, no Were would be here today".

Mum turned slowly around the fire pit, looking at all the faces captivated by her story. No one dared speak or interrupt her as she went. As the story drew to the end, the emotions around the fire were obvious. All stories about the Goddess lead to heightened emotions.

Mum smiled brightly and lifted her hands to the sky as she got down on her knees.

"We give you our thanks, Selene, and we recognise your sacrifice" she called out.

My father joined her on his knees and raised his hands also. The rest of the pack followed the lead of their Alpha. Zelena turned to look at me and I nodded at her to follow. We got down on our knees and lifted our hands to the sky.

"In the Goddess we love" we all chanted together.

The pheromones in the air were thick and tense. Everyone's emotions were running hot. My father picked up my mother and sat her straddling his lap. Other pack members began to pair off and go their separate ways. Some didn't bother to leave the fire and started roughly kissing and groping in full view. Lust filled growls and groans echoed through my ears, and I could smell the desire and heat all around me. Zelena stood and looked up at me with confusion. She's so sweet, so innocent. I can't wait to have her for my own. I felt the possessive growl vibrate in my chest before I knew what I was doing. I wanted her, right now. I grabbed her hand and pulled her off to the side. I could feel my heart starting to race as my desire grew, the hardness in my pants was straining to get free. I'm not going to last. I dragged Zee behind a cabin and lifted her up, pinning her against the wall. I was panting heavily and my skin was burning. I smashed my lips into hers and she wrapped her legs around me, taking my tongue into her mouth greedily. I kissed her hard and fast, tasting every inch of her mouth. I pulled her dress up to her hips and slid my hand under the material and up to her breast, squeezing it in my hand.

"Gunner" she moaned into my mouth, her fingers twisting into my hair.

Not taking my lips off hers, I slowly glided my hand down her stomach to her crotch. I pressed the palm of my hand against her pussy. The heat coming from her was maddening. I howled inside my head and felt my canines push forward. I could feel her juices seeping through her panties, and it was my undoing. I pulled her panties to the side and stroked her wet lips. She shuddered and moaned loudly. I breathed in deeply through my nose, taking in her delicious scent. I growled lowly, letting it vibrate through my body. I swiped my fingers across her again and sighed into her cheek.

"I want you to" she breathed out heavily.

Fuck, what am I doing? Get a hold of yourself, Gunner. I'm letting my wolf take control, not even trying to fight it. I let go of her panties and pulled her dress back down. I kissed her a few more times, trying desperately not to grind against her. After a beat, I managed to pull back, resting my forehead on hers. Taking long deep breaths, I forced myself to calm down. I let Zee down and stood leaning over her, caging her in with my hands on either side of her head.

"Why'd you stop?" she panted, her arms hanging limp at her sides. I looked at her beautiful face, her cheeks were flushed, and her lips were swollen. I gently brushed my fingers over her plump lips. The soft feel of them under my thumb sent a burning sensation back through my chest. Stop it Gunner, I scolded myself.

"I'm sorry, I wasn't in control" I said standing up straight and running my fingers through my hair.

She looked up at me through her lashes, a disappointed pout on her lips. She is too damn cute. I chuckled and gripped the back of her neck. Leaning down slowly, I watched her eyes dilate, then gave her a quick kiss. She wants me. She may not know it, or understand it, but she's just as hungry as I am. I pushed off the wall and let the night's cool air wash over her.

"Come on my love, it's late, let's go to bed" I said, taking her hand in mine.

We walked back around the front of the cabin and towards the main house. The firepit was now on the verge of an all out orgy. Zelena looked over at the scene with surprise and curiosity. There was a lot of kissing and growling and some very sexual grinding. In the distance, in almost every direction of the village, loud sexual moans echoed through the air. They were all well on their way to a steamy night. Zelena watched as I led her back to the porch, her eyes darting in every direction. We stopped at the door and she turned to me and giggled with a blush across her cheeks.

"Not so PG-13 huh?" I joked.

"No, but it's kind of hot" she huffed with an excited giggle.

I looked at her in shock and held her face between my hands.

"You are full of surprises, little wolf" I smiled kissing her sweet lips. The overly sexual display would be frowned upon by humans. Weres are more openly free with their sexual desires, we are run on animal instincts after all. I half expected her to be disgusted by it all. But her fast heartbeat and the scent of her arousal was proof enough that her own animal instincts were drawn to the scene. Keeping my hands to myself tonight is going to be very difficult.

Chapter Eleven

Zelena

So, today we're going running, like in our wolf bodies. Running as a wolf. I'm excited and honestly a little scared, my last change seems like such a blur now. It happened so quickly, and I don't even know how I initiated it. I remember the heat and the pain of my breaking bones, but that's all. I mean I didn't even know I was changing into a wolf back then. Wow, it feels like a lifetime ago. Gunner thinks he can help me trigger it, though I'm not sure how he'll do it yet. I just hope that I don't disappoint him. I hate the idea of letting him down and not being the kind of wolf that he deserves.

We headed out to the flower field, silently walking hand in hand as I thought about last night. It was the most amazing night that I've ever had. We danced, we kissed, we laughed, and I finally felt like I belonged somewhere. Meeting Gunner's parents and the senior pack members, and then getting accepted into the pack, it has been the highlight of my life so far.

I loved the story that Roe told, about Selene and her lover. It was magical. That's where werewolves came from, that's where I came from. I'm a little envious that Gunner has grown up hearing these stories all his life. He has known who and what he is from the moment he was born. This world is still so new to me. Once the story ended, things got very interesting. The weird heat and desire I felt as the pack chanted for the Goddess, seeing them all attack each other with so much hunger and desire. Not to mention the passionate attack from Gunner. Phew, it was enough to blow my panties off. But seeing the pack so raw and sexual, it excited me, more than I thought it would. Not Gunner though apparently, well at least not enough to warrant more than a steamy make-out before going to sleep. The fact that I am dying for him to touch me, yet he is so resistant to do so, is really making me question if Roe was right about us.

I got to talk with Nat some more, and I really like her, she is so sweet and always seems happy. I think we could become the best of friends, or at least I hope so. She convinced me to go shopping with her in the city, and even though he wasn't exactly thrilled about it, Gunner finally gave in and said yes, only when Nat agreed to let him come along.

The weird actions from the tall girl by the fire were still playing on my mind a little, I want to ask him about her again, but later, I don't want to think about all that right now.

We finally got to the field and I saw Smith and Cole sitting in the grass, of course they would be here too. I waved and smiled at them, they stood up as they saw us.

"Hey fellas" Gunner beamed.

"Hey boss man, boss lady" Smith said with a smile and a wiggle of his fingers at me.

"You ready for this?" Cole asked looking at me with a slight frown.

"She's ready" Gunner answered looking down at me. His confidence in me made me feel warm and happy, but what if I can't trigger a change, will he be angry with me, or even disappointed?

"What if I can't do it?" I asked Gunner,

"You'll be fine, it just takes time" he said with a calm tone.

"You boys can hang back, we're just going to get in the right head space". Cole and Smith sat back down in the grass a few paces away from us, but they could still see what was going on.

"Okay, so now what, what am I meant to do?" I asked looking from side to side and shrugging my shoulders.

"Well, anger is the best way to start for most wolves. So, think of something that makes you mad". Gunner stood in front of me and crouched down a little to be more at my eye level. Mm, he is sexy. Nope, that's not anger. Shit, I've got to focus. He is too distracting, I closed my eyes and tried to concentrate. Okay, something that makes me mad. A lot of things make me angry, but they make me sad as well. My dad makes me mad, the fact that he never showed that he loved me, or even liked me. A small tingle ran through my arms. Why couldn't he love me? A parent's love is meant to be unconditional, why was I not worth loving? Tears began to well in my eyes and the tingle disappeared. I shook my head clear. I don't want sadness, I want anger.

"You can do it, Babe, concentrate on something that really infuriates you" Gunner said softly.

What infuriates me? Demi. She infuriates me. Demi and her little pack of imbeciles. I had never done anything to them and yet they made my life at school a living hell. The tingle came back, and pins and needles ran through my arms and up my legs. Why was she such a bitch to me? What did I do to her to deserve that kind of torment? I always kept to myself and tried to stay out of her way, but she made the time to bully me regardless. She went out of her way to make me miserable. My skin prickled with a heat waving over me.

"That's it, Zee" Gunner cheered.

She is the worst. She needs to be taught a lesson. No one should be subjected to endless torture and harassment like I was. Demi needs to be stopped. I could feel my legs shaking from underneath me, my wrists and fingers tensed and tightened. I clenched my teeth together as the pain intensified. I should be the one to teach her a lesson. I should be the one to stop her. I want to make her hurt and scared like I was, I want to taste her blood. My knees gave out and I fell to the ground. My back curved and twisted through the breaking of my bones. My skin felt like it was on fire, ripping and burning off in giant pieces.

"Yes, Zelena, YES!".

I will show her, I will show Demi what pain really is when I tear her throat out. I cracked my neck to the side, and then to the back, and let out a harrowing scream. My scream echoed through the field but melted slowly into a howl. Then the pain stopped, and the burning sensation was gone. I looked down at my hands, but they were now midnight black furry paws with long black claws. I looked behind me down my back and waved my tail through the air. I looked over at Gunner and he was now sitting on the ground with his legs crossed, staring at me.

I walked over to him and stood in front of his face. He didn't try to touch me and didn't say anything, in fact, he barely moved. I looked over his shoulder and saw Cole and Smith were now standing, watching us closely. I looked back at Gunner and sniffed at his face, he had bacon for breakfast, and I could still smell it on his breath. I sniffed at his hair, he smells like sunshine. There was another smell though, a funny, almost sour like scent, it was like he was nervous or something. He slowly started to lift his hand to the side of my face, he was acting weird, and it was freaking me out a little. I think he's scared of my wolf. I pushed my head into his hand, and he gently stroked my fur from my ear down my right shoulder. I leaned forward and pressed my head against his and he relaxed. I felt him ease, and the weird smell went away. I nuzzled my nose into his neck and licked his face.

"Ah, my little wolf" he laughed grabbing me and falling onto his back. I laid on his chest and continued to lick his face as he laughed and ruffled his hands through my fur. He even tastes like sunshine.

"You are magnificent, your wolf is the most beautiful colour I've ever seen" he smiled. His eyes were full and happy and there was this sweet smell coming from him, like happiness or love. I heard a soft crunch and looked up to see Smith and Cole had come closer to us. Smith was smiling and had his hands out in front of him, Cole was still a step behind him. Gunner sat up as he noticed them come closer.

"Easy guys" he said looking at me cautiously. I didn't understand why he was being so weird, like he thought I was going to attack them or something. I walked over to Smith's feet and he froze. I looked up at him and he just stared at me. I was about to rub my head against his leg to let him know it was okay, but Cole growled quietly from behind him. I looked up at Cole and cocked my head to the side. What the fuck, Cole, was he growling at me?

What was that for?

I thought to myself. I was caught off guard by another voice in my head.

He thinks you might attack Smith

I looked behind me and saw a huge silver wolf, it was glorious. Tall and muscular, way bigger than me and a little intimidating.

Gunner?

Yeah it's me

How can I hear you in my head?

We're flashing

No shit, cool

He huffed and shook his head and walked over to me, rubbing his head along my side and up my neck. Wow, he is incredible, is it any wonder this wolf will one day be the Alpha.

Why does he think I will attack him? I would never do that

Well now that I can hear you, I know that, but it's not always that way with newborn wolves. They are usually very aggressive and temperamental

Oh, am I like broken?

No of course not, you're just very mature. It's actually pretty incredible

He pressed the side of his body against mine and looked up at the boys. They both immediately relaxed.

"She's beautiful" whispered Smith as he stepped closer to me. He held his hand out in front of me and I pressed my head against it. He scratched the top of my head and sat down in the grass. Cole was still standing and watching us. I wanted to make him feel a bit more comfortable and to get him to trust me. I walked to his legs and rubbed my head against his thigh and pressed my nose into the palm of his hand. He didn't respond right away but then he brushed his fingers through the fur on my head.

"You sure are different" he breathed heavily as he ran his hand over my ear.

Gunner walked up next to me and nuzzled his head into mine, he then jumped up and pushed Cole over. My ears pricked up and I stood up tall. Was Gunner trying to fight him? Cole rolled

Gunner off and jumped on him wrapping his arms around Gunner's neck. I started to growl but Smith stood beside me and put his hand on my shoulder.

"They're just wrestling, they do it all the time" he said with a chuckle.

I looked back over at them as they were rolling through the grass. I noticed Cole's arm bend the wrong way and his back arch funny. There was the sound of a snap and a then crack, ripping clothes and in a split second, he was changed. A big chocolate brown wolf took his place, not as big as Gunner but still huge. He changed so quickly, and he didn't yell once. I couldn't help but scream in pain through my change, but he and Gunner could change in a snap of their fingers.

Cole jumped on Gunner and chomped at his neck and then Gunner grabbed Cole's leg. They wrestled through the grass biting at each other. I looked up at Smith who was watching and laughing. I nudged his leg with my head and whined at him. Is he going to change too? He looked down at me and grinned.

"My turn now, ay?" he smiled and stepped back, taking off his shirt. He knelt down on all fours and closed his eyes. He knelt there for a few seconds and then scrunched up his nose, his right arm snapped to the side and then his left. He arched his back up high and his neck cracked to the side. This is what we look like when we change? No wonder it friggin' hurts. Reddish brown hair sprouted through the skin on his arms and chest and his face morphed into the shape of a wolf. He lowered his head again and lifted his back, I could see his spine twisting like a snake under his skin. His bare back quickly disappeared under the fur as his head was turned to the side. And then it was done, he didn't make a single sound either. How is it so easy for them?

Smith shook off from his head down to his tail. His fur was a dark red brick colour and he was not too much bigger than me. He trotted over to me and did a little jump and roll, stopping at my feet.

Hey Princess
Holy crap we can flash?
Of course we can

I thought it was just with my Mate
All members of the pack can flash each other when in wolf form
Gunner flashed as he and Cole walked over to Smith and me.
Oh wow, I had no idea. This is awesome!
I jumped around a little, bashing into Gunner. He laughed and
shoved me with his head.
So, what now?
You and I are going to do a bit of wolf training
And them?
They're coming too
We're just going to hang back for this one, let you two do your thing
Oh okay, I thought we were going running though?
Ha, we are, you'll see. Smith, scout ahead and check things out, Cole, pick
up the rear. You, little wolf, just stick close, if you can keep up
Smith took off through the trees, Gunner gave me a little shove
and took off behind him. I followed after them and caught up to
Gunner easily. I think he is running slower for me. We ran
through the forest and it was just like my first change. The wind
flowing through my fur and the dirt under my paws. I really like
being in wolf form.
What do you see?
Huh?
Look around you as you run and tell me what you can see
I looked at a tree in the distance and like a camera lens, my eyes
focused in on it. I could see the details on the bark and each
individual leaf. I looked ahead of me to a bird's nest on a branch,
I could see the twigs making up the nest and the bird sitting inside
it.
I can see everything, like things I shouldn't be able to see. I can see small
details at impossible distances
Very good, now what can you smell?
I sniffed into my nose, at first it was just the smell of the dirt and
forest air, but as I continued to sniff I could start to make out
different scents.
I can smell the feathers of the birds and there's a creek to the right
What else?
I can smell you and I can smell Smith
Who can't smell Smith?
Cole chuckled through our flash.

Shut it, keep going, Zee

I sniffed hard at the air, sucking it in through my nostrils. A foul metallic scent hit me. Kind of like blood but different, not human, and maybe rotten, it was off somehow.

I think it's blood, but it would have to be animal blood, and it's old, at least a few days

You're doing amazing, now listen, use your ears and listen to the forest

I concentrated on my paws hitting the ground and the dull thudding they were making. I can hear the water trickling over rocks from the creek and there are so many birds. I focused up ahead to a thumping sound, but what was it? I followed the sound and then it all came together, once I used all my senses together it's like I was transported. I was suddenly running behind Smith, but not really running, more like hovering or flying. I don't know.

It's Smith, I can hear his heartbeat, and I can smell him, I can see him. Or it's like I can see the path he is running

Seriously?

I don't know, it's weird. I can't physically see him, but I can still see him, you know, like in my mind. The sound of his feet on the ground and his heart thumping and his panting, add that to the trail of his scent and I can picture him, like I'm running right behind him

Duuuude what?

Everyone halt

Gunner skidded to a stop and stood in front of me. I could hear Smith had stopped, and Cole was walking in our direction way back behind us.

You could see Smith, in your mind, without actually being able to see him?

Yes, you can't?

No Zelena, I can't. No one can do that. At least not anymore

What do you mean not anymore?

Well, if I'm right, it's called Drakos-Mati, the Dragon's Eye. It's from the story last night, one of the gifts Selene gave to her human lover was the sight of her dragon

Do you mean dragons are real too?

Of course not, maybe they were once, but not for thousands of years

I'm not following

Selene's chariot is pulled by dragons.

Uh, huh?

Um, it means you can see things in your mind without having to see them in person

Oh, okay

Never mind, it's only a story. You're just intuitive and have a great wolf mind is all

Oh well that seems fair, I'm pretty great at this whole wolf thing

I pranced around him swishing my tail on his face. He snapped at me playfully, taking me by surprise. He bowed his front quarters, waving his tail in the air. He was just like a puppy in prance mode. The sight made my heart melt a little. I pounced onto him, taking his ear in my mouth. He rolled over onto his back taking me with him. He growled and snapped at me as we wrestled through the trees.

We came to a stop, panting softly, with me lying half on top of him. He licked my face, and I nuzzled my head into his neck. His fur was so soft and inviting. I could imagine my naked body engulfed in his fur, tickling and touching my bare skin. The thought was turning me on. He began to growl softly, his whole body vibrating along with it. Mm even in wolf form I was still aching for him.

I breathed him in deeply and a burning sensation sent waves through my body. As I nuzzled my snout into his fur, I felt a hot dizziness and a sharp pinch. I winced and lifted myself off Gunner, noticing my human hands against his fur. He sat up and looked over my naked human body. He stood up, leaving me sitting on the ground, and began to circle me, still growling. It's very intimidating and a little scary, he is huge standing in front of my tiny frame. He moved his face directly in front of mine and I gasped at his glowing silver eyes. I lifted my hands to his face and gently stroked his fur. He pressed his head against mine and made a rumbling purr like sound. He pushed me back onto the ground and licked my face, I giggled at his slobbery kisses.

The fur between my fingers disappeared and was replaced by warm sculpted muscles. Gunner had changed and his naked human body was now laying on top of mine. He began kissing and biting at my neck, sending shivers through my veins.

"You are irresistible" he growled lowly, his voice sounding a little strange, deeper, and more dominant than usual. He kissed me roughly, digging his fingertips into my thigh. He was somewhat different, almost animalistic in his roughness. I like it, my body does too. I can feel the wetness pooling in my crotch and my skin start to heat up. His hard member was pressed against my stomach, there's nothing between our nakedness, just skin on skin. My skin prickled where he was touching me, which was all over my body. This was it, he was going to take my virginity right here in the forest.

"I want more" I moaned in his ear. He moved his hand from my thigh to my crotch and gently rubbed his finger against my wetness. The sensation of his touch, right there, made me shudder with pleasure. He flicked and teased my clit sending pulsating quivers through my body. My moans got louder as he teased me. He placed his other hand over my mouth and whispered.

"We're not alone out here". I don't care who heard us, I couldn't stifle my pleasure. He inserted two fingers ever so quickly and started sliding them in and out. The filling feeling was foreign and unusual but gave way to an immense pleasure pulsating through my blood. He was not holding back now, being out here in the wildlife, I've never felt him like this. He was rough and raw, I loved it. He muffled my screams as he brought me close to climax.

"You're mine, yes?" he growled seductively in my ear.

I nodded in response as he kept his hand over my mouth. He trailed his kisses down my neck to the top of my shoulder and bit down gently. I was nearing the edge when his movements got faster. I could feel my insides start to tighten around his digits. My body shook and quivered and right as I hit my peak, Gunner sunk his teeth into my shoulder harder, definitely breaking the skin. The pain was hot and sharp but was overshadowed by my jolting pleasure. I screamed into Gunner's hand as my body jerked and bucked and then slowly relaxed into the cold ground. He withdrew his teeth and licked over my neck.

Gunner let go of my mouth and grinned at me devilishly, a small line of my blood dripped from the corner of his mouth. He lifted his hand and licked my juices from his fingers.

"Mm little wolf, you are scrumptious" he smirked.

I blushed brightly at his remark. He stood up in front of me in all his naked glory, still fully aroused. I gasped at the sight of him. He turned to look at me and smiled.

"Oh, yeah" he chuckled looking down at his naked body.

He knelt down and shook his head and was instantly changed back into his wolf form. It was easy for him, and so quick. I sat up and crossed my arms across my naked breasts, feeling a little embarrassed. He nudged me with his big head and licked the side of my face.

Come on little wolf I'll take you back to the clearing to get some clothes
"I'm not walking back naked"
I'll shield you it's okay, besides, Cole and Smith aren't close enough to see you

My stomach dropped and I felt sick, I completely forgot about Smith and Cole. Did they see that or hear that? Oh, my god, I'm so embarrassed. Gunner rubbed his head into mine and nudged me again to get up. I stood up, keeping one arm across my breast, Gunner stood beside me and I leaned my hips into his fur. We walked together back to the clearing and found the bags the boys had left, I pulled out a yellow dress and pulled it on over my head. Gunner stood up slowly back in his human form. I lost myself in the sight of him, he is so god like, so handsome. The sun bounced off his muscles, defining every perfect curve. His soft skin glistened in the light. Mm, I just want to lick him from head to toe.

"Zee" he shouted, snapping me out of my daydream.

"Can I have my pants please?" he chuckled at my adoring stare.

"Hm, no. I think I like you better this way" I teased.

"Yeah but I don't" snorted Smith as he and Cole walked through the tree line. They were both wearing only shorts. Cole was tall and lean, with well defined muscles. I was surprised by Smith, he was ripped. I knew he was strong but under that shirt he was hiding some serious hotness. I blushed and threw the shorts to Gunner turning away from the boys.

"Can we go eat now? I'm starving" Smith groaned.

"You're always starving" Cole laughed.

"Well, I'm a growing boy" sneered Smith as he jumped on Cole tackling him in a headlock. I giggled as I watched the boys wrestle. Gunner wrapped his arms around my waist and rested his head on my shoulder.

"Ouch" I hissed as his chin pressed against the fresh bite mark. I looked it over. I hadn't noticed the dried blood on my chest before.

"You bit me" I exclaimed. Not sure if I was asking a question or just making a statement. I looked up at Gunner and a hot flush flew across his face.

"Ah, yeah, s-sorry" he stuttered.

"Oh, shit" breathed Smith as he noticed the blood and the mark.

"Come on, let's give them a minute" Cole said as he pushed Smith out of the clearing.

"I'm so sorry, really I am. I don't know what came over me" he rushed out.

"I was still in my wolf mind, and being in the forest, and seeing you like that, all naked and free. I just kind of went a little wild, I'm sorry, I didn't mean to mark you, fuck I'm an idiot" he spoke so quickly, and his voice started to shake.

"It's okay, I'm okay" I said grabbing his hands from his face.

"I should have asked you first" he said softly.

"Asked me what?"

"If I can mark you".

"What does that mean?" I questioned confused. Mark me? Is that what this bite is, a wolf mark? He gently traced his fingers over the bite mark, sending tingles dancing over my skin. I felt this warmth come from him, like pure love.

"A mark is what a wolf does to claim his Mate. No other Were can Mate you now" he said gazing at the mark on my neck.

"I don't want any other Were, I just want you" I whispered. He picked me up in his arms and held me tightly. I wrapped my legs around his waist and kissed his cheek. He gently kissed the mark on my shoulder and whispered.

"You're mine". It felt so filling, to be claimed by him, to be loved by him. My heart just felt full.

"I'm yours" I agreed.

"It's for forever now" he said pulling his head back to look into my eyes.

"Even that wouldn't be long enough" I mused, smiling at his gorgeous face. He pressed his lips against mine and started walking, keeping me firmly in his arms. I belong here, right here in the arms of this Adonis of a man. Now, and apparently forever.

Chapter Twelve

Zelena

I think I've been awake for about ten minutes now, but Gunner is still asleep holding me and I don't want to wake him yet. I rolled over as carefully as possible so that I was facing him. He looks so young when he's sleeping. I know he's only eighteen, but I've always seen him as this big, tall strong, and protective man. But right now, with his cheek squished on the pillow and his mouth partly open, he is baby cute. I leaned my head forward and kissed him on his soft lips. He stirred a little and smiled but didn't wake up.

I lay still and watched him sleep for a while, but couldn't hold still any longer. I reached out and traced my finger from his forehead over his nose and lips and down along his chest, all the way to his belly button, and then back up again. He moaned a little and rolled onto his back. I was enjoying teasing him in his sleep, so I pulled myself up and planted little kisses around his neck and ear.

"Why?" he moaned without opening his eyes. I tickled my finger over his chest, tracing around his nipples and belly button. He grabbed my hand and held it still.

"That tickles" he groaned. I jumped up and sat on his lap, straddling him. I rested my hands on his shoulders and leaned down kissing his lips.

"It's time to wake up now" I whispered as I planted more kisses on his cheeks.

"We're going shopping today" I said in a sing song voice then kissed more of his face. I went to sit back up but he grabbed my face and kissed my lips one time more.

"I like waking up like this" he grinned opening his eyes.

"Get used to it mister, because you're mine now" I leaned down and gave him another kiss. I then got up and sat down on the floor with my three bags of clothes to pick out and outfit.

"I'm so excited"

"I know, you told me five times last night"

"I've never been shopping before"

"I know, you told me that too"

"Are you sure you want to give me money? I feel really weird about it" I said turning on the floor to face him. He was now lying on his side with his hand propped under his head.

"Of course I do, you are part of the pack now, and you're my Mate, so it's your money too" he said with a smile.

"Okay, I'm having a quick shower". I jumped up and put my clothes on the end of the bed and ducked into the shower. I picked up the body wash on the floor and examined it. I might even get myself some nice body wash and decent shampoo I thought. I got out of the shower and wrapped my towel around me and walked back out to the bedroom. Gunner was standing by the dresser with just his jeans on, he turned his head to look at me, lowered his chin and growled.

In a blink he had me up against the wall, lifting my legs up around his waist. He pushed his hips into my hips and held me there, smashing his lips against mine. I opened my mouth and rubbed my tongue along his. God, he tastes so good. I put my hand around his neck grabbing hold of a hand full of hair. My other arm was holding up my towel. He kissed down my neck to the top of my shoulder where he left his mark. He sucked and licked and nibbled at the skin, then he sunk his teeth into the same place. A small burst of pain shot through my skin around his bite, but it quickly transformed into pleasure. I moaned pulling his hair and dropping my towel, letting it fall to my belly and exposing my breasts. He released his jaw and slowly moved his lips down my collarbone to my chest, kissing and licking along the way, he grabbed my breast and squeezed it gently. He traced his tongue around my nipple, flicking it a little before taking it in his mouth, sucking and biting softly. I lifted my head back and groaned.

"Oh shit" I breathed wanting more. My chest was heaving, my fingers gripped tightly in his hair, and my lips parted in sweet bliss, when we both jumped, startled by a bang on the door.

"Zelena, you need to come with me" Nat's voice called through. A soft growl emanated from Gunner as he let me go, putting his hands on the wall on either side of my head. I grabbed my towel to keep it from falling any lower.

"Zelena, are you awake?" she yelled again still banging.

"I'll be out in a sec, just got out of the shower" I called back.

What the fuck Nat seriously, things were just getting good. Gunner had his fingertips pressed hard into the wall, he was shaking his head and mumbling to himself.

"Fucking Nat, always with the perfect timing" he snarled with a chuckle. He stood up straight and let his gaze roam my body with a hungry smile. I pulled the towel up over my breasts and he frowned. Leaning forward he kissed me again on the mouth and then kissed my shoulder where he had bit.

"You better go see her before she breaks the door down" he grumbled. I dropped my bottom lip and put on my best puppy dog eyes. He kissed me again and smacked my butt.

"Don't tease me or we'll miss your shopping trip". He walked back to the dresser and pulled on a maroon shirt. Agh! I quickly got dressed and walked to Nat's room, at the other side of the pack house. The door was open, but I knocked anyway, I've not been in Nat's room before.

"Hey?" I called out for her. She came out of the walk-in robe dressed like a magazine model. She had subtle makeup on, and her hair was straight and shiny. She had on big beige wedges and blue jeans, with a striped crop top that was tied in the front. She looked gorgeous, I would love to be able to wear clothes like that, but I just couldn't pull it off.

"Finally, I need to do your hair and makeup" she exclaimed, grabbing my shoulder and sitting me down in a pink fluffy chair at a desk that was covered in makeup.

"Aren't we just going to the shopping centre?" I asked.

I was honestly a bit taken aback by the spread of beauty products in front of me.

"Yes, but there's no harm in looking fabulous. Now hold still, I've been wanting to do this for days". She started with my hair, pulling the top and side parts up leaving only the back part down, and then made it wavy. She turned me away from the mirror so I couldn't see what she was doing. She had a little pink sponge and lots of different brushes. After a few minutes, and lots of poking and stroking and brushing, she spun the chair around.

"Voila, my masterpiece" she exclaimed proudly. I examined the new face in the mirror looking back at me, I couldn't recognise myself. I had pink rose cheeks and gold glimmery eyes with long black lashes. My skin looked soft and smooth, my lips were pink and full. I look kind of nice, and for the first time ever I don't hate what I see in the mirror. No scars, no bruises, no cuts and scabs. I can finally see it, what Gunner has been telling me all this time. I'm actually kind of pretty.

"Wow" was all I could manage to say. Nat laughed.

"I'm not ugly" I said touching my face.

"You've never been ugly, you just didn't know where your beauty was hiding" she smiled and half hugged me over the back of the chair.

"Thank you so much" I smiled brightly.

"Anytime, now let's go".

Nat grabbed a small handbag and took my hand, we walked down the stairs together and onto the porch. Gunner, Cole, and Smith were standing at the bottom of the steps waiting for us. Of course, he would never go anywhere without his boys.

Cole was standing with his feet wide apart and his arms crossed over his chest, Smith stood with a bounce in his toes, while Gunner had his back to us. I stepped down the first step and Smith stood up straight with his mouth dropped open. Cole lifted his brows with a surprised look and lifted his chin as an indication for Gunner. Gunner turned around to see what they were looking at, and his body seemed to stiffen. He stared at me with his eyes wide and his mouth open. Smith whistled and smiled up at me brightly. Gunner quickly snapped his head over his shoulder at Smith and growled. Smith put his hands up and laughed before quickly retreating around the side of the house.

As I got to the bottom step, he had already walked to meet me, grabbing my hips as I stepped down the last step.

"Holy shit" he breathed tilting his head to the side.

"You are positively the most beautiful thing to walk this earth" he whispered and kissed me had and fast.

"You like it?" I asked a little breathlessly.

"I fucking love it" he beamed,
"Do we have to go shopping, or can we just take our clothes off and go back to bed?" he smirked, kissing me again. I hit him on the chest and walked past him.
"Yes, we're going. Nat worked really hard on this" I said while gesturing to my whole body.
"Like it's hard making you look gorgeous" he teased sarcastically. I blushed and lowered my head. Compliments are uncomfortable. I looked around the clearing confused, they weren't expecting to run there were they?
"How are we getting there?" I asked.
"We drive, of course" Nat said grabbing my hand and leading me towards the back of the house. As we came around the side, I saw a row of cars lined up. Not just beat down rust buckets either, they were shiny fancy rich people cars. Exactly how rich are these guys.
"We're taking the SUV" Gunner called from behind us.
"Shotgun" yelled Smith.
"Not a chance" I giggled opening the front passenger door. Gunner climbed into the driver's side, and the others piled into the back, with Smith in the middle. Gunner started the car and Nat stuck her head through the middle of the seats.
"Don't forget the epic road trip jams" she said plugging in her phone and turning up the volume. A soft pop song started to play, I hadn't heard it before, but then again, I hadn't heard a lot of songs before. We headed off down the dirt driveway, it was long and winding, zigzagging through the trees. We came out onto the main road and sped up towards the city. I was gazing out the window at the forest, as Smith and Nat sang along to the songs on the stereo. Gunner took my hand and lifted it to his lips, kissing it, and then held onto it, resting our hands on his lap. I turned around and looked at Nat, she smiled back, still singing, Smith was doing a little air guitar and Cole sat quietly looking out his window.
The drive felt pretty quick, we even played a bit of Eye-Spy on the way, Smith won but Gunner argued that spying an ant was a cheat move. We eventually pulled into the underground parking lot and got out of the car. I lifted my arms and stretched out. Cole and Smith climbed out of the door behind me, I smiled at Cole, but he just nodded with a forced closed mouth grin and turned

away. Had I done something to make him angry, we haven't really hung out or talked much so I'm not sure. I walked behind him to the back of the car where Nat and Gunner were. Gunner took my hand and we started walking to the entrance.

"So, me and Zelena are going to hit up some shops and then we'll meet you guys later in the food court" said Nat jumping around in front of us.

"Yeah, no way" grumbled Gunner.

"Come on seriously, I let you come with us, you don't have to follow us around the shopping centre" Nat whined.

"I'm staying with Zee" he said firmly.

"Ugh, fine" growled Nat.

"Well I'm not going to the girly shops" Smith chuckled nudging Cole.

"You coming with me, or following them?" he asked.

Cole looked at Gunner, and then me, and back at Smith again.

"I'm with you man" Cole said throwing his arm over Smith's shoulder.

We got through the doors and I was shocked. This place was massive. There were three levels, all lined with shops with an open middle section cordoned off by a railing. Looking up you could see each floor, all the way to the large glass roof. It was bright and smelled like perfume. It was about ten thirty in the morning and already there were so many people strolling around. I started to get butterflies and needed to pee from excitement.

"I'm so excited, but I gotta pee" I said turning to Nat.

Gunner nodded at Cole and Smith and they walked off, I assume they were flashing.

"Okay, this way". Nat grabbed my hand and started skipping down the walkway, dragging me along with her with Gunner on our tail. We ducked into the bathroom leaving Gunner by the corridor entrance.

"Where are we going first?" I asked Nat who was busy checking herself out in the full-length mirror.

"Leave it to me, girlfriend, I got our path all figured out" she answered,

"As long as I get to buy some body wash and fancy shampoo"

"Of course, and some makeup of your own" she chuckled.

I flushed the toilet and washed my hands and we headed back down the corridor. Gunner was still waiting for us, but he was now surrounded by three girls giggling and smiling. Walking slowly towards them I focused my hearing.

"My friend thinks you're cute" a short blond one wearing a tiny skirt giggled.

"Uh huh" Gunner mumbled.

"So can I get your number to give to her?"

She was playing with her hair and pushing her chest out. At that moment, listening to her desperate little voice, I could feel the heat burning through my body. That's my man you stupid skank, get away from him. I went to run but Nat grabbed my arm stopping me, we stopped walking and waited in the corridor listening.

"I don't think so" Gunner grunted.

"Aw why not, don't you think she's cute?"

"I'm taken" he said firmly. She stepped forward closer to him. A hot flash swept through me, one more inch and I will end that little tart. If she touches him, I will rip her perfectly manicured fingers from her hand.

"I bet I could make you feel a little less taken" she whispered suggestively. Nope, that was it. I walked right up to Gunner, pushing between him and the girl, purposefully shoving her back with my hip. I grabbed his face and pulled him down to me, kissing him passionately, making sure that the little slut could see my tongue swirling with his.

"What the fuck" I heard the skank say to her friends. I moved Gunner's hand to my ass, and he squeezed it hard, I kept kissing him, using my tongue generously. After a minute I let him go and turned to face the three girls, pulling his hands around my body. They had taken a few steps back and had filthy jealous looks on their faces. I gave them a wink and they turned and left. Gunner kissed my neck and whispered.

"Was someone a little jealous?"

"Jealous no. But you're mine, I was just making sure she knew it".

"Okay that was like super gross and also super fucking awesome" Nat laughed.

"Did you see their faces? Zee, you are a savage"

"Don't call her Zee, only I can call her that" snapped Gunner.

"Wait, seriously?" she questioned.

"Yes seriously" Gunner responded in a mocking big brother type of tone.

"Ugh whatever, come on Lena, we have things to buy". Nat sarcastically smiled at Gunner and grabbed my hand pulling me out of his arms. He growled softly but didn't respond.

The first shop we went to was covered in pink, yellow and orange coloured clothes. I'm not really keen on bright colours, I usually stick to my blacks purples and blues. I was browsing through a rack of tiny little dresses when I pulled out a maroon dress with long sleeves and pockets like a hoodie, it was a tight dress, but I kind of liked it. I took it to the changing room and put it on. Examining myself in the mirror it didn't look too bad, it was definitely tighter than anything else I have worn before, but my butt looked amazing. I came out of the little room where Nat was waiting for me.

"You aren't going to show me?" she scoffed.

"Nope, you can see later. But I love it" I smiled. Nat clapped her hands and squealed.

"Yay! Your first purchase". She grabbed my wrist and dragged me to the register plopping the dress on the counter. On a stand on the counter was some silver jewellery, I turned the little rack around and spotted a tiny little crescent moon. How cute I thought picking it up and studying it closer.

"Ooo I like that" Nat said from beside me. She snatched it from my hand and put it with my dress. The cashier put it through and I handed her Gunners card. With that first shopping bag in my hand the excitement started to grow.

"What's next?" I asked Nat with a giant smile.

"I think someone has the shopping gene" she giggled skipping out of the store.

The next few stores were much more my style. I found some jeans and some tops, and even got a pair of denim short shorts, thanks to Nat's persistence. Gunner stayed close, always watching us, but keeping his distance and letting Nat and me do our thing. Next door to the beauty shop was a store with all kinds of sexy underwear. I bet if I wore something like that, there is no way Gunner would be able to hold back any longer. I'd have to beat him off with a stick. We walked into the beauty shop and Gunner waited by the entrance, just inside the door. I pulled Nat to the back where I didn't think he couldn't hear us.

"I want to buy some sexy underwear from the shop next door" I whispered in her ear.

"Eww, Babe I do not want to know that" she frowned.

"No, I need you to distract Gunner so it can be a surprise"

"Ugh, I don't want to know about my brother's sex life. But fine whatever, I can probably get you like five minutes, ten tops" she grunted and stomped over to where Gunner was standing. As she pulled him towards the smelly soaps, I crouched down low and snuck out the door, and dashed into the lingerie store next door. Okay, wow. There is so much to choose from, and I am way out of my comfort zone here. A shop assistant spotted me right away and sauntered over.

"You look a little overwhelmed, love" she smiled sweetly at me.

"I've only got a few minutes to pick something before my boyfriend finds out" I tell her. She smiles and looks around at the racks.

"Okay over here quickly" she whispered. She hurries to a rack in the back, waving me along with her. Once there she pulls out a bright red lacy bra with lots of straps and buckles. It was way kinkier than I was expecting.

"Uh, I think that is a little out of my league" I say holding one of the buckles.

"Got ya, what about something more like this". She put the kinky red set back and holds out a white one-piece lacy bodysuit. It's cute but too angelic. I want him to think I'm hot, not sweet.

"Hm, it's too gentle"

"Alright, I know just the one".

She goes to a rack on the other side and holds out a black lacy bra with matching panties and waist belt thing. It was pretty sexy, I could see myself in it for sure.

"Ooo I like this" I said taking it from her with a wide smile.

"What is this thing?" I ask holding the belt.

"It's called a garter belt, and it holds up these" she said holding up a pair of black thigh stockings. A smile spread across my face, I can just imagine his reaction.

"I love it"

"I thought you might" the woman said turning back to the rack.

"Now, you look like a 30b" she said over her shoulder.

"So, you'll want this one". She pulls out my size and hands it to me, then waves me over to the counter. She must be pretty good at her job to get my size right, just by looking at me. So, she must know what she's doing, I think I can trust her judgment on choice of lingerie.

"$89.95 in total" she smiles. Holy fucking shit, underwear is expensive. I pull out Gunner's card and hand it to her. It'll be worth it, I suppose. She puts the items in the bag and hands it to me.

"Have fun" she giggles. I smiled and rushed back to the beauty shop, shoving the little bag inside one of the other shopping bags as I went. Walking back into the body shop I grabbed a red bottle of body wash from the first shelf I saw and took it over to Nat and Gunner. Now to act like nothing has happened and I'm not panting with anticipation.

"I don't want to smell the fucking soap, you can figure it out yourself" Gunner grunted angrily. Nat saw me coming and smiled, Gunner turned quickly to look at me with furrowed brows.

"Where were you?" he snapped.

"I was over there smelling all the body wash, I picked this one, what do you think?" I lied holding up the bottle to Gunner's nose.

"Hm strawberry, simple yet delicious" he smiled. Phew that was lucky. Nat had already found some shampoo for me, apricot and almond oil, smells pretty good.

"Okay, let's go to Sephora" Nat said cheerfully. Gunner walked to the door and Nat and I went to pay for our things.

"Did you find something?" she whispered.

"Sure did" I giggled quietly.

"Here you go ladies" the woman at the register said handing over our bags. We walked to the front of the shop where Gunner was waiting, I leaned into him hugging him around the waist.

"You had enough yet?" he asked putting his hand over my shoulder and taking my shopping bags for me.

"Not yet" I smiled looking up at him. He leaned down and gave me a quick peck.

"The boys are going to the food court for lunch, are we ready to meet them?" he asked looking at Nat.

"We'll just pop into Sephora, and then we can go and eat" Nat said as she turned and began walking. Gunner and I followed behind her, with one arm around his waist and the other holding his hand that was draped over my shoulder.

"Are you having fun?" he asked.

"Oh I really am, this place is awesome, thank you so much for bringing me here"

"Anything for you, little wolf" he said squeezing my hand. We got to the makeup shop and it was super busy, there were heaps of people in there. The lights were bright, and the music was loud, usually I think it would be a pretty cool place, but it just made me feel nervous. I gripped onto Gunner's shirt and gulped.

"Do you want me to come in with you?" he asked looking down at me. I nodded my head and he took my arm from his waist. Holding my hand, he led me slowly into the shop, trailing not far behind Nat.

We were looking at a giant rack of lipstick when I heard a familiar voice from behind me. The shop was really loud, but I knew who it was right away, and a sickness flooded my stomach.

"Well, if it isn't Romeo and Juliet" screeched Demi.

"Haven't seen you two for a while".

I squeezed Gunner's hand, digging my fingernails into his skin. He stepped slightly in front of me as we turned around. Demi stood there, hand on hip, with her usual tiny skirt and skin-tight top. Her minions were standing on either side of her, dressed almost the same.

"Trying to find some makeup to disguise Frankenstein's monster?" she giggled to her friends.

"Who's this bitch?" Nat scoffed, looking at Gunner and back at Demi.

"Aw, the freak made a friend" she laughed looking Nat up and down and smacking her lips. Demi was sizing her up. Probably taken back by how gorgeous Nat is. Demi isn't exactly used to not being the prettiest girl in the room. And with Nat here, she was far from winning that title. Demi sneered and curled her lip back, feigning a disgusted look on her face. But I could see it, in her eyes, she was intimidated by Nat. Nat stepped towards Demi, but Gunner quickly put out his hand to stop her.

"Demi, leave" Gunner growled.

"Or what? You're going to throw me across the room again" she snapped. Nat looked up at Gunner, she looked surprised, so she obviously doesn't know what happened on our last day at school.

"Where's my little freak? Aren't you going to say hello to me, I haven't seen you in ages" she said peering around Gunner.

He pushed me further behind him, I could feel his growl vibrating through his chest. Shit, he was about to lose it. I quickly stepped out from behind Gunner and stood in front of Demi. My confidence disappeared, if I even had any. I just knew I had to protect Gunner and stopping him from killing Demi in the middle of the shopping centre was the first step. Gunner's warm hand settled on the lower half of my back and a rush of strength blew through me. I swallowed deeply and smiled.

"Hey Demi, you look nice" I chirped. She stumbled a little on her feet as she saw me, she'd never seen my face so clearly, no one from school ever had. Also, I never spoke to anyone at school either, so I guess she wasn't expecting me to talk. But after everything I have been through, with my dad nearly killing me, finding Gunner, and discovering I'm a wolf, Demi, and her petty bullying just didn't seem so scary anymore.

"Ha! Someone's had a makeover" she sneered, eyeing me up and down. The friends behind her followed suit, also looking me up and down, then whispered to each other.

"Who's that?" one said.

"That's the weird chick from school, Zelena" the other one answered.

"No way" the first one gasped.

"A lot has changed" I said keeping my calm and trying to hide the smirk that was threatening to push through.

"Yeah, I can see that. So what, a little makeup, some new clothes and you suddenly think that you're better than me?" Demi frowned, crossing her arms over her chest and pushing up her boobs. How was I ever scared of this trash bag. I see her for what she really is now, an insecure little girl, off putting her own fear through bullying and intimidation.

"Not at all, I'm just not afraid of you anymore" I smiled shrugging my shoulders. She stepped forward right up to my face.

"You think you're hot shit now" she snarled. I could feel the heat from Gunners body behind me and heard the soft growl on his lips. I put my hand back, resting it on his stomach. To both hold him back and to calm him down.

"Demi, can't you just leave me alone and find something else to occupy your time?" I said politely.

She lifted her hand to my face quickly, pretending she was going to slap me. I guess she thought I was going to flinch like I used to. Nat growled along with Gunner. I reached out with my other hand and grabbed Nat's wrist. I could feel her blood pumping fast under her hot skin. Demi looked disappointed that I didn't flinch at her threat. I've had enough of this shit. I've taken her abuse for years, never fighting back. But no more. Gunner's skin under mine was hot. I didn't need superhuman instincts to know he was furious. But this time, I don't need him to fight for me. I can do it myself. I'm going to do it myself. I stood up as tall as I could, my face just inches away from Demi's.

"Get out of my face before I rip your fucking throat out" I growled slowly at her.

She stepped back, her eyes wide, and her face a little pale. She froze for a moment, I suppose weighing up her options. After a long second, she huffed loudly. Then quickly turned on her heels and hurried out the store with her minions in toe. I can't believe I actually stood up to Demi, I felt so strong and powerful. I smiled and turned around to look at Gunner, he had the most adorable proud look on his face.

"I am so hot for you right now" he smirked, pulling me into his chest.

"Um, excuse me, who the fuck was that raging psychopath?" Nat snapped.

"No one important" I chuckled with a smile.

"Let's pay for this and go eat, I'm starving" I said while holding up my basket.

I felt so untouchable, like I slayed the dragon and conquered the beast. Demi and the pain she once inflicted meant nothing to me anymore.

We got to the food court and found Smith and Cole already stuffing their faces. We put our many bags on the table next to them and sat down.

"You will never believe what Zelena just did" Nat said excitedly.

"Oh shit, what she do?" Smith asked through a mouth full of food.

"She just gave a total smackdown to this self-important beauty queen that was all up in her face. It was EPIC!" she laughed tossing her head back.

"Ay what, Who?" Smith said looking over at me.,

"Demi" Gunner smiled, answering his question.

"For real?" asked Cole surprised. He lifted his head and looked at me with a quirked eyebrow.

"Yeah" I chuckled, feeling a soft blush grace my cheeks.

"Nice one" Cole smiled at me brightly.

"You little demon you" smiled Smith proudly.

I couldn't help but smile. Even Cole was impressed with me standing up for myself. Maybe he doesn't hate me so much after all. This has turned out to be the most awesome day ever. Gunner went and got us some sushi and spring rolls while I chatted with Smith and Cole.

"So, you smacked Demi, for real?" Smith said with his eyes wide.

"No I didn't hit her, I just told her I was going to rip her throat out" I laughed.

"Daaaaaamn Zelena, that's dark girl" Smith chuckled raising one eyebrow.

"She totally deserved it though, she was all up in Lena's face calling her a freak and shit. And then she pretended like she was going to hit her, and Gunner was growling and I started to lose it, and Zee was all like nah bitch, get away from me". Nat spoke quickly waving her arms around as she told the story.

Gunner brought the food over and sat down next to me, kissing me on the cheek as he handed me a fork. I looked around at the boys and Nat as they chatted excitedly, I felt an overwhelming wave of happiness sweep through me. As far as friends go, these guys are pretty great.

"So, I'm thinking movies and popcorn tonight, what do you guys reckon?" Nat asked everyone

"Yeah, I'm in" said Smith.

"Me too" I squeaked.

"Sure, why not" said Cole.

"What are you thinking?" asked Gunner.

"Something scary I think, what about you Lena?" Nat said looking at me.

"Well I've only seen like three movies, and they were all for school, so I'm up for anything" I smiled.

They all looked at me surprised and with a bit of pity. I guess sometimes it's easy to forget my life before this.

"Okay, well you're easy then" Nat said breaking the silence

"Smith, you're super weird and disturbing so you can pick the movie. Zelena and me will organise the snacks" she said rubbing her hands together.

"Uh thank you?" Smith said slowly with a light frown.

"We have just a couple of shops left, and then we can get out of here, are you guys going off on your own again, or coming along with us?"

"Who knows who Zelena will try and fight next, I'm not missing that" chuckled Smith.

"Yeah, I'm coming too" agreed Cole.

We finished eating and put our trays on top of the bins, then headed for the top level. I found a couple more things in the last few shops we went to. I found a pair of strappy heels, a dress, and a bikini swimsuit that Gunner was pretty excited about. Once we were all done, we headed back to the car and shoved our stuff in the trunk. There were a lot of bags, I can't believe how much we all got. I like shopping, especially with Nat, she's a really cool girl and I think we are becoming great friends. We climbed into the car and began the drive home.

Chapter Thirteen

Gunner

I was standing by the entrance to the bathrooms, waiting for Zee and Nat, when I noticed them. Three girls, about my age, maybe a year or two younger. All wearing, or not wearing, tiny little clothes. Short skirts and tight little tops that showed every bit of skin they could. I can't believe I used to like that sort of crap. Now that I have Zee, I see things a lot differently. A girl flirting with me, I used to find cute, but it's now just annoying. Suggestive remarks from random girls were once an ego boost, but now they are just gross. Girls dressed in barely any clothes, I thought it was sexy, now it's just disgusting. But if Zee did any of that stuff, I would love it, it would drive me crazy with lust.

The girls walked up and stood in front of me. A short little one with blond hair stepped forward, twirling the end of her hair around her finger.

"Hey, I'm Penny" she said smiling and fluttering her lashes suggestively. I lifted my chin in acknowledgment but didn't say anything.

"Aren't you going to tell me your name?" she cooed. I shook my head, just hoping that they would give up and walk away.

"Why's that, are you shy?" she squeaked giggling over her shoulder to her friends. I shook my head again and rolled my eyes.

"My friend thinks you're cute".

"Uh huh" I grumbled,

"So, can I get your number to give to her?" She really wasn't getting the picture.

"I don't think so" I mumbled,

"Aw why not, don't you think she's cute?"

"I'm taken".

She stepped forward close to me, pushing out her chest, I held down the desire to gag and laugh obnoxiously in her face.

"I bet I could make you feel a little less taken" she whispered seductively. Oh Goddess, could she embarrass herself any further? I could smell the desperation on her. How pitiful.

Just then, Zee pushed herself between me and the blonde girl, grabbing my face and pulling me down to her lips. She kissed me fast and rough, I liked it. She was marking her territory in front of the girls and shaming them at the same time. She grabbed my hand placing it on her ass, I accommodated by squeezing it tightly. She let my cheeks go and turned to face the girls, pulling my arms to wrap around her shoulders. I smiled at the girls as their shocked faces turned and walked away. I kissed Zee's soft neck, I love how protective she is.

"Was someone a little jealous?" I whispered,

"Jealous no. But you're mine, I was just making sure she knew it" she said firmly. Nat walked over laughing,

"Okay, that was like super gross and also super fucking awesome. Did you see their faces? Zee, you are a savage"

"Don't call her Zee, only I can call her that" I snapped. Zee is my nickname for Zelena, I came up with it and I don't want anyone else to use it.

"Wait, seriously?" she questioned,

"Yes seriously" I responded mocking her like the big brother I am.

"Ugh whatever, come on Lena, we have things to buy". Nat exaggerated the new nickname she gave Zee as she sang sarcastically, pulling Zee out of my arms. I growled at her as she walked away with Zelena. I know that Nat likes her, and I know she wants them to be like sisters. It's hard letting go of that slice of possessiveness I have. Zee is mine and I'm growing tired of

Nat getting in the way. But I think it's better to give Nat the day to bond, and then I can have Zee for myself when we get home. I do need them to get along if we're going to keep a peaceful household. And who knows, maybe Nat will help draw Zelena out of her shell a bit more.

We went through a few shops and I stood by the door mostly, just keeping an eye on them and making sure no one got too close. Zee looked happy, her smile didn't fade from her face for hours. She and Nat were laughing together and trying on clothes and jewellery. Looking at her from a distance you would never know the terrible ordeals she's lived through. I know that she has no idea how beautiful she is. I will make it my life's mission to tell her every day. We got to the shop with all the soaps and candles, the smell was intense. I crinkled my nose and immediately wanted to leave again. Nat came over to me and gripped my wrist.

"Come look at these, I want to buy something nice for Mum" she said pulling me to the scented candles.

"What about this one?" she held up a candle to my nose and I gagged,

"Eh no, that's gross" I said pushing it away.

"This one then?" she says holding up another,

"Better but not great" I grumbled. I looked around the store, I've lost sight of Zee, she must be behind one of the shelves.

"Okay, well maybe some soap then, come over here". Nat dragged me towards the back of the shop. There were rows and rows of different coloured soaps, most of them were cut into rectangles, but there were some shaped like flowers and seashells. They look pointless, who wants to wash their hands with a seashell. Nat began lifting up soaps and shoving them under my nose. This went on for about twenty different soaps. I still couldn't see Zee in the shop, I lifted my nose and sniffed for her scent, but the products were too overpowering. I can't see her anywhere, and Nat was pissing me off now.

"I don't want to smell the fucking soap, you can figure it out yourself" I snapped at her, she smiled at someone behind me, and I turned to see who it was.

"Where were you?" I snapped at Zee, she looked a little flustered and had blushed cheeks.

"I was over there smelling all the body wash, I picked this one, what do you think?" she said holding up a bottle to my nose. Great another thing for me to sniff. She seemed a little nervous or anxious, something was off. Even with her standing right in front of me, I still couldn't smell her scent over all the soap and incense in the store. I held the bottle to my nose and sniffed,

"Hm strawberry, simple yet delicious" I smiled. This one wasn't too bad, she has good taste.

"Okay, let's go to Sephora" Nat said cheerfully. They went to the register, and I headed for the door when Smith flashed me,

Gunner, where are you guys? We're going to eat

The girls are just paying for some stuff and then we'll head down

Okay, meet you there

Zee walked up carrying her bags and pressed herself into me, hugging me around the waist. It's still such an amazing feeling to have her touch me and show her affection unprompted. It's not something I will tire of easily. I will drink in her offered affection greedily every time.

"You had enough yet?" I asked her, hugging her back.

"Not yet" she smiled and looked up at me. Her beauty will never bore me. I leaned down and kissed her lips softly before I turned to Nat,

"The boys are going to the food court for lunch, are we ready to meet them?" I asked her.

"We'll just pop into Sephora and then, we can go and eat" Nat said turning and walking off. Zee and I followed behind her, she held my waist, and I rested my arm over her shoulder. Being with Zee was so natural and easy.

"Are you having fun?" I asked,

"Oh, I really am, this place is awesome, thank you so much for bringing me here"

"Anything for you little wolf" I said holding her hand a little tighter.

~

I'm in awe. Complete and utter awe of her. Did I miss it? When did Zelena turn into such a badass? After telling off Demi, she turned around and smiled at me as the bitch and her little crew of slags marched away in a huff. I felt so proud of her, she has come such a long way in such a short time. This confident and brave side of her is hot as hell, and surprising. It really turns me on. As I looked at the proud smile she wore on her face, I wanted nothing more than to kiss her, really kiss her, like everywhere. I could feel the tightness in my pants growing.

"I am so hot for you right now" I blurted out, I pulled her to my chest and held her. She really dominated that dumb cow.

"Um, excuse me, who the fuck was that raging psychopath?" Nat snapped. Zee smiled at her and giggled,

"No one important. Let's pay for this and go eat, I'm starving" Zee smiled at us both.

She has become so fearless and strong. I don't even see the scared little girl from before anymore. I think she is ready to seal the bond, I sure as shit know I am. I've been holding back from it for too long, and I'm about ready to explode.

We finally got to the food court and the girls sat down at the table with Cole and Smith, who were already eating. I went to get some food for Zee and me as they all talked among themselves. I watched her as I waited for the food, she fits in so perfectly into our little group. I could tell Cole was warming up to her more, I think our talk at the beach really helped. Smith is already smitten with her, but I know that after my rage out the other day, he won't touch her again. At least he better fucking not. Nat has always wanted a sister, thankfully her and Zee are the perfect match. I have no doubt that Zelena will make an amazing Luna. I took the food to the table and kissed Zee on the cheek, giving her a fork. I came into a conversation about a movie night.

"What are you thinking?" I asked,

"Something scary I think, what about you Lena?" Nat said turning to look at Zee.

"Well, I've only seen like three movies, and they were for school, so I'm up for anything" she smiled. Of course, she hasn't seen any movies, of course her dad never let her watch TV. I clenched my fists at the thought of that bastard human. There was an uncomfortable silence between us all. She's so different now, so normal, they forget what she had to endure before coming to live with us.

"Okay, well you're easy then" Nat said turning everyone's eyes from Zee.

"Smith you're super weird and disturbing, so you can pick the movie. Zelena and me will organise the snacks"

"Uh thank you?" Smith said slowly and awkwardly,

"We have just a couple of shops left, and then we can get out of here, are you guys going off on your own again, or coming along with us?" Nat asked, facing Cole and Smith,

"Who knows who Zelena will try and fight next, I'm not missing that" snorted Smith with a crooked smile.

"Yeah, I'm coming too" agreed Cole.

Once we had all finished eating, we headed up the escalators to the top level. We were in a surf shop, I was on one side of the rack while Zelena was on the other. Smith and Nat were joking around and trying on hats and sunglasses, their loud laughter was filtering all through the shop. I have no idea where Cole had disappeared to again. Zee held out a dark green bikini and showed it to me. It was small, like string small, with tiny little triangles. Mm, yes, please. I would love to see her in that. I think she was joking, she looked like she was joking, but I nodded enthusiastically anyway. She giggled with a shrug of her shoulders and dropped the bikini into her basket. I can't wait to get her into that, only to take it off her again.

A couple of shops later we were all done and headed back to the car. The girls filled the trunk with shopping bags, so many shopping bags. We all climbed into the car and I started the drive home. Smith fell asleep on Nat's shoulder as she and Cole played games on a phone. Zee sat quietly looking out the window, while gently stroking my thigh. The drive home was much faster this time. By the time we arrived back at the pack house, the sun was already setting. Cole and I grabbed the bags from the trunk of the car and carried them upstairs for the girls.

"Did you get it?" I asked Cole once we were alone. He pulled out a little velvet bag and handed it to me. I opened the bag and tipped the contents out into my hand. It was perfect, I held it up to my face and looked over it. It was a little silver chain bracelet with a silver heart pendant hanging from it. I grabbed the heart and turned it around. On one side engraved into the metal were the words 'My heart, my soul', and on the other was our pack symbol. She'll love it, I hope.

"Thank you, brother, I knew I could count on you" I hugged Cole tightly,

"No problem" he said hugging me back.

"Let's go before Smith picks a shit movie". I smiled as we headed out the door and down to the cinema room. Smith had already pulled the blankets and pillows out of the cupboard and laid them out over the couch.

"Where are the girls?" I asked,

"In the kitchen getting some food" Smith responded. He was sitting in the middle of the couch with the remote pointed at the giant screen scrolling through the movies. Cole sat down in the corner spot and pulled a blanket over him. The girls walked in holding a big bowl in each hand and placed them on the table in front of the couch.

"Gunner come and help us with the rest" Nat called walking back out the door. I followed them to the kitchen and picked up a big plate of chocolate biscuits and mini chocolate bars and a bowl of popcorn. I took them back to the cinema room and sat them on the table, the girls brought out two more bowls of popcorn and a tray of soft drinks.

"What, no beer?" Smith jeered.

"Ha, yeah right" Nat said sitting down beside him. I sat down on the other corner of the couch and Zee cuddled in next to me.

"So, what's on Smith?" Nat said picking up a bowl of popcorn.

"Well, I know how much you like clowns Nat, so I picked a real good one for you" he smiled holding up the remote.

"I thought we were watching something scary, what's so scary about clowns?" Zee asked. Oh, the poor thing was in for a very rude awakening.

"You'll see" chuckled Smith, Cole laughed as well. She looked up at me confused, I smiled weakly and nodded. This is going to be great. Smith started the movie and I lifted Zee in close, resting her between my legs, and pulled a blanket up over us. During the movie Nat and Zee both screamed and jumped multiple times, even Cole muffled a quiet scream here and there. I don't think Zee really watched any of the movie, she had her hands over her face, or she buried herself into my chest for most of it. As the movie ended, we all kind of giggled and grunted at the scariest and most disturbing parts of the film.

"Yeah okay I get it now, clowns are definitely scary" Zee admitted.

"That clown is straight fucked up" Cole exclaimed.

"Who's ready for Chapter Two?" Smith chuckled.

"There's another one?" Nat yelled.

"Sure is, and we're watching it now".

Zee cuddled into me further with her head up close to my neck and the blanket up over her shoulders. She slipped her hand under my shirt and tickled my chest with her fingers. As the movie played, she covered her face with her hair and the blanket and barely watched any of it. Her hands moved smoothly over my torso, each pass of her gentle fingers set off a new round of goosebumps. Eventually, they slowly moved from my chest to the top of my jeans. She slowly undid the button and started pulling down the zip. I grabbed her hand and looked around at the others. Cole was still in the other corner with a blanket pulled up halfway over his face, he was staring at the screen, fully invested in the movie. Nat and Smith were sitting next to each other sharing a blanket, they were screaming and cuddling into each other during the scary parts. None of them were paying any attention to us. I let go of Zee's hand and she continued to unzip my jeans.

She slid her hand down my pants and over the top of my boxers. She lightly stroked my cock through the boxers as I started to get hard. She nuzzled her face into my neck, kissing me softly. She rubbed her hand a little harder and I was at full attention. Her hand pulled away and she started to lift the band of my boxers. I turned my head and kissed her soft lips, I licked her bottom lip and she opened her mouth slightly, I pressed my lips harder against hers and rubbed her tongue with mine. She had moved her hand under my boxers and gently wrapped her fingers around my throbbing cock. I looked back at the others and they still weren't paying us any mind. She started to move her hand up and down along my shaft. I bit down on my lip to stop myself from moaning.

I pulled her hand away and zipped my pants, she growled at me and I shushed her.

"Zee's tired, we're going to head to bed" I said standing up and lifting her to her feet. She smiled at me as she realised what I was doing.

"Don't lie, you're not tired, you're just too scared" Smith chuckled.

"You got me, this movie is going to keep me up all night" Zee responded. I almost laughed out loud, it's not the movie that's going to keep her up.

"Good night" called Nat and Cole and they all went back to the movie.

We walked out the door and I scooped Zee up into my hands, she giggled as I ran for the stairs. We got to the bedroom and I kicked the door open. Zee jumped out of my hand and closed the blinds partway, as she stood in the light of the moon, I felt a surge of guilt run through me. I don't know if she is really ready for this.

"Are you sure about this?" I asked her, stepping closer to the bed.

"Oh definitely" she smirked putting her hands on the bed and leaning over, her cleavage on clear display from the top of her shirt.

"It'll be different this time, you know that?" I said softly. She stood up straight and looked at me confused.

"What do you mean, this time?"

"I mean with me, you know?"

"No, I don't know, who else are you talking about?" she snapped. She was getting angry with me, I could feel it. Shit, I'm ruining this. I wanted to protect her from it, I don't want to have to say it so blatantly.

"I mean sex with me will be different for you, compared to before" I explained gently.

"I've never had sex before" she barked. Her face burning red with her anger and her hands placed firmly on her hips, she glared me down.

"You think I've been sleeping around? Are you fucking joking?"

"No that's not what I meant, please don't be mad, I just mean after what your dad did, raping you. This won't feel like that".

She didn't respond just stared at me blankly for a moment and then slumped down on the bed. I quickly sat next to her and took hold of her hands. I said it. Out loud. I just basically threw her brutalization in her face, and she's going to hate me for it.

"Gunner, why do you think my dad raped me?" she whispered,

"Well, when I found you in the basement, you were half naked, so I just kind of assumed". I spoke slowly and softly trying to read her face in the dark of the room. She leaned forward and kissed me holding my cheek,

"My dad was a monster, there's no question there. He may have beaten me bloody and tortured me, but he never raped me or did anything sexual like that" she said, her tone careful. I sat back and analysed her face. She was serious.

"But you were naked" I mumbled.

"Yes, because my clothes ripped off in the parking yard when I changed, remember? That's why he beat me so bad that night, because he caught me sneaking back home without clothes on".

Oh, I'm such an idiot, how could I be so ignorant. I could kick myself.

"Is that why you keep pulling away or shutting me down, because you thought I was raped?" she asked,

"Well, yeah" I huffed. She leaned forward kissing me again, she got on her knees and pushed me back onto the bed and sat on my lap.

"I love you, you are amazing. You're sweet and considerate, but you don't have to worry about that. I really, truly want to, for me and you, but mainly for me". She kissed me hard and I sat up, holding her on my lap. That's all it took, I was convinced. There was nothing that was going to stop us this time. I gripped the back of her shirt and ripped it off, throwing it on the floor. She sat back and looked at it, and then back at me,

"I liked that shirt" she smirked.

"Lucky you went shopping today then". I dragged my lips along her neck. She pushed me back and jumped off me.

"Where are you going?" I grunted,

"I almost forgot I have a present for you" she said picking up a bag off the floor. I rolled my eyes, now really.

"Can't you give it to me later?" I reached out for her, but she went to the bathroom door holding the bag.

"Trust me, you will love it" she said closing the door. I groaned and threw myself back on the bed, this had better be good. I sat back up and pulled my boots and socks off, dropping them on the floor next to the bed. I stood up and pulled off my shirt and jeans and left them on the floor. I sat back on the bed in my boxers and crossed my ankles lifting my hands and holding them behind my head. I watched the bathroom door, impatiently waiting for Zee.

The door slowly opened and she stood there in the doorway with the light behind her. I sat upright and my mouth fell open, a rush of hot desire blew through me. She was wearing black stockings with lace on the top and small straps leading up to a garter belt. She had on small black lacy panties and a matching bra. The bra is basically see-through, and I could make out her raised pink nipples.

The animal inside me came alive. I crawled to the end of the bed and onto the floor, I lowered my eyes and growled, a growl that vibrated all through my body. She was breathtakingly, agonizingly sexy. She was my prey and I was the hungry predator. I crawled on my hands and knees across the floor to her feet. She is perfection, she is light and love, she is fire and desire, she is a Goddess in her own right. And she is all mine.

I grabbed her foot and lifted it to my shoulder, another growl rumbled in the back of my throat as I dragged my teeth up her leg to the top of the stocking. I bit down on her inner thigh and she gasped quietly. I lifted my hand to the straps on the belt and pulled them free. I moved my mouth to the stocking and grabbed it with my teeth, slowly I pulled the stocking down her leg and over her foot. I kissed her toes and the top of her foot, making my way back up her leg, kissing as I went. I reached the top of her thigh and put her foot back on my shoulder, I breathed in deeply. I could smell her juices, her aroma sent a shiver down my spine, and I felt an urgency to kiss and taste her. I pressed my lips against her panties and kissed hard, I slowly ran my tongue between her legs, along her lips through the lace. She groaned and her body shivered. I slid my hands up to her perky ass-cheeks and pushed her hips forward, harder into my mouth. I undid the clips on the belt, and it fell to the floor, I took the top off her panties and tugged on them a little. I looked up to her face. She was holding either side of the door frame with her head back, she looked down at me and nodded with blushed cheeks. She put her foot back on the ground and I pulled the panties down to her ankles. She slowly stepped out of them and I held them up to my nose and breathed them in. Her scent was intoxicating, I wanted more.

I grasped her hips and lifted her off her feet and half onto my shoulders. I turned around and placed her on the bed. I stood above her, admiring her magnificent body, running my hands up her legs and over her stomach to her neck. I put my knee between her legs forcing them apart, I leaned down and kissed her mouth pushing my tongue in, she accepted it openly and grabbed my neck, kissing me back. I traced my finger down her torso, over her belly button, and pubic bone, and along her soft wet lips. She bit down on my bottom lip and I gently stroked her clit, circling it with my middle finger. She moaned, pushing her hips forward,

"Mine" I growled lowly as I inserted my finger. I want to make this last. She was warm and moist, her skin soft and inviting. She put her arm over my back, digging her nails into my skin, she pulled me down so that my body was on top of her.

"More" she whispered biting onto my earlobe. She tugged at my boxers pulling them down over my ass, I slid them down my legs to my ankles and kicked them off. My throbbing erection was pressed against her dripping sex. I kissed her mouth rough and fast, taking her tongue in my mouth and giving her mine.

"Are you ready?" I whispered, nuzzling my face into her neck. She lifted her legs, wrapping them around my waist, then she grabbed my face and kissed my lips hard. I pushed my hips forward, my cock resting at her entrance. She groaned softly and I slid into her slowly. I paused a moment, listening to her little gasps. Then I pushed forward until I was fully sheathed inside her. Zee moaned, lifting her head back. I dragged my teeth across the base of her neck. Her luscious pussy felt tight and hot, like my dick was being enveloped by a warm moist and loving cloud. I thrust forward pushing into her deeper, my penis engulfed with pleasurable feelings. Tingles ran through my body. Zee moaned with each thrust, the sound of her pleasure resonated inside me, driving my desire. She scratched her nails deeply down my back, the pain was incredible, only adding to the thrill. I reached down grabbed hold of her ass, and lifted her hips higher, the angle let me push into her deeper. I bit harder into her neck, breaking the skin. She squealed, tightening her legs around me. As I began to thrust faster, I could feel my body begin to tense. The fire was climbing up my arms and legs towards my crotch. I could taste Zelena's blood on my tongue, the wildness of my wolf was screaming inside me. Her pussy tightened around my cock and her body was quivering beneath me. One last thrust and the fireworks exploded through my balls and down my shaft. My body tightened and spasmed, and then a numbing wave of relaxation flowed through me. Zee was panting, her body warm and sweating. I put my hand on her cheek and looked into her eyes, her face was flushed and her lips bright pink.

"Are you okay?" I whispered gazing at her. She smiled and nodded, lifting her head she kissed me softly. I pulled myself out of her and rolled over onto my back, she cuddled into my chest.

"That was…" she breathed out,

"That was amazing" I smiled kissing her forehead.

"I love you" she whispered,

"I love you too".

Chapter Fourteen

Gunner

She must be exhausted, I know I am. I think it was nearly sunup when we finally went to sleep. But at least today we don't have to go anywhere or do anything, we can stay in bed together all day. I laid still, watching Zelena sleep. The sunlight through the window bounced off her naked back. Her skin is smooth and soft, glowing in the light. There's not a single scar left, as impossible as that is, but she has completely healed.

I lifted my head and studied her bare back, the way it bent and curved as she lay sleeping. I raised my hand and gently traced the words 'I Love You' across her skin. I ran my fingers over my bite mark on her shoulder, she is mine, now and forever. As I put my head back down, I met her gaze. She was awake, her golden eyes staring into mine.

"Good morning" she smiled sleepily. I leaned forward and kissed her soft pink lips.

"Good morning my love"

"What time is it?"

"It's about noon". She giggled softly, lifting up off the pillow and rubbing her eyes,

"Is it really?" I wrapped my arms around her and pulled her on top of me.

"Yes, it is, but we aren't going anywhere today. So, you're all mine". I kissed her again as I slid my hand down her back and grabbed hold of her ass. She lifted her leg up over my hip and kissed me a little harder. I reached down a bit further and brushed my fingers against her waiting pussy. She arched her back, raising her hips higher and I slowly slid my finger in. She lifted her body higher onto mine so her breasts were in my face. I took her nipple in my mouth, sucking softly as I flicked it with my tongue and she moaned quietly. I slipped in a second finger and she gasped, then I started slowly moving them in and out. She is delicious. She put her hands on my shoulders and sat upright on my lap. I slipped my fingers out and grabbed her hips. She reached her hand down and took hold of my hard cock, positioning herself above me, she slowly slid down taking my entire length inside her moist warm pussy. I moaned, holding onto her hips, she is so tight. She moved her hips forward and back, slowly grinding along my shaft.

She had her hands on my shoulders and her head tilted back. I grabbed one of her perfect perky breasts, gently pinching the little pink nipple. She dug her claws into my skin and started moving her hips faster, I could feel my orgasm growing with her movements. I held her hips, to try and make her slow down. She growled dragging her claws down my chest.

"Zee" I groaned,

"I'll cum".

"Cum with me" she moaned. She lifted her hips up and back down. The sensation sent shivers down my legs, my body tensed as my balls throbbed,

"I'm coming" I breathed heavily. She thrust her hips forward, hard, and I couldn't hold on any longer. She thrust again, I lost control and the fireworks started. Another thrust and I exploded, my whole body quaked, and I let out a muffled cry of pleasure as I emptied myself into her. Zee squeezed her thighs as her body quivered, her pussy throbbed around my cock and she moaned through one last thrust. I melted into the bed my whole body feeling weak and spent. Zee fell forward, collapsing on top of me, panting heavily. I wrapped my arms around her and rolled her onto the bed beside me. We lay side by side in each other's arms, slowly cooling down again.

"I don't know if I ever want to leave this room" she smiled looking into my eyes.

"If only we had a mini fridge, I'm starving"

"Oh my god, me too"

"If only Uber Eats delivered to the bedroom door" I chuckled. "If only they delivered to the island at all" she laughed.

"I'll run down to the kitchen and grab some food. Want anything special?" I asked,

"No anything will do, I'm going to have a shower, I need it".

I pulled her in closer and licked her neck up to her cheek. She squirmed in my arms giggling.

"You taste pretty good though" I teased,

"But I reckon I don't smell as good" she cooed back.

I lifted myself up and hovered above her, I lent down kissing her lips,

"You'll always smell good to me, but yes, have a shower" I smiled, stifling a laugh as she punched my shoulder.

"Asshole" she huffed. I kissed her again and stood up, looking around the room for my sweats.

"Hm, that ass though" Zee whispered. I turned to look at her and she was perched up on her side, biting her lip.

"Ha! Easy girl" I chuckled. I pulled on my sweats and walked out the door, closing it quickly behind me. I walked down to the kitchen, my knees and legs feeling weak and wobbly. I walked in the door, froze, and then quickly walked back out again. What the fuck did I just witness! I walked back in just to check, yep, I did see that. Nat jumped down from the counter and Smith was putting his shirt back on.

"What the fuck?" I said stupidly, watching them both fumble around.

"Gunner, what are you doing down here?" Nat mumbled nervously,

"We, uh, we were just um" Smith stuttered,

"Yeah, I saw what you were just doing" I teased,

"Gunner don't" snapped Nat.

"Don't what? I didn't say anything. I'm just surprised is all"

"You're not angry bro?" Smith asked shakily.

"Nah, I figured it would happen sooner or later" I said with a careless shrug of my shoulders. I'm not blind to their closeness. I've been watching them flirt incessantly for months now.

"Wait really?" Nat questioned,

"Yeah whatever, it's fine". They both looked at each other wide eyed, not saying anything, yet they appeared to be having a silent conversation. Wait! Are they flashing?

"Hold up, are you two flashing right now?" I yelled and pointed between them. Smith looked at me sheepishly and Nat smiled nervously.

"Well we, uh, we are kind of Mated up" Smith said quietly.

"Holy fucking shit" I exclaimed.

"SERIOUSLY?" I yelled, they both stood quietly looking at me. Flirting and hooking up is one thing, but Mating is another. I can honestly say that I didn't expect Smith to settle for one she-wolf, like ever. Now that I think about it, I don't know if I'm happy it's with my little sister, or worried. So, I laughed. Maybe a little more than I should have.

"Well shit, the famous ladies' man Smith has settled down" I said with a heavy breath. I wasn't mad, just super surprised. Smith chuckled a little and Nat elbowed him in the ribs hissing at him. Yep, I am leaving that one alone. I walked to the cupboard and grabbed a bag of chips and then a loaf of bread and some ham from the fridge, setting it all down on a carry tray. Nat and Smith just watched me, not saying anything. I went to the door and looked back at them. Holy fucking shit, Nat and Smith. Smith and Nat. My sister and my future Delta, Mated. Okay. I wonder how long they have been hiding their feelings from me. Actually, nope. Not my problem. I laughed and walked out the door.

I walked up the stairs slowly, still chuckling to myself. I don't know who I should feel more sorry for, Nat or Smith. I went through the bedroom door and put the food on the bed. Zee was in the shower. I lifted my arm and sniffed my pit. Hm... I could probably use a shower too. I took off my sweats and walked into the bathroom, I opened the shower door and Zee spun around surprised. There was a strong energy rolling around in the shower cubicle, like a weird heaviness. Zee looked like she saw a ghost, I must have really startled her.

"Oh, hey you" she smiled awkwardly,

"Need an extra pair of hands?" I said stepping in. She took my hands and pulled me under the water hugging me tightly. The water was steaming hot, just how I like it. The water poured over her head, so I picked up her new shampoo and poured it into my hand. I moved her out of the waters stream and rubbed the shampoo into her hair. She tilted her head back and let me keep washing her hair.

"Mm that feels really nice" she smiled,

"Good, it smells nice too". She turned around and rinsed her hair out under the water.

"Your turn now" she smiled looking up at me,

"Uhh… hm" she hummed as the realisation hit that she couldn't reach my head, I chuckled at her puzzled face and got down on my knees.

"Ah, that's better". She started to rub the soap into my hair, but standing there naked at that level, my brain had other plans. I put my hands on her hips and pulled her closer. I kissed her belly from her hips to her ribs, all over. She giggled trying to step back but I held her tight,

"You're going to get soap in your eyes" she cried out,

"I don't care" I mumbled with my lips pressed against her stomach. I trailed my kisses down to her crotch,

"Gunner" she gasped. I growled at her jokingly and kept kissing. I lifted her leg and put it over my shoulder.

"I'm gonna slip over" she squealed,

"No, you won't, I got you girl". I pressed my mouth against her pussy and rubbed my tongue along her lips. Sucking her clit into my mouth I flicked it with the tip of my tongue.

"Oh shit" Zee breathed, grabbing the top of my head. I continued licking and sucking at her dripping pussy, she tasted amazing and sweet. I pushed my tongue inside her, swirling it around and dragging it back up over her lips to her clit. I sucked hard on her clit before standing up and pushing her against the shower wall. I want to bury myself deep inside that delicious pussy. To feel her walls clench around my cock as she comes. I kissed her mouth hard pushing my tongue against hers.

"You taste good" I whispered between kisses.

"Well you can do that any time you want" she giggled,

"I'll remember you said that". I kissed her a few more times until my stomach growled, echoing through the bathroom. We both stopped and looked at each other before bursting out laughing.

"Okay I think we're clean enough, let's go eat" she said turning off the water. I grabbed her towel and passed it to her then picked up my own, wrapping it around my waist. I sat down on the bed and opened the bag of chips. Zee dried off and slipped on a loose black dress with skinny straps. She twisted her hair up in her towel and sat it on top of her head. She looks gorgeous, without even trying. No makeup and still a little damp and yet she is heavenly. She sat down next to me, opening the bread bag, and started making a sandwich. When she turned around and got up to grab the laptop off the dresser, I noticed a mark on the back of her neck.

"What's that, Babe?" I asked her.

"What's what?" she responded looking back at me. I stood up and moved the towel from her neck and there it was, as clear as day. A bright red triple moon emblem, just like the symbol of the Moon Goddess. When Zee was unconscious after her attack, I remember seeing a pale pink crescent moon on the back of her neck. But this is different, the colour is darker and its grown. It's not just the crescent shape, now it's the whole marking. That's not exactly a commonly shaped birthmark.

"What is it?" Zee asked,

"It's uh, well, I don't know what it is" I stuttered. She put down the laptop and sandwich and went to the bathroom mirror. She turned her head from side to side, twisting and bending her neck.

"I can't see anything" she said looking at me, her face started to look worried.

"Here I'll take a photo of it" I said grabbing my phone from beside the bed. I snapped a photo and passed the phone to Zee. She stared at it for a few minutes, studying the red waxing, full and waning moon shapes on the phone screen, before trying to see it again in the mirror.

"I've never noticed it before" she said confused,

"That's because it wasn't there before" I said back,

"What do you mean it wasn't there before?" she snapped at me, I could hear the fear making its way into her voice.

"I don't know, it just wasn't there, not like that". She looked at me seriously, rubbing the back of her neck. She was scared and I could smell her anxiety growing. I need to make this better, to calm her down somehow.

"I saw a pale pink semi-circle on your neck the night I brought you here, but it wasn't that dark, and it wasn't that big" I told her honestly.

"Where did it come from then?" she questioned. I know the symbol, and I know what it means to our people, but I've never seen it on a person before. I think I need to talk to Mum, she knows everything about this sort of stuff. She'll be able to tell us it's nothing, and then we can get back to lazing around in bed for the rest of the day.

"I think I should go get Mum" I said slowly. Zelena whipped her head around and stared at me wide eyed,

"Why?" she snapped,

"Is something wrong with me?". Her fear exploded and the smell flooded the room. I wrapped Zee in my arms and squeezed her tight.

"There is nothing wrong with you" I whispered,

"But the mark is in the shape of the Moon Goddess symbol, and Mum knows everything there is to know about her. She'll know what it is" I said as calmly as possible. Zee's breaths were sharp and fast, she was panicking. I let her go and crouched down in front of her and held her face in my hands. A tear fell from her cheek and I wiped it away. I gave her a kiss and smiled weakly,

"Everything is fine Zelena, it's just a birthmark, you don't need to worry". I looked down at my legs, I was still wearing the towel.

"First, I should put pants on, and you should put some underwear on" I smiled and she giggled. Good, she was laughing, I didn't mean to stress her out. I'm worried though, I don't know what this means or if it's important. Mum has told a lot of stories about the Moon Goddess, but I didn't always pay attention to them. I pulled on a pair of shorts and a baggy tank top and Zee pulled on a pair of panties. She took the towel off her head and shook her wet hair loose.

I took her hand and led her downstairs. I stuck my head in the kitchen, but Mum wasn't in there.

"Mum" I called out, no answer. I looked in the library, but she wasn't there either. We went out onto the porch and I saw Mum on the swing drinking a cup of tea.

"Hey Ma" I called. She looked up from her cup and smiled brightly as we walked over to her.

"Hello, my Darlings, how are you?" she cooed, putting down her cup and standing up. She gave me a hug and kissed my cheek and then did the same to Zee. She sat back down, and I pointed to the swing for Zee to sit next to her, and so she did.

"What's wrong Baby? You look worried" Mum said frowning and looking up at me, she knows me too well.

"Well Mum, I found a mark on Zelena's neck, and I just wanted to see if you knew what it was". Mum nodded and turned to

Zelena who was half smiling nervously. I nodded at Zee and she turned her back. But before she lifted her hair, Mum noticed the bite mark on her shoulder. She grabbed at Zee's shoulder and examined the bite. She looked up at me pursing her lips together and frowned,

"Gunner" she hissed,

"You didn't have to mark her, she's your True Mate, she isn't going anywhere" she snapped glaring at me. I rolled my eyes at her,

"Is this what you are showing me?"

"No Mum, never mind about that"

"I AM going to worry about that, marking a Mate is very possessive behaviour"

"MUM!" I yelled, trying to get her to pay attention. She looked at me, clearly surprised at my sudden outburst.

"Sorry, I didn't mean to yell" I stuttered,

"It's not the bite, it's the back of her neck". Mum brushed the hair off Zelena's neck and Zee reached back to lift it up. She leaned in a little to get a better look at the mark, then quickly jumped up off the chair and gasped, putting her hands over her mouth.

"That's not possible" she whispered,

"What's not possible Mum?" I snapped. Zee stood up and turned to look at my mum. I grabbed her arm and pulled her close to me, holding her tightly. My mother's reaction made me nervous and an instant urge to protect swept over me.

"Mum!" I yelled, but she didn't answer. She started pacing on the porch in quick little steps, shaking her head, looking at the ground, and mumbling.

"Roe?" Zee said shakily,

"Please" she pleaded. Mum stopped pacing and stared at Zelena. Her face was pale and her eyes were huge. She stepped forward and quickly grabbed both our hands.

"Quickly" she whispered,

"Into the library". She pulled us both back into the house and to the library. She left us in the middle of the room and ran to the shelf in the back corner by the window. She furiously started pulling out books and flipping through them, paying little care to the rough way in which she handled them.

"Mum, will you answer me?" I said loudly but she didn't answer. She kept pulling out book after book, flipping through the pages and then throwing it on the ground. I've never seen my mum so careless with her books, she's always so calm and gentle. 'Books are to be respected' she always told us. She was mumbling to herself as she went, I was starting to get really worried.

"Gunner I'm freaking out a bit" Zee said gripping my shirt,

"Yeah, I'm with you there" I whispered,

"Mum, for fuck's sake, what are you looking for?"

"A book" she snapped,

"Yeah, I can see that, now will you tell me why you're going crazy?"

"I'm not crazy, I know that I saw it here somewhere" she muttered,

"Ah yes" she cried.

"Here it is, look, look, look!" she yelled waving us over to her. I walked over to where Mum was standing with Zee behind me, still gripping my shirt. Mum had a big blue book in her hands and was pointing to a page. I took the book and looked at it closely. There was a silhouette of a girl with the same marking on her neck as Zee, three moons in different stages of phasing. I read the blurb next to it out loud,

"The symbol appears on the skin of the next chosen daughter of the Goddess. It will only appear once the girl becomes a woman. The mark will appear at either the base of the neck or the wrist. Only a female Were from the descended bloodline of the first daughter can inherit the mark. With it, she can take on the powers of the Moon"

"I guess you've sealed your bond then" Mum giggled. I looked down at Zelena in disbelief. This isn't real, it can't be. Mum had her hands on her cheeks and was staring between the book and Zee. I continued to read,

"Not all chosen descendants can wield the powers of the Moon, only a select few throughout time have been blessed with the gifts. The powers have been known to include, but are not limited to; Telekinesis, the power to move objects with the mind. Hydrokinesis, the power to move water and manipulate the tides. Aerokinesis, the power to manipulate air and weather. Shapeshifting, the power to morph oneself into another form. Gravitokinesis, the power to manipulate gravity".

"Mum. Are you for real with this?" I said closing the book.

"I absolutely am" she said snatching the book from me,

"Come sit, sit" she said ushering us to the sofa. Mum sat down on the coffee table in front of us and leaned in close.

"I thought the line had disappeared years ago, the last known descendant was living in Northern Alaska, but their pack was wiped out by hunters, I think not quite twenty years ago. There hasn't been a known Triple Goddess for more than a hundred years"

"Are you trying to tell me that you think I'm some kind of god" Zee laughed.

"Oh no, my Darling, you are not a god" Mum chuckled holding Zelena's hand,

"You are the chosen daughter of the Moon Goddess, you are a descendant of the first daughter Selena, that must be why you were given this name. They are quite similar don't you think?"

"But how, my father is just a human?"

"Yes, Darling but what about your mother? The Goddess is passed from mother to daughter. What do you know about your mum?"

"I don't know anything about my mother. All my dad ever said was that I was a waste of his time and he couldn't believe that I came from her. She died when I was a baby, I don't know what she looks like. I don't even know her name". Mum pulled Zee into her arms and hugged her,

"Oh, my sweet thing" she whispered. Mum turned to look at me and sighed,

"Gunner, baby, I know how you will feel about this, but I think we need to talk to Zelena's father"

"WHAT?" I screamed, standing up.

"Are you fucking kidding me, there is no way 'that' man is getting anywhere near Zelena"

"Gunner" Zee said softly reaching for my hand,

"It's not going to fucking happen" I demanded and stormed out the door.

I went out on the porch for some fresh air. How could she even consider letting that bastard talk to Zelena? I stomped back and forth along the porch trying to cool down. It wasn't working though. There's no way this is happening, NONE! Has she lost her damn mind, superpowers, and daughters of the Goddess. How fucking crazy is that? Mum has completely lost it. Holy shit, what if she hasn't lost it, what if she's right. HA! No. No way. I saw Dad walk over from the fire pit and stand at the bottom of the steps.

"Son, if you keep stomping like that you're going to break through the floorboards" he said sarcastically. I looked at him and snarled. I'm not in the mood for jokes.

"Funny" I snapped,

"You want to tell me what's got you all pissy?" he teased.

"I'm not pissy"

"Oh really, this is you not pissy then?" he chuckled. I held in the growl that was sitting on my lips and frowned. Oh, I'll show you that I'm not pissy.

"Your fucking wife has lost her fucking mind" I screamed as I stopped pacing and turned to look at him.

"She's in there talking about the daughter of the Goddess, and how Zelena has superpowers now and all that crap. AND she wants to invite Zee's dad to dinner. How about that?" I rushed out in a single breath. I was panting heavily, and I could feel my bones cracking and creaking inside me. Just the thought of seeing that man, of him being close to Zelena again, it was setting off a serious rage. Dad walked up to me and grabbed me by the shoulders.

"Gunner, first of all, take a bloody breath. Second, Zelena's father is NOT coming for dinner. And finally, why are you screaming about your mother?" I took a deep breath in, and then let it out again slowly, my body slowly started to cool down. Okay maybe I'm acting a little pissy. I looked at my father's face and told him what is going on.

"Zelena has a mark on her neck in the shape of the Moon Goddess' symbol. Mum has now got it in her head that Zelena is a long-lost descendant of the Goddess and therefore she has magical superpowers. But to make sure that her theory is correct, she wants us to go and have a nice little chat with Zee's father and find out more about her parents". Dad stared at me blankly for a moment, contemplating what I had just told him. He let go of my shoulders and stood up straight.

"Where is your mum?" he asked,

"In the library with Zee" I told him.

"You know that she knows more about our history than anyone else?"

"I know Dad, but this is just ridiculous". We both looked at each other in silence for a moment, I think we were both stalling. If this is true, then everything will change. Do I want it to be true, or do I want to live this normal boring life we were talking about? "Come on son, let's go have a calm conversation with your mum and your Mate" he said patting my shoulder. I took another deep breath, nodded my head, and turned around, walking for the door.

Chapter

Fifteen

Zelena

Nerves skittered across my skin as I pushed the door and let it slowly swing open. I stood in the doorway on full display. I let my hands dangle at my sides, fighting the urge to cover myself from him, as I took in the shocked look on Gunner's face. His mouth dropped open, and he stared at me, a dark and ravenous gleam flashed over his face. A low seductive growl came from deep inside him, making my legs tingle. He crawled across the floor to my feet, grabbed my ankle, and lifted it to his shoulder. He bit down on the top of my foot and slowly dragged his teeth up my leg, all the way to my inner thigh, where he then bit down again. His growl was doing something to me, I felt the wetness soak my panties and a fire flow through my veins. The sensation sent pleasurable electric shocks through my legs and into my stomach. Using his teeth he pulled down the stocking and took it off. He kissed each of my toes and trailed his kisses back up my leg, without missing a beat he pressed his lips hard against my crotch. I held onto the door frame as my knees started to shake. He ran his tongue along my panties, the pressure on my lips sent a shiver through my body. The garter belt fell to the floor, and he pulled on my panties. I looked down at him meeting his gaze. His eyes were full and dark, it made him look wild and insatiable. I nodded slowly, I want him to take them off. I want this, I want him inside me. He slowly pulled them down my legs and I stepped out of them. He lifted them to his nose and inhaled deeply. A heated blush burned my cheeks, as I watched. At least they're clean, I thought to myself.

He grabbed hold of my hips and lifted me onto his shoulders, I had to hold in the squeal as he spun me around and laid me on the bed. He slowly ran his hands up my body to my neck, and using his knee he nudged my legs apart. I was completely at his mercy, exposed and vulnerable. It made my body quiver with excitement, a hot burning desire flushed through me repeatedly. Gunner kissed me eagerly, I clutched his neck pulling his mouth harder into mine. He glided his hand down my belly and over my curls to my waiting wet lips. His finger slid along the slit, up and back. He tickled my clit with his fingers, and I bit down hard on his bottom lip. As he slid his finger inside me, making me moan loudly, I pushed my hips forward into his hand. I moved my hands down to his back and pulled him down on top of me,

"More" I whispered into his ear and bit his earlobe. I pulled his boxers down releasing his huge erection. His cock was pressed against my throbbing core, I was ready, I want to feel him. I kissed him hard and fast, giving my tongue generously and taking his into my mouth.

"Are you ready?" he whispered nuzzling into my neck.

I wrapped my legs around his waist and kissed him hard again. He slowly pushed his hips forward a little, and the tip of his hard cock was at my entrance. I moaned into his mouth urging him to give me more. He pushed his hips further forward and his length entered me. A gasp got caught in my throat and the pain caught me by surprise. I tipped my head back and groaned loudly, a stab of pain and a burst of pressure, and my virginity was gone. It felt tight and unnatural at first, but with each gentle drive forward of his hips, a tingle began to grow in my stomach and my pussy began to accept his length eagerly. Gunner bit into the base of my neck as he thrust into me deeper. My mind was fuzzy and I felt as though I had no control over my body, I moaned with each push forward. The pressure I felt inside me was unlike anything I could have imagined. Gunner lifted my hips higher and drilled into me deeper, as he did, he bit down harder into my neck. I cried out loudly and my body tensed, the sudden burst of pain on my shoulder and the deep pressure in my vagina was the perfect mix. He began to thrust faster, and a warmth started to spread through my body, I could feel my insides contracting. My whole body tightened and then released. I had pins and needles in my toes and my head felt like it was spinning. Gunner's body went stiff, he groaned and then melted on top of me. I was panting and my skin was hot, and so was Gunner's as I rubbed my hands up and down his back. He put his hand on my cheek and stared into my eyes.

"Are you okay?" he whispered. I smiled, nodded, and kissed his beautiful lips. He slowly pulled himself out of me, the release was strange and uncomfortable and I instantly missed the feel of him inside me. He rolled over onto his back and I cuddled into his chest.

"That was…" I paused,

"That was amazing" he smiled and kissed me on the forehead.

"I love you" I whispered gazing up at him.

"I love you too" he said squeezing me tighter.

"I almost forgot" Gunner blurted excitedly, pulling his arm out from under my head and leaning over the edge of the bed.

"I got you something too". He sat back up and handed me a small black pouch. I looked up at him and smiled. I've never been given a present before, this is exciting. I opened the top of the pouch and reached my fingers inside and slowly pulled out a small silver link chain. I held it up and saw a little heart pendant attached to it. I turned the heart around to examine it. There are three crescent moons all connected, the same symbol that is on that old book I found on the shelf. On the other side of the heart, in very small cursive writing are the words 'My Heart, My Soul'. Oh wow, this is the sweetest thing ever. I could feel the tears welling up in my eyes, this was so beautiful and so special. I love him so damn much.

"Do you like it?" he asked watching me. I held it to my chest and smiled at him, trying to hold back the tears.

"I love it. I love it so much, thank you" I cooed,

"It's our pack symbol" he said opening my hand and pointing to the three moons,

"You are part of the pack now, so you need your own token".

He took it from my hand and clipped it around my wrist. I held up my arm and turned my wrist around in front of my face and watched the bracelet dangle around. Gunner laid back down on the bed and I snuggled into him. I kissed his chest and tickled my fingers in small circles across his skin. As I lay in his arms, it dawned on me that we really don't know anything about each other. We have this amazing connection that came on so fast and we got swept up in it. We've never really had a full conversation about anything important. I want to know everything that there is to know about him.

"Gunner?"

"Yeah Babe"

"What's your last name?"

"Mathers, why's that?" I sat up and smiled at him and he perched himself up on his arm.

"I just wanted to know. Now, what's your favourite colour?"

"What's this, twenty questions?" He chuckled,

"Yes, it is, I don't know anything about you"

"You know that I love you"

"I do know that, but I don't know any of the little stuff, will you just tell me?". Gunner sat up and huffed,

"Okay but if I have to answer then so do you, deal?"

"Okay deal" I smiled.

"So, favourite colour, was it?" he asked,

"Yes"

"It's dark blue, and yours?"

"Mine is purple"

"Of course it is. Okay, do you have a favourite song?"

"Um, well I've never really had access to music or movies or TV, anything like that. I was never allowed to watch TV or have my own phone or anything, so I guess I don't know enough songs to have a favourite". Gunner was silent, he sat with his head down fiddling his hands. He lifted his head and looked at me.

"Can I ask you about it?" he said softly. I knew what he meant, and as scary as it is to open up about it, I know that I can trust him. So I nodded.

"When did it start?" he whispered.

"For as long as I can remember. I don't remember a whole lot from when I was really young, I just remember the fear of getting into trouble. The youngest I remember was when I was seven or eight, he locked me in the basement for a few days. It was dark and I didn't have any food, when I cried because I was hungry, he whipped my hands with a belt. So I just stopped crying. After that, it was just an open hand or a belt or something like that, never my face or anything too visible. As I got older the beatings got worse. He would use chains and whips, he'd kick and punch with more and more power". Again Gunner was silent, he dropped his hand and clasped his fingers together.

"Did he ever take care of you, like afterwards?" he finally asked, breaking the silence,

"Take care of me, as in fixing the damage he caused?"

"Yeah, did he ever try to help you?"

"Nah, he got used to keeping bandages and band-aids around, because he knew I'd fix myself up. There were some broken ribs, and I think my wrists a few times, but I always tried to do it myself. There was a time when I was about eleven, I think, he got called into the school because one of the teachers saw the bruises on my arms. He was so mad at me for letting someone see, even though it was an accident. I really thought he was going to kill me that night, I couldn't breathe properly for a few weeks after that". I looked at Gunner's hands as I spoke, he was gripping them so tight that the veins were bulging and his skin was turning white.

"You never asked anyone for help?"

"No"

"But why?"

"I was too scared. I didn't want anyone to know about it because I didn't believe that anyone could do anything. Especially after that time with the teacher. The only thing that changed after that meeting was that he became more conscious of where he was hitting me, but the hitting didn't stop. If anything it got worse, more brutal. But then you came along." I smiled weakly and placed my hand over his.

"Don't do that" Gunner sniffed.

"Don't do what?"

"Don't act like it's all okay, it's not okay. He should suffer for what he did to you"

"But what would that change? It happened, I lived through it and I found you. The rest doesn't matter anymore". It wasn't a lie. I am ever grateful to have found Gunner, despite the road I had to take to get here. I crawled over and laid my head in his lap, I reached my hand up and stroked his cheek. He smiled down at me and gently ran his fingers up and down my arm.

"Are you scared about being the Alpha?" I asked, trying to change the subject.

"I used to be, but not anymore" he answered without hesitation,
"Why not anymore?"
"Because I have you to help me now"
"Yes, you do" I grinned bopping his nose with my index finger.
"How did you picture your future?" he asked,
"Honestly, I never did, I didn't think I would live this long. What about you?"
"I figured it would look just like my mum and dad's life"
"Why do you make it sound like a bad thing?" I questioned him.
"It's not a bad thing, I just always thought of it as boring". I thought about what he said for a minute. Boring? I would have given anything to have a boring life, instead of the one I've had so far. He's lucky.
"The life you have here, the life I have here now, with you, it's all I could have ever wished for" I told him earnestly.
"Don't get me wrong, now that you are a part of it, everything is different. I don't think of it as boring anymore. As long as I have you with me, I will be blissfully happy"
"Aww Gunner, that was really sweet" I cooed.
"Shut up" he chuckled poking my stomach.
"No really, that's the nicest thing anyone has ever said to me. And for the record, Alpha or not, you're all that I want".
I sat up and kissed him softly, then again, and again. I moved my legs over and sat on his lap, straddling him. I licked his lips and pushed my tongue against his. He ripped the blanket out from his lap and pulled me in closer. He moved his kisses down to the bite mark on my shoulder and kissed it softly,
"Mine" he whispered. I could feel his erection growing under my ass, I wanted it again. He rubbed his fingers up and down my back as he kissed me passionately. He unclipped my bra and pulled it off my arms, we were both naked now.
"Again" I whispered in his ear and he sucked and bit along my neck.
He lifted me by my hips and gently sat me back down on top of his dick. It slid right in, and I felt that same pressure and tightness. I moved my hips forward and back slowly. I was in control this time, I like it. I wrapped my arms around his head and grabbed hold of his hair. He put his hands on my ass and squeezed as I thrust my hips forward faster. Sitting on him like this, it felt incredible. I moaned loudly, and Gunner was groaning. It was

happening faster this time. The warmth spreading and the tightness in my stomach, it was building quickly.

"I think I'm coming" I moaned,

"Me too, just keep going". I moved my hips faster, I could feel his cock pressing against the inside of me. I started to quiver, and my clit was throbbing. I thrust my hips hard, and my pussy contracted.

"Ah shit" Gunner groaned. I thrust forward again, and my body began to shake. A few more times and everything inside me was exploding. I cried out and squeezed my thighs. My pussy was convulsing, and it didn't stop, I closed my eyes and tilted my head back. The pressure began to subside, and I felt weak and tired. I sat in Gunner's arms, panting, and rested my head on his shoulder.

"Holy shit, Zelena" Gunner breathed.

"I'm sorry, was I too fast?"

"No Baby, you are a Goddess. A sex Goddess". I giggled shyly and slowly pulled myself off him. I flopped down on the bed feeling completely spent. Gunner laid down next to me and rested his arm across my stomach. I was staring at the roof, listening to him breathe. He was going to be the Alpha, which means I'll be the Luna one day. But I still don't know much about being a wolf. There is still so much that I haven't asked.

"Gunner?" I asked, not moving,

"Yeah"

"Can you teach me more about the wolf stuff?"

"Absolutely, what do you want to learn first?" He propped himself up and leaned on the headboard.

"Uh... well some basic stuff, I guess. When did you first change?"

"My wolf was born not long before my thirteenth birthday"

"Is that what you call it? Being born, like a baby?"

"Well yes, another part of your body and soul is born the day that you have your first change"

"And is that the age most people first change?"

"Firstly, we use the term Weres, not people. And for males it's usually between thirteen and fourteen but for females it's very random. The youngest has been twelve and, well, you've been the oldest that I know of"

"Why didn't I change sooner?" I asked thinking about it some more. If I had changed a few years ago, I would have been able to stand up for myself. I could have fought off my father and saved myself years of torture and abuse.

"I've thought about that a little bit actually. I think it was because of your upbringing. You suppressed that side of yourself for some reason. Well, I can assume to know the reason, but it would only be a guess. Once I found you and the True Mate bond started, your subconscious wolf recognised that it was time. Well, that's my theory anyway".

That's a pretty good theory, it sounds like he has thought about that a lot.

"You can change really quickly, with like no pain" I said, not sure if asking a question or noting the fact.

"Yeah, I can" he agreed,

"So, how long did it take you to learn to do that?" I asked him,

"Learn control?"

"Yeah"

"I think I had it mastered at about sixteen".

Three years, it took the son of an Alpha three years to learn control over the change. I dread how long it will take me to learn.

"Wow, that's a long time" I breathed out.

"There's no rush, you'll get it when you get it"

"And what about the other stuff, like the flashing in human form, and healing, and whatever else there is"

"Well I think it's safe to say your healing is just fine" he chuckled,

"Yeah, but that was you giving me your power, I heard Roe and Artemis talking about it"

"Oh, you did ay?" he said nervously, rubbing the back of his neck.

"Nmhm" I hummed,

"It's dangerous isn't it, sharing power like that?" I asked with a grumble,

"Ah well, it can be if you're not careful. I passed out a couple of times giving it to you"

"Gunner" I yelled sitting up and hitting him in the chest,

"Why would you do that? You could have hurt yourself".

He leaned forward and grabbed my hand as I went to hit him again. He held it up to his face and rubbed his cheek with the back of my hand.

"Because you were so weak, and I knew that I wouldn't survive if I lost you. I had to help, I had to make you better. I loved you then, even if I didn't realise it. I still love you now".

Oh my. It felt as though my heart grew three times bigger. How could I have ended up with this man, what have I done to deserve him. I tilted my head to the side and gazed at him lovingly. I think actual hearts popped out of my eyes.

He's perfect

Gunner's eyes opened wide as he sat up straight and put my hand down.

"You flashed me" he said surprised,

"I did?" I asked, feeling a little surprised myself.

"Yeah, you just said 'he's perfect' just now". Oh shit, he heard that?

"I did say that, I said it to myself"

"No, you said it to me" he smiled brightly,

"Try it again" he demanded excitedly.

I closed my eyes and tried to concentrate. 'Gunner' I said in my head. I opened an eye looking at him and he shook his head. 'I love you' I said. I looked at him again, but still nothing.

Ah fuck

He laughed out loud.

Shit, did it work?

He nodded still laughing at me.

Will you stop swearing at me?

Holy crap, I heard his voice in my head, just like when we were wolves. This is awesome.

Say something else

You are saying something

I am. Fuck yeah

Gunner leaned forward and kissed me, his whole face was smiling. "With flashing you can also share images of things, try that" he said proudly.

"But what do I show you?"

"Show me anything, maybe like this".

A picture of a purple flower growing out of the side of a tree popped into my head. It was a gorgeous image. It's like I could see it for real, like it was from my own memory.

"Wow, what's that?" I asked him,

"I saw it the other day and it made me think of you" he smiled. Okay, I can do this. Just think of something nice, think of something special. My mind took me to my old basement and the chains on the floor that Dad used to use to hold me still. Uh no, not that, stop it. Think of something different.

"What was that?" Gunner asked slowly, his face contorted into a wince.

"What was what?"

"You gave me a picture of yourself, kneeling on the floor with your arms in chains. There was so much pain attached to it" he talked slowly with his face scrunched up as he gripped at his chest, like he was in physical pain.

"I didn't mean to, sorry. After what we were talking about, it was just the first thought that came to me. I'm sorry"

"That was real?" he yelled, kneeling up taller. I had a rush of fear blow through me. I needed to cower, to cover myself. I flinched, closing my eyes and I whimpered. I leaned back turning away from him and I lifted my hands to protect my face. I felt cold and angry, and sick to the stomach.

"Shh, it's okay" Gunner said softly. He gently placed his hands on my skin and ran them down my arms, he carefully grabbed my wrist and turned me back around. Moving slowly and carefully, he moved his hands to rest on both sides of my face.

"I'm sorry, Zee. Shh, I'm sorry, I didn't mean to. That was my fear, I pushed it onto you. I'm so sorry, it was an accident. Please look at me" he pleaded. I opened my eyes and gazed at his face, his eyes were full of worry and his bottom lip was shaking.

"I'm sorry, I would never hurt you, please know that" his voice was shaky and urgent. I sucked in a deep breath, slowly blew it out, and relaxed. The fear had passed, just like that, it was gone. That was so weird.

"It's okay" I whispered,

"I'm sorry too". He pulled me into his lap and hugged me tight.

"You don't need to be sorry, that wasn't your fault. I pushed it, please forgive me"

"It's okay really, that was such a weird feeling"

"I know, I know, I didn't mean to, it just came out" he said stroking my hair.

"What was it?" I asked him.

"When you showed me the picture, I felt the pain with it. It scared the hell out of me, to see you like that. I forgot that our minds were still linked and I pushed my fear into you"

"You can do that?"

"Ah well, we can, you and me, because we're True Mates. I don't think we could do it to anyone else though"

"Oh". Gunner held me in his arms and continued to stroke my hair. It felt so nice and comfortable, I felt warm and safe. My body felt exhausted and although I wanted to know more and practice more, my head was heavy and my eyes started to drift. I shuddered awake as Gunner started to lay me down on the bed. "Shh, go back to sleep, I'm still here" he whispered laying down with me. He pulled me into his arms spooning me and I drifted right back off to sleep.

Chapter

Sixteen

Zelena

I'm not a virgin anymore. A whole night of sex with that sexy animal has thrown me for a loop. I am so sore! My legs are aching, and my poor vagina has been seriously worked out this past twelve hours. Worth it. My stomach grumbled loudly, and I chuckled. I should definitely take that hot shower while Gunner gets us some food. Plus, I'm sure it would help my aching body.
 I stood up and nearly fell back down. Holy crap my legs feel like jelly. I couldn't help but giggle to myself, this is a sign of great sex, right? Standing by the bed still naked, I slowly and very wobbly walked to the shower. I could feel his cum running down my leg, it's a weird, warm kind of feeling. I don't hate it. I turned on the tap to let the water heat up and then stood in front of the mirror. The bite mark on my shoulder was a dark red, and fresh teeth marks were now present over the old ones. It didn't hurt though, it felt more like a dull pressure, almost enjoyable.
I stood under the water and instantly felt better, my whole body relaxed under the heat. I tilted my head back and let the water wash over my hair and face. Ah, that's so good. Relaxing and calming. The sensation of the water hitting my skin made me feel like I was unwinding. Everything around me felt free and weightless. I bent down to pick up my new shampoo bottle and froze. That's not normal. The water drops from the shower hit the floor and bounced up again, and kept floating up, and up and

up. They weren't falling back down, just kind of hanging there. In mid-air. How is that possible? I stood up slowly, following the little drops of water with my eyes. What the fuck was going on? I looked around the shower and noticed hundreds of drops of water all floating around me. I lifted my hand and touched one of the droplets, it burst at my touch and fell to the ground. I touched another and it did the same thing. This is so weird, what is happening? I let the bottle of shampoo slip out of my hand, but I didn't hear it hit the floor. I looked down and it was just hovering there, in mid-air, just below my fingers. I reached to touch it but was startled by the shower door opening. I spun around quickly and heard the bottle hit the floor. It was Gunner,

"Oh, hey you" I said with a smile, I looked down at the bottle now laying on the floor. Did he see the floating bottle of shampoo?

"Need an extra pair of hands?" he asked stepping into the shower. I guess not.

I grabbed his hands and pulled him under the water, hugging him tightly around the waist. My eyes darted around the shower, no more floating water either. I must have been hallucinating, maybe I'm more tired than I thought I was. What a trip, I'm definitely losing my mind. Gunner pulled out of my arms and picked up the bottle of shampoo. He gently shifted me out of the stream of water and turned me around so that my back was to him. I tilted my head back and let him rub the soap into my hair. His fingers rubbed into my scalp, nice and slowly, making smooth circles through my hair. I closed my eyes and just about melted into him.

"Mm… That feel's really nice" I groaned,

"Good, it smells nice too" he said continuing the scalp massage. He tipped more shampoo into his hand and ran his fingers through my long locks, rubbing the soap into the lengths.

"All done" he said proudly.

I turned around and rinsed my hair out under the water. I opened my eyes and found Gunner was watching me closely, clearly enjoying the view of my naked body under the water.

"Your turn now" I said smiling up at him. Hm, he is like two feet taller than me, how am I meant to do this?

"Uhh… hm" I hummed studying his tall frame. He chuckled and got down on his knees facing me.

"Ah, that's better". I began rubbing the soap into his hair, copying the circular motions on his scalp. He groaned happily and grabbed my hips, pulling me into his face. He was kissing my belly all over, it tickled and made me giggle. I tried to step back but his grip was too tight.

"You're going to get soap in your eyes" I giggled,

"I don't care" he mumbled through his kisses.

He started trailing his kisses down to my crotch, I stretched out my hands to brace myself against the shower walls.

"Gunner" I gasped as his lips pressed against my pussy. He growled at me softly and lifted my leg, putting it over his shoulder.

"I'm gonna slip over" I squealed, grabbing his shoulders in an attempt to push him away.

"No, you won't, I got you girl" he said before rubbing his tongue along my lips.

"Oh, my" I breathed softly. He traced his tongue along my slit, teasing me. Oh, wow this is something else. He circled my clit with his tongue before sucking it into his mouth. He flicked my pulsating bud with the tip of his tongue as he sucked hard. My knees felt weak and bursts of pleasure were shooting through my veins.

"Oh shit" I breathed heavily, grabbing a handful of his hair. I tossed my head back and closed my eyes tight, everything else around me disappeared. All I could focus on was Gunner's mouth on my pussy. He was sucking and licking, setting fireworks off inside me. He stopped, standing up and pushing me against the wall. He kissed me passionately, rubbing my tongue with his.

"You taste good" he smirked,

"Well, you can do that any time you want" I panted softly.

"I'll remember you said that". Our kisses were interrupted by Gunner's stomach screaming, I looked up at him and we laughed. Nm... I really don't want to stop where this is headed, but I'm also pretty hungry.

"Okay I think we're clean, let's eat" I said turning off the tap begrudgingly.

Stepping out of the shower, Gunner passed me a towel and I wrapped it around myself. I started rummaging through the dresser drawer looking for something to put on. I pulled out a black singlet dress and slipped it on. I twisted my hair up in my towel and sat down on the bed. I started fixing a sandwich, getting hungrier by the second. I think we might watch a movie,

Gunner's got heaps of movies on his computer, and I kind of need to catch up on the cinema world. I got up and took the laptop from the dresser.

"What's that Babe?" Gunner asked,

"What's what?" I asked back confused.

~

It was hard to follow, all this talk of Goddess' and magical powers. Surely this can't be real? Surely, Roe's not serious. I was trying to keep my cool, stay calm, and chill, but I was on the verge of laying down on the floor and curling into the foetal position. When she mentioned my father and seeing him again, I felt the vomit rise up in my throat.

"It's not going to fucking happen!" Gunner yelled angrily. He pulled away from me and stormed out of the room. I was about to follow him out, but Roe grabbed my arm and held me there,

"Let him go, Sweetheart" she said softly.

I sat back down and stared at her, thinking about what she was suggesting. This whole thing is past the point of crazy. All this talk about superpowers and Goddess', it's not possible. Is it? I tried to listen, I tried to take it all in. But the more Roe spoke, the more unbelievable it sounded. I'm not a Goddess or some special chosen daughter, I'm nothing, no one. How could this be possible. My father, Hank, he couldn't know anything. Surely not. At least I don't think so.

"Do you really think my dad could know something about this?" I asked softly

"I don't know Darling, maybe. At the moment we don't really have many other options, do we?" she answered.

I looked down at my hands, I really don't want to see him, but I must know if this is true or not. Would he even know anything? He never let on to it, or at least I didn't realise if he did. Plus, the shower thing was weird, with the water and the shampoo bottle. Could that be one of the powers in the book, did I do that to the water?

"Roe, something happened in the shower, I think I should tell you about it" I said quietly,

"Go ahead, Darling" Roe answered with an encouraging tone.

"Ah, well um, the water from the shower head was kind of floating"

"Floating?"

"Yeah, like, it hit the ground and bounced up again, but then it just kept flying up. And when I dropped the shampoo bottle it didn't fall, it was hanging in mid-air. Do you think that I did that, maybe?" I was looking at my fingers in my lap as I spoke. Nervous to know the answer.

I looked up at her face and she was staring at me with a huge smile on her face. I thought her eyes were about to burst out of her head.

"Oh Zelena" she breathed heavily, putting her hands to her chest, "It sounds like you either have Hydrokinesis or Telekinesis. However, it could also be a gravitational power. Being in the shower surrounded by water, it would be hard to tell exactly which power it is. A water gift would be spectacular. The glorious things you could do" she cooed happily. But then her face dropped a little and she looked off to the wall.

"If it is Gravitokinesis, we must be very cautious, it's a very strong power, one of the strongest there is. So much of the gift can be beautiful, but a lot can also go wrong" she said turning very serious.

Okay, so I apparently have superpowers now. Great, I thought sarcastically. Will the surprises ever stop coming, I don't know how much more weirdness I can take. Like seriously. Enough now, please magical Moon Goddess.

"Roe, I-I don't know about this, isn't it just a little too far-fetched?" I asked looking at her with my head tilted.

She half smiled and closed her eyes, taking in a deep breath.

"I understand how confusing this must be for you, my dear. Not four weeks ago you didn't even know that were-kind existed, and now I'm telling you that you're a daughter of the moon and have unimaginable powers. It would be a lot for anyone to hear. But please trust me, my entire life has been dedicated to learning and teaching others about our history. I would never intentionally lead you astray, this is real, and this is happening." she said looking directly into my eyes.

Roe and I were pulled from our conversation by Lupus walking through the door, followed by Gunner. Gunner looked flushed and agitated.

"Hello Zelena" Lupus nodded at me, I smiled weakly in response. He sat down next to Roe and Gunner sat next to me, taking my hand in his and kissing my cheek.

"I'm sorry I lost my temper" he whispered.

"It's okay" I said kissing his lips.

"Roe, tell me what's going on would you please" Lupus said turning to his wife.

"Zelena has the mark of the Goddess, my love. She is the chosen descendant and has already begun to exhibit powers" Roe said confidently.

Gunner snapped his head to look at me,

What is she talking about?

Something happened in the shower before you came in and I told her about it

Why didn't you tell me?

Because I thought I was hallucinating

You still should have said something

I didn't know Gunner

"Stop flashing you two, talk to us" Roe growled,

"Sorry, Gunner was asking about the powers"

"I'd like to hear it too, if you don't mind" Lupus grumbled.

"I was having a shower and the water started floating upwards, and I dropped a bottle of soap and it didn't fall to the ground"

"Are you certain?" Gunner questioned,

"It's kind of hard not to notice"

"Will you show me? Like I taught you last night" he said turning to face me.

"That didn't turn out so great, in case you forgot"

"Just try, Baby, please" he pleaded. I huffed and nodded. It was a hell of a lot harder to concentrate with the eyes of Roe and Lupus on me now as well.

Ready when you are

I closed my eyes and pictured the scene in my head, the water drops floating around the shower and the shampoo bottle hovering. I then pushed it out, giving it to Gunner. I heard him gasp and snapped my eyes open. He was looking at me wide eyed.

"I saw it, holy shit" he exclaimed.

"Gunner" Roe hissed,

"Sorry Mum"

"Well, okay then" Lupus huffed,

"So that's it then, she is really the Triple Goddess?" Gunner breathed,

"Yes. See, I told you" Roe smiled.

I sat back in my chair and huffed. Okay, so they were easily convinced. Roe sure is excited about it, and Lupus hasn't exactly disputed her theories.

"How do we know for certain though?" I asked not looking up.

"Artemis, he will know how to test you and prove it true" Roe said standing up,

"I'll go fetch him" she said cheerfully,

"I'll come with you" said Lupus. They both left the room and I sat in the chair, completely spinning out. I feel like I'm dreaming, this is all just one big elaborate dream. Finding out about werewolves is one thing, but now this. Gunner squeezed my hand and sat back next to me.

"So, this is quite the revelation" he said looking up at the roof.

"You think? I've just been told that I'm some kind of magical Goddess with superpowers, like I'm not enough of a freak already"

"You're not a freak Zee, you're incredible. I knew you were special, and I could always feel that you were very powerful. I would have never guessed all this though"

"What will this mean? Am I going to be studied or experimented on, or something?"

Gunner sat up and looked at me seriously.

"I would never let that happen to you, nothing has to change if you don't want it to. Our pack will love and respect you and even worship you"

"But Gunner, I don't want to be worshipped, all I wanted was a family" my voice cracked and I could feel the tears starting to well in my eyes. My emotions were being overwhelmed, the picture I had of our future together had now shifted. We were never going to have that simple, happy and boring life together. Especially not if the pack think I'm a Goddess. This will change everything. I have changed everything.

Artemis burst through the door breathing heavily, he searched the room before his eyes fell on me. He stared at me, wide eyed and amazed.

"Triplí Theá" he whispered and rushed to my feet, kneeling down in front of me. A bead of sweat dripped down his forehead and his face was flushed. He smelt strange, like anxious, mixed with excited, mixed with terrified. It came off him like a hot sour smell.

"Please, I see?" he gestured to my neck.

I nodded and turned around in my chair lifting my still damp hair. He gasped and leaned closer to me. I could feel his breath on the back of my neck, it gave me goosebumps.

"I touch?" he asked, I nodded again.

He placed the palm of his hand on my neck at first, and then rubbed at the mark with his fingers. After a moment of poking and humming, he moved away. I turned back around, Artemis was kneeling again with his head bowed and his hands held out flat in front of me. I didn't know what he was doing but it made me very uncomfortable. I looked at Gunner and back at Artemis and then Gunner again.

"Artemis, my friend, you don't need to do that" Gunner said softly putting his hand on Artemis's shoulder.

Artemis hissed and lowered his head further, yeah, I definitely don't like this.

"Artemis, please will you stand up" I whispered trying to keep my voice from breaking.

He quickly jumped to his feet but still bowed down with his hands out,

"Yes, my Goddess" he whispered.

"Seriously Artemis, you don't have to do that" I snapped.

He stood up straight but didn't look me in the eye.

"Artemis, do you need to test her?" Lupus asked,

"No test, I see her. She is chosen daughter, I feel her magic" he said not looking up.

Lupus and Roe looked at each other and then back at me, then they both too knelt down, bowing their heads and holding their hands out flat. Why is the Alpha bowing to me, this isn't right. I looked at Gunner confused, and he just stared at them clearly confused himself.

"Dad?" he questioned,

"What are you doing?"

Neither Lupus nor Roe answered him. I stood up and Artemis took a few steps back from me, his retreat and the reaction from Lupus and Roe, brought it all to the surface. I went from being treated like the scum of the earth, to having people I care about bow to me. It's too much. I don't want this. I felt my heart contract and my head spin.

"Stop it" I shouted.

The coffee table in front of my feet began to slowly lift off the ground, and the multiple bookshelves around us started to shake. "Stand up! Stop doing that, both of you please, get up" I sobbed. My body felt heavy, like every inch of my small frame was being pulled to the ground. I could feel my chest tightening as a dull ache ran through my arms. I don't understand what is happening. The shelves on the bookshelves snapped in half sending all the books falling to the ground. They all hit the floor with a collective thud, and then began to float around the room. I felt a weightlessness in my head and an electric energy circle around me. Roe and Lupus got up and stood by Artemis. Gunner was now standing behind me with his hands on my shoulders. They all looked around the room at the flying books and then back at me.

"Please, I don't want this, I just wanted a family" I croaked weakly. The tears were falling down my face as Gunner put his arms around me. The books started to fall and rise, over and over.

"We're sorry, Darling, we are just showing our respect to our Goddess" Roe said quietly.

"I don't want to be your Goddess, not if it means you will start treating me differently"

"This is our way, this is how it is done" Lupus said firmly.

"Well I don't care! If you want me here and you want me to be your Goddess, or whatever, then you can't do that. Lupus, you are the Alpha, I don't want you to bow to me, you are all my family now, why can't we just be a family?" I shouted through my sobs. Parts of the table began to crunch and break.

Everything I had hoped for, a family, love and acceptance, having a normal life, I felt it all slipping out of my grasp. I felt helpless and lost, like a darkness was looming overhead. Roe stepped forward, around the coffee table, and carefully took my hands.

"I'm sorry, my Darling, nothing has to change, not between us. You are right, we are family. Right Lupus?" she said reaching for her husband's hand.

He stepped forward and put his hand on ours, a wave of calm brushed the darkness away. I instantly felt better, the heaviness let go and my chest relaxed. All the books hit the floor with a loud thump, everything had stopped flying.

"Thank you" I whispered taking a deep breath.

Lupus and Gunner both wrapped their arms around us and squeezed. My body felt weak and tired. I couldn't place my emotions or pinpoint how I was feeling. After a minute they let me go. Artemis was still standing with his back against the wall, staring at me with this amazed and terrified look on his face. I looked around the room, there were books all over the floor. I did all this?

"Oh Roe, your library, I'm so sorry. I didn't mean to" I said as I surveyed the mess I had made.

"I know, Darling, it's okay. It was quite the sight to see" she cooed with a smile.

"I can't wait to see what you can do when you learn to control it" Lupus huffed with an odd hint of pride in his voice.

"I can control when this happens?"

"Yes, you need training. Right away" Artemis spoke from across the room.

"Okay, but for now can we keep my new abilities on the down low? I don't want to scare anyone else"

"You don't want the pack to know?" Gunner asked,

"Not right away, just let me get a handle on it first"

"I think that's reasonable" Lupus said, picking up some books.

"I can clean this up, why don't you two go and relax for a bit. Maybe talk some things out?" Roe said suggestively to Gunner and me.

"No, I made this mess, I'll clean it up"

"Oh nonsense, it was just an accident. Go on now".

Gunner took my hand and led me toward the door.

"Tomorrow, my Goddess" Artemis called. I turned to look at him.

"Tomorrow, you come. We train."

"Okay, sure" I answered slowly.

He nodded his head and Gunner and I went upstairs. I sat down on the bed and Gunner stood in front of me.

"Are you okay?" he asked softly.

"I'm fine"

"That uh, that was different"

"I'm sorry, I really didn't mean to, I just got so upset"

"I know, I could feel it too". He sat down next to me on the bed and took my hand.

"I don't know what happened, your parents were being weird and I just kind of burst" I said quickly,

"It's okay, it was actually pretty cool" he chuckled.

We sat quietly on the edge of the bed. I need to tell Gunner that I have to see Hank, but I know he won't make it easy. I don't know for sure if Hank has any answers, but I have to find out, and I can't just let it go. Did my mum know about this, did Hank know about this? There are too many unanswered questions and so many unknowns. It will end up driving me crazy if I just try to forget about it.

"Gunner, please don't get mad" I said softly,

"Why would I get mad?"

"I need to talk with my dad"

"Zelena, NO!" he snapped.

"I have too, if I'm going to get answers about my mum, and about this Triple Goddess thing, then I have to start with him" I pleaded.

"I'm not just going to hand you back over to him". I could feel his skin starting to burn under my hands, he was ready to rage out.

"I don't want you to just hand me over. I need you to come with me. Please, I can't do it alone". I tried to stroke his arm, as I spoke, to calm him.

"I will kill him, Zee" he growled lowly,

"No, you won't, for me, because I need this". I sat staring at him while he thought about it, I couldn't read his face and his emotions were changing too fast for me to get a smell of them. I was going to do it with or without him, that decision was already made.

"Okay" he eventually whispered,

"But not alone, Cole and Dad will come as well"

"That's fine" I agreed,

"And maybe Smith"

"Sure" I smiled to myself, okay we're making progress.

"We'll bring him to you though, I'm not taking you back to that house" he growled,

"You want to bring him here?" I said slowly. He isn't going to show Hank where we live, is he? No, of course not. He wouldn't do that, not if he planned on letting him go again afterwards.

"No, not to the village. We have another place"

"Ah, okay" I mumbled. I have no idea where he is talking about.

"Tomorrow at sundown, when you've finished with Artemis" Gunner said with finality.

"Oh, so soon?" I said softly, as my heart rate increased,

"You don't have to" he said looking down at me, like he was expecting me to back out now.

"No, no, tomorrow is good. Let's do it".

Gunner was quiet for a few minutes before he frowned and stood up off the bed,

"I'll go sort it out with Dad" he said as he turned for the door.

I jumped up and ran to him, launching myself onto his back. I held onto him like a little koala and kissed his cheek.

"It'll be okay, you'll see" I whispered and kissed him again.

He turned his head and gave me a weak smile and a peck on the lips. Then he took my hand from around his neck and lifted me back down and onto my feet. He walked out the bedroom door, closing it behind him. He was so cold and distant, not the warm and loving Gunner I've grown used too. I sat back on the bed and breathed out heavily, am I really ready to face my father again?

Chapter Seventeen

Gunner

The moment that both of my parents dropped to their knees, mimicking Artemis, I knew shit was about to go down. Once Zee stood up, I swiftly followed her, staying just behind her.

"Stop it" Zee shouted.

The little table in front of her lifted off the ground. Holy fucking shit, this is her, Zelena is doing this. The bookshelves and everything on them started to shake. I could feel this dull vibration coming from Zee, like pulsating waves.

"Stand up! Stop doing that. Both of you, please get up" she shouted as she sobbed.

In a snap, all the shelves on the bookshelf broke in half, sending everything falling to the ground. They hit the floor and then started to float around the room, circling us. Mum and Dad stood up next to Artemis, out of the path of the flying books. In an instant, I grabbed Zelena's shoulders, hoping to calm her down, but instead, I felt a deep fear flow through me.

"Please, I don't want this, I just wanted a family" she cried desperately.

The feeling rolled through me. I thought I was going to be sick. My body felt laden and heavy, but my head was airy and light. I wrapped my arms around Zelena to calm her. But the moment I had her in my arms, I nearly pulled away from her again. A frigid darkness filled her emotions. She felt scared and lost. I couldn't let her go, I needed to calm her down. The books stopped spinning and started falling and rising again and again.

"We're sorry, Darling. We are just showing our respect to our Goddess" Mum said quietly, taking a small step forward.

"I don't want to be your Goddess, not if it means you will start treating me differently" Zee cried, while shaking in my arms.

"This is our way, this is how it is done" Dad growled,

"Well, I don't care! If you want me here and you want me to be your Goddess or whatever then you can't do that. Lupus, you are the Alpha I don't want you to bow to me, you are all my family now, why can't we just be a family?". I could feel how desperate Zee felt. I could feel the intense fear and anxiety coursing through her. It was like picks of ice stabbing against my skin, all the while my head felt like it was going to pop off and float away.

Mum stepped around the coffee table and took Zee's hands,

"I'm sorry, my Darling, nothing has to change, not between us. You are right, we are family. Right Lupus?" she said reaching behind her for Dad.

He stepped toward us and wrapped his hands around theirs, the heaviness in the room evaporated instantly. Everything hit the floor at once and didn't rise up again. Zee's emotions stabilised and I felt the strange darkness dissipate.

"Thank you" Zee said softly.

Dad put his arms around me and pulled us all in together for a hug, and then he flashed me,

Son, she must be protected

What? I flashed back as I eyed the side of his face.

Together you will be the most powerful Weres in history. You must make sure her pain and fear do not overcome her or else they will take hold of you as well

I won't let that happen, Dad

If you do, you will have the power to destroy us all

I understand

Dad let us go and looked at Mum, they were flashing now. Zelena looked around the room at the mess,

"Oh Roe, your library, I'm so sorry. I didn't mean to" she said with a sniff.

"I know, Darling, it's okay. It was quite the sight to see" Mum smiled, she was enjoying this.

"I can't wait to see what you can do when you learn to control it" Dad huffed.

"I can control when this happens?" Zee asked,

"Yes, you need training. Right away" Artemis spoke from across the room. I honestly forgot he was there.

"Okay, but for now can we keep my new abilities on the down low? I don't want to scare anyone else"

"You don't want the pack to know?" I questioned,

"Not right away, just let me get a handle on it first"

"I think that's reasonable" said Dad while picking up some books.

"I can clean this up, why don't you two go and relax. Maybe talk some things out?" Mum said, obviously trying to get us out of the room so that they could talk.

"No, I made this mess, I'll clean it up" Zelena argued,

"Oh nonsense, it was just an accident, go on now".

I grabbed Zee's hand and started walking her to the door,

"Tomorrow, my Goddess" Artemis called,

"Tomorrow, you come? We train"

"Okay, sure" she answered slowly.

We went upstairs and back to the bedroom to talk it out some more. Afterwards, I sat on the bed next to her and held onto her hand. I still can't believe this is all happening. Mum told us stories about the daughter of the moon and the she-wolves with powers when I was a kid. But of course, back then, I just thought they were stories to make us feel good. I don't like this plan, of going to that human scum for answers. I mean there's no way he'll cooperate anyway. The guy is an absolute monster, why would he tell us anything. Unless we torture him a little bit first. Maybe I can get on board with this plan after all. I could get a little payback for all the horrendous things he did to Zelena, and I can get Zee her answers.

"I'll go sort it out with Dad" I said standing up and walking for the door. Zee jumped up onto my back, like an adorable Koala bear, and kissed my cheek.

"It'll be okay, you'll see" she whispered.

Fuck I love her, the power she is emanating makes it hard to resist. At least I can now recognise it as power, pure power, and not just pure animalistic need and lust that has me so magnetised toward her. I wanted to stay there and rip her clothes off again, I hungered for the taste of her lips. But I need to make plans with Dad before I let this anger go. I half smiled and kissed her quickly before getting too caught up in those lips. I took her arms from around my neck and put her back on the floor and walked out the door, closing it behind me. I took a deep breath and leaned my head against the door. I thought this uncontrollable lust was meant to ease off after sealing the bond. That has clearly not been the case here. I shook my head clear and then headed downstairs. Mum and Dad were still tidying up the library, but Artemis had already left. They had piled the books up on the floor and the broken shelves were gone.

"Are you both alright?" I asked walking into the room. They both turned and looked at me at the same time.

"Yes, we're okay" Dad grumbled,

"Were you affected?" he asked,

"What do you mean? Like, by her powers?" I questioned,

"Yes, did you feel them" Mum asked urgently,

"I don't know, it was a weird feeling".

Mum rushed forward and grabbed my hand, pulling me down on the couch to sit next to her.

"Gunner, she has Gravitokinesis. Do you know what that can mean?" Mum asked leaning towards me.

"Ah... she can make things fly around the room" I said sarcastically, gesturing to the ample amount of debris.

"No son, if she can access the full extent of gravity, then her powers are almost limitless" said Dad with a very serious frown.

"Is that a bad thing?"

"No, Baby, but it is very dangerous. With your True Mate bond heightening her emotions and the unpredictability of these powers, she will either lead the entire Were species into a new age of greatness or she could wipe us all out completely. Did you feel anything when she was accessing her powers?" Mum said seriously.

"Uh, I don't know what I felt. I felt heavy, like I was being pulled into the ground, but my head was like flying into the air. When I held her, I just felt lost, like I was stumbling in the dark"
They looked at each other with raised eyebrows.
"What?" I demanded with a grunt.
"We talked it over with Artemis and have all agreed that because of your True Mate bond, and your ability to share your powers with each other, it is very possible that you too will be able to access the powers of the Goddess" Mum said sternly,
"Wait seriously?"
"We aren't sure, there has never been a male Triple Goddess as the powers are only passed from mother to daughter. But because you aren't inheriting them it means you're not a God or Goddess and could instead access them through your True Mate bond. However, if you use the power, you may offend the Moon Goddess causing her to retaliate against you" Mum continued,
"Couldn't that hurt Zee? If I use her power, will it weaken her like sharing my healing strength did to me? Would the Moon Goddess retaliate against only me, or her as well?"
"I can't answer these questions, Gunner. There has never been anything like this recorded in our history. A True Mate bond is rare enough on its own, but adding a Triple Goddess to the mix is just unheard of" Mum answered with a wave of her hands.
This was the first time I had ever heard my mother sound so unsure. She knows everything about Were-kind and the legends of our species. To hear her speak with uncertainty was nerve-racking.
Everything has changed so fast, I really haven't had a moment to take it all in and think about it. There have been some weird feelings, like sudden surges of emotions. Her control over her wolf and the speed at which she is learning is unusual. But there was nothing to indicate that Zee had powers. Last night's sexual marathon was definitely not what I was expecting. I've only slept with someone once before, and it didn't feel anything like what I have with Zelena. With Zee, it's almost animalistic, there's an urge and an unrelenting desire to always be near her and to touch her. With Zoe, it was uncomfortable and forced and just felt unnatural. Is that the bond, or the powers, or is it just love? I have this constant nagging feeling of fear. With this new revelation comes an unending list of threats and dangers.

"What are we going to do now?" I asked with a heavy breath,
"Do about what, Darling?" replied Mum,
"About Zee and her new status, we can't keep her hidden from the pack forever, they deserve to know"
"I agree, they deserve to know, in time. But, this is Zelena's choice. She has to be the one to decide when they find out" Mum said soothingly.
"But what about after that? You know that this news won't stay here, it will travel worldwide. When the other packs find out, and they will, they'll come for her and not all of them will be friendly"
"They can try" growled Dad.
"You will help then, help me protect her?"
Mum pulled me into her arms and squeezed me tight.
"You don't even have to question it, Gunner, Baby" she squeaked. My mother pulled back and cupped one of my cheeks,
"Zelena is a Triple Goddess, yes. But more importantly, she is your True Mate, and she belongs here with you, the pack will fight for her if need be" Mum said firmly. Dad nodded along, placing his hand on my shoulder.
"Okay good" I said pulling myself from my mother's arms,
"Dad, I need your help" I announced, standing up and turning to face him.
"With what?" he asked, slowly standing also.
"We need to get Zee's father and take him to the cabin. If he knows anything more about Zelena and her mother, then we are going to find out what".
"You're sure?"
"Definitely" I answered with a strong nod.
Dad stood up a little taller, straightening his back and squaring his shoulders. He nodded his head in agreement, with a deep grunt.
"Okay, well I'm going to go and get dinner started, you two can talk business" Mum said softly as she stood up and headed for the door.
"We will take Spartan and Cole with us" Dad announced. Even though I had already assumed as much. They are Beta and future Beta after all.
"What about Smith?" I questioned,
"He will stay and watch over the girls in the house. Mazz and Julian will guard the pack"

"Do we need the extra guards?"
"We don't know anything about this man and how he came to raise the Triple Goddess, but it can't just be an accident".
I hadn't thought of that before. Why was a human raising a Were? And not just any Were, the Triple Goddess. Dad's right, it's not just a coincidence, there's more going on here.
"Okay, I agree. When?" I stated,
"As soon as possible, it's like you said, we can't contain this for long and we need all the information we can get"
"Well, tomorrow then, while Zee is training with Artemis. From what I understand, he doesn't have a job, so he'll probably be at the house"
"Okay. Call Cole and Smith, tell them to come to the hall".
Dad sat back in his chair and closed his eyes, he was flashing with Spartan, Mazz, and Julian. I flashed Cole and Smith,
Cole, Smith, I need you to come to the house immediately
Dad just told me, we're on the way
I'm in the forest, I'll be there in a minute, I have to change back
Why are you wolfing?
I needed to get away from my mum, she's extra clingy today
We'll be in the hall
Gotcha
Okay
Dad opened his eyes and looked at me, I nodded my head and we both got up and walked to the hall at the back of the house. The hall is where Dad does his pack meetings. There's a big round table with the pack symbol on it and ten chairs around it. On the back wall is an old map of Cape Breton Island with our territory marked out. I took the most recent town map from the shelf and laid it out on the table. Spartan and Cole walked in together and stood on either side of my father and me. Cole was eyeing me cautiously.
What's going on?
Just wait for the others, Dad and I will explain
Mazz and Julian came in, nodded to my father, and stood on the other side of the table.
"Okay, let's get going" Dad bellowed,
"Just waiting for Smith" I said quickly.
Dad looked at me and frowned.
"Where is he?" he grumbled,

"He was out running, he won't be long" I told him.

Smith, where are you?

I'm outside, I can't change back

Don't worry about it, just come in

Okay

Smith walked through the door in his wolf form, Dad and Spartan looked at him and frowned. Not being able to control your wolf is a sign of weakness. It ties into your emotions, which is why getting angry can trigger a change. Being scared or sad can bring out your protective nature, and your body will always stay in its strongest form when it feels unsafe. Smith has always had trouble with his change, I think it goes back to what happened to his father, hence the wolf currently inside the house.

"He said he's sorry, he couldn't change back fast enough" I told them.

"Okay, before we start, I need you all to understand that this is a very sensitive matter and needs to be handled discreetly and quickly. Gunner, do you want to continue?" Dad said looking at me.

He's never let me lead a meeting before, even if it is just with a couple of us. Was he testing me or is he letting me take the lead because it's involving Zee? I stood up straight and cleared my throat.

"We are making plans to capture a human. We need to take him to the cabin for questioning" I offered the small group,

"What human?" Spartan asked without hesitation,

"Zelena's father" I answered him,

"And why should we care about him, if he is just a human?" he grumbled in response,

"He is, but he may have certain information that we need"

"What kind of information?" Mazz interjected. I looked around the room at the waiting faces, I don't know how they are going to believe this without proof. It's a far fetch, I know that. Dad nudged me gently and nodded his head for me to go on.

"He may have critical information about Zelena, her mother, and their ancestry" I continued,

"Mate, I know she's your True Mate now, and you want to look out for her, but how is this critical?" Cole asked confused.

"Don't we have more important things to do than kidnap humans?" spat Mazz.

Dad growled deeply and everyone in the room went silent and bowed their heads.

"Carry on Son" he said to me, using his firm and authoritative voice,

"Zelena has the mark of the Triple Goddess and has started displaying gravitational powers" I blurted out in one breath.

They all stood silently and stared at me with blank expressions. Then all at once, the room erupted into shouting and laughing.

"Is this a fucking joke?" laughed Julian,

"You summoned me here to talk about fucking fairy tales?" Spartan yelled,

"SILENCE!" Dad screamed, his voice shook the room and filled it with a heavy energy. They all stopped and looked at him sheepishly.

"See for yourself" he said angrily.

Dad closed his eyes, I think he is flashing them pictures of the library. I flashed Cole and Smith, the image of the table floating and the books flying around the room. Spartan looked across at me wide eyed, and Mazz stumbled on his feet, clutching the table for support.

"This can't be" Julian whispered.

"Artemis has confirmed it. Gunner, myself, and your Luna have witnessed. She is the chosen daughter of the Goddess and her powers are already very strong" Dad spoke firmly, standing above the pack members.

I fucking knew she was wicked

Smith flashed as he jumped in a little circle and shook his wolf head.

"What does this mean for the pack?" Spartan demanded,

"It means the pack has been blessed by the Goddess herself. Not only will your Alpha-Son have a True Mate bond, but your future Luna will hold the powers of the Moon Goddess. This is a gift greater than any other" Dad spoke firmly, as if challenging the other members to question him.

"But Lupus, this news will bring threats from all across the globe, it could be dangerous for the pack, 'she' could be dangerous for the pack" Spartan interjected,

"She is part of the pack!" Dad said raising his voice and turning to Spartan,

"Well, maybe she shouldn't be!" Spartan shouted back.

Dad pushed his chest against Spartan, and Spartan did the same. They growled at each other not breaking eye contact. Spartan was challenging the decision of the Alpha. I stood beside my father and growled at Spartan, how dare he even subtly suggest that we exile Zee. Cole put his hand on his father's shoulder and tried to pull him back.

"Dad, enough" he begged. Spartan held my father's gaze as he growled but quickly snapped his head away and stopped his challenge.

"I'm sorry my Alpha, you are right, this is a blessing for the pack" Spartan grumbled, standing down and offering his hand to my father. They took each other's hands and quickly pressed their foreheads together, in a show of respect that we call Sevasmo.

Sorry mate, you know he's hot headed

I know Cole

We will protect her, I promise

I looked at Cole and nodded. Even though I know that he isn't exactly fond of Zee, he still has my back. I can trust him to put whatever animosity aside and look out for her. I can always count on him, no matter what.

"So, what's the plan then?" Mazz asked looking directly at me. Everyone in the room was looking at me to lead them now. I swallowed any hesitation and nodded. Alright, let's do this.

~

"Here's the house" I said and pointed at Zee's old house on the map. We'd been at it for a while now. I'd explained my wish to question the man in private. I wracked my memory, trying to remember all the smallest of details from the night I rescued her from that Goddess-awful place. But like a fool, I wasn't paying attention to that stuff. My one tracked mind was focused purely on Zelena and getting her out.

"According to Zelena, he doesn't work, so he should be home. We really don't know anything about this man. He could be just a useless human or he could be a trained fighter, he may even be a Were" Lupus offered,

"The night we found her, he didn't seem exactly surprised to see you change" Cole added,

"No, he didn't, so, he could very well be expecting us" I said cautiously,

"I saw no weapons in the basement, but he could be keeping them elsewhere".

"You're telling me we're going in blind" Julian huffed,

"Not all of us, no. Mazz and Julian, you'll stay behind to guard the pack. Only Spartan, Dad, Cole, and I will go"

"What about me" Smith asked from the corner, he had finally changed back to his human form.

"You need to stay close to Zee. She trusts you and if her training with Artemis goes wrong, you'll need to calm the situation until I can get back"

"Can do boss man" Smith nodded in agreement.

"We need him alive and conscious for questioning, so attack to disarm only. I don't want to be around this mongrel any longer than we have to be, so let's keep it quick and clean".

I looked around at the table as I spoke, and they were all nodding their heads.

"We meet at the fire pit at first light" I told them,

"Okay"

"Got it"

"Alright" they all mumbled back in agreement.

"Thank you, my brothers. We will see you tomorrow".

The senior pack members nodded and filtered out of the hall. Cole paused and patted my shoulder, then followed after his father.

"Smith, hold up" I commanded once everyone else had left the room,

Smith stood by the table and waited. My father stood in front of me and placed his hands on my shoulders.

"You did well my boy, I'm proud of you" he smiled and tapped my cheek and then left. I turned to face Smith.

"I'm trusting you with this Smith" I said sternly

"I know mate, I won't let you down"

"She has taken a liking to you and she truly does trust you, but she has no control over her powers. This could go south"

"Gunner, I'll look out for her, you have my word"

"Keep in contact at all times"

"Of course, my brother".

I pulled him in for a quick hug and then we left the hall together. Okay, tomorrow it's on.

Chapter Eighteen

Gunner

I walked through the bedroom door, closing it behind me. Zee was sitting on the armchair under the window with the pack history book on her lap. She looked up at me and smiled.

"Hey beautiful" I said laying on the bed.

"You were gone a while" she said softly.

"Sorry, just making arrangements"

"Are you going to like, I dunno, just go and pick him up?"

"It may not be that simple, Zee"

"Why not?"

"What if he fights back? Or what if he is a Were? There's a lot we have to account for"

"Oh".

She bit her lip and looked back down at the book. She smelt a little anxious and sad. I rolled onto my side to watch her read.

"Found anything interesting?" I asked,

"A few things, I can't believe how far back this book goes. You have your entire history laid out right here in front of you. I don't even know my mother's name".

I stood up and took the book from her hands and placed it back on the shelf. I held out my hands for her and lifted her up out of the chair.

"What?" she groaned, drawing out the word.

I pulled her into my chest and held her, wrapping my arms around her and resting my head on hers.

"What's this for?" she mumbled,

"Nothing, I just wanted to hold you"

"Oh" she huffed,

"This is nice".

I held her there for a while slowly rocking back and forth. After a few minutes, Zee looked up at me,

"Gunner?"

"Yes, little wolf" I smiled at her,

"I never got to eat that sandwich"

"Huh?"

"I'm really hungry"

"Okay" I chuckled,

"Let's go eat".

We headed down to the kitchen and I could already smell Mum's cooking from the foyer. I walked in the kitchen door with Zee behind me. Mum had pots on the stove and different food spread across the benchtop. She turned to smile at us as we came in.

"Mm... smells good Roe" Zee hummed licking her lips,

"Can I help you?"

"You don't have to do that, sweet girl" cooed Mum,

"Oh, I know, but I want to" Zee squeezed my hand and walked over to my mum. I sat down at the breakfast nook and watched them in the kitchen. Mum grabbed one of her aprons from the cupboard and put it over Zee's head. They giggled and chatted happily, moving about the kitchen together. Zelena was a natural cook and it looked like Mum really enjoyed having her there. Seeing them both so comfortable and happy together, put a smile on my face. She really does belong here, it just wouldn't feel the same without her now.

"Gunner, baby, call your sister and father in for dinner will you"

"Sure, Mum" I smiled and walked out of the kitchen. Nat was in the movie room, I could hear the TV from here. I poked my head in and saw her and Smith snuggled on the couch together.

"Hey, love birds, dinner's ready" I winked at Smith and then went in search of my father. He wasn't in the hall and wasn't outside. I eventually found him in the library, reading a big blue book. Dad isn't usually a big reader, so I was a bit surprised.

"Hey Dad" I called from the door,

"What's up son?" he said looking up at me,

"Dinner's ready"

"Thanks, buddy".

I stepped through the door and walked over to where he was sitting.

"What are you reading?" I asked eyeing the book. It was the same one that Mum had found earlier. He rubbed his brow and showed me the cover. Selena, the first daughter, it said.

"Just reading up on our newest pack member" he said looking up at me with a frown.

"Oh" I exclaimed and sat down beside him,

"You're not regretting accepting her in, are you?"

"Of course not son, I just want to be able to help and protect her the best I can. She isn't going anywhere Gunner" he said putting his hand around mine.

"Lupus" Mum yelled from the foyer.

"Come on kid, we better go" he said standing up and walking to the door. I looked at the book again before getting up and following him to the dining room. Everyone was already sitting around the table. Dad kissed Mum on the head before he sat down. I sat down next to Zelena and kissed her cheek.

"Smells good ladies" I cooed, giving Zee's hand a squeeze.

"I'd like to give thanks before we dig in" said Mum standing up. She motioned for us all to hold hands and then closed her eyes.

"Beautiful Goddess Selene, we give you our thanks for your love and your light. We thank you for blessing us with your chosen daughter Zelena. We promise to love, cherish, and protect her. From now until forever. In the Goddess we love"

"In the Goddess we love" we all chorused.

~

The sun was not far from rising. I lay on the bed and gazed at Zelena's naked silhouette lying beside me. In the time she has been here, she has put on a bit more weight. She was sickly thin before, but has thankfully started to get a little extra meat on her bones. Her skin has completely healed. Not a single scar is left, as impossible as that is. She smiles all the time and is constantly emitting this glow of happiness. I want desperately to run my tongue along her bare skin, but I can't wake her. I carefully slipped out of the bed without disturbing her. I slid on my jeans and grabbed my boots and a shirt. I stood over Zelena's body and very gently kissed her temple. She groaned and rolled over but didn't wake. I crept through the door and down the stairs. I took an apple from the kitchen counter and went out the front door. Cole and Spartan were already waiting for us.

"Gunner" Spartan nodded as I walked over with the apple in my mouth. I nodded back in acknowledgment. Mazz walked over and grumbled good morning. I looked over to Smith's cabin and saw him sitting on the front step. He waved as I caught his eye. Finally, Dad walked up to the fire pit and took Spartan's hand in greeting. "Okay, let's go catch us a human" Dad said rubbing his hands together. I looked back at the house that had my sleeping Mate inside, then over at Smith. A great wave of worry fell over me. Since first bringing her here, I've not left her for this long before. Nor have I gone this far away from her. Something about this plan doesn't feel right.

Go, Gunner, she'll be fine

I nodded at Smith and kicked off my boots. Spartan and Dad were already changed, and Cole was just pulling off his pants. I laid my clothes on a log and got down on my hands and knees. A quick snap and a jump forward and I was changed. Cole nudged me with his head and we ran to the tree line where Dad and Spartan were waiting.

Lead the way, son

My dad's large dark grey wolf stepped to the side to let me pass. He nipped at my hindquarters and we took off into the forest. We bounded through the trees with my dad staying close to my left flank, Spartan staying close to his left and Cole on my right. It's not often the Alpha gets involved in this sort of task, he usually sends fighters for this stuff. I suppose this isn't exactly a normal task though. I'm thankful for his help. It would have been so simple to just cast Zee out and keep the pack out of it. But not my dad, he is an incredible Alpha. I can only hope to one day be half the leader that he is.

We reached the tree line across from Zelena's house in minutes. I looked at my father to hear his first order but instead, he nodded at me, again insisting I take the lead.

Cole, scout around the rear of the house and check for visible dangers. Once you have confirmed that it's clear, hang back in case he tries to run. Spartan, follow him to the back and wait for my mark. When I say so, enter through the back door and make your way to the front of the house.

Dad and I will come in through the front door. Remember we need him alive and able to communicate.

Cole and Spartan nodded in unison and slinked away through the trees. We gave them a minute to take position and then I nodded to Dad. We slowly emerged from the tree line and trotted over to the front of the house. The sun had made its appearance and the morning sky was slowly starting to brighten in the daylight. We stalked slowly up the wooden porch steps and stood by the front door.

I focused my ears to the sounds inside the house. A tap was dripping into a sink and the TV was playing the news, among that noise I could make out the grunts of a snoring man.

Ready?

All clear here

In position

Go now. I commanded.

I put my head down and barged into the door, it easily came off the hinges. It's probably still damaged from my last abrupt entrance into this house. The smell was horrible, mouldy food and alcohol mixed with stale body odour. I took a few steps through the door and turned to the room on my left, I was greeted right away by a baseball bat smashing into my face. I stumbled back and winced at the pain to my snout. I guess he was expecting us after all. Dad's angry roar echoed through the house as he grabbed the wooden bat from Hank's grip and snapped it between his teeth. Hank ran from the room, passing my father, but was blocked by Spartan, his enormous brown and grey wolf stood by the basement door with his teeth bared, growling ferociously. Hank began to step back away from Spartan but was stopped by the chest of my father. He growled lowly and huffed at the worthless meat bag. The power and authority rolling off my father's wolf was enough to make any lesser wolf submit, for a human though, it would be a very unnerving feeling.

Hank froze in his place looking around at the three giant wolves surrounding him.

"Fuck" he breathed, seeming to accept his capture.

The short grubby man wore a faded navy singlet that was covered in holes and stains. His brown greasy hair sat in messy curls atop his head. His face was chubby and covered in a nervous sweat. He looked nothing like my beautiful Zelena. How could someone so grotesque raise a Goddess like her? I snapped my head to the side and changed back to human form. Hank looked at me and his eyes widened in terror,

"You!" he exclaimed.

"Me" I mocked wiping the blood from my nose and stepping toward him,

"So then, which one of you is my darling daughter?" he chuckled looking between Dad and Spartan. So, he did know that Zee is a Were, though clearly not what her wolf looked like. He was trying to keep it cool, but the stench of his fear was pouring out of him. Seeing his smug face and being in this house, plus the hit he got to my nose, it drew all my anger to the surface.

"Now" I snickered. I was standing in front of him now, so I grabbed his shirt and pulled him close to me,

"You and me are going to have a little chat". With that, I readied myself and snapped my head forward. I smashed the hardest part of my forehead to the bridge of his nose. The satisfying crunch of his breaking nose brought a smile to my face. Hank fell back out of my grip, landing at Spartan's legs. Dad growled softly but kept his stance.

Ha! Got him

Spartan flashed, kicking Hank away from his paws.

"You broke my fucking nose" he cried out grasping at his face. I took a slow step toward him, grabbed his scraggly hair, and lifted him to his feet.

"If you cooperate, then that is all I will break" I hissed at him. Hank's face twisted into a crooked smile, he then spat his blood over my face and cackled.

"Good luck" he laughed spitting out more blood. Dad stepped around me in his human form and grabbed Hank by the shoulders. With one swift movement, he snapped his head forward, headbutting Hank. Dad let him go and his body fell to the floor like a sack of potatoes, knocked out cold.

"We didn't come to play with the fucking man" he growled, throwing me a t-shirt that was hanging on a chair.

"Clean yourself off" he grumbled. He then turned to Spartan and pointed at Hank on the floor,

"Spartan, pick that bag of dicks up, and let's go" he said stomping out of the house. I wiped the blood off my face and threw the shirt on the ground. Spartan was now in his human form and pulled on a pair of shorts that he picked up from the ground. He easily lifted Hank up and threw him over his shoulder. I got down on my knee and snapped my head back and changed into my wolf again.

I followed Spartan out the front door, Cole and Dad's wolves were waiting for us by the tree line. We kept a decent pace through the forest towards the cabin. I'm so damn mad at myself for losing my temper like that, it's not what we planned. I just kept remembering the picture Zee showed me of her beaten body chained to the floor.

I'm sorry fellas

It's all good mate, if you didn't hit him I would have. Cole huffed with a nod of his head.

Thanks, brother

You let your temper get the better of you

I know Dad

Will it happen again?

No sir

We made it to the cabin in good time, it was not yet midday and Hank was still out cold. Dad really knocked him good. Spartan threw Hank on the ground and went inside, emerging again with a handful of shorts. Dad, Cole and I all changed back and pulled on the shorts Spartan threw us. Dad grabbed Hank by the ankle and dragged him into the cabin. Cole and I followed and we all made our way to the underground cell.

The cell is like an old basement that was re-engineered a little. The walls are covered in sheets of thick iron and the floor is concrete. There's a sink and toilet in one corner and a small metal bedframe with a dirty mattress in the other. No windows, and only one door, which was secured with round metal bars. It doesn't get used much, mainly for roaming Omegas that cause drama. Maybe the occasional feral as well.

We put Hank on a steel chair and chained his arms and legs down. I got a bowl of water from the sink and threw it over him. He coughed and lifted his head and looked around the room.

"What the flipping fuck?" he groaned, spitting out some of the water.

"Are you Hank?" Dad's loud and commanding voice caught his attention.

"Some say that" Hank replied

"Are you, or are you not Hank?" Dad asked again, hiding his irritation.

"Yeah, sure I'm Hank"

"You know of our kind?"

Hank huffed and spat on the floor and glowered at my dad.

"I'd say that's a yes" Spartan said quietly.

"Yeah, I know about you filthy mutts" he growled. Spartan stepped forward and growled, my father lifted his arm to stop him.

"You are clearly not a Were"

"Of course I'm fucking not, I'd die before becoming one of you parasites"

"That can be arranged" I muttered quietly.

"So, how then, did you come to raise a wolf?"

"A wolf? You mean Zelena that snivelling little whore?"

A sudden rage burned through my veins at the sound of his words. I stepped toward him ready to rip his throat out. But my dad beat me to it and hit Hank across the face with the back of his hand. One of his teeth flew out of his mouth and slid across the floor.

"You fucking dog" Hank spat with blood dripping down his chin.

"You do not speak of the girl again, understood?"

"Fuck you!" he screamed and tried to break free of his chair.

Dad hit him again on the other side of his face, this time tipping the chair over, Hank along with it. Dad motioned for Spartan to pick the chair back up.

"I'll fucking kill you, you worthless dog" he yelled shaking and fighting against the restraints.

"Not yet you won't, first you will answer my questions" Dad's voice remained calm and steady.

"I'm not telling you shit" Hank yelled.

"Is Zelena your daughter?" Dad asked, ignoring the yelling and cursing or the stupid idiot,

"Fuck! You!" Was his answer.

Dad nodded at Spartan and he stepped forward, punching Hank in the stomach. He coughed and spluttered and gasped for air.

"It doesn't have to go this way, you just have to answer some questions and then you can go home". Dad spoke softly as he grabbed a chair, placed it in front of Hank, and then sat down.

After a few moments of wheezing from Hank, and silent staring from Dad, he finally spoke,

"So, are you ready to talk?" Dad asked tilting his head to the side.

"How do I know you won't just kill me afterwards?"

"Fucking coward" Spartan hissed. Dad raised his hand to silence him but did not turn his gaze from Hank.

"I give you my word as Alpha, I will not kill you".

I growled at my father, why would he make such a promise to this worm? Hank looked at me and smirked, knowing all too well that's not what I wanted.

"Yeah, alright, I'll answer some questions" he said with a devilish grin.

"Is Zelena your daughter?"

"No" he said bluntly, turning his gaze back to my father.

"Where is her father?"

"Dead"

"Why is he dead?"

"Because I killed him" he said proudly. A growl escaped my mouth and the hot rage set back in.

"Why?" Dad asked sternly. Hank looked back at me and chuckled.

"Because that's what I do" he paused before looking at my dad and whispering.

"I'm a hunter".

Cole and Spartan growled and bared their teeth, stepping toward Hank in attack positions. Dad stood and held them both back.

Not yet my brothers, not yet

He's a hunter, he needs to die

Soon, we still need more information

Cole's mother was killed by hunters when we were five. Along with Smith's Dad. The fighters of the pack tore the clan of hunters to pieces, but not before they killed eight of us. One of which was Cole's mother. After that, he swore to kill every hunter he came across. In the region that we're in, being so isolated and a somewhat reclusive pack, we thankfully don't cross paths with hunters often.

Hank was screaming to Dad's back, taunting them with his words.

"If I had known you mongrels still lived in these parts, I would have hunted you down years ago" he yelled manically.

While Dad was distracted, I lunged forward and with all my strength, landed a punch to Hank's eye. The chair tipped over and

Hank was out cold. They all turned to look at me and Cole burst out laughing.

"Gunner" Dad growled with annoyance,

"What? I didn't kill him".

If he isn't Zee's father, then why was she with him? And he's a hunter, if he knew or even thought that she was a Were, why wouldn't he just kill her? When has a hunter even shown mercy to a wolf? What would he have to gain by raising her?

We stood and waited for a few minutes for Hank to come too again. I got another bowl of water and threw it on him. Nothing. Dad tapped on his cheek a bit while I got more water. The skin below his eye was split and bleeding, and his eye socket was swelling fast. Payback is such sweet candy. He started to moan and groan as he was waking up.

"You little fucking prick" he mumbled. Cole and Spartan chuckled quietly.

"Why did you have Zelena?" I yelled,

"Because I took her" Hank said groggily.

"Why would you keep her?"

"They told me to".

He's working with other hunters

He said they

"Who are they?" Dad demanded,

Hank let his head fall back and laughed a little,

"They're coming for you, they're coming for your little wolf bitch" he chuckled in a sing song tone. My skin burned with a thousand hot needles, I felt like my head was on fire. My wolf took control and my eyes blacked over. I raged out.

"WHO ARE THEY!?" I yelled rushing in for another punch to the face. My fist only just connected with his jaw, as Dad grabbed me around the waist, pulling me back. He lifted me off my feet and pushed me toward the door of the cell.

Get him out of here

Dad flashed. Cole grabbed my arms and kept pulling me up the stairs.

"I'll fucking kill you, you psycho cunt" I screamed down the staircase. I could hear Hank laughing behind me. Cole got me outside and shoved me hard away from the cabin door.

"Take a breath Gunner" he said calmly. I tried to rush past him back into the cabin but he caught me. I screamed in frustration and turned to punch the closest thing to me, it was a tree. The bark splintered and the tree creaked at the force of my fist. I hit it again with my other fist, then again. I screamed as I punched the tree, again and again until it cracked from the repeated force and fell to the ground with an echoing thud.

"Feel better?" Cole joked,

"Don't laugh, you heard him, there's more coming" I snarled as I put my bleeding hands on my head. I turned to face Cole, whose face was now void of any amusement.

"Yes, I heard him. I heard him say that he's a hunter" Cole snapped angrily. I looked down at my bleeding fists and watched the skin stitch back together. I huffed a long breath and looked back up to my best friend.

"There's hunters involved. This isn't just about Zelena anymore" Cole said with low and deadly voice. His face was full of hurt and anger. Having a hunter so close must be torturous for him. I walked to him in four quick steps and pulled him into my arms.

"I'm sorry brother" I whispered.

I squeezed him tight and he hugged me back. He patted my back and we both took a deep breath, the fury slowly simmering back down.

"So, let's evaluate everything so far" Cole said pulling himself from my arms. I nodded in agreement.

"He was given orders to take her, but not to kill her. Plus, he knew she is a Were" Cole spoke slowly, thinking about the words he was saying.

"Could that be why he was beating her? To bring on the birth of her wolf" Cole asked.

"Do you think maybe he knew she was special?" I asked him, ignoring his last question. I still can't bear to think about that monster touching her.

"He knew of her line" Dad said walking out the door and coming over to us while wiping blood off his hands.

"Huh?" I questioned looking at him intently,

"He knew that she's descended from Selena, but he doesn't know she is the Triple Goddess"

"He said that?" I snapped,

"Not in so many words" Dad smirked.

I growled and went to go back into the cabin. I'm going to kill this worthless heap of crap. Dad grabbed me before I could go past him,

"He has nothing more that he can tell us" Dad said sternly,

"I'm going to test that theory" I growled and tried to shake out of his hold.

"Gunner, enough" he growled back. I stepped back and curled my hands into fists, I lifted my chin and screamed.

"Fuck!" I shouted into the air.

I turned away from my father and ran my fingers through my hair. I think Zee is in more danger than I first thought. If hunters know about her line and they kidnapped her because of it, then they must know of her power and possibilities. If they are coming, it won't just be a couple of hunters. It will be a whole fucking army.

"Son?" Dad said softly,

"Yeah?" I answered turning to look at him.

"He uh… he wants to talk to her"

"Are we sure that's a good idea?" questioned Cole.

I know that she wants to talk to him herself, she said as much. But that was when she still thought he was her father. Now though, with the light of this new information, I'm not sure. Can I really keep her from him though? Is that fair? She deserves to ask her own questions. Perhaps I'm being selfish in wanting to keep her from this revelation. I sighed to myself and flashed Smith.

Smith?

Yeah boss man

How is she?

She's actually really fucking great

I growled with jealousy seeping into me. The growl sounded through the link to Smith.

I mean her training is really great. Gunner, she's a natural

He wants to see her

Oh?

Do you think she can handle it?

I think you need to give her a little more credit man

I looked at Cole, who was listening to our flash. He nodded, agreeing with Smith. I snarled at myself. I fucking hate this plan.

Okay then, bring her to the cabin

Alright

And Smith
Yeah?
Try and prepare her a little
For what?
This isn't what she's expecting
Okay?
It's not good, it's going to hurt her
We got her man, she'll be alright
I turned to tell my dad, but he was now whispering with Spartan.
I tilted my head at them curiously,
"What?" I questioned,
"It can wait, Son. Is Zelena coming?"
"Yes. Smith is bringing her in" I answered.

Chapter Nineteen

Zelena

I reached my arm behind me but there was nothing there. I pushed myself up and looked at the other side of the bed, no Gunner. The slit in the curtains revealed the sun was only just starting to light the sky. Gunner was gone already, gone to get my father. The thought sent a lump to my throat and a pain in my stomach. Oh god, my father. I slumped my face back into the pillow and groaned loudly. I really hope he can tell us something about my mum or about me. Any info on this Goddess thing will be accepted.

Wait, I flew up on the bed. Training with Artemis today. Why am I excited by that? I mean it could turn out to be the one thing in my life that I can actually control, right? Considering my hormones, my species, my unknown past, and basically my entire future are all out of my control. I could maybe have just this one thing.

I sat up on the bed and swung my legs over the side. As I let my legs hang there, I closed my eyes and listened to my body. It felt tired and weak, another night of sexapades with Gunner had taken its toll. But I just can't help myself around him, his body is too seductive. Everything about him is irresistible to me. From the way he smells to the way my skin prickles when he touches me. My body aches for him when he's not around and my mind is clouded by constant visions of him. A small hot throb sounded in my core as I pictured Gunner in my head.

I'm not going to shower this morning, I want to be able to smell him on my skin all day. The idea of his essence on my skin, an intimate kind of marking, the thought alone made my clit pulse. I held my hand to my forehead, I was making myself all hot and bothered getting lost in my horny thoughts.

I pulled on a pair of jeans and a navy blue top that clung just a little too tight for my liking. I've put on a little extra weight from Gunner and Roe constantly overfeeding me. I have a bit more of a curve to my hips now and my breasts were filling out a little. I like it. I look more like a girl and less like a pre-pubescent boy.

I slipped on my boots and made my way down to the kitchen for breakfast. As I walked through the door, I got a nose full of bacon and my mouth began to salivate immediately.

"Good morning my sweet girl" Roe cooed, as I sauntered over.

"Good morning" I smiled at her as I reached for the tray of bacon and pulled it close to me. She turned around and leaned against the counter, watching me intently.

"Big day for you, love" she said softly,

"Mhm" I hummed with a mouth full of bacon.

"Are you nervous, about training your gifts?"

I shook my head and tried to speak but a piece of bacon fell out of my mouth, Roe laughed. I swallowed my food and smiled at her.

"No, I'm not nervous. Actually, a little excited" I said with a little bit too much cheer in my tone.

"Well, good. Just take it easy sweet thing, don't push yourself",

"I won't, promise".

Roe stepped forward and cupped my cheek. She looked at me adoringly, the kind of way I imagine a mother would look upon her daughter. It sent a warm feeling spreading through my body, I felt loved. I smiled fondly at her for a moment and then looked away, growing a little uncomfortable with the prolonged show of affection.

"Well, I'm off" I said standing up,

"Okay, Darling, be careful" Roe cooed as she turned back to the sink.

I headed out the front door and down the porch steps. The morning air was still fresh but was warming up quickly. A few pack members were wandering around the village, they nodded and smiled and greeted me as I passed them. Artemis lived in a small wooded cabin at the very far corner of the clearing, away from the rest of the pack. His cabin was shaded by a large tree and had vines crawling up the walls, bright wildflowers grew at the front. Depending on the way you look at it, it could either be a magical cabin lost in the woods or a haunted witch's home. As I stood staring at the little wooden house my nerves started to grow and butterflies took up flight in my stomach. I heard a snapping twig behind me. I whipped around and found Smith with his hands up in surrender.

"Hey, Killer, it's just me" he chuckled,

"Hey Smith" I breathed out with a half-smile,

"You scared me".

"Aw, I'm not that ugly, am I?" he said with an over exaggerated pout. I giggled softly and a blush burned across my cheeks. He knows all too well that he is stunning. He stood up a little taller and he pushed his chest out slightly at my reaction.

"Well, let's see what you're made of" he chuffed as he walked to the door of the cabin and knocked loudly.

"Come in" Artemis called out. Smith pushed the door open and motioned for me to go in. I hesitated for a second but walked through the door with Smith closing it behind me. It was dark inside and smelled of moss and wet leaves. The walls were covered with flowers and what looked like herbs. There were a lot of small plants scattered around the floor. Artemis stood before me and bowed holding his hand out in front of him.

"My Goddess" he whispered. Smith looked at me with his eyes wide and mouth pulled down. I forgot he hadn't seen this kind of reaction to my presence yet. I shrugged and shook my head, indicating for him to ignore it.

"Hi Artemis, shall we get started?" I said uncomfortably.

"Yes, my Goddess" he turned around and stood up straight a walked to a rug laid in the middle of the floor. He motioned me over and sat down on a pillow crossing his legs, I followed his lead, taking a place on a pillow opposite him. Between us sat a large silver bowl. I looked around the cabin again, noticing small statues of heavenly bodies and wooden wolf carvings. Some looked kind of old and tribal, others looked beautiful, almost regal.

"My Goddess?". Artemis snapped me back to attention and I scrunched up my nose at the name he insisted on calling me.

"Please, could you call me Zelena?".

He pursed his lip into a straight line and his eyebrows frowned together.

"Or not, that's fine" I quickly rushed out and his face relaxed slightly. He stared at me blankly, not saying a word. I burned under his intense gaze, like he was trying to see into my soul. I small sweat broke out on my brow.

"Sooo, what now?" I said slowly trying to break the silence.

"First close eyes and relax, take big breaths" I did as I was told closing my eyes and breathing deeply. But the relaxing part was hard, I could still feel his eyes on me.

"Relax now" Artemis snapped. I opened one eye and glared at him.

"I'm not going to relax with you snapping at me" I said coldly, he was visibly embarrassed and turned his eyes away from me. I took a few deep breaths and kind of let my body relax, like I was melting into the floor.

"Good" Artemis whispered,

"Now you listen to me, only my sound. Keep big breaths and think of moon".

I pictured the moon in my mind, its shape and colour. I saw its pale shape sitting in the clear blue sky during the daylight. Then I pictured the moon in the night sky, surrounded by stars. I saw the light that it brings and could feel the glow on my skin. A flush of light air blew over my body, I felt weightless and peaceful.

Feeling completely relaxed I sat waiting for Artemis to tell me what to do next, but he was silent. I opened one of my eyes but he was no longer in front of me. I opened my other eye and immediately noticed that I was no longer sitting in front of Artemis, I was now floating above him. He and Smith were staring at me, gobsmacked. All I could do was blurt out a shocked laugh and I fell to the floor, landing hard on my hip. I turned to Smith ecstatic and proud.

"Did you see that?" I screeched at him,
"Pretty hard not to see it" he said with raised eyebrows. He lifted an arm to brush his fingers through his hair, all the while staring right at me. The intensity of his gaze made me feel warm with embarrassment. I turned back to Artemis with a huge grin.
"What's next?".
He breathed heavily as he stared at me, quickly shaking his head to focus again. He reached behind him and placed a rock in the bowl.
"You lift rock".
"Ah okay, I lift the rock" I paused,
"How do I lift the rock?".
"What did you think before? When you float".
"I was thinking about the moon, and the way its light glowed in the night sky",
"Okay, then think of moon. Moon is mother, she guide you".
I looked down at the rock and focused on it the best I could. I thought about what the rock would feel like in my hand, if it was cold to touch or warm. Then I started I wondered if this rock were like the rocks on the moon, would they be similar in any way?
The rock slowly began to lift out of the bowl, rotating in mid-air. My excitement grew as I watched the rock rise. A smile took over my face and my heart began to race. The rock started to spin faster until it suddenly flew upwards breaking through the roof of the cabin and off into the sky.
"What the?" I stuttered as I looked at the small hole that the rock created. I looked back at Artemis with an apologetic smile. He was staring at me intently, taking in my face and studying my expression.
"S-sorry" I mumbled.
"You let feeling take over, rock fly away. You stay balance and calm, rock obey" he said firmly, not taking his eyes off me. His accent was at times hard to understand but his point always managed to get across.
"Again" Artemis said placing another rock in front of me. This rock was small and round with a greyish white colour. It instantly

reminded me of the moon. The rock lifted out of the bowl easily as I looked it over. Twirling in the air it moved closer to my face, as I moved my eyes slowly around the room, the little white rock followed. As I felt my excitement grow, the little rock jerked a bit. I breathed deeply and relaxed my mind and the rock continued to glide through the air smoothly. Without thinking about it I lifted my hand out in front of me and the rock slowly came to rest in the palm of my hand. I looked up at Artemis again and this time his expression had changed. His face had softened and I could tell he was trying to suppress a smile.

"Very good my Goddess, you have this" he lifted his hands to his head and then shot it around in front of him,

"You move with mind".

"Telekinesis" Smith chimed in from behind me. I had forgotten he was there, I didn't know he could go this long without talking.

"Yes" Artemis nodded.

"But I thought my powers were related to gravity?" I questioned tilting my head to the side.

"Yes, that too, you use two together".

"I have two powers?"

"Yes Goddess, maybe more, don't know yet".

"We think she has the Dragon's Eye as well" Smith chimed in again.

"Drakos-Mati" Artemis asked, moving his eyes to Smith. Smith nodded his confirmation.

"Very good, very strong and very power, lots of power" Artemis nodded, struggling through his broken English.

I sat up a little straighter, maybe a little too excited by this revelation. Two powers, maybe three, that we know of. This is kind of amazing, I never would have imagined my life going down this path. I slipped the little white rock into my back pocket, I want to keep it as a memento.

"I have questions" I announced to Artemis, putting my hands on my crossed knees.

"Yes, my Goddess" he replied with a nod of his head.

"Can I only use my powers on small things, or could I lift a car if I wanted to?"

"You train you get strong, how strong, I don't know" he said with a shrug of his shoulders.

"I used the Dragon power in wolf form, does that mean that I can use my other powers in wolf form too?"

"This maybe".

I looked down and my hands, scared to know the answer to my next question. I shifted my body uncomfortably in my seated position and eyed Artemis again.

"Am, am I dangerous?" I asked slowly.

"Zee" Smith sighed behind me, shifting closer. When did anyone other than Gunner start calling me Zee? Though, I kind of like it.

"My Goddess" Artemis said, leaning a little closer and looking at me with a softer face,

"You strong and have big power. Danger come with emotion. Be calm, relax and stay control. Be sad or angry, maybe hurt on mistake".

I let his words resonate a bit as I swirled them around in my head. If I remain calm and not get too emotional, then I can keep control of my powers, but if lash out because of sadness, or anger, or fear, I could hurt someone, maybe kill someone. My mind instantly went back to what happened in the library. A pain stung in my chest at the realisation that I could have really hurt my new family. With the way my hormones have been behaving lately and the never-ending supply of new and unknown information, I don't like my chances of staying neutral. A tear slips out and slowly rolls down my cheek and I quickly wipe it away. No Emotions I tell myself.

"Okay, let's keep going" I said with a forced confidence. Sensing my anxiety and sadness Smith shuffled forward a little more.

"Zelena, you can take a break" he said placing his hand gently on my shoulder. The contact was welcomed and comforting. His skin on my skin sent a warm feeling through my body, making me lean into his touch. After the incident with Gunner and my hugging him, I didn't think he'd be game to even stand close to me anymore. I appreciate the risk he took in order to comfort me. I reached up and stroked his hand affectionately.

"It's okay I want to do this". I patted his hand before I cleared my throat and repositioned myself on the pillow. I looked to Artemis to continue and he nodded. Reaching behind him he pulled out a wooden stick, about fifty centimetres long and an inch thick, and placed it on the ground.

"With gravity power, you can make heavy or you can make lite, with this I want you to make too heavy for he to lift" Artemis pointed at the stick and then at Smith and I nodded slowly.

"Remember moon mother, her light help you".

I stared down at the stick and lifted it into the air, this power I think I've got the hang of. How to make it heavy though, I have no clue. I tried to think back to science class and our lessons on space and how gravity on each planet is different. I pictured the video of the astronaut jumping on the moon and how easy it was for him to leap. Then I pictured Jupiter and the fact that the gravitational field on Jupiter is stronger than any other planet. I felt a heaviness in my head and the stick dropped a little. I held onto that thought and focused in on it. The stick fell to the ground with a thud.

"Okay, try now" I said keeping my eyes on the stick. Smith stepped around me and bent over to pick up the stick but nearly fell over as he failed. He looked at me wide-eyed and grabbed the stick with both hands, grunting as he pulled at it hard. It lifted slightly off the ground before he let it go in a huff.

"Nah, fuck that" he panted. I smiled and chuckled at his red face, leaning forward I picked up the stick and waved it in his face. He frowned at me and I laughed loudly. Artemis twitched his lip, refraining from giving over to his smile. Smith sat back down scratching the back of his head. I'm feeling pretty pleased with myself, nothing in my life has ever been easy, but this whole 'powers' thing is working out nicely.

"One more, then you rest" Artemis said pointing at the large bowl. I lifted my eyebrow and looked at him with curiosity.

"You make small" he said bringing his hands together slowly like he was trying to burst a balloon. Okay make it small, how the heck do I make it small? I stared at the large bowl and tried to focus but I don't know where to start. The rest was easy, I just thought about the moon. But what does the moon have to do with making something small. I lifted the bowl off the floor and spun it around in the air but nothing else happened. Getting slightly frustrated I lifted my hand to my lap and clenched my fist. When I did that a small bend appeared on the bowl. I lifted my hands and outstretched them towards the bowl. Bringing my fingers in and twisting them around, the bowl started to follow suit. I pictured the bowl as a shining silver ball just like the moon in the sky. It twisted and turned in mid-air, folding, and compressing at the will of my fingers. I held out my hand and the now small apple sized silver ball came to rest in my palm. I glided my fingers over the perfectly smooth surface. I did it, I actually did it. I looked up from the shining ball to see Artemis with a tiny smile on his lips. Smith had come and sat on the floor beside me, his leg pressed to my leg. I huffed in amazement and stared at me, his eyes glittering in awe. "Wow" he exclaimed. The fact that he was impressed with me made me feel good. A sense of pride swept through me, heating me from the inside out. I tossed Smith the little ball with a smile, "For you" I said as he caught it in his lap. He held it up to examine it closely. His eyes glazed over slightly as he stared at it and then turned his head to me, not saying a word but also not really looking at me. After a minute he blinked a few times and stood up, holding his hand out for me.

"Come on" he said sternly. I grabbed his hand and he pulled me up. The skin of my hand where he touched me felt unusually hot.

"Come on where?" I asked,

"Gunner is calling for you" Smith answered, soundly a little frustrated, maybe, I couldn't tell.

"Why wouldn't he just flash me himself?"

"You can ask him that yourself".

"We're going to see him?"

"Yes, it's time to see your dad".

"Oh" the bottom of my stomach sank and I felt nauseous instantly. Still holding my hand, Smith went to pull me out the door. I quickly pulled my hand from his and knelt down in front of Artemis taking his hands in mine. He was shocked and clearly uncomfortable about my actions.

"Thank you, Artemis" I said softly. He squeezed my hands a little and nodded,

"Yes, my Goddess".

"Again tomorrow?" I asked hopefully,

"Yes tomorrow" he nodded again.

"Come on Zee" Smith said quietly nodding to Artemis and taking my hand again. We walked out of the cabin and the bright sunlight caught me off guard as I lifted my arm to block my eyes. Still holding my hand Smith began to lead me into the forest. I was a little confused by his hand holding mine. I thought other males were not allowed to touch me. Why was he so suddenly comfortable with this? His skin was burning against mine, it was such a strange sensation. I don't mind it though, it feels kind of nice, but he isn't Gunner so it doesn't feel right. I pulled my hand from his and he frowned a little. What is that for?

"Where are we going?" I asked trying to ease this weird tension.

"To the holding cabin, Gunner's waiting for you" he said without looking at me,

"It's a long walk, will be quicker if we run".

"Okay sure" I was about to start jogging when he grabbed my arm to stop me. Again, my skin burned at the contact.

"Not that kind of running" he smirked and pulled his shirt up over his head. I turned my eyes away surprised at his openness.

"Ah... wa-w-what are you doing?" I stuttered,

"I don't want to rip my clothes" he said pulling off his boots,

"You might want to do the same, that's if you want to have something to put on again when we get there".

I looked back at him and he now stood in nothing but his boxer briefs with his hands on his hips, staring directly at me. A breath got caught in my throat. I have only ever seen Gunner this naked before. Smith is seriously good looking and he was making no attempt to hide himself. A heat ran through my body and I felt a tingle in my legs and an ache in my lower abdomen. What the fuck is wrong with me right now? I love Gunner, so why would I be ogling another man? Something about Smith felt different though, he smelled different to me now, almost alluring. I cleared my throat and turned away from him. I started pulling off my boots and heard the sound of bones snapping. I glanced back at Smith and he had started his change. I unzipped my jeans and pulled off my shirt. I heard a growl behind me and Smith was now in his wolf form, watching me undress.

"A little privacy" I snapped at him. He growled again and turned around. I slipped my jeans off, but I'm not willing to take off my underwear, I can still feel Smith watching me. I crouched down, deciding to leave them on. I remembered what Gunner said about using the anger. So, I pictured Demi and her hateful words. I began to feel my bones snap and twist immediately, the pain was excruciating. It didn't last as long this time, though. With a snap of my neck and a loud howl, I was changed.

I shook out my fur and turned to Smith. He was watching me with his head low and ear back. His hair was standing up and it looked like he was trembling.

You'll want to carry these in your mouth

He was snuffling his snout in my clothes on the ground so, seeming to sniff them, maybe? I approached slowly and picked them up gently between my teeth once he moved away. I could taste him on the clothes. And I liked it.

Okay, let's go Smith flashed in a gruff tone.

Stay close he said as he swept passed me, brushing his tail across my face. The sensation made me shiver. Without another word, he took off through the trees, and I stayed right on his heels.

As we ran through the trees at top speed, Smith would occasionally nip at my ear or give me a little shove. He was so playful as he chuckled at me. The ache in my abdomen started to get a little worse. Now in my wolf form, my senses were better and I could smell the lust and desire coming from Smith. It made me feel uneasy, but I enjoyed the smell. I didn't want to let on that I could smell it on him though. Plausible deniability and all that.

We started to slow down and I could hear Gunner's voice ahead of me. The sound sent shivers all through my body and a deep burning ache between my legs. What is going on? We came through the trees and I spotted him standing in just a pair of black shorts and nothing else, he was talking to his father and Cole. The sun shone through the gaps in the trees, bathing his bare golden skin in the sunlight. Just like that, it was like I lost all control of my body. I dropped my clothes, ran right up to him, and pounced, pushing him to the ground and rubbing my head against his.

"Hey little wolf" he laughed. I licked at his face and he ran his fingers through my fur. The sensation sent a pleasure firing to my groin. I whimpered at his touch. Oh shit, please touch me again, I thought.

"Gunner" Cole growled stepping closer. I jumped up to face him and snapped my jaw. He's mine Cole, back off I growled to myself. "Easy Zee, it's just Cole" his voice said soothingly. He stood up and froze on the spot, pointing his nose in the air.

"Gunner" Cole growled again. His growl was making me angry but also really turned on. What the actual fuck. Gunner stepped in front of me taking a defensive position and growled lowly at Cole. What was he doing? Smith stalked over and stood beside Cole and they both growled deeply, only they weren't growling at Gunner, they were growling at me.

Gunner growled again, and this time it echoed through the trees. I felt a sharp sting in my belly and an intense heat washed through me. I fell to my knees in my human form. Sitting in the dirt in my nakedness, I was panting hard and my skin felt like it was on fire. Both Cole and Smith's growls grew louder. I wanted to go to them, but in the back of my mind, I knew I couldn't. I dug my nails into the dirt as another blast of heat rushed through me, drawing a pained moan from my lips.

"Take her into the forest son" Lupus said putting his arms against Cole and Smith. Smith looked near rabid, his teeth dripping with saliva and his fur standing on end. Cole's teeth were fully extended and his body was shaking with tension. Both of them were still staring directly at me, completely unfazed by Lupus' hold on them, and Gunner's warning growls. In an instant, Gunner scooped me up and carried me off through the trees, running deeper into the forest and away from the others. Being held in Gunner's arms against his bare chest, I could smell his heated skin, I could feel his own desire alight with desperate need.

I felt an overwhelming urge to lick the sweat from his golden skin. I felt the mindboggling urge to bite into his skin.

"What's happening to me?" I panted trying to hold my aching teeth back.

"You're in heat" he growled and I shivered.

We came to a stop and he put my feet on the ground, only for me to be pushed backward, and slammed against a tree. Without warning, Gunner's hungry lips crashed against mine. I moaned into his mouth, eagerly returning his kiss. He took hold of my ass cheeks and lifted me off the ground, I wrapped my legs around his waist and growled desperately. I clawed at his back, trying to pull him to me harder. Gunner pushed his hard dick into my already dripping pussy and growled back at me. The feel of him inside me did nothing to diminish the burning heat and desire in my loins, if anything it made me feel more ravenous for him. He pounded into my hot core, slamming my back against the tree with each thrust. I moaned and growled loudly while clawing at his back, his arms, his shoulders, everywhere I could reach. His bare chest was right in front of my face, and I couldn't stop myself, I lifted my mouth and sank my pointed teeth deeply into his flesh. He hissed and growled and slammed into me harder, more savagely. The taste of his blood was intoxicating and made my head spin. I groaned and growled, swallowing down his blood while my core clenched around him. Gunner grabbed my hair roughly and pulled my teeth off his skin. He forced my head to bend back so that I could look at him. His blue eyes were dark and full of lust, a glint of silver flashed through them. His lips were curled back in a growl and I could see fangs poking out from behind his lips. I don't know if I need to fight him or fuck him. I bared my teeth and growled at him, snapping my jaw forward. He let go of my hips and swiftly turned me around, pushing my face into the tree. He entered me again from behind and continued to thrust into me hard and fast. The growling, groaning, and sound of slapping flesh echoed through the trees, only making the animal in me feel more wild.

Gunner pressed his chest against my body and pulled my head back, we were cheek to cheek with my neck completely exposed.

I needed more, more of his touch, of his taste, just more. I could feel my orgasm building and was almost at my tipping point. Gunner leaned over and bit down hard into the side of my neck. I screamed at the pain and pleasure that hit me hard. I gripped onto his hair, pulling roughly, keeping his teeth in place. My pussy lips started to throb as my orgasm began, my whole body contracted and released over and over again, and I screamed out with unintelligible words of pleasure. Gunner kept pounding into me, prolonging my orgasm, dragging it out for delicious second after delicious second. My knees gave way and my eyes rolled back, if Gunner wasn't holding me up, I would have crashed to the ground. Two last deep long thrusts and Gunner released inside me on a strained groan. His seed was an immediate antidote to the aching heat, like a cool balm to ease the ache. He took his teeth from my neck and we both fell backwards onto the ground, with me landing on top of Gunner. He wrapped his arms around me and held me to his chest. I was panting hard and sweat was covering my body. We lay on the ground until I had enough air to speak.

"What the fuck was that?" I breathed into his chest. I have never felt so desperate, so uncontrollably horny. It was like I had no other option but to fuck. It was that or death.

"That was your first heat" Gunner answered with a small chuckle.

"My first, you mean there will be more of whatever that was?"

"Every month, little wolf".

"Holy shit". I don't know if I can handle that every month. The loss of control I felt was nauseating. Am I just meant to get used to it?

I laid on Gunner's chest and he drew circles on my bare back with his fingers. I sat up and straddled him, looking down I saw my bloodied bite on his upper peck, between his collarbone and nipple. I gasped and gently traced over it with my fingers.

"I'm so sorry, Gunner, I bit you" he lifted his head and looked at my mark. He chuckled and dropped his head again.

"I guess we've both been marked now". He lay on the ground with his eyes closed and a wide smile spread across his kissable lips.

Seemingly completely unbothered by the bite on his chest, the entire last few minutes, or however long that just was.

A breeze hit my back, reminding me that I'm completely naked. I looked around at the empty forest and shivered. Gunner slapped my thighs, startling me, and then propped himself up on his elbow.

"As much as I love seeing you like this and having you naked on my lap, we have people waiting on us" he said with his eyes falling over my body and his other hand sliding down my chest.

"Oh, I forgot about that" I reluctantly stood up and let Gunner stand as well. I looked around again, the full reality of my weird sex-crazed moment hit me and I was filled with shame.

"I uh, I left my clothes back there" I said meekly.

"You can wear these, and we'll pick up your clothes on the way". Gunner held out the black shorts he was wearing earlier and I took them gladly. I slipped them on and turned to Gunner taking in his magnificent God like physique. I licked my lips hungrily and without realising it, I reached out and slid my hand down along his torso. A soft growl rumbled in the back of my throat and a flash of heat hit my groin. I want to bite him again.

"Zee" he growled back. I snapped my hand back and smiled up at him, embarrassed.

"Sorry" I blushed. He stepped forward and cupped my cheeks in his hands and pressed his lips to mine.

"Don't be sorry. Your heat isn't over yet, we still have time" he said into my lips. I licked my tongue across his bottom lip, teasing him. He growled again and pressed his lips hard against mine. My body reacted, melding against him while my arms curled around his neck.

"Buuuut, just not right now" he said while slowly pulling away from me. I grumbled, crossed my arms, and pouted. He quickly grabbed my chin and pulled me back to his face.

"But I already can't wait till next month" he smirked quickly pecking my lips. He let me go and turned around tapping his back. My eyes right away noticed the claw marks all over his skin, but he didn't seem to care or even notice.

"Climb on, I'll piggy-back you" he said with a devilish smile. I sighed and jumped up, wrapping my arms around his neck and pressing my breasts to his back. We began walking back to the cabin and I thought about what just happened.

"Why did Cole growl at me?" I asked,

"He could smell your heat and he wanted to fuck you" Gunner said bluntly. I blinked, completely taken aback at his gruff response.

"Cole wants to fuck me? I didn't think he even liked me".

"He doesn't have to like you, when an unmated male wolf scent a female in heat it sends them a bit crazy".

"But Smith's with Nat, why was he acting weird?".

Gunner stopped walking and snapped his head to look back at me, an angry growl fell from his lips.

"What did he do to you?" he snapped.

"He didn't do anything, he smelled weird and was acting strange but that was all" Gunner frowned and jerked me higher on his back and kept walking, seeming to ignore my question about why it happened to Smith too. A delicious pain fizzled through my groin and I blushed.

"That uh, that was like really rough" I whispered awkwardly.

"It can be rougher".

"It can?" I squeaked. Gunner chuckled at my surprise.

"I was fighting it, and I was being as gentle as I could manage. With unmated wolves, they don't usually care as much. There can be blood and broken bones and a lot of claw and bite marks. I think we were pretty tame" Gunner mused.

I looked down at the marks I had left on him. Deep gashes still marred his arms and back. I had a few scrapes from the tree, but nothing like what I did to Gunner. A pang of guilt flooded over me. Gunner must have caught on and he squeezed my thighs for reassurance.

"Oi, I'm okay, don't worry about it" he said softly. I kissed his neck and rested my head on his shoulder. We walked for a bit longer until I could hear Cole and Lupus up ahead.

"We're here. Where did you drop your clothes?" Gunner asked.

"Uh, over there, I think" I pointed to where we ran in. He walked over to my clothes and let go of my legs, I quickly slipped out of his shorts and started pulling on my jeans. Gunner slapped my behind, causing me to squeak. I slipped my top on over my naked chest. Man, I should have taken off my underwear before I changed. I turned to Gunner who was waiting for me. He looked down to my chest at my protruding nipples and a quick darkness flashed across his eyes. He stepped forward and rolled my nipple between his fingers. I gasped and bit my bottom lip.

"I'm not so sure about this top" he growled softly leaning down to my face.

"I ripped my underwear when I changed" I said breathlessly. He leaned in and kissed my waiting lips, sending another small ache to my stomach. Gunner breathed in hard through his nose and licked my lips gently.

"We can't be here long, or I'll be fighting off rabid wolves trying to get to that sweet kitty of yours" he whispered, tracing his fingers along the front of my jeans. I huffed out a breathy gasp and leaned toward him. But he stood up and grabbed my hand, leading me over to the waiting Cole and Lupus. I sighed heavily and followed along.

"Damn Gunner" Cole huffed as he turned to us. His eyes showed humour, but his body was stiff and his movements jerky. Lupus let out a tremendous laugh and smacked Gunner on the back as we came over.

"She got you good boy" Lupus bellowed. Gunner hissed at them both, warning them away. My cheeks burned red, I can't believe they know what we just did. Oh god, I hope that didn't hear it too.

"Yeah alright" Gunner chuckled and shoved his father off him.

"Just try not to breathe through your nose okay, I don't want to have to rip your limbs off" Gunner snarled semi playfully. He pulled me into his hip and held my waist tight against his body. The chuckling died down as Lupus turned to me. He held my gaze, not once looking at my body. I appreciated his effort to maintain my humility.

"He's ready for you" Lupus said in a calm gentle tone, while nodding his head to the door of the cabin.

Chapter Twenty

Zelena

I clung onto Gunner's arm as we walked slowly down the stairs to the cell. I turned and buried my face into his chest.

"Don't leave me" I whispered.

"Never" he wrapped his arms around my shoulders and squeezed me tight.

We got to the bottom of the stairs and found Spartan waiting by the cell door. He looked at me and his body tensed, a deep growl came from the back of his throat. I froze as my eyes went wide. Gunner growled back and Spartan quickly snapped his eyes to him and shook his head.

"I'll wait upstairs" Spartan huffed, keeping his eyes on me. As he walked by his huge chest slowly brushed against my arm, a small whimper fell from my mouth and a flush flew over my face. He growled again but stepped away quickly. Gunner stared him down with his teeth bared until Spartan was up the stairs.

"You're not making this easy on everyone" he said brushing his lips against my neck. A move that would usually get my legs shaking but I couldn't focus on anything other than the cell door. I don't want to wait any more, I just want it over with. I stepped forward and reached for the door handle, but Gunner grabbed my hand.

"What?" I snapped a little more harshly than I anticipated,
"Zee, he uh, he didn't exactly cooperate" Gunner said with a hint
of uncertainty.
"So, what?",
"So, he got beat a little".
"He did?" I couldn't help but smile at the thought of Hank finally
getting a beating of his own. I dreamed for years of having
enough courage to fight back, but I was never strong enough to
put those thoughts into action. Imagining Gunner and the others
beating up my decrepit father makes me slightly happy. Shit, is
that, bad? If the idea of another person being hurt brings me joy,
maybe I'm not as good as everyone seems to think. Gunner's
brows raised as he looked at my quickly changing expressions
curiously.
"Zee?" he questioned.
"Huh?" I huffed, coming back to the moment and finding Gunner
gazing at me with concern.
"It's fine, just let me in" I pushed passed him and turned the
doorknob, pulling open the big steel door. I walked in and looked
around at the scene before me. The air was cold and damp. The
stench alone was enough to make me nauseous. There was blood
splattered on the floor and one of the walls. In the middle of the
room sat my father, chained to a chair with his head slumped
forward. I crept forward, basically tip-toeing, and stopped to
stand in front of Hank, but he didn't move. Oh my god, is he dead?
He was wearing the usual muck-covered singlet shirt and grey
cotton shorts full of holes. He was wet, why was he wet? Gunner
stepped up beside me and tapped him hard on the cheek and then
quickly stepped back again. Hank stirred and shakily lifted his
head, locking his eyes on mine. I'd almost forgotten what he
looked like. Almost. His face was still present in my nightmares,
but seeing it again in front of me now made fear shake through
my body. His face was covered in blood, his eye was swollen over
and he had open cuts on his lip, chin, cheek, and eyebrow.
Underneath that I could see that his skin was pale and clammy, he
had been beaten around a lot, clearly. He smiled at me and half
huffed, half laughed.

"Ah daughter" he groaned groggily,

"Come to let Daddy out of this shit hole, have you?". Gunner growled a warning from behind me.

"Don't growl at me mutt" Hank yelled, causing me to jump at his ever familiar aggressive voice. He struggled in his chair trying to free his arms.

"I'll fucking kill you once I get out of here, you fucking dog. You're dead, you hear me?" he snarled and mumbled eyeing Gunner as he fought.

"St-stop it, please" I said shakily.

He turned his eyes back to me and raked them slowly over my body. I felt so exposed and vulnerable under his heated glare. The mere feel of his gaze drinking in my body made me feel dirty.

"I see it didn't take long for them to make you into a proper whore, look at you with your tight fucking clothes and your tits out for those mangey dogs. You're one too though aren't you, a fucking dog. I see that disgusting bite on your neck, and on his" he spat with disgust in his voice. Gunner growled viciously at his harsh comments. Hank looked back over at him and tried again to fight his way out of the chair, mumbling and cursing to himself. I forgot how his words could make me feel, so dirty and insignificant. It was like a whole other life ago that I got those comments on a daily. But they didn't make me feel small and worthless anymore, they just made me angry.

"Dad" I snapped recapturing his attention. He turned his crazy gaze back to me and smiled again. The smile was not from happiness though, behind it was just pure evil and it made my skin crawl. He chuckled a little looking back at Gunner again,

"You didn't tell her?" he snickered. I snapped my eyes to Gunner and he was glaring angrily at my father.

"Tell me what?" I demanded. They were both silent for a minute neither one answering my question.

"Tell me what!?" I screamed. A wave of emotion rolled off me, hitting Gunner and my father like a stiff breeze. They both looked back at me wide eyed. Then Hank laughed again.

"I'm not your father, you stupid little slut" he hissed. Gunner leaped forward and punched Hank in the mouth, his head snapped to the side and he spat blood across the floor. Not completely able to grasp what Hank just said, I stumbled back onto the chair behind me and slumped down. I put my hand to my chest a breathed deeply. Hank groaned in pain while Gunner paced in front of him.

"You're not my dad?" I spoke aloud after a few moments.

"I would never sire a little beast like you" he spat. Gunner growled and stepped forward again.

"Enough, Gunner" I snapped at him, holding my hand up. He looked at me and paused, with a reluctant huff he stood back, leaning against the wall.

"If you're not my dad, then where is he?"

"He's dead, I killed him" he chuckled maliciously. His words sent a sharp pain running through my body and into my heart. He killed my father, my real father. I'll never know him, or where I truly came from. A tear fell from my eye before the red hot anger in my stomach began to burn.

"Why?" I demanded glowering at Hank.

"Because he was a filthy wolf and got in our way",

"Who's way?"

"My clan". I balked and blinked a couple of times. His what now?

"You're what?" I asked, barely keeping my annoyance out of my voice.

"My clan of hunters" he hissed in response. I gasped. His words hit me like a punch to the chest. A hunter. I was raised by a werewolf hunter. But why? I heard whispers of hunters around the pack, it wasn't until this moment that I understood how prevalent that information was.

"W-Wha-Why?" I stuttered.

"Because we know where you came from. We know who you are. The line of the great and powerful Selene, the dirty witch that cursed this land with your wretched wolf kind" his voice got louder and louder as he preached at me.

"You're an abomination on this earth!" he yelled, his words were full of hatred and disdain. He truly despised me and my species. But if so, why would he keep me, why would he make me believe that he was my father?

"Why did you keep me alive, if you hate my kind so much, why not just kill me?" my voice was starting to shake and the anger was rising in my stomach, bubbling up like bad indigestion.

"Because we also know what the whores from your line are capable of. Special powers they say. What a joke! Look at you, you worthless fleabag, there's nothing special and powerful about you! Seventeen years I've wasted with you" he yelled, thrashing about in his chair. So much hatred. All these years, all the torture, the beatings, the starvation. I endured all of it, and for what? I stared at him blankly, how could he know all this? About me, my bloodline, my power. I don't even understand it. How could he, why did he? Then it dawned on me, like a door of my mind flew open unincumbered.

"My mother" I whispered. His eyes lowered and that evil grin returned to his face.

"Your mother" he repeated in confirmation.

"Where is my mother?"

He tossed his head back and cackled.

"She's dead" he snickered. I flopped back into the chair and pressed my hands to the side of my face. My mother. My father. My entire family, they are all gone. Hank was babbling, but his words were muffled by the screaming in my head. He killed my family. He took away any chance I had to know who I am. He needs to pay for it. I stood again and listened as he mumbled on.

"Now she, she was formidable, an incredible creature. As beautiful as a monster could be. Fought to her very last breath she did. Killed a lot of us before we finally took her out" his voice was void of any emotion and he didn't look at me as he spoke of her.

The burning anger inside me erupted like a volcano. I could feel it spilling out of me as I stared at the murderous bastard who raised me. My skin was alight in burning heat, like lightning shooting out of my pores. I felt my feet lift off the floor as I floated in front of Hank. A look of terror flooded his face as he watched me rise.

"It can't be" he whimpered shaking his head.

I reached my hand out to him and flexed my fingers. I didn't even need to think about it, it was a natural instinct. Hank cried out in pain as the chair began to collapse beneath him.

"You killed my mother" I screamed, twisting my hand as he called out for me to stop. I thought back to every time he hit me, every ounce of pain he inflicted on my body. I was going to give it all back to him now. I clenched my fingers again and his chair folded into the floor his legs shattered and compressed along with it.

"Zelena stop" I heard Gunner yell. I pushed out my hand toward him, keeping him from stopping me as I took out my revenge on my surrogate father.

"Did you enjoy it, Hank, torturing me all those years? I was innocent" I screamed at his crumbling body.

"You're not innocent, you're a monster" he wailed as I turned my hand over him again. I could once again feel the blows of his fists to my body, the whips and burns and slashes to my skin. Every torment and torture he inflicted on me was now replaying in my mind's eye. My past pain echoed through me once again. The chains holding him down broke apart and his arms snapped and twisted and compacted inwards. His torturous cry only fuelled my rage. A darkness descended upon me, filling every inch of my being. I could feel the cold icy chill of it slithering its way through my veins. I lowered my eyes and opened my mouth, an agonizing scream filled with the memories of my childhood trauma shot out from deep inside me, crashing over Hank like a wall of water. With one last flex and turn of my hand, his head crunched back and snapped to the side and his screams stopped. I looked down at his mangled body and a wave of satisfaction breezed over me.

I fell to the floor but was caught in Gunner's arms. I felt weak and drained, my eyes got cloudy and my breath hitched in my throat.

"Zelena, what did you do?" Gunner questioned. His face was horrified and filled with sadness. I reached up to cup his cheek in my hand.

"I had to" I whispered. My head fell back and my eyes blurred over. A darkness blanketed over me and I was gone.

~

I blinked my eyes open and looked about the room, I was back at the pack house in mine and Gunner's bedroom. I sat up on the bed and frowned. Where was Gunner? I swung my legs over the side of the bed just as the door opened.

"Oh, Zee you're awake" Gunner rushed over. Kneeling in front of me, he buried his face into my stomach and wrapped his arms around my waist. I brushed my fingers through his hair and little shots of electricity ran up my arms.

"How long have I been out?" I asked,

"Coming on five hours now, Artemis said you wore yourself out" he replied looking up at my face. I grabbed his cheeks and kissed his forehead. I looked into his worried silver eyes and he stared at me with his usual adoring look, but something had changed. Deep in his eyes, he was trying to hide something. I pulled him back to my stomach and rested my head on top of his. A flash of memory came back to me and I saw Hanks's deformed and broken body lying on the floor before me. I gasped at the memory. Nausea rolled through me. How could I do that, how could I let myself get so angry that I would not only kill someone but do it so violently. I started to pant rapidly, my chest tightened, and I couldn't breathe. Tears fell uncontrollably from my eyes and a sweat appeared on my brow. Gunner looked up at me and swiftly picked me up in his arms and cradled me in his lap.

"Shh it's okay, you're okay. It's over now, little wolf" he said trying to calm me down. He stroked my hair and rubbed his finger up and down my arm.

"I-I-I killed him" I sobbed hard into Gunner's chest. I'm not at all sorry for the death of that monster, he deserved it no question. But this dark side of me that managed to take hold and cause me to lash out and do something so savagely violent, it was terrifying.

"It's okay my love, it's over now" Gunner soothed. He rocked me in his arms as I continued to sob and shiver. I can't get the image out of my mind. I'm a monster, just like he said I was.

"I'm a monster" I wailed.

"No, baby, a monster would not feel remorse. You are anything but. Even after all that you heard and everything he did to you, you still feel guilty for giving him his just dessert. That is not a monster, that is a Goddess. You little wolf are a Goddess" he spoke with such confidence and conviction it was hard not to trust his words. I slowly started to calm down and after a while my breathing normalised.

"Did I hurt you?" I asked softly,

"When I pushed you back"

"No, my love, I wasn't hurt. It just felt like I was pushing against a wall."

"Okay good"

"It was a surprise though. You had so much control and so much power. How did you learn to do all that after just a couple of hours?" his voice hitched a little, he was trying to stay cool, but I could tell he was impressed if not shocked by what he saw.

"Artemis is a good teacher"

"Ha! No shit" he laughed, his warm chest bouncing under me.

"Well, he demanded that I give you a full feast to get your strength back, so let's go stuff your face" Gunner lifted me off his lap and stood up off the bed. He took my hand and went to pull me out the door but I pulled him back to me, wrapping my arms around his waist for another hug.

"Thank you" I whispered,

"For what?"

"For not running away from me, for not being afraid".

Gunner sighed and picked me up into his arms, I wrapped my legs around his waist and held his shoulders. He cupped his hand on my cheek and smiled at me.

"I'm not going anywhere" he pulled my face to his and pressed his lips to mine ever so gently. I felt a slight pang of heat in my stomach, my heat was still not over. But right on cue to kill our moment, my stomach screamed at us. He chuckled and put me down again.

"Come on" as we got to the top of the stairs he stopped and faced me.

"If they act weird around you please don't take it personally" he said cautiously.

"What do you mean?"

"Well, Dad and Cole and Spartan, they were there, they saw you using your powers"

"They're afraid of me now?" I said lowering my head. Of course I would do something to ruin this good thing I have here. I guess I knew it couldn't last forever, I suppose I'll be kicked out now. Gunner put his hand under my chin and lifted my head again,

"No, no, no, the opposite. They all feel a lot more protective of you now. They were in awe of you actually"

"Wait seriously?"

"Seriously"

"Even Cole?"

"I don't know why you think he doesn't like you, he just isn't as open as everyone else"

"He never even speaks to me"

"Well, I have a feeling that may change" he said with a smirk,

I huffed and started stomping down the stairs. Gunner came up behind me and grabbed me around the waist and ran me down the rest of the stairs. He started tickling my sides making me laugh and squirm in his arms.

"Don't stomp away from me missy" he laughed pressing his fingers into my ribs.

"Stop, you'll make me pee" I screamed with a giggle, fighting against his strong arms. He started to nibble and lick my neck and earlobe and I squealed with joy.

"Say you're sorry" he chuckled into my hair,

"Never" I giggled trying to free myself from his hold. He pressed his fingers into my ribs again and I yelled,

"Okay, I give, I give. I'm sorry" I squealed, now panting. He slowly put me down and turned me around to face him. His smile covered his whole face, reaching up to his eyes. He looks so young and carefree when he smiles like that. He stepped forward and cupped my cheeks. As he bent down to kiss my lips, I stuck out my tongue and licked him from his chin up to his forehead. I laughed and ran for the kitchen door,

"Oh, no you didn't" he chuckled chasing after me. I burst through the kitchen door and slammed face first into a rock-hard chest.

"Shit" I mumble falling backward but I was caught and steadied by two hands on my shoulders. Rubbing my nose, I looked up and saw Lupus's amused face. Gunner came up behind me panting,

"Hey Dad" he breathed putting his hands around my waist.

"Kids" Lupus grumbled with a smile,

"Glad to see you're up, Zelena, there's food in the fridge for you" he stepped aside and let us through the door.

"Thanks, Lupus" I smiled ducking around him and making a beeline for the fridge.

"Hey boys" I called to Smith and Cole at the breakfast nook, both devouring a plate of food. I pulled open the fridge door and examined the contents. Gunner's arms snaked around my waist and he rested his chin on my shoulder.

"I know what I want" he said lowly,

"Yeah, what?" I asked. He nibbled on my chin leading down my neck. A dull ache returned to my stomach and my cheeks flushed red.

"Some of this would be nice" he mumbled into my neck. I quickly pushed his head back and grabbed a plate of lamb chops. If I don't eat now before he gets my hormones going again, then I never will.

"Food first" I said kissing his cheek and spinning out of his arms.

"You two are gross" Smith mumbled with food falling out of his mouth. I squeezed in next to him and started gnawing into a cold lamb chop.

"Don't you want to heat that up?" Cole chuckled at me. I was a little taken aback by it. I don't think I've heard him laugh or make any kind of happy sound before.

"Meh" I shrugged.

"Can't take her anywhere" Gunner huffed grabbing my plate and putting it in the microwave.

"That was quite the show you put on earlier" Cole leaned back in the chair and put his hands behind his head, raising his eyebrow at me.

"I told you she was wicked" Smith mumbled again. Cole smiled and shook his head,

"Yeah, I see that now" he said winking his eye at me. All I could manage was a crooked awkward smile. Who the heck was this guy? Where is the sullen, silent Cole that I'm used to? I just stared at him with my mouth open, completely dumbfounded. Gunner put the plate back in front of me and I blinked a few times and continued chomping away.

I told you he likes you

Or he's been body snatched

Gunner snorted out loud and soda flew out his nose. He turned to look at us with liquid pouring down his face. I looked back to Cole and we all burst out laughing. This was great, feeling so at ease and enjoying the little things. After everything that has gone down today, I didn't think life here would feel so normal and natural again. Gunner sat down on the edge of the seat next to me forcing me to shuffle closer to Smith, who then shuffled around further giving us more room. He rested his hand on my thigh and dug into his food.

We sat together eating and laughing and just being teenagers again. Life has been moving and changing so quickly, it's nice to just sit down and be a kid for a few minutes. Cole threw a potato wedge at Smith hitting him between the eyes. He then picked up a piece of carrot and threw it at Cole, just before it made contact with his cheek, I stopped it. The piece of vegetable floated for a moment in mid-air, right in front of Cole's face. Curling my fingers a little, I pulled it back and pinched it out of the air then popped it in my mouth. I smiled at the boys and they all just stared at me with their eyes bulging.

"I will never get used to that" Cole said as he flung another potato wedge at Smith.

"Hey, why are you saving his pretty face but not mine?" Smith whined with a laugh.

"Because I'm prettier" Cole chuckled standing up with his plate. I hadn't noticed that Gunner was gripping my leg just a little tighter and was leaning down a bit. I looked up at him and he crashed his lips to mine. He slowly started to harden his kiss, moving his lips more urgently.

"Well, that's my cue to leave" Smith grunted, sliding all the way out of the other side of the booth. I grabbed Gunner's chin and sat up a little higher.

"I mean, you could have waited till we left" Cole grunted. I heard the boys shuffle towards the door, I waved my hand at them but didn't move my mouth away from Gunner's. The kitchen door opened and closed again, they were gone. Gunner quickly grabbed me under the arms and lifted me onto the table in front of him. His tongue explored my mouth forcing a moan from my lips. The ache in my lower stomach intensified and a heat crawled along my skin.

"I can smell your heat" Gunner growled into my mouth. The vibration made me tingle and I could feel the moisture in my panties. I wrapped my arms around his shoulders and pulled him into my body. He stood up holding me up by my ass. I wrapped my legs around his waist and he started walking. His taste was addictive, I just couldn't get enough. I found myself licking and sucking on his neck, the urge to bite was getting stronger. I was suddenly tossed off his body and landed bouncing on the bed. He had carried me up the stairs and to our room in no time. He quickly pulled my jeans off and crawled on top of me, growling softly. In one swift move, he grabbed the tank top I was wearing and tore it off me, discarding the shredded pieces on the floor. He trailed his teeth along my jaw and down my neck and chest to my stomach, leaving little bites along the way. I was feeling restless and full of energy, like I couldn't lay still. I quickly lifted my legs and wrapped them around his shoulders, trapping his head between my thighs. He growled lifting his eyes to look at me. Looping his fingers through the band of my panties, he ripped them off and tossed them across the room. With a growl and a devilish grin, he slammed his lips into my core, using his lips and tongue he hungrily enjoyed my waiting wetness. My head fell back and a loud cry escaped me. I gripped my fingers into his hair and arched my back, lifting my hips into his mouth harder. Gunner's mouth sucking hard on my swollen clit, I could feel the tremors coming, starting to pulse through me. I thrust my hips into him with each wave of pleasure falling over me, and yet he didn't let up, only intensifying my orgasm. Finally, my legs gave out and I released my grip on him. He slowly crawled back up on top of me and pulled my chin down to look at him.

"I'm not done with you yet" he smiled cheekily.

"Good" I growled, playfully snapping my teeth at his nose.

Chapter Twenty-One

Gunner

I stared in amazement as her body slowly lifted off the ground, just like she was flying. Can Zelena fly now? Hank mumbled something and started shaking his head, clearly as surprised by this as I was. Suddenly, the legs of the chair he was on folded underneath him, with his legs along with them. His painful scream hurt my ears.

"You killed my mother" Zelena screamed. I looked back at her and she had her hands outstretched towards Hank. She was doing something funky with her fingers, moving and flexing them weirdly. Hank continued to scream and cry in pain. I was frozen, I could see it happening in front of me, but I couldn't understand what was happening. My eyes shot from Hank to Zelena and back again. A violent and powerful rage started boiling up from inside me. I felt a heaviness in my legs, like I was being pulled into the ground. Of course. It hit me like a freight train. She's using her powers on Hank. It's not my rage, it's hers.

"Zelena, stop" I called to her, stepping forward. I needed to calm her down, to take her focus away from her rage. She quickly glanced at me out of the corner of her eye. I got a glimpse of her glowing yellow eyes, shining brightly like stars in the night sky. They were beautiful. I'd never seen her eyes do that before. A small panic joined the confounding rage inside me. Zelena reached her hand to me in a stop gesture, and I was sent sliding back across the floor. I tried to walk to her again but I couldn't move, there was some kind of invisible wall blocking me. It this... A force field? I pushed against it, but I couldn't get through. The power that I was able to feel coming from her dissipated, along with the overwhelming rage and sorrow. Was she blocking me now too?

Dad, Spartan, and Cole appeared at the door across the room. I tried calling to them but they couldn't hear me, the force field was blocking the sound of my voice.

Don't go near her. I flashed Cole as I smashed my hands on the invisible wall. I must have looked like one of those creepy French mimes.

She's going to kill him, Gunner

Then he'll die. Just don't touch her, stay back

Zee was unpredictable, I couldn't risk them getting hurt unintentionally. I saw Cole's lips move and then Dad nodded in agreement. They stood still in the doorway watching, eyes fixed on Zelena. She turned her hands and flexed her fingers. The muffled screams from Hank were barely audible to me. His legs were crumpled sacks of meat of shattered bone underneath him. His arms were slowly curling and twisting into his sides. His mouth hung open wide with a pained expression plastered on his face. I turned my gaze back to Zelena. Floating there in the air, her hair looked as if it were caught in a gentle breeze, waving slightly around her shoulders. Even with her furrowed forehead and glowing eyes, she looked almost angelic. She opened her mouth and a white wave of haze surged from her body, crashing over Hank.

Hanks's body lay crumpled and broken on the ground, his head twisted and bent in an impossible way. I looked back to Zee as her hands fell to her side. I felt the wall holding me evaporate and I ran to Zelena, just in time to catch her as she fell back down. I sat down on the ground and held her tightly in my arms, her face had never looked paler. Her eyes were struggling to stay open and her breaths were short and ragged.

"Zelena, what did you do?" I asked softly. She was fading, her strength dwindling. She reached up to cup my cheek in her hand. "I had to" she whispered, her eyes closed and her head fell back.

"Zelena?" I gently shook her body.

"Zelena, open your eyes" I placed my hand on her cheek, her skin was still warm. I leaned my ear closer, I can still hear her shallow breaths. I looked up to see my father standing over us.

"She passed out" I told him. I looked over to Cole and Spartan, they were inspecting what was left of Hank's body.

"This is incredible" Spartan said lifting what looked like an arm. He dropped it again and looked over to me.

"She can do this, with just a wiggle of her fingers?" his voice was uncertain, impressed, but laced with a bit of fear. Which is highly unusual coming from Spartan.

"She's the Triple Goddess, she can do anything" my father said still looking down at where I held her on my lap.

"Come on son, let's get her to Artemis" Dad grabbed my shoulders and helped me to my feet with Zelena still in my arms.

"Cole, you go with Gunner back to the village, Spartan and I will clean up here"

"Yes Alpha" agreed Cole.

We made our way out of the cabin and started through the forest. We walked in silence for a while, my worry for Zee occupying most of my thoughts.

"Gunner" Cole said clearing his throat,

"I'm sorry, mate" he said softly.

"Sorry for what?" I asked not looking at him.

"I'm sorry I didn't give her a proper chance. I was too wrapped up in my own feelings and jealousy, and I didn't see how happy she was making you".

"It's okay brother".

"No really, I was selfish and I'm really sorry",

"Cole, I know. It's okay".

He grabbed my arm and stopped us short then stood in front of me. Placing one arm on my shoulder and the other on Zee's hand resting on her stomach, he looked directly into my eyes.

"I swear to you, here and now, I will give my life to protect her and you. She is truly amazing and I can't believe I'm only just seeing that now. She will be the greatest Luna our pack could have ever asked for, and I'm sorry for doubting that".

His oath took me a little by surprise but it warmed my heart.

"Thank you, brother" was all I could say. The threat of emotion in the back of my throat kept me from declaring my appreciation. Cole leaned his forehead against mine for a moment before standing up straight again.

"Well come then, our Luna-to-be needs to be checked out" he said slapping my shoulder. We picked up the pace to a light jog. I'm glad Zee is so tiny, she fits perfectly in my arms. As we neared the edge of the forest Cole took off ahead of me, I'm assuming to go and find Artemis. I broke through the trees and made my way to the pack house.

Artemis is in your room

Thanks, Cole

I got to the door just as Cole opened it for me. Mum rushed over and placed her hand on Zee's face.

"Is she okay baby?" she asked with a shaky voice.

"She passed out, I'll fill you in after we've seen Artemis" I walked upstairs with Cole and Mum trailing behind. Artemis was standing by the bed waiting for us. I laid Zee down and took a small step back. Artemis glided his hands through the air above her body and hummed loudly. He rested the back of his hand on her chest over her heart and then stood up again.

"She do too much, get weak. She need rest and big food, then be okay" Artemis nodded to me and headed for the door.

"Thank you, Artemis".

"Yes" he replied as he left.

"Okay, come on then, let's let her sleep" I said while ushering Mum and Cole out the bedroom door. Once out the door I closed it behind me and turned to face Cole.

"Cole, gather the senior pack and the lead commanders, tell them that they are needed at the hall immediately".

"Gunner baby, your dad..."

"Dad will expect me to get things started" I interrupted my mother.

"Yes, but get what started my boy, what is going on?" Mum asked urgently.

"Cole, go. When both our father's get back, tell them where I am. Mum, come with me, I'll fill you in". With that, Cole nodded his head and ran to the front door. I took Mum to the kitchen and sat down at the counter.

"If the pack are coming, I better get some food ready" she said then went rummaging around the fridge and cupboards. She dropped the food on the bench and started preparing the snacks.

"Well?" she said, not looking up from her cutting board.

"Zelena was kidnapped as a baby and raised by a hunter, he knew of her lineage and was ordered to keep her in the hope she would bear the powers of the Goddess" I blurted out in a single breath. No point dancing around the truth, right? Mum gasped and dropped her knife to the floor,

"You can't be serious?" she said softly.

"He said they were coming for her Mum, there's a battle coming and I have a feeling it's going to be a bloody one".

Hearing the words come out of my mouth made it all that much more real. I had been pushing the thought away since first hearing it from Hank. Until this moment, I wasn't ready to accept it, now I have no other choice. We need to be ready and I need to keep Zelena safe.

"Can you flash Dad, find out how long he'll be" I lifted my eyes to my mother, a single tear was slowly rolling down her cheek. She picked up her knife and continued chopping away at the vegetables in front of her, not pausing for a second.

"They're on the way" she said softly. I nodded my head and looked down at my hands, rolling my thumbs around each other.

"Gunner?" Mum whispered,

"Yeah?" I asked looking up at her.

"What happened at the cabin, with Zelena?" she was now staring directly at me with both hands on the counter. I took a deep breath and steadied my nerves.

"She killed her father" I paused, took in her expression, and continued.

"After he told her about the kidnapping and the hunters and killing her real parents, she let her anger take control and her powers were unleashed. She flew into the air and crushed his bones into a pulp"

"Oh, my word"

"It was incredible, she was incredible. So much power and in total control of it. If I didn't know better, I would have been terrified" I couldn't deny the smile that the memory brought to my face. My Mate is seriously a force to be reckoned with.

"Sweetheart, you look like you believe this is a good thing?"

"Isn't it though? She's the most powerful wolf I have ever seen and she belongs to our pack, she belongs to me, she's my Mate"

"Yes, my love but we spoke to you about the potential danger. If she lets her anger take her into the darkness, she could destroy us all"

"Zelena isn't like that Mum, she is kind and gentle and she cares about us"

"I know she does Gunner, but she has suffered, more than almost anyone else. That kind of pain can change you"

"Well I won't let it, neither will she".

Mum stared at me intently, her face was painted with worry. A weak smile grew on her lips and she nodded her head.

"I trust you" she said and returned to her cooking. I sat and watched her for a few minutes, she smelled of anxiety and her brows were fixed into frown lines on her forehead. She was really worried about this, about Zelena's gifts. I know that Zee won't do anything to hurt us, any of us, she sees the pack as her family now. She is strong and she can control it, I believe in her. I was about to reach for Mum's hand to comfort her when Cole's voice in my head startled me.

Everyone is in the hall

Thanks, man. Any sign of Dad?

Not yet

Keep me posted

Got it

"Mum I'll be in the hall" I said standing up,

"You're not going to wait for your father?" she questioned with one brow raised,

"I don't need to wait, he knows I wouldn't wait. It's okay Mum honestly".

She pursed her lips together and nodded her head. She doesn't like that I'm doing this without Dad's approval. He is the Alpha and everything is meant to be run by him first. Other pack members could see my pre-emptive actions as a challenge against my father's authority, but I just know that time is of the essence here. Dad will see that too and he'd understand, I think.

I pushed open the hall door and walked in. The faces of the men turned to look at me but quickly went back to their conversations once they realised it was just me. Mazz and Julian were here as well as four others, the commanders. Smith sat quietly in the back corner of the room. He was avoiding eye contact with me, he must still be embarrassed about his reaction to Zelena's heat. I stood at the head of the table and cleared my throat loudly.

"Settle down, let's get things started" I called to them. One of the young commanders turned and scoffed,

"Thanks, pup, but we'll wait for the Alpha" he spat with a sarcastic laugh. I think his name is Jackson.

"The Alpha is on the way, in the meantime, I will be leading this meeting" I said sternly.

"Pfft" the commander turned his back to me and went back to talking to the others. His disrespect and arrogance made my blood boil. Mazz and Julian were now watching me, waiting for my reaction to the commander's behaviour. Smith sat up straight and was also watching me, waiting. If I let him speak like this to me now, I will never have his full respect, even when I take the Alpha role. My skin burned and tingled with rage. I slammed my fist on the table and jumped up on it. I grabbed the commander by the neck, lifting him up and slamming his back onto the table at my feet. My protruding claws were digging into the skin of his neck. I crouched down and leaned far forward, growling ferociously right in his face, my fangs now only centimetres from his face.

"When I tell you to shut up, you will shut the fuck up and listen" I growled at the arrogant asshole.

"You're not Alpha yet, pup" he choked out. I roared angrily, lifting the commander's body and slamming it again back into the table.

The hall door flung open with such force I thought it was going to fly off its hinges. Dad stood in the doorway growling lowly. He looked around the room and then down at me. I was crouched on the tabletop with the commander sprawled across it at my feet, my claws gripped around his neck. It would have been a sight to see, I have no doubt that looked like a wild animal.

"Explain" he growled stepping into the room with Spartan and Cole close behind.

"I was about to give this jackass a lesson in respect" I growled looking back down at the commander's reddening face.

"What the fuck have you done to earn my respect?" he yelled trying to pry my hand off his neck. I growled again, squeezing my grip harder, until my father's hand landed on my shoulder.

"Release him" he ordered.

"But…"

"Now, son" he cut me off. I growled again, pulling back my fangs and claws, and let go of my grip on the commander's neck. He quickly stood up and growled, baring his teeth and leaning toward me. In a blink, my father had his hand around the commander's neck and his back pressed against the wall. Dad lifted the commander's feet off the ground and growled so loudly that the walls shook.

"That is your Alpha-Son and the future Alpha of this pack. That title alone earns him your respect. However, the strength, bravery, and compassion for his pack that he has displayed throughout his entire life is more than deserving of your respect and loyalty" Dad bellowed.

"Yes Alpha".

"Challenge his command again and I will tear your arms from your body. Is that understood?"

"Yes Alpha".

Dad lowered him back onto his feet but didn't release the grip on his neck. Dad leaned closer and growled with his teeth bared.

"I apologize my Alpha-Son, I will not disrespect you again" he said with a shaky voice. Dad threw him into a chair at the back of the room and ran his fingers through his hair in an attempt to put his calmness back together.

"Gunner, please continue" he huffed standing beside me. I smirked at the commander and glanced at the other men, they were all now giving me their full attention.

"Hunters are coming, they mean war and they will kill every Were in the village to get what they want" I paused and waited for their onslaught of questions.

"How do you know this?"

"When?"

"Impossible"

"What do they want?"

I raised my hands to command silence, and this time, they obeyed. I looked to my dad and he nodded, it was time to tell the pack about my Mate.

"Early this morning we captured a hunter that had been residing in the town for the past seventeen years, unbeknownst to us".

"How did you find him out?" one of the older commanders interrupted. I know him only as Rex, but he's been around longer than I have.

"He was apprehended for questioning about his relationship to my True Mate, Zelena".

"Your True Mate?" Rex interjected again. Not asking disrespectfully, just curiously.

"Yes, my True Mate" I confirmed.

"There hasn't been a True Mate pairing for decades, why would there be one now?" Rex asked with a slight bow in order to show he was not challenging me, but just asking.

"That question is best directed to the Goddess herself" my father answered.

"And the relationship, between the hunter and your Mate, is what?" the newest commander, Felix, asked stepping forward to the table.

"She was raised to believe that he was her father, during his interrogation he revealed the truth of his identity and his motivations". I paused again for more questions, but the room was quiet. They were now allowing me the time to explain uninterrupted.

"The hunter known as Hank, was ordered to kidnap Zelena as a babe from a pack we suspect was in Alaska. In doing so her birth parents were killed along with the remainder of their pack".

"My Alpha-Son" another commander interrupted, he placed his hand on his chest and bowed his head slightly as a show of respect and submission.

"Jonathon is my name. Why would the hunters go to such lengths for your True Mate? True Mates can be powerful, but they couldn't have known what she would be to you, especially as only a pup". His question was valid, but the theory he was working on was far off. I felt all eyes burning into me, waiting for the answer to his question.

"It's not about her being my True Mate. In fact their motives aren't tied to Tri-Moon at all" I began, again no interruptions, just silence.

"Zelena is the last known female descendant of Selena, the first chosen daughter of the Goddess. She bears the mark of the Moon Goddess and harnesses her powers as well. Zelena is the newborn Triple Goddess". There were multiple gasps and muffed swears, and then a deafening silence. None of them would dare challenge my word now, but it would still be difficult for them to believe.

"You are sure?" Rex asked.

"With the confession from the hunter, and the few of us that have witnessed her powers in use, plus Artemis has confirmed it, the fact can no longer be denied. The Triple Goddess has been born again, and she is of the Tri-Moon pack" my father spoke strongly, with not a hint of doubt in his voice. They all looked around at each other and then back to my father. Their expressions quickly turned from disbelief to shock, to fear, to excitement, and then landed on what appeared to be pride or respect. Then collectively they turned to face me and bent a knee to the ground and bowed their heads. My father did not kneel but he did bow. In one unified voice that echoed around the hall, as if they had practiced it, they chorused together,

"For the Alpha and the Goddess".

I felt a wave of energy crash through me and like a warm glow prickle across my skin. I looked at my dad and he was still bowed but looking at me with a proud smile. I know what this was meant to be, I've been told about since I was a pup. But this isn't how it's meant to happen.

"Dad?" I whispered running my hands along my arms, feeling the warmth.

"Dad, was that...?". He stood up straight and placed his hands on my shoulders, leaning his forehead against mine his spoke softly, "My Alpha" his words sparked in my ears like electricity. Everyone else stood up slowly and stared at me. My father stepped back and Cole took his place, repeating the same action.

"My Alpha" he said proudly. The remaining pack members followed suit. With each embrace and each call of the Alpha, I felt my connection to the pack grow. I could feel my muscles spasm and grow beneath my skin, my spine straightened and my tingled with renewed power. Once everyone in the hall, even Jackson, had acknowledged me as their new Alpha, I turned back to the table.

"Thank you, my brothers, I will not fail you and I will fight every day to prove that your faith in me is warranted. But for now, let's turn our attention back to the matter at hand" I tried to sound confident, and they all seemed to believe me. This was unprecedented, for an Alpha to ascend at only eighteen. Especially when the former Alpha is still alive and perfectly capable of continuing his role. There is meant to be a ceremony, held in front of the entire pack to bear witness. But this impromptu and unexpected changing of hands was far from the norm. I have trained and prepared for this my entire life, but I still don't know if I'm actually ready for it.

Everyone gathered around the table and we began our preparations. We would call to our allies, the Blue Moon pack that resides a few hours away, and the Crescent Wolves, that lived further away still. Both packs were strong and had great fighters, we never had to called on them before, but they had always remained loyal to our alliance. Mazz, Julian and Smith will head out at first light.

The pups, the elderly, and wolves that can't fight will be taken to our emergency housing located in a warehouse near the docks in the human town. I tasked each commander with their own role.

Rex the elder commander was to oversee the extra security of our borders. Jonathon and Jackson were to lead their fighters to guard the forest entrance. And Felix is to set traps and other defences around the village. Cole, who I announced as my Beta, was to assist and lead the commanders in the completion of their tasks.

"As my ascension to Alpha happened somewhat unexpectedly and without the pack to witness, we will need to address that before we commence the relocation" I told the group.

"Mazz, Julian, tonight will you both spread the word that the Alpha has requested the pack to gather in front of the porch of the pack house at dawn".

"Yes Alpha" they chorused.

"I will inform the pack of the incoming threat after the ascension announcement. Remember we don't know when the hunters will arrive, so we need to be prepared for their attack as soon as possible. The relocation to the town safe house will be done tomorrow afternoon. Is everyone clear on their responsibilities?"

"Yes Alpha" they answered in unison.

"Thank you, my brothers, I trust in you and I appreciate your strength and courage. Spend tonight with your families and rest up. I will see you at sunrise".

"My Alpha" Jonathon said as he tipped his head and left the hall, Rex and Felix we right behind him. Mazz and Julian both put their hands to their chest and nodded as they left.

"My Alpha" Spartan said with a smile as he pulled me in for a hug. Spartan isn't usually one for showing affection. I knocked my fist on his back and grunted as he squeezed me tightly. He let me go and smiled before leaving. Jackson walked over with his head bowed avoiding eye contact.

"My Alpha, I apologize again for my disrespect earlier" he said sheepishly.

"All is forgiven, though I expect it won't happen again?" I asked strongly.

"No, my Alpha, you have my respect and my loyalty" he blurted out placing his hand on his chest and bowing.

"Thank you, Jackson, we'll start fresh".

"Thank you, my Alpha," he stood up straight, tipped his head in a bow and left.

Smith approached me with a smirk.

"My big strong Alpha" he chuckled with a bow. I pulled him in for a hug and he hugged me back.

"You're not mad?" he asked into my ear,

"I'm furious, but I also know how damn good she smells, and I can't hold that against you" I chuckled a little. I let him go and he stood with his hands on my shoulders.

"I'm truly sorry, it caught me off guard, and I..."

"Smith" I interrupted,

"It's okay, I know you. Stay for dinner yeah?"

"Definitely" he smiled and headed out the door. Cole gave me a wink and smacked my shoulder and followed Smith. Dad stepped in front of me and pulled me into a strong hug, lifting my feet off the ground.

"I'm proud of you son".

"Thanks, Dad". He put me down and held my shoulders.

"You conducted yourself well and organized those old dogs with ease. You are every bit the Alpha I hoped you would be" he said proudly with a wetness welling in his eyes.

"You taught me well Dad, thank you". We looked at each other for a moment before he cleared his throat and dropped his arms.

"I'm going to get some food and fill in your mother" he said rubbing his belly.

"She's going to be pissed that she missed the ascension".

"Oh yeah" he huffed on a laugh.

"Well, I leave that with you. I'm gonna go check on my Luna" I said heading out the door.

"Son" Dad called after me,

"Yeah?" I answered turning back to him,

"Make the most of tonight, a lot will change come sunrise".

I nodded my head and walked away heading up the stairs. My Luna, I thought. I'm the Alpha now, and Zelena is the Luna. Come tomorrow the pack will know about the new Alpha and his True Mate, their Luna and Triple Goddess. I know that the senior pack and commanders see my mating with Zelena as the ultimate advantage, and they aren't wrong. Everything leading up to this point has proven that we will reign together as one of the most powerful pairs in our history.

Chapter Twenty-Two

Gunner

I lay in bed staring at the dimly lit ceiling. The light from the bathroom was enough to illuminate the room. Zelena was resting her head on my chest, quietly humming while tracing circles across my bare stomach. I tickled my fingers up and down her naked back, her skin was so soft and smooth. I still can't believe it was once riddled with scars. I could lay with her like this all night. She is everything I could have hoped for in a Mate and a Luna.

"Zelena" I spoke softly.

"Oh no, you're using my full name" she said nervously.

"I need to tell you something" I said perching myself up on my elbow,

"Okay" she said slowly angling herself up, putting her chin in her hands and looking at me.

"While you were resting, I met with the pack council. My dad, and the commanders…"

"Commanders?" she interrupted,

"Yeah, they're the leaders of the pack fighters, kind of like the generals of an army. Anyway. With everything your dad, I mean Hank. Everything that he told us about the other hunters, well we had to prepare".

"Prepare for what?"

"Well, to prepare for battle".

"What battle, Gunner what's going on?" Zelena asked as she perched up a little higher.

"The hunters that are coming, are coming to kill. They're not just coming out here to talk to us" I said gently.

"You don't know that" she squeaked. I gave her an 'are you serious' kind of look and she nodded in agreement.

"That's not all" I huffed hesitantly.

"Oh god, what?" Zelena grumbled. I could only just hold back the smirk playing on my lips, she's so cute when she's grumpy.

"Well, I had to tell the commanders why the hunters were coming. I had to tell them about you, your lineage, and your new status".

"You mean about me being this Triple Goddess?"

"Yes".

"Oh" she looked off out the dark window for a few minutes. I could smell a small amount of anxiety from her, but it quickly disappeared. She turned back to me with a smile.

"Well, they were going to find out sooner or later. I suppose now that I have pretty good control of myself, now is a good a time as any" she tried to sound confident but her voice cracked a little mid-sentence. I gripped her hand and smiled softly at her bravado.

"I'm glad to hear that, because there's more" I said with an awkward smile.

"Oh, god. What is it?".

"Well…" I paused trying to figure out the best way to word this without freaking her out.

"Well, um... Once I told them about you, I told them about our True Mate bond as well",

"Mhm" she hummed,

"After they were all caught up, and the full gravity of what I was telling them sank in"

"Ha, gravity" she giggled. I flicked her nose and continued,

"They kind of initiated my ascension".

"Ascension to what?" she tilted her head to the side.

"To Alpha". Zee flew up on the bed now sitting on her knees and staring at me wide eyed. I was distracted by her nakedness and her perfect perky breasts staring right at me.

"Alpha" she said snapping me back to reality,

"You're the Alpha now?" she asked urgently.

"Yes. It wasn't supposed to happen this soon and it usually happens during a special ceremony in front of the whole pack".

"You're the Alpha" she said again, like she was trying to convince herself.

"Yes, little wolf, and you're the Luna". I sat upright and cupped her cheek in my hand.

"No I'm not, your mum is the Luna" she scoffed with her nose crinkled.

"She was, but the moment I became Alpha, you became Luna".

"Holy shit" she slumped back and kicked her legs out from under her.

"One more thing" I said sheepishly.

"Fuck, what more could there be?" she growled.

"I've called the pack to meet in front of the house at first light. We are going to announce our ascension to Alpha and Luna, and the incoming threat from the hunters".

"Oh, the hunters" she said putting her hands on her cheeks with a terrified look in her eyes.

"You're the Alpha now and I'm the Luna. We have to protect the pack, it's our duty now, our responsibility. Gunner, what are we going to do?" she spoke quickly as her panic started to rise and she started getting flustered in her own thoughts. I pulled her close to me, grabbing her face and kissing her forehead.

"Calm down, everything will be ok. I'll tell you the plan" I said smoothly, gently rubbing my thumb on her cheek.

~

Zelena and I sat at the breakfast nook with Nat, Mum and Dad were standing at the kitchen counter. Clearly all of us were feeling a little anxious about this morning's announcement. The sun was not far from rising and already I could hear members of the pack starting to gather outside.

"Are you ready for this?" I asked Zee giving her hand a squeeze.

"Sure am" she smiled. She looked every bit the Luna this morning. Wearing a dark purple dress that flowed to her knees, clinging to her body in all the right places. Her hair was pulled back into a ponytail and Nat helped her put some makeup on. She looks absolutely stunning, beautiful, and mature with a glow about her. Mum took the news pretty well. She only cried and cooed over me for about five minutes, I was expecting it to be more like twenty or so. Nat was pretty chill about it as well, she was more excited about her new sisters' powers than anything else. Zee floated a few things around her head to calm her down and to show off a little. I don't mind it though, I will never tire of seeing Zee's powers.

Dad and I are waiting on the porch
Thanks, Cole

"Cole and Spartan are outside" I said looking at Dad, and he nodded in response.

"Smith is here now too" Nat said standing up from the table.

"Alrighty then" Mum said before kissing Dad on the cheek. They all turned to look at me, waiting for me to move. I'll have to get used to this. It has always been Dad that we turn to, that makes the first move. It's my role now. I stood up and offered my hand to Zelena.

"Let's do this" I said smiling down at her. She grabbed my hand and I lifted her to her feet. Pulling her to my chest I pressed my lips to hers in a brief kiss.

"Together" I whispered against her lips.

"Always" she whispered back.

I turned to my family and nodded my head. Taking Zelena's hand, we walked out of the kitchen to the front door with the rest of the family following behind. I squeezed Zee's hand and pulled open the door. The sky was still a little dark but the early morning sun was slowly starting to lighten things up. I nodded to Cole and Spartan as we walked to the porch railing. Mum and Dad stood on Zee's left and Cole stood to my right. Smith walked up the stairs and kissed Nat on the cheek before standing beside Cole.

"Good morning, Tri-Moon pack, thank you for coming out so early to meet us" Dad's voice bellowed across the village clearing. The crowd of faces all looked at him with respect and adoration. He was a brilliant Alpha, and the pack has a lot of respect for him. I can only hope that I live up to his reputation.

"There are a few things we need to address here today. First and foremost, I'm sure you all felt the power shift in the atmosphere late last night. Well, during an emergency meeting with the pack council, your Alpha-Son Gunner, ascended to his new position as Alpha of the Tri-Moon pack".

Soft murmurs and gasps broke out throughout the crowd. My gaze landed on some of my friends who were all beaming with excitement, but I couldn't help but notice the few disappointed and confused faces as they whispered to each other.

"We understand that this momentous occasion usually happens with a ceremony that includes you all, however this is a rare and special occasion. Please welcome your new Alpha to continue this morning's announcement". Dad stepped back slowly with his arm out to me, signalling for me to step forward. I gulped down the breath that was caught in my throat and stepped up, putting one hand on the railing and the other on my chest.

"I swear to honour, protect, and serve you as your Alpha, until my last moon has shone". I bowed my head to the pack and then stood up straight. In unison, the crowd all got down on their knees, bowed their heads, and chanted,

"For the Alpha".

Their acceptance sent a wave of energy flowing through me. I again felt the warm prickling of my skin and a new connection to each of them. I blew out the breath that I was holding in. feeling somewhat relieved that they accepted me without a fuss.

"Thank you, my brothers and sisters, I will do my best to not let you down" I called while roaming my eyes over the gathered crowd.

"However, this is just one small part of our announcement this morning" I continued.

"As many of you already know, the beautiful Were to my left is my new mate, Zelena. What you do not know, is that your new Luna and I are not chosen Mates. We have instead been blessed by the Goddess with a True Mate bond".

The crowd was silent for moment. Looking around at each other before back to Zelena and me. A small cheer broke out and quickly the whole pack was shouting and cheering along, screaming their praise and congratulations to us. I looked at Zelena and her face was overtaken by a smile so bright and happy that it could infect anyone that saw it. They accepted our bond and accepted her as their Luna. I smiled out at my pack, filled with joy and pride. They love her already. Well, that didn't take a lot of convincing, thankfully.

My chest was tight with emotions, the most prominent being pride. My pack, my family, and everyone I have ever known and loved, they have all welcomed Zelena without question or hesitation. My smile was wide as I looked out over my pack.

"Thank you, thank you" I raised my arms to settle them down, and after a minute they were quiet again.

"Your new Luna is not just my blessing, but she is yours as well. Zelena here hales from an old pack in Alaska. Unfortunately, that pack was wiped out many years ago, however her lineage still holds great significance and importance to the Were community" I paused, swallowing hard before letting the next piece of impossible information be know.

"Zelena's earliest known ancestor is Selena, the first chosen daughter of the Moon Goddess".

Shocked gasps and hushed profanities came from the pack.

"Now I understand that this may be a shock, as it was rumoured that the line of Selena was abolished long ago. Some of you may choose to not believe. However, it has been confirmed and tested over the past few days that Zelena, your new Luna, bears the mark of the Moon Goddess and is the new chosen daughter".

Mumbled and hushed voices grew louder as I spoke until I was near on yelling the last few words. I lifted my hands trying to get them to settle down again.

"Please, quiet down. Please let me finish" I called over the crowd. "Zelena has the mark of the Goddess, yes, but she also wields her powers. She is, without a doubt, the Triple Goddess".

The crowd was silent, so silent that you could hear an ant fart in the forest. The tension was thick in the air and my previous proud confidence quickly dwindled. Perhaps I am asking too much of them too quickly. To accept a True Mate bond is more realistic than to accept a Triple Goddess. With my panic slowly rising, Zelena stepped forward and grabbed my hand, squeezing it tight. I could feel her nervousness, but I could feel her love and support more. I turned to look at her and she smiled up at me sweetly. It was all the push I needed. The pack then burst out in inaudible cries and calls. I whipped my head back to face them, but I could only make out a few of their words.

"Bullshit"

"Impossible"

"Prove it"

I turned to look at Zee once more. Her smile had morphed into uncertainty. She was a little pale and was chewing on her bottom lip. Her eyes were bouncing around the crowd, full of worry and panic. I squeezed her hand and breathed deeply.

"Zelena, my love, will you come forward and show your pack the mark of the Goddess?" I spoke, loud enough to be heard by the crowd.

She hesitated at my request but slowly stepped forward in front of me. At the sight of her coming forward, the crowd became quiet again. Zelena turned her back to the pack and lifted the hair off her neck, exposing her Goddess mark. After a minute she let her hair fall back down and turned to face them.

"I know this is a lot to take in, believe me, I struggled with the revelation myself" Zelena's voice carried like Christmas bells around the village. She spoke with so much confidence, it caught me off-guard. The entire pack was enchanted by her. Listening intently to every word.

"I understand your scepticism, I truly do. So, if you require further proof, please just watch" she quickly glanced at me and winked with a smirk. Fuck me, she's incredible. All signs of her previous doubts were gone. Gone was the shy little girl I found at a human high school, before me now stood a magnificent and strong Luna.

Zelena slowly lifted both her hands into the air and stretched them out in front of her. From between each of the pack members, small rocks floated up off the ground and into the air above their heads. The pack remained silent, their eyes all following the rocks. Zelena spun her arms around and the rocks mimicked her action. They twirled and flew through the air in a circular motion. While standing close behind her as she used her gifts, I could feel the raw power dripping off her. There was a subtle glow to her skin and a serene softness to her aura. This was so completely different from her persona in the cabin. Though she still looked and felt angelic, this was calm and gentle, there was no heaviness or danger about it.

Zelena flexed her fingers as she spun her arms, before slowly bringing them to a halt. She calmly lowered her arms and the rocks followed suit until they hung in the air, just above the heads of the pack.

"Please, take them" she called out. Different hands begun to reach up and plucked the little rocks from the air. Amazed and surprised voices were heard as they each examined their rocks. Zelena brought one over to me and it hung in front of my face. I took it from the air and turned it over in my hands. It was now a perfectly smooth marble shape.

"Wow" I exclaimed, looking back at my mate.

"Goddess" a woman's voice called.

"Luna" came another. And then another and another. Soon the whole pack were on their knees calling to Zelena, calling out to their new Goddess, their Luna. It was like a scene from a movie, they looked to her, called for her, like she was their saviour. In a way, I guess she is. I stepped forward and wrapped my arms around her waist, burying my nose into the crook of her neck. I couldn't be more proud of her.

"They love you" I whispered. She placed her hand on the back of my head and turned to offer me a soft kiss.

"Yes, maybe they do now. But will they still love me after we tell them about the danger that I have brought on them?" she asked softly.

"Of course they will" I assured her, kissing her once more before standing up straight and facing the pack.

"Please quiet down" I called out waving my arms.

"Please, quiet, there is one last thing" I called a little louder. Zelena raised just a single hand and the pack was silent. I looked at her with a raised eyebrow and she shrugged her shoulders. She already had more control over the pack then I did. Clever little wolf.

"As overjoyed as I am that you have accepted your new Luna as your Goddess, unfortunately, there is no time to celebrate just yet. A threat is fast approaching our pack and we must act quickly. Hunters are coming. They wish to take your Luna, but we will not let that happen." I spoke loud and clear, my voice carried through the village. Angry voices and remarks were hauled from the crowd, not aimed at Zelena or me, but instead at the idea of hunters coming to harm their new Luna. It was clear then that the pack would join in my mission to protect Zelena, without hesitation.

"Measures are already underway to ensure your safety and to put an end to the incoming threat. This afternoon two transport vans will be taking the young, the old, the weak, and anyone else who wishes to go, to alternate housing away from the village. It is only temporary, but it is necessary. Please pack only essentials and be ready by three o'clock. Any of you that wish to fight for your pack, please make yourself known to your new Beta, Cole Thomas, son of former Beta, Spartan." I pointed to Cole who took a step forward, his chest was puffed and he stood tall and proud. The pack stood still for a few moments, taking in what I had just told them. They slowly started to peel off and headed in different directions around the village. A large group stood waiting at the bottom of the steps, waiting for Cole. I turned and put my hand on his shoulder.

"Take note of who wants to stay and report back to me in a few hours". He nodded his head in agreement and turned for the stairs. I took Zelena's hand and began to pull her with me back to the door.

"Zelena" Cole said, calling for us to wait. We stopped and he quickly came to stand before her. I don't know why I was suddenly scared. My best friend, facing off with my Mate. Cole has assured me his trepidations towards Zelena had changed. But what if they hadn't? Cole put his hand to his heart bowed his head low in front of Zelena, showing his acceptance and respect.

"My Luna" he spoke proudly. Zee placed her hand on his shoulder and he stood. He gave a half smile before turning to go about his task. Zelena hurried over to my side, her smile just about splitting her face in two.

"Did you see that? He called me Luna" she whispered excitedly as we went back into the house. I smiled and wrapped my arm around her shoulder, kissing the top of her head. I was worried for nothing apparently.

"Go get your bag packed and ready, I have some stuff to do before I see you off" I told her, gently pushing her towards the stairs. She spun around and glared at me.

"I don't need a bag, I'm not going to the other house" she said sternly.

"Uh, yes, you are" I replied stepping toward her.

"No, I'm staying here, with you" she took a step back away from me and crossed her arms across her chest.

"Zelena, I'm not arguing about this. You will go with the other woman and children to where it's safe".

"I'm not arguing either, and I'm not hiding. They are coming for me and I'm going to stay and fight" she huffed angrily and glowered at me like the matter was done. Her stubbornness sent a fire through my blood and my anger erupted.

"Exactly Zelena" I shouted, throwing my hands in the air.

"They are coming for you, for MY Mate. I'm not going to let you put yourself in danger so that you can prove how strong you are. I'm not going to risk you getting hurt. You will go with the others and that's final" my anger only grew as I yelled at Zelena. The fire in my stomach was slowly spreading. She glared at me, not saying a word. I could feel her anger radiating off her skin, it mixed with my own in a delicious dance of dominance. She quickly flicked her wrist at me and I flew back across the floor hitting the door with my back. I stumbled on my feet but quickly regained my balance. I looked over at Zee and growled a warning to her.

"I will stay, and I will fight" she spat across the foyer. Her hands dropped to her sides and her tiny hands curled into tense white fists. I started to walk towards her with my eyes lowered, glaring from under my lashes. She dared question my word, I'm the Alpha. She held up both her hands and I was stopped mid stride. She put up that force field thing, just like the one in the cabin. I banged my fists on the invisible wall and pushed as hard as I could. The anger and fury inside me grew and grew. I was blinded by it, so much so that I couldn't recognise that I was feeding off her anger, just as she was feeding off mine.

"Let it down" I screamed with another bang of my fist. She shook her head with a wicked smirk. I placed both my hands against the wall and pushed. I yelled in frustration and pushed again with all my might. Zelena suddenly slid back a few feet along the floor, though she managed to stay on her feet. I felt a wave of energy fly from my hands and a heaviness in my legs. My skin prickled and a warmth spread through my fingers. It was remarkable, like nothing I had ever felt before. I felt strong and unstoppable. The feeling could quickly become addictive. Zelena dropped her hands to her sides and stared at me with a blank expression.

"That is enough you two" my mother's strong voice echoed from behind me. I quickly glanced at Mum's angry face and looked back over my hands. Did I actually just do that? I looked back to Zelena and she was still staring at me, shocked and a little frightened. Oh Goddess. I ran to her and picked her up in my arms, squeezing her tightly into my chest.

"I'm sorry, baby, I'm so sorry. I didn't mean to" I mumbled into her neck. I can't believe I just did, I used her own powers against her. I could have hurt her, unintentionally or otherwise. I'm so fucking stupid.

"Gunner" Zelena breathed out, her hands pushing on my chest.

"Gunner, you just used my power". I put her on her feet and she grabbed at my hands, turning them over in her hands, examining my fingers and palms.

"How, how did you do that?" she asked. I didn't know how to answer her, because I didn't know how I did it. I know what I did but how is another story.

"It's your bond" Mum said from behind us,

"Because your True Mate bond allows you to share your gifts, now, that apparently includes the powers of the Goddess too".

"But you said it could be dangerous if that happened" I said concerned.

"I did, and it still may be. But I also said this kind of pairing has never happened before, so we don't know what to expect".

I looked back down at Zelena and cupped her face in my hands, lifting her chin to look at me. My beautiful little wolf, my Goddess. So strong and yet so precious. How could I ever let her leave, I'd never be able to concentrate not know where she was, what she was doing, if she was safe. I hate it, but the safest option for her could only be one thing.

"I'm sorry my love, you can stay. But you have to promise to stay close and do exactly as I say". She was about to argue, I could see the thought play in her eyes and the words at the tip of her tongue. The stern look on my face must have made her rethink it. She smiled and wrapped her arms around my waist, pressing her cheek into my chest.

"I will I promise" she squealed.

I don't like it, not one bit. But she has proven herself strong and capable. The use of her gifts will help protect her, plus I will die before letting anything bad happen to her. She will be safest by my side.

Chapter Twenty-Three

Zelena

As I sat at the huge table in the room that Gunner called the hall, I was listening to him and Cole talking. Cole announced that more than half of the pack had elected to stay behind to help in the fight against the hunters. As much as I tried to argue with Gunner about sending them away with the others, it was useless. He just kept reminding me that he didn't force them to stay and the more wolves to keep me safe, the better. I didn't like the idea of normal people, or Weres, fighting against trained killers. Once Gunner told me about all the time each pack member is made to spend in battle training during their younger lives, it made me feel slightly better. I'd never actually seen them train, but I had noticed multiple times when the village gets unusually quiet through the day. Makes sense now where they all disappeared to. Apparently, battle training is now an enforced requirement after an incident that happened a long time ago.

Gunner and Cole were organizing where to position the extra pack members when Lupus pushed open the door.

"Son?" he said as he stepped through the door,

"The Blue Moon pack fighters have arrived, joined by their Alpha".

"Their Alpha?" Gunner questioned.

As the words left Gunner's lips, the tallest man that I had ever seen stepped through the door and stood beside Lupus. He was monumentally gigantic. He doesn't look to be too much older than me and Gunner though. His skin is a deep dark brown with a smooth and airbrushed look to it. His large strong muscles were protruding through the material of his t-shirt. His shaved head allowed the light to bounce off his scalp. His lips were full and perfectly plump. His dark eyes which looked nearly black were pointed directly at me. I felt small and insignificant under his gaze. Everything about this colossal man screamed intimidating and powerful.

"Hello" he spoke, his voice like smooth silk, deep yet friendly.

"I'm Tobias, eldest son of Alonzo Gilliano, Alpha to Blue Moon pack" he was speaking and facing Gunner, yet his eyes didn't move from me. Gunner stepped forward, his body now blocking me from Tobias.

"Hello Alpha Tobias, I'm Gunner, the newly appointed Alpha of Tri-Moon. I offer my sincere thanks for answering our call" Gunner offered his hand and Tobias took it, they both lent forward and pressed their foreheads together. I've seen this action a few times now, I believe it is a show of respect when greeting someone of a high rank, but I haven't had a chance to ask about it.

They parted and Gunner took a small step back to the table, once again putting me in full view of the giant Alpha.

"If you'd like to..." He held his arm gesturing to the papers laid out on the table,

"I have been told you are mated to the Triple Goddess" Tobias interrupted, stepping towards my chair. Gunner quickly moved between us and stood before Tobias, chest out, claws ready to surface, and a growl rumbling through his teeth.

"I mean her no harm, young Alpha" he chuckled at Gunner's protective stance,

"I only wish to offer my undying loyalty and services to our Goddess" he flicked his eyes to Gunner and quickly back to me again. The air was thick with tension. Gunners muscles rolled under his shirt, his distrust obvious to everyone with a nose. He walked backwards to stand at my side and placed his hand on my shoulder, squeezing it slightly, a show of possession perhaps.

It's okay, Gunner. I flashed Gunner while gazing at the tall male. The sight of him alone was intimidating, but as I looked deeper,

I saw more, I felt more. I don't know what it was or how to explain it, but I trusted him immediately.

He is still a stranger, little wolf

He just wants to meet me, you knew that some people would act this way

I don't like how he's looking at you

Gunner growled softly but nodded his head to the huge man. Tobias stepped forward and got on his knees in front of my chair. Even on his knees, he was still at eye level with me. He bowed his head and held his hands out to me. His stance resembled Artemis in the library the other day. I forgot to ask Artemis the meaning behind it, and what I am meant to do about it. Like, am I meant to take their hands, or are they showing me they have no weapons, or something totally different? This is still kind of weird. For some reason, I felt compelled to touch the enormous hands in front of me, like I was being pulled to reach out to him. I slowly put my arms up and gently placed my hands in the centre of his palms. A sharp shock fizzled where our skin touched and the air around the room filled with calmness. His fingers wrapped around mine tightly, but he didn't raise his head. A quiet whispered voice blew past my ears, and a gentle wave of relaxation swept over me. I felt Gunner's grip on my shoulder loosen. I wanted to melt into the chair, bask in the feel of the stranger's warm hands on mine. But the voice, where did it come from, what does that mean? Tobias looked up to meet my gaze and he smiled,

"I knew it" he whispered through his breathtaking grin.

"What was that? What does 'guardian' mean?" I rushed out looking over the smiling face in front of me.

"You heard it too?" he said excitedly,

"Heard what? I didn't hear anything" Gunner said in an irritated tone.

"Yes, I did. You didn't answer my question though" I said, ignoring Gunner's question.

"A few weeks ago, the Goddess came to me in a dream and told me I was to watch over and protect her chosen daughter. She said I would be called to her and when the time came, I needed to answer the call" he interlaced his fingers with mine, holding them between us.

"I am to be your guardian, to help your Mate keep you safe. My Goddess, I offer you my loyalty, my servitude, my allegiance and my life". There was no hint of teasing or joking in his voice. Every word he spoke was said with the utmost sincerity and seriousness. It was a little unnerving, having someone offer you their life. But this feeling, this gut turning certainty that he is meant to be here, that our lives are tied together, be it by fate, coincidence or Divine will, I can't ignore it.

"Well, this is new" Lupus said, still standing by the door.

"Uh, th-thank you" I mumbled, trying to calm the swell of emotions inside me.

"Do you accept me as your guardian, my Goddess?" Tobias asked, staring deeply into my eyes. I looked up at Gunner, just needing another branch to hold. He never took his eyes of Tobias, but his face was more serene now, no more of the previous uncertainty. Can he feel this too? Gunner gave one slow nod of his head, it was all I needed.

"Yes, I accept" I answered turning back to the Alpha.

"Excellent" he bellowed jumping to his feet. I jolted in surprise, pressing myself into the armchair.

"Alpha Gunner, please show me your plans and instruct me where to place my fighters" he called, slapping his hand on Gunner's shoulder. Gunner squeezed my shoulder once more and went back to the table with Tobias, where Lupus and Cole were waiting.

After some introductions, they started chatting over battle plans and the fighting abilities of the wolves. With the four of them in the room, and another new revelation playing on my mind, I felt small and uncomfortable. I have a magical guardian now. First, I learned that there are Werewolves in the world, and I am one of them. Then that I have a soulmate, and that we eternally belong to each other. Also, I'm a daughter of the Moon who has magical powers, and my father wasn't my father. And now this? A super-solder dedicating his life to protect me. Is this going to be a regular thing? Random Weres, strangers, pledging their lives to me?

It's too much. It's too much too fast and I can't breathe. I needed to find a bit of space for myself to process. I stood up from my chair and walked to the door. Gunner turned his head to look at me, I gave him a weak smile.

Just going for a little breather
Don't go far from the pack house
I won't

He looked back to the table and I went through the door, closing it behind me. The air right away feels lighter out in the foyer, I take a deep breath letting the air fill me to the brim. As I let it out, I saw that the front door was wide open, and I took in the busyness outside. There are new faces gathered around the fire pit, about twenty maybe a few more. They must be the fighters from Tobias's pack. I want to make them feel welcome and thank them for coming. Roe has been in the kitchen with a few other ladies all day, she'd have some snacks prepared to offer them, no question.

Once in the kitchen the chaos was undeniable. There were six ladies, plus Deena and Roe, all cooking and running about the kitchen. It smells amazing, whatever they are baking.

"Hi Roe" I called out.

"Zee, Darling, do you need something?" her voice came from behind two other women.

"I was thinking I should offer the Blue Moon fighters some food or something".

"That is a lovely idea, sweet thing. Grab a tray of sandwiches off the breakfast table".

I looked over at the breakfast nook and the whole bench was covered in trays of food. I picked up the biggest one, filled with wraps and sandwiches, and left the kitchen again. As I walked out the front door and down the porch steps, the men gathered at the fire pit started to notice my approach. One of the men who looked very similar to Tobias, just not as gigantic, stepped forward to greet me.

"Hi there" I said as I neared him,

"Hello, little Miss, what can I do for you?" he spoke. His voice sounds similar to Tobias as well, though I don't get the same feeling from him like I did with Tobias. They have to be related.

"I thought you could use a snack" I said smiling down at the tray in my hands.

"Now I'm assuming that you're talking about that tray of food you're holding and not that scrumptious little body of yours" the man said while pulling on his bottom lip. His tongue poked out slightly, coating his bottom lip and the tip of his finger. I believe he meant for the gesture to be seductive, but it only made my stomach turn and a distasteful feeling washes through me. I stared at him blankly, lost on words. His bluntness caught me by surprise.

"I uh... I um..." I mumbled. He chuckled and waved his hand dismissively.

"They're so shy here in Tri- Moon. I'm just kidding little one, calm down. Thank you, that is very kind of you" he said gesturing for one of the other men to come forward and take the tray.

"I am Marius, brother to Alpha Tobias and Beta wolf of the Blue Moon pack. Who might you be?" he asked with a cocky tone. He tilted his head to the side with a smirk and let his eyes scan over my body as he licked his lips again.

"I'm Zelena, I guess I'm the Luna now" I said taking a small step back, feeling very uncomfortable with his hungry inspection of my body. He snapped his eyes back up to mine, the smirk gone and his eyes wide. He dropped to one knee and placed his hand over his chest, bowing his head.

"My Goddess, please forgive my rudeness, I offer my sincere apologies" he said with a slight panic in his voice. The men behind him mimicked his action and all got down on their knees.

"It's okay, please stand up" I said stepping toward him again. He quickly stood and took a retreating step away from me. Even though he made me feel icky in the stomach, the action saddened me, I don't want people to be afraid of me.

"I just wanted to tell you thank you, for coming to help us against the hunters. We are very grateful" I offered a big warm smile and his body relaxed a little.

"Anything for you, my Goddess" he responded bowing his head again. I nodded to him and smiled at the men behind him, offering them my thanks as well. I waved goodbye and turned on my heels to head to the pack house. This is really going to take a while to get used to, the whole bowing and 'my Goddess' thing. It just feels weird.

I was stopped in my tracks by a massive pair of boobs in my face. I looked up at the owner and recognised her from the bonfire. She's the girl that was glaring at me from across the fire. Her brows were frowned together and she had her arms crossed under her chest.

"Uh, hi" I said confused at her angered appearance.

Her lip curled up into a snarl and she huffed.

"Can I help you?" I asked,

"Yeah, you can leave" she snapped, her voice a little too high pitched for my liking.

"Sorry what?"

"I said, you can leave. You don't belong here" she whined.

"And who are you?" I snapped with a growing frustration.

"I'm the one who is meant to be with Gunner, I'm the one he was going to Mate. That is until your pathetic bony ass rolled into the village" her voice was like venom, why would she think that she was meant to be with Gunner?

"Are you being serious right now?" I huffed in shock with a hint of rage.

"I'm dead fucking serious princess. Look at what you've done, bringing hunters to our pack, endangering us all. Why don't you just fuck off with your little flying rock tricks and take your hunter friends with you!"

Her words hurt me a little. I know that I'm the reason the hunters were coming, but it's not like I invited them here. And I'm sure as hell not running away from them. This bimbo is way out of line and I really don't feel like dealing with petty jealousy. I have enough on my plate already. I went to walk past the tall woman, but she stepped to the side making me run into her airbags and bounce back. She growled at me, uncrossing her arms and spreading her fingers by her side, claws at the ready.

"Move girl" I snarled.

I took in her stance, her readiness to fight, and my anger burst inside my stomach. She growled again and stepped towards me. I held out my hand and pushed her back with my power, she stumbled on her feet and fell onto her ass. She jumped back onto her feet and charged at me letting loose a wild howling scream. I lifted my arm to shield myself, but the action sent her body flying across the clearing landing nearly twenty meters away. She rolled a bit before stopping on her hands and knees, facing me. Her eyes were filled with hatred and her face was scrunched up in anger. I watched on as she changed into her small brown wolf, just a little faster than what Smith could. She let out a howl and charged towards me again. This bitch is relentless, and she has really pissed me off now. I stood facing her charge, my feet planted into the ground. I reached out my arms and lifted her wolf into the air. She struggled and fought against her weightlessness, still growling and barking in my direction. I threw my hands back down and her wolf followed, slamming hard into the ground. She let out a yelp but got back up, not putting her front left paw down. She started to charge me again, a little slower this time and with a hobble, because of her injured foot. I again picked her up off the ground and held her in the air.

"ENOUGH!" a strong voice, filled with an earth bending authority bellowed from the porch. I turned around and saw Gunner's angry face watching down at us. He jumped over the railing and was quickly standing in front of me. I looked at him and then around the village. I hadn't noticed that everyone had stopped what they were doing to watch me and the girl. All eyes were on me and my hands, still holding the bitch up in the air. Oh, no. This isn't good.

"Zelena, let her down" Gunner said firmly. I dropped my hands and she fell back to the ground. She lay there in the dirt for a minute before changing back to her human form. Her naked body stood up and she snatched a towel hanging from the railing of one of the cabins. She hobbled over to where Gunner and I were standing, stopping a few meters away.

"Gunner, baby, she..." the girl started to talk,

"Quiet" Gunner stopped her.

"What happened?" he demanded now looking at me.

"She came up to me and told me that I needed to leave" I said softly, now that my anger had died down a bit, I was feeling seriously embarrassed.

"And?" he pressed,

"And that it's my fault the hunters are coming".

"Is that all?"

"No, I tried to walk away but she got in my face growling and saying shit about you two being mated".

Gunner turned to look at the girl and growled at her through his bared teeth. She stepped back a little with her eyes wide.

"Baby..." she sooked at him. Why the fuck is she calling MY mate 'Baby'. The sound of her whining started to anger me again. A growl escaped my lips and I could feel my skin starting to prickle.

"Enough Zoe" Gunner yelled. Zoe is her name, perfect name for a big boobed bitch I thought.

"We are not Mate's. She is my Mate" he growled at her, pointing back to me.

"She is a good for nothing freak that is going to get the pack killed" Zoe snarled.

With that, growls erupted from all around us. Marius and his fighters were in a defensive stance facing Zoe. A few other pack members were growling as their gaze flew from me to Zoe and back again. An earth-shaking growl came from behind me, I whipped around to see a giant black wolf with a white crescent moon shaped patch on its chest. The enormous animal was standing at my back but towering over me. It was huge, way bigger than Gunner's wolf. I could probably walk under its legs without having to crouch down. It wasn't looking at me though, its black eyes were fixed on Zoe.

"Tobias" I questioned, staring at the humongous wolf. He huffed and nodded his head, keeping his eyes fixed on Zoe. Just his presence alone made me relax slightly.

I turned back to Gunner. I could see his muscles shaking, he was on the verge of changing. The anger coming from him was overwhelming. Zoe took a few steps toward Gunner and reached out for him. The action made my own anger spike again. I stepped closer to him and growled loudly. Tobias followed suit, still standing above me. Zoe looked at the giant wolf and froze.

"G-Gunner, I still love..." Zoe stuttered.

"Silence" Gunner snapped, making the simpering harlot bite her jaw closed.

"For attacking your Luna with the intent to harm or kill, you are banished" he said loud and firm.

"You are no longer of the Tri-Moon pack. You have until nightfall to be out of my territory".

Zoe fell to her knees clutching the towel to her chest. She breathed heavily looking up at Gunner, tears began to fall from her eyes.

"P-please" she breathed out.

"We're done here" he sapped.

As he turned from her, she let out a high-pitched wail. As angry as I was two minutes ago, the sound of her cries made me feel for her. Gunner took my hand and nodded to Tobias. He pulled me to the porch as I looked back to Zoe sobbing on the ground. No one helped her or went near her, she sat there alone. Everyone that had gathered around to watch went back to whatever it was that they were doing. Completely ignoring the girl crying in the dirt.

"Gunner, are you sure about this?" I asked still looking at Zoe over my shoulder. He pulled me around and into his arms. He crouched down to look into my eyes and cupped my face.

"She tried to hurt you, she's lucky I didn't kill her". He kissed my lips and wrapped his arms around my shoulders bringing me into his chest. Someone clearing their throat behind me broke our hug. I turned to see Tobias back in human form, wearing only a pair of blue basketball shorts. His shorts hung low on his hips, revealing that sculpted V shape like Smith has, only his dark skin made his eight pack and hairless chest more defined.

"Well, little one, you just made my guardian status feel completely useless" Tobias chuckled. I smiled shyly with a hot blush grow across my cheeks.

"If you can do more of that to those hunters then you won't even need us" he smiled down at me. Gunner's hands found a protective hold on my waist. He doesn't trust Tobias yet, clearly.

"I don't want her fighting" Gunner said coldly,

"I think I have proven myself more than capable" I argued, looking up over my shoulder at him.

"I know you are capable, but all it takes is one bullet, one arrow, one lucky hunter with a good shot and you're gone" he growled tightening his grip.

"I will fight" I growled back.

Tobias laughed out loud, interrupting our bickering.

"I am happy to fight beside her, young Alpha. I assure you that I will let no harm come to your feisty Mate" he said with a small chuckle and smile at Gunner.

"She is mine to protect" he growled.

"Gunner" I snapped, elbowing his ribs, feeling slightly embarrassed at the way he was talking to our guest. Tobias raised his hands in surrender and laughed again.

"She is yours Alpha Gunner, I only wish to protect her. It is in my nature to keep her safe, as blessed so by the Goddess".

"I'm sorry Tobias, Gunner is very protective. It's a consequence of our True Mate bond" I said, softly pinching Gunner's arm. Tobias huffed and tilted his head.

"You are True Mates?" he questioned.

"Yes" Gunner said firmly. What is up with him?

"We are, yes" I confirmed again, glaring up at Gunner's hard stare.

"Incredible" he exclaimed,

"You two are truly remarkable. It is an honour to serve beside you both" he put his hand on his chest and bowed his head. He lifted his eyes and smiled at me through his thick dark lashes. A breath caught in my throat and I pressed back into Gunner's chest. Tobias is seriously handsome. Gunner's fingertips dug into my hips and I hissed.

"Ow" I mumbled pulling at his fingers.

"Excuse us, Alpha" Gunner grunted as he pulled me through the front door. Once away from Tobias, he scooped me up into his arms and in a flash ran up the stairs to the bedroom. He kicked open the door and threw me down on the bed.

"Gunner" I howled as I bounced on the mattress. He quickly closed the door and came back to the bed, placing himself above me. He grabbed my hands and pinned them above my head. He pressed his face into the crook of my neck and inhaled deeply.

"Gunner" I whispered breathlessly. The feel of his skin on my neck was sending tingles down my thighs.

"What was that down there?" he growled lowly.

"What was what?" I asked pulling my leg from under him and throwing it over his waist.

"You like the Blue Moon Alpha" he said, not a question more like a statement.

"Huh?" I breathed. Why was he bringing up Tobias right now? He growled and bit my neck, not breaking the skin. The feeling sent more tingles down my thighs and into my stomach. He continued to rub his nose and lips along my neck.

"You like the Alpha" he growled.

"He seems nice" I arched my back and pulled down with my leg, bringing Gunner's bulging pants into my crotch. Something about his dominance really gets me going.

"He turned you on" Gunner said pressing his hips harder into mine. I moaned softly at the pressure.

"No" I whimpered as my breathing quickened. Using his free hand, he lifted my dress over my knees. In a painfully slow movement, he brought his hand up my thigh to the lining of my already moist panties.

"You're lying" he growled into my ear, biting on it.

"No" I breathed. He pulled my panties to the side and gently slid a finger over my wet lips.

"I could smell your desire" he said as he roughly plunged his fingers deep inside my pussy. I gasped and threw my head back. He moved his fingers in and out, pressing deep inside my core. I cried out as he rolled his thumb over my clit.

"Do you want him?" Gunner rumbled, moving his fingers faster.

"No" I moaned, arching my back further and pressing my groin into his hand harder.

"Who do you want?" he growled seductively, biting into my neck. He inserted another finger, making my breathing fasten and my stomach tighten.

"I want you" I cried.

"Whose are you?" he demanded, continuing his assault on my throbbing pussy.

"I'm yours" I moaned feeling my climax looming. I tried to wriggle my hands free, but he held them tighter. As he drove his fingers into me harder, I could feel my legs shake and my insides contract.

"Gunner" I groaned as the first wave of my orgasm hit. My toes curled and my clit throbbed, but he didn't relent. He curled his fingers inside me, setting off a new wave after wave of orgasmic bliss. His fingers slowed and he released his hold on my hands. I felt completely spent, slumped on the bed with Gunner kissing my neck softly. He removed his hand and sucked the juices from his fingers.

"You're mine, I don't care how big the Alpha is, this is for only me" he sucked my cum off his middle finger and smiled at me wickedly.

"Gunner stop it. I don't want him, I just want you" I cooed wrapping my arms around his neck. He leaned down and kissed me hard. I could taste myself on his tongue, and surprisingly, I enjoyed it. Abruptly he jumped up and off the bed, smoothing his hair with his fingers.

"Come on little wolf, enough play time, we have a fight to get ready for" he smirked. I huffed and threw my head back onto the pillow. He walked over and kissed my cheek,

"Don't wash off either, I want to smell you like this for the rest of the day" he whispered in my ear. A shiver ran down spine as his words got me excited all over again. Is this still the heat? I don't even care, I just love how he effects my body.

Chapter Twenty-Four

Zelena

As I stomped back down the stairs, I found Gunner talking with Tobias, Cole, and a man I hadn't seen before. He was a bit shorter than Cole and a lot older, but still clearly very fit and in good shape. His long light brown hair was tied back in a ponytail and his beard was well kept. As I reached the bottom step, all the men turned to face me. Their faces were blank, but I could feel the tension in the air around them. It prickled across my skin uncomfortably.

"What's going on?" I asked walking to Gunner's side.

"Smith is headed back, he reached the Crescent Wolf pack" Cole paused,

"And? Are they coming too?" I questioned. Cole looked to Gunner and the new man and back to me, his eyes dropped a little. Something didn't feel right.

"Not exactly" Gunner inserted.

"Hello Luna, I'm Patrick, I've come from Crescent Wolf" the new man spoke, his voice somewhat breaking the awkward silence.

"Hello sir" I said softly. I felt an unease settle in my stomach. Something was wrong, but they were all dancing around it, trying to avoid telling me.

"What?" I snapped looking at Cole and then up to Gunner.

"Crescent Wolf were attacked, Patrick here came to ask for aid" Tobias finally spoke. Gunner growled softly at him. Attacked? A heaviness filled my chest, it had to be the hunters.

"Was it the hunters?" I asked, even if I felt that I already knew the answer.

"Yes Miss, we suffered a lot of casualties. Most of our fighters are gone, the ones that are left are leading the remaining pack to safe houses" Patrick said, his voice shaking slightly.

"Bring them here, we'll help them" I said urgently. The unease in my stomach turned to guilt, I felt nauseous and anxious. I did this. Because of the hunters, and their search for me, they have now attacked an innocent pack. What have I done?

"We can help, we have to help them. Oh god, this is all my fault. Gunner, please bring them here, we have to find them, we have to go to them".

Tears were flooding my eyes. I had to find them, I had to help them, I needed to make it right. My arms were shaking and my legs felt weak, the panic overtook me and I felt like my feet lift off the ground. I closed my eyes tight and when I opened them again, I was floating above a bloody scene. All I could see were dead bodies splayed out in a grass field. Small white houses, riddled with bullet holes, were lined up along a tree line. The grass below me was red with blood. I can see the bodies of children, all huddled together in the grass, though none of them were moving. Dead wolves with blood stained fur and torn apart human bodies scattered the grounds. The whole thing was horrifying. Off in the distance, I can see walking figures. Who were they? In a blink, I was now floating above them, looking down as they marched. Men and women, so many of them. All dressed in black army clothes, each of them carrying big bulky guns and crossbows, and all sorts of other weapons. It's the hunters.

I gasped for air as I came to again. I was lying on the foyer floor with Gunner holding my head. He took a deep harsh breath and quickly looked down at me wide eyed and confused. I burst into tears as what I saw played back through my mind. As impossible as it was, I knew it wasn't my imagination. The things I saw, the bodies, the blood, it was real.

"My Goddess! Goddess! Can you hear me little one?" Tobias's rushed voice echoed around the foyer as he knelt next to us holding my hand in his.

"Zelena, are you ok?" Gunner panted, his pale face and wide eyes filled my vision.

"I saw them, Gunner" I cried out,

"I saw the Crescent Wolf pack. They were all dead" I sobbed loudly as he pulled me up into his lap. I pressed my face into his chest and let the tears fall.

"I know little wolf, I saw it too" he whispered stroking my hair.

"And the hunters, I saw the hunters".

"What does that mean, she saw them?" Tobias asked.

"She has the Drakos-Mati" Gunner replied.

"Impossible" Patrick gasped.

"Does she really?" Tobias questioned again. They spoke like I wasn't laying on the floor in front of them. But I was glad for it, I don't know what I could say, how I could describe what I saw. I was thankful not to be interrogated this very second. Granted, Gunner knows a lot more about all this than I do, so it makes sense that they direct some of their questions to him.

"She does. This time she took me with her. I could see what she saw" Gunner finally answered. Wait what?

"You saw it too?" I demanded, lifting my head to look at Gunner. He brushed his hand over my tear stained cheek and nodded his head solemnly.

"But how?" I sniffled,

"You were scared, your fear allowed you to shared it with me, not flashing, but more like you shared your gift".

"The Drakos-Mati, the dragon story you told me in the forest?"

"Yes, not just a story, my love".

"You're serious?" Tobias exclaimed. Gunner just nodded his head, not turning his eyes from me. Three confirmed gifts. More power to get control of. Oh my, this life is going to be a crazy ride. I recalled the vision I had. It was like I was flying, such a strange feeling. My body felt weightless and yet power coursed through me. The sight I looked down on though, I shuddered, it was horrifying.

"It was awful" I whispered.

"I wish you didn't have to see that Zee, I'm so sorry".

The torn and bloodied bodies of the children hung in my mind. How could anyone hurt a child, Were or not. What kind of monsters are they? My own childhood pain echoed in the back of my mind. The hurt Hank had caused me replayed in my memories.

He was one of them, a hunter. I knew exactly what kind of monster they were. My anger grew and I could feel the heat in my skin rising.

"We're going to kill them all" I hissed looking up at Patrick. I want to feel the life of every last hunter as it leaves their bodies. I want to crush them under the weight of my power. I want to taste hunter blood on my tongue and feel ripped flesh between my teeth. I want to end them all. I felt my canines slip down and my claws break through the skin at the tips of my fingers.

"Zelena" Gunner said cautiously. I stood up and took Patrick's hand, staring directly into his eyes.

"I promise you I will kill them all, every hunter that hurt your pack. They'll pay with their lives". I could feel the venom of my words, my fury was bubbling over and infecting the men around me. Patrick growled excitedly and Cole smirked, lowering his eyes. I turned around to face Tobias and Gunner, crossing my arms over my chest. Gunner was studying me cautiously, he must feel my rage through our bond. Tobias had his lips curled back baring his growling teeth.

"They're coming. Let's do this" I said firmly. Tobias smiled and nodded. Gunner was red hot with anger but his eyes only held worry. The urge to sooth his anxiety pulled me towards him, dousing some of the heat. I stepped into his chest and wrapped my arms around his neck.

"I need to do this, you need me to help you do this" I pushed him.

"Zelena it's dangerous, you saw how ruthless they are" he pleaded.

"Don't fight me on this Gunner. I will fight them with or without your blessing".

He let out a slow breath and lowered his head. He knew my stance on this was too strong to argue, especially after seeing what they had done at Crescent Wolf.

"Okay, fine" he conceded reluctantly.

"I will not leave her side, Gunner. I give you my word" Tobias said placing his hand on Gunner's shoulder.

"You better not let anything happen to her" he snarled snapping his head to glare at Tobias.

"I promise, I will earn your trust young Alpha" Tobias promised. I already know that I can trust him. The moment that our hands touched, and I heard the voice of the Goddess whisper to me, the guardian bond was undeniable. Now I just need to help Gunner understand it as well.

The front door opened a little and Lupus poked half his body through it,

"The vans are ready to leave, son" he said.

"Thanks, Dad" Gunner called,

"Come and see them off, they'll want to see you".

Gunner took my arms from around his neck and kissed my hand. Together we each took a deep grounding breath to calm down, before heading out onto the porch. The village looked so empty, I could see men and wolves gathered at the tree line towards the edge of the clearing. A few more people were headed to the front of the house, but there were no happy voices or laughter. No sounds of kids playing, or the smell of food cooking. Nothing.

Gunner and I headed around to the driveway while the others went back to their preparations. The first bus was already loaded and ready to go, and the second was still putting bags in the storage hold. Roe was standing with two men, assisting them with the bags. A lot of men were standing waving up to the busses, both older and younger men, fathers and their sons, I guess. A few strong looking women were sprinkled into the crowd as well. It didn't occur to me that the females could stay and fight as well. But why wouldn't they? Girls are just as strong and capable as boys. Seeing the women made a sense of pride fill my heart.

We were walking through the small crowd, over to where Roe was.

"Are you taking this one?" Gunner called to her, getting her attention.

"Yes my boy, just finishing up with the bags" she answered with a smile. She walked over to us and pulled Gunner's head down to kiss his cheek. She gave him a tight hug and whispered in his ear. She then turned to me and pulled me into her arms.

"Take care of my baby boy, okay" she said softly,

"I will" I assured her.

"Take care of yourself as well, sweet thing"

"We'll be okay Roe".

Roe was every bit the mother that I wished I had. She spread the love and affection onto everyone around her. I'm so thankful and glad that I have her to turn to, I love her like my own Mum. She kissed my cheek and let me go, standing in front of us she grabbed my hand and Gunner's hand.

"Both of you be careful, I couldn't bear to see either of you hurt" she smiled weakly as a tear rolled down her cheek.

"We'll be okay Mum, you just look after this lot and leave the rest to us" Gunner said confidently.

"Can I kiss my woman now?" Lupus chuckled from behind us.

"She's all yours" I smiled squeezing her hand before letting it go.

"I love you Mum" Gunner said giving her another hug.

I stepped aside and let Gunner have a moment with his parents. I turned to go look around for Nat and swiftly spotted her standing at the back of the bus. I rushed over to get in my goodbye before she left with her mum.

"Can I get a hug?" I asked as I neared her.

"Lena" Nat squealed jumping towards me, she grabbed my shoulders and pulled me in for a hug.

"I wasn't sure if I was going to see you before we left. I can't believe Gunner is letting you stay, I was sure he was going to lock you in a dungeon or something. I don't like this Lena, you should be coming with us, what if something happens to you. I just got a sister I can't lose you now…."

"NAT!" I yelled with a small chuckle,

"You're nervous rambling".

"Oh, sorry" she said letting me go and holding my hands. I smiled at her fondly, I've come to love having a sister and a girl friend. I never would have been able imagined someone like Nat. She sweet and kind, but determined and fierce. She makes me feel special and wanted. I have been truly blessed to get not just Gunner, but his whole family too.

"You'll be okay, won't you?" she asked softly,

"Of course I will, we all will" I said squeezing her hands.

Lupus shouted for the last of the pack to get on the bus, so I pulled Nat in for one last hug.

"We'll see you soon, okay" I choked out trying to hold back tears,

"Okay, take care of Smith for me, I'm pretty fond of the big goofball" she said kissing my cheek.

"I will, now go quick". I pulled myself out of her arms and she ran over to her dad giving him a hug and a kiss on the cheek before climbing onto the bus. Gunner came up beside me grabbing my hand. He looked down at me and smiled sweetly and wiped away a tear from my cheek.

We waved to the kids smiling brightly at the windows of the first bus, blissfully unaware of the incoming danger. I know it's for the best but I don't like having to send them away. I should be with them to protect them, but I have to stay and fight. I'm needed here more. The busses headed off down the driveway, I watched until they were completely gone from view.

"Where are we at with planning?" I asked turning to face Gunner.

"With the new info from Patrick and your Drakos vision, we can estimate that they will get here not long before sunrise. We are expecting their numbers to be close to a hundred. Most are on foot with only nine or ten small tactical vehicles. Tobias brought thirty-eight fighters with him and Smith flashed saying he had gathered another twelve from Crescent Wolf. With our own fifty-seven fighters and the pack members that elected to stay behind with have just over one hundred and fifty wolves".

"Oh, wow. Will it be enough?" I asked with a deep breath,

"It'll be more than enough, so much so that we really don't even need you".

"Gunner, don't start".

"Okay, okay, you can't blame me for trying. I love you, Zee, I would die if anything happened to you".

"I love you too, you don't need to worry about me. I am so ready for this".

"Okay warrior, let's get back to the hall, I have to get an update from Rex and Felix".

~

Night fell quickly, with Gunner busy and Nat and Roe gone, the house felt cold and empty. Sitting on the porch looking out over the near empty village, I could make out some of the booby traps set up by one of the commanders. If you didn't know where they were, you wouldn't be able to tell they were there. That commander has a seriously dark and twisted mind. Brilliant but scary. He's set up some terrifyingly brutal traps. Gunner made sure I studied the placement of every single one, seeing as he ordered that I remain in the village when the fighting starts. I wouldn't want to accidentally get myself caught by one. All the lights in the village had been turned off to make it harder for the

318

hunters to see the traps, but thanks to our werewolf vision and the light of the moon, we could all still see just fine.

Roe and the other ladies had prepared a huge feast before they left. Our troops were more than thankful for the sustenance. Can I call them troops? That makes them sound like soldiers in a war. I guess they kind of are though, aren't they? I haven't been able to shake the dreaded feeling of guilt playing in my mind. All these people, these wolves, they were here because of me. I hate the idea that so many of them could die because of my lineage, because someone thinks I'm valuable. My gifts are both a blessing and a curse.

Smith, Mazz, and Julian returned a couple of hours ago. They have been in the hall with Gunner ever since. It was not long after midnight now, and everyone was in place and ready to go. All we can do now is wait. But the waiting, alone with my thoughts, it was driving me a little crazy. Tobias had picked up on my anxiety and thought it best to give me some space to clear my thoughts and prepare myself. I couldn't stay in the deathly quiet house alone anymore, that's what brought me out here onto the porch. Tobias stalked around the grounds in front of me, keeping close. A couple of his pack fighters were hanging close too. I assume they are my very own private security detail. The light from the moon blanketing my skin made me feel so much better, and more energized. Kind of like the shining light was the power source, charging me up like a battery. It seeped into my pores, my blood, my bones. And I drank it up thirstily, letting it fill my soul. I couldn't help but melt into the silvery light, feeling like I belonged there.

I laid my head back on the wooden chair and closed my eyes. I've used this Dragons Eye power twice now, no idea how I did it, but I did. With Artemis gone to the safe house, I had to try and figure it out on my own. The first time I was trying to work on my wolf senses and it just popped up. The second I was overwhelmed by fear and guilt and the power just took hold of me. But bringing it on by command was proving difficult. But I have to try. If I can locate the hunters, it'll help Gunner and the others.

I took deep breaths and relaxed my body, letting myself melt into the chair. Although the night air was cooling down, the light from the moon was keeping my skin warm. The hunters, where are the hunters? I tried to concentrate and picture them in my mind. The moonlight danced across my skin like lightning. I inhaled deeply and felt my body lift off into the air. The next thing I knew, I was high in the sky, looking down at a winding road. I could see six big black identical trucks, driving one behind the other. Where are the hunters? I quickly flew closer to the ground, the sky flashed past me like I was in fast forward. I came to a stop and was floating among the treetops. Below me were rows and rows of people, all dressed in black and carrying huge weapons, Just like the ones from the last vision. I found them. I flew back up higher into the sky and could see the coast in the distance with small lights splattered around it. I know where this is. It's the island, They're already on the island, and closing in fast.

I gasped loudly as I lurched forward in the chair. Tobias was standing in front of me with concern written all over his face.

"GUNNER!" I screamed.

"What is it little one?" Tobias urged me,

"They're nearly here" was all I could say.

Gunner came flying out the front door with Smith and Lupus following close behind. He pushed past Tobias and crouched in front of me taking hold of my hands.

"What's wrong?" he rushed out.

"They're here, I saw them. They'll be at the borders any minute". I flashed him parts of my vision, the trucks on the winding road, the hunters walking, and the view of the coast in the distance. His brows pressed together in a frown as he nodded to me and stood up. I followed suit and stood up also, I looked at the men gathered around me. Gunner, Tobias, Lupus, Smith. Goddess, please protect them. Gunner's eyes glazed over, he was flashing with someone. I looked at Lupus and he was doing the same. A loud bang off in the distance, from the other side of the house, broke them out of the flash and got everyone's attention.

"The spikes" Gunner breathed,

"They're at the end of the driveway. Cole reported them approaching the southern border" he said quickly.

"Spartan reported them at the western border too" Lupus inserted.

"To your positions and show no mercy, as no mercy will be shown to you" Gunner snapped. He, Lupus, Smith, and Tobias threw their heads back and howled loudly, signalling the start of the battle. The sound echoed through the village and into the forest, no doubt reaching the ears of everyone nearby, human and Were alike. It made my hair stand on end, and my ear twitch with the desire to change. Lupus turned and jumped from the porch, changing into his wolf mid-air, and bounded towards the furthest tree line. Smith was already on bended knee, mid-way through his change. Gunner grabbed my face and pulled me to him roughly, he crashed his lips to mine and kissed me hard. I grasped onto his shoulders and held him tight.

"I'll be back for you, stay safe little wolf" he whispered before pulling away. He joined Smiths wolf at the bottom of the porch steps, he glanced at me once more before snapping his head to the side and changing into his wolf. His beautiful silver wolf had grown. He was taller, more muscular and he oozed power and dominance. They took off around the front of the house, leaving Tobias and I alone on the porch.

"You ready for this little Goddess?" he asked looking down at me.

"Definitely" I answered with a smirk. I cracked my knuckles and headed down the porch steps.

"Oooh, this is going to be fun" Tobias chuckled behind me.

Chapter Twenty-Five

Gunner

"No, we need to spread them out more, here" Cole said pointing to a section of the forest on the map that was splayed out on the table.

"We already have two battalions in this area, they can cover that ground as well" I replied.

"Yes, but now we have the extra wolves to utilize, and that forest area is thick, they could use the additional eyes" Cole rebutted.

Cole has taken to his new official role as Beta Wolf with ease. We always knew that he'd become the Beta at my ascension, but doing the job and training for the job are two different things. I trust him one hundred percent and that's why I'm letting him argue his point, even if the Alpha's word is final.

"Okay, I hear you. Place another ten there and there, others here and here" I agreed as I pointed at parts of our borders on the map.

"Son" I heard Dad's voice from the ajar door behind me. I spun around to see him and nodded for him to continue.

"The Blue Moon pack fighters have arrived, joined by their Alpha" he told me as he stepped through the door.

"Their Alpha?" I echoed. It's unusual for an Alpha to leave his territory for the war business of an ally. They usually send the Beta or commanders. Why would the Alpha come as well?

~

I really don't like the way the Alpha is looking at her, like he is trying to see her soul. It's making my hair prickle.

"Do you accept me as your guardian, my Goddess?" Tobias asked Zelena. I fought against the snarl pulling on my top lip. Every part of my Alpha nature and my protective instincts are telling me to get him away from her. I don't want anyone else to touch her. and I sure as hell can protect her on my own. I don't need help, and she doesn't need a babysitter. As much as I don't want to admit it, there is something about him that seems genuine, something kind of calming. I don't know if that's the word I should choose, but there is something there, something different. Besides, if he was sent by the Goddess as he claims, then I couldn't refuse him. Zee looked up to me and I reluctantly nodded my head. I better not regret this.

"Yes, I accept" she said softly.

"Excellent" Tobias bellowed as he jumped to his feet and slapped his hand to my shoulder.

"Alpha Gunner, please show me your plans and instruct me where to place my fighters" he said with a smile. I gently squeezed Zee's shoulder once more before releasing her.

"This is my Beta, Cole" I said turning back to the table. They shook hands and we all leaned over the maps on the table.

"So far we have placed thirty-five fighters along this border. This section of the forest is very dense and would hold good cover for the hunters. We have traps set here, here, here, here and many more spread out through here" Cole spoke clearly and firmly as he pointed everything out on the map. Tobias nodded along, taking in the information we were telling him, offering alternatives and suggestions at certain points. His mind for battle was impressive, he pointed out things I didn't even consider. I need to get better at this.

A cold snap of anxiety slithered up my spine, it was coming from Zelena, she was worrying about something. I heard her stand up and shuffle her feet, I turned my head to look at her and she was standing holding the doorknob. She smiled to me but it was a forced smile, not reaching her eyes.

Just going for a little breather

Don't go far from the pack house

I won't

I turned back to the table as she left, picking back up where Cole was at with Tobias.

"Our best fighters have been positioned here, it's a more open area and easily accessible should the hunters enter from this direction" Cole continued.

"My men are highly trained warriors, with extensive combat knowledge and experience. They can be spread out and placed with your men here, here, and here. Have you heard from the Crescent Wolves yet?" he asked looking at me.

"No, no word from our scouts yet" I answered his question. We should have heard from Smith by now, I wonder what is taking him so long. I need to remind myself to check in on him soon.

"So far roughly forty pack members have elected to stay and fight. More will join them before the buses leave. They are trained in basic combat but not to the level of our fighters. We will be holding them back around here and using them as mostly clean-up crew. Once the fighters have taken out most of the hunters, they will be there to pick off the stragglers" Cole explained.

"You're allowing your untrained pack to fight?" Tobias questioned turning to face me.

"I have not ordered them to stay, they volunteered. They want to protect their Luna, their Goddess. They aren't useless, they can handle themselves" I snapped, I don't need to defend myself to this man I huffed to myself.

"That's admirable, I can respect that" he smiled with a nod and leaned back over the table. Okay, I didn't expect that response. Maybe I am judging Tobias too harshly. Fuck, I don't want to like him, but dammit I just might.

I felt a sudden tinge of fury burn through my chest. I stood up straight, placed my hand on my chest, and took a deep breath.

"Are you okay, Gunner?" Cole asked peering over at me.

"Something is happening" I panted. I focused my hearing and tried to make out what was going on outside. An all too familiar howl burst through my ears and I knew Zelena was in danger.

"Fuck" I spat as I stormed out of the hall and onto the porch. I looked down at the people all gathered to watch the scene unfolding in front of them. There I spotted Zelena standing strong with her arms outstretched before her. I followed the direction of her hands and saw a small brown wolf struggling to get itself free from the air.

"ENOUGH!" I roared, my new Alpha tone seeping into the words. I jumped over the porch railing and quickly dashed to stand in front of Zee.

~

My patience is on its final string, one more stupid, ridiculous, off-the-fucking-rails crazy thing, and I will snap completely. Goddess help whoever is close by when that happens. I can feel my control waning. I can feel the tension in my blood, boiling inside me, along with my steadily increasing anger.

First, this damn Alpha staring at Zelena like she is a snack he wants to sink his teeth into, and then that pathetic excuse of a she-wolf, Zoe. Maybe I was too easy on her. I should have punished her, tortured her, for attacking the Luna, for attacking MY Mate. Fuck! Why did I send her away? Releasing this built-up anger on her would have been so much more satisfying. That dumb greedy bitch. I told her multiple times that we were done, and yet she still persisted. Screw her, she earned her banishment. I definitely let her off too easily though, I should have ripped my damn claws over her throat.

I was already feeling possessive, especially after the way this Alpha was drooling over Zelena. But the way she looked at Tobias when he was half dressed, it made me crazy with jealousy. The connection they share is undeniable, I can sense it. Why Selene? Why did you have to send him to her? I don't like it. I can take care of her myself, I don't need his fucking help. She wanted him, I could smell it on her. It can't still be her heat, Artemis said most of it burned out of her when she used her power to kill Hank. The rest we worked out through the night. It had to have been a natural attraction. I'm at the end of my tether, if it happens again I will lock her away, force her to stay away from him. And Tobias! I will fucking kill him. I already have the urge to. One more wrong look, one more touch, I will end him.

~

Fuck I needed this. Her. Her taste, her smell, the warmth of her skin. The little sounds she makes when I touch her, when I push my fingers inside her. Her body is the best medicine. Cole's voice in my head interrupted my romp with Zelena.

Gunner, you need to get back down here now

I growled internally and pressed a hard kiss to Zelena's lips, forcing my tongue into her mouth. Then I jumped up off the bed, with a wicked smile, I can still taste her on my lips.

"Come on little wolf, enough play time, we have a fight to get ready for" I grinned at her. She huffed and threw her body back onto the bed. Oh my little wolf, I feel your frustration believe me. I gently kissed her cheek and whispered in her ear,

"Don't wash off either, I want to smell you like this for the rest of the day"

With that, I quickly ran out the bedroom door before I lost my self-control and started up again. I got to the foyer and Tobias and Cole were waiting for me, as was another man. Tobias sniffed at the air and smirked at me. Is this guy fucking serious with me right now?

"Gunner, this is Patrick, he has come from Crescent Wolf" Cole said gesturing to the new man. He put his hand on his chest and bowed his head.

"Alpha Gunner, it is my absolute honour to meet you" he said before standing up straight again.

"Are you a commander?" I asked, expecting that he would be here to answer our call for support.

"No Alpha, unfortunately, I bring no aid" Patrick answered.

"Why are you here then?" I grunted, annoyance growing in me.

"Gunner, Crescent Wolf were attacked by hunters" Cole answered for him.

"What?" I huffed.

"My Alpha sent me to you as the fighting broke out. We were caught unprepared and it was a slaughter, more than half the packed killed in the first two minutes" his sadness was evident in his voice. I felt for him, I really did. But I couldn't get my mind past the fact that the hunters were closer than we thought.

"Survivors?" I asked urgently.

"I am not so sure, Alpha, I intercepted your scouts on my way here. They said to continue on to you and they would check back on the pack".

"Thank you, my friend, a moment please" I said softly as I closed my eyes to connect with Smith.

Smith, Smith, are you there?

I'm here Gunner

Report

Crescent Wolf has been destroyed, we found a small pack of survivors
Alpha Titus, did he survive?
Still unknown, his Luna and children are with the survivors. They are
headed to safe houses now
How many?
There are sixty-two survivors with the Luna, there could be more spread
around.

Only sixty-two survivors. Crescent Wolf was a large and powerful pack, if they could be diminished to this magnitude, we may be in for a bigger fight than I was expecting. Cole was relaying the flashed conversation to the others as we spoke.

I need you back here right away, we will send aid to them once the fight
is done
Already headed back, twelve fighters are joining us
Good man, I'll see you soon.

I turned to look at Patrick, he looked defeated and pale. I placed my hand on his shoulder and he sniffed, clearing his throat and standing up straight.

"I will fight with you" he announced with a nod of his head.

"You don't have to do that" I assured him. He paused for a moment before answering.

"No, I do, for my pack" he said strongly.

Zelena made her way down the stairs and came to stand by my side.

"What's going on?" she asked nervously. This will hit her hard, I'm sure if it.

"Smith is headed back, he reached the Crescent Wolf pack" Cole told her.

"And? Are they coming too?" She questioned. We all looked at each other awkwardly, none of them wanted to be the one to break the news to her.

"Not exactly" I croaked,

"Hello Luna, I'm Patrick, I've come from Crescent Wolf" said Patrick piping up, seemingly excited to see her, despite his obvious grief.

"Hello sir" she said softly. We all stood quietly for a moment until Zee broke the silence,

"What?" she snapped looking around at us.

"Crescent Wolf were attacked, Patrick here came to ask for aid" Tobias finally spoke. He could have said it a little more gently, this will devastate her. I growled at him softly.

"Was it the hunters?" she asked.

"Yes Miss, we suffered a lot of casualties. Most of our fighters are gone, the ones that are left are leading the remaining pack to safe houses" Patrick said, his voice shaking slightly.

"Bring them here, we'll help them" she said with her voice breaking,

"We can help, we have to help them. Oh god, this is all my fault. Gunner, please bring them here".

Tears were flowing from her eyes and her whole body was shaking. Her eyes rolled back and she then began to fall to the ground, Tobias caught her before she hit the floor.

"Zelena" I cried out as I slumped down on the floor above her head. I placed my hands on either side of her cheeks and was sucked into darkness. I could see dead bodies everywhere. The little white houses indicated that I was looking at the Crescent Wolf village. I've been there twice, I remember what it looked like. But how is this happening? The amount of blood all over the ground was daunting. There's a pile of pups laid on top of each other, all dead. There are wolves and human pieces spread out across the open field. In a quick flash, I was now looking down at men and women dressed in black combat gear, carrying ArmaLite rifles, automatic shotguns, and high-powered crossbows. This is high-tech military equipment. These hunters are the real deal, not some rag-tag group of wannabees. I tried to count how many hunters I could see, but I was pushed back into the darkness.

With a deep breath, I was back in the foyer, sitting on the floor. I looked down at Zee, she was also awake again. That can't be possible, surely not. I recalled what Zelena told me that day we went running in the forest. Drakos-Mati is just a story, she couldn't really have the eye. But then again everyone thought the Triple Goddess was a myth, look how that turned out. That vision, or whatever it was, that was real. It had to have been. Zelena had never seen the Crescent Wolf pack, there's no way she could have known what it looked like. This girl will never stop surprising me.

"Zelena, are you ok?" I asked breathlessly.

"I saw them, Gunner" she cried, tears pouring from her scared golden eyes.

"I saw the Crescent Wolf pack, all dead" she sobbed loudly. I pulled her up onto my lap and pulled her face into my chest. Wrapping my arms around her shaking frame, I tried to calm her down again.

"I know little wolf, I saw it too" I said softly as I brushed my hand through her hair.

~

"We have this section of forest secure, the tree cover will give our fighters a boost. We have blocked the path through here and here. This section of the forest was already nearly inaccessible, we have downed a few trees to make sure that nothing can get through". Rex my eldest commander was pointing out the parts of the forest on the map as he spoke. He's a great Were, strong and capable. It will be a hard hit to the pack the day that he retires.

"I have traps set here and here for any incoming vehicles. More traps are set along this section of the border. The exterior of the pack house is secure and the village has been rigged here, here, here and here" Felix pointed out the cabins in the village and the other parts of the pack land. He has done very well in the limited amount of time he had. I like his initiative, his work ethic, and his focus. He is a high contender for the top commander position after Rex.

"I want Zelena to stay in the village during the battle, it's at the centre of our territory and it should be the safest place" I said looking to Felix, internally questioning his trap placement.

"As long as she stays in this vicinity and doesn't go near this cabin or this one, then she will be fine. This is definitely the most secure position for her" Felix confirmed.

"I want extra warriors here and here, closer to the pack house in case anything happens" I said pointing to the map.

"Of course, we will split a squad and spread them around these sections" Rex responded.

"Excellent. Thank you, my brothers, you have done brilliantly. Please return to your posts" I stood and offered my hand to both of my commanders. Rex took it first and bowed his head as he shook, Felix next and he placed his other hand on his chest.

"Thank you, Alpha" he said as they turned to leave the hall. Cole stepped forward from the corner that he had been standing in, silently watching my interaction with the commanders.

"Are you sure about this?" he asked me,

"About what part exactly?" I answered, I ran my hand through my hair and eyed him as he came to stand at my side, looking down at the table.

"About letting her stay, letting her this close to the fight".

"I don't have a choice" I groaned.

"Of course you do. Send her away Gunner, get her out of here. It's not safe. What if they get through, what if she gets hurt? I don't know how any of us will cope if something happens to her".

"You've really changed your tune" I smirked at him.

"I didn't give her a chance before, I admit that. But I see her now, she's… she's pure. She's good for you, good for this pack" he said not looking at me in the eye.

"Are you saying this because she's the Triple Goddess?" I asked him, leaning back on the table and crossing my arms over my chest.

"I can't lie to you, so yeah, that helps. But you were right about her, right from the beginning. She's special, not just because she is powerful, but because of how she has already changed the atmosphere in the pack. She's brought with her a glow, and it's infection everyone she touches" Cole chuckled in a far off way, clearly thinking about Zelena and the pack.

"They already love her, and she's only been here for what two weeks? It's incredible. I just don't know about this arrangement, about keeping her this close, even with Alpha Tobias staying with her". I growled at the mention of Tobias's name and Cole barked out a laugh,

"I knew you were only playing nice with him" he laughed.

"It's not funny. I don't like him" I growled.

"Why? Do you think he is lying about being sent by the Moon Goddess?"

"No. I don't know. Maybe. I just don't like the way he looks at her".

"Ahh, so this is about jealousy?" Cole chuckled. I growled at him and stood up straight. He threw his hands up in front of him in surrender and stepped back.

"Okay, chill out mate, I was just teasing" he smiled.

"Why would Selene send him to her? Does she not think I can take care of her? A fucking guardian, really? Why would she do this?" I groaned and paced around the room.

"Gunner, since when do you question the will of the Goddess? You know better than that. If she has sent Zelena a guardian then there must be a real reason behind it. You can't think of it, of him, as anything more than what it is, it will make you crazy, and we all know what a crazy Alpha is capable of. Throw in the fact that you are True Mates, it only makes you more volatile. Please try to stay calm. She loves you and only you" Cole pleaded with me. A lot of what he said makes sense. Deep down, I know he is right, and I need to stop questioning it and second guessing our connection. But it's hard to push that part of me aside. The possessive Alpha wolf inside me, all instinct and no brain. The thought of her having any kind of bond, with any other male makes me want to kill.

"Fuck" I whispered to myself. Cole came to stand in front of me and gazed intently into my eyes.

"You're right" I said to him.

"I know" he replied.

"You're a good friend, a good Beta. Thank you".

"Any time. I'm with you, Gunner. Always". I pulled him into my arms and hugged him tight.

"You swear it?" I asked him as he wrapped his arms around my back,

"Huh?"

"Do you swear it? To always make sure I'm not being a dick". Cole laughed and pulled back, keeping his hands on each of my shoulders and looking right into my eyes,

"Alpha Gunner, I vow to always be at your side, to protect the pack and uphold your leadership. As your Beta, I will always make sure you are strong and true. As your best friend, I will always make sure you are not being a dick" he said with a wide smile. I chuckled and pulled him back into my arms.

"Thank you, Cole" I said into his ear,

"Any time" he said back.

"Okay, go on then, you have Beta shit to do and I have a Mate I need to prepare". I let go of my grip on him and he stepped out of my arms,

"Yes Alpha" he smiled as he walked out the door. I watched him go with a smile on my face. I'm lucky to have him, as my Beta and as my best friend. Mostly I'm glad that he has come to like Zelena, they are both too important to me to not get along. We need to hang out more, after this, we all need a little bonding time. I'll work on it.

Zelena, I need you to come to the hall please

Is everything okay?

Yes, I just need to go over a few things with you

Okay, I'm on my way

A few minutes later Zee walked through the door and came straight to my arms. She wrapped her arms around my waist and hugged me tight. I pulled her into my chest and squeezed her small body against mine.

"What do you need to show me?" she asked looking up at me. I took her hand and led her to the table.

"When the fighting begins you are to stay here, in the village" I said pointing at the map,

"But Gunner…" she was about to protest.

"Just listen" I stopped her. She frowned but nodded her head and I continued.

"Felix has traps set up at these positions, it is vital that you stay away from these cabins. I will be fighting in this area and Smith and Cole will be here and here. Tobias has sworn to stay by your side, he will have four of his men with him. More warriors will be here if you need them" I said pointing out all the areas.

"Gunner I…" she started to argue again but I stopped her once more,

"I know how badly you want to help, but the best thing that you can do is stay here and not get killed. If I keep thinking that you're in danger or you're being irresponsible, then I won't be able to focus on the fight. I need you to promise that you won't do anything stupid Zelena" I looked over her face, and although I could tell she wanted to fight me on it, she didn't.

"Okay" she said nodding her head.

"Okay?" I repeated,

"Yes, Gunner okay, I will stay in the village".

"Well okay then. Take this map and study it, you need to be one hundred percent aware of the traps around you. I will show Tobias and he can inform his pack fighters". I rolled up the map and passed it to her. She looked uncertain, she was trying to hide it but I've come to know her facial expressions pretty well. I stepped forward and placed my hands on her shoulders.

"Zee, you don't have to do this, it's okay if you want to back out. No one expects you to fight".

She was quiet for a minute, taking in my words.

"It's not that, I want to fight, I'm ready for it. I'm just so scared for our pack and for you. So many people are putting themselves in harm's way because of me. I don't like it and I don't want them to get hurt". Her eyes welled with tears as she spoke. My beautiful little wolf, already thinking like a Luna.

"Zee, this isn't just about you. Hunters have been killing Were-kind for hundreds of years, they have plagued our kind since the first wolf. Our pack and our allies aren't just fighting because you are a Luna, but because you are their Goddess. You may not understand because you weren't raised as a Were. The Moon Goddess gave us life, she gives us hope. And the line of the Triple Goddess is her continued gift to Were-kind. Any wolf would give their life for the Goddess and her chosen daughter, regardless of who she was. So, you see, you are a beacon of hope for all Weres. You are worth protecting, not just because they love you, but because they need you. You are important, and I'm not the only one that thinks so." Tears were flowing freely down her cheeks now and her aura had changed, she was exuding pride.

"Do you understand now?" I asked smiling down at her beautiful face. She sniffed and smiled then nodded her head. I pulled her into my chest and held her tight, breathing in her scent.

"Okay, now go and study that map. I have a few more things to do" I said as I pulled her out of my arms.

"I love you Gunner" she said smiling up at me. I grabbed her cheeks and placed a kiss on her lips.

"I love you too" I whispered.

Chapter

Twenty-Six

Gunner

I was talking over the final details with Smith and Dad when Zelena's voice screamed through the hallway. I dropped my half eaten muffin and raced out the door to her side.

"They're here, I saw them. They'll be at the borders any minute" Zelena rushed out. She flashed me pictures, I saw the hunters converging on the borders and an aerial view of forest around our village and the coast in the distance. She had another Drakos vision, which is excellent. However, the hunters were definitely closer than we predicted, they had to be only minutes away from the borders now.

Cole report

They are at the edge southern border, with heavy weapons and high numbers of soldiers

How close?

Two minutes maybe less

An explosion, a loud bang, and the sound of bursting tires brought me out of my flash with Cole. They've hit the traps at the end of the driveway.

"The spikes. They're at the end of the driveway. Cole reported them approaching the southern border" I said turning to my father.

"Spartan reported them at the western border too" he informed me. They have us surrounded, just as we predicted.

"To your positions and show no mercy, as no mercy will be shown to you" I snarled quickly. I tossed my head back and howled to my pack, readying them for the start of the battle. Tobias, Smith, and Dad howled along with me. I could hear the replied howls from the pack and fighters almost instantly. Dad jumped down from the porch, changing through the air, and took off to his position at the western border. I stepped forward taking Zelena's face and kissing her hard. She had better listen to what I've been saying. I know she is powerful, but I don't need her acting like a hero. I just need her alive.

"I'll be back for you, stay safe little wolf" I said softly before running down the porch steps to where Smith was waiting for me, already in his wolf form. I looked up at her once more before initiating my own change.

It was almost instant this time. I hadn't changed into my wolf since before my ascension. I felt stronger and more powerful, my wolf had transformed into a true Alpha now. He was bigger, faster, stronger and his senses were way more magnified. I could smell human in the air, mixed with gun powder and metal. I could hear their boots stomping through the forest and their erratic heartbeats. I was now the ultimate predator and protector.

I dug in my claws and took off around the front of the house to the driveway with Smith tight on my heels.

Fight well my brothers and sisters

I flashed to my pack, they growled, barked, and howled in response. I could hear the hunters at the end of the driveway, yelling and crying out from their burning cars. A large dark grey wolf ran over from the edge of the tree line, followed by four more smaller wolves. I couldn't flash with him, so he's not from my pack. He bowed his head slightly and growled, nodding towards the end of the dirt road. I growled and clawed at the dirt three times. Gunshots began to echo through the night air, my ears prickled up registering the direction that they were coming from. I crouched down and launched myself off in the direction of the hunter's vehicles and the gunfire. I could hear the heavy thumping of paws and excited growls behind me. Smith and the other wolves were following close. The light of the fire was visible ahead as we closed in on them. Three dead human bodies were laid in front of one of the cars, the smell of their burning flesh filled my nose.

My Alpha

Rex

Rex's sandy blonde wolf threw the body of a hunter to the ground as we passed the first car. I saw movement behind him to the right. A hunter was lifting his gun and taking aim at Rex. I leaped over him and twisted my body through the air. Angling my head back I gripped the head of the hunter in my jaws as I continued through the air. I felt the warm metallic taste of blood and the satisfying sound of a crunch and a rip. I landed back on all fours and the hunter's body rolled through the dirt ahead of me. The sound of a gun clicking caught my attention, I spat out the hunter's head and turned to the source of the sound. A hunter leaning against an overturned vehicle was fumbling with his gun. I stalked forward as he looked on at me in terror, he finally lifted his gun to point at me. I struck my paw out and smacked the gun from his hands, sending it skidding across the dirt. The sound of his terrified scream echoed around me as I leaped forward taking his throat between my teeth. His blood spilled over my coat as I ripped his jugular apart.

Alpha we are taking heavy fire and being pushed back. We need more wolves at the northern forest

Backup is coming, Felix

I looked around at the other wolves, the visiting fighters were exceptional. I spotted Smith tearing the head from a hunter's body, he was handling himself well. I puffed out my chest and filled it with pride as he leapt onto the next hunter. I heard a whistle blow past my ear and then another, closer this time. I ducked my head down as I looked over to where it came from. Three hunters were standing side by side, marching forward as they rang off shot after shot. Who trained these idiots, because they are useless. I growled and bounded towards them, another shot flew past me and another landed at my feet. One of the hunters suddenly flew backward through the air and let out a loud scream. That's when I saw the dark grey wolf behind them. He had the hunter pinned to the ground and his teeth around his neck. I jumped onto the next hunter who was quickly taking aim at the grey wolf. I tore his arm from his body and he shrieked in pain, I clamped my jaws around his neck and pulled making his head pop off like a cork. The grey wolf jumped over my body and landed on the last hunter. Picking him up with his teeth he tossed him through the air with ease. The hunter crashed into a tree trunk with a loud crunch, that would be his spine.

Pleased with the fighter's abilities I growled and nodded my head, ushering for him to follow me. He understood and nodded in agreement. We raced off toward the north and quickly reached Felix and his battalion. They had been forced back far from the borders edge. I took in the scene before me. Bullets were flying all around, I could see a few unmoving wolves sprawled out on the ground.

We can't get through without them picking us off

Felix flashed. He was shielded behind a large tree trunk, his fighters were doing the same. I looked up, following the trunk of the tree, then peered out at the other trees. Large trunks with strong horizontal branches, the idea hit me. Perfect trees for climbing.

The trees, use the trees to get behind them

Climb

Felix's brown wolf jumped onto the tree trunk he was taking cover behind and began the climb. I launched onto a tree and dug in my claws, climbing onto the first branch and then easily jumping to the next one up. The remaining wolves followed suit, climbing up and then jumping across to the next tree. The hunters were oblivious and continued to shoot at our previous positions. We leaped from tree branch to tree branch until we were above the hunters. They had still not noticed our new vantage point. I looked over the trees around me, the wolves were waiting for my command. I waited until the hunters had marched further forward so that we could take them down from behind.

NOW!

On my command, the wolves all began to leap down from the trees landing on and near the hunters. My paws hit the ground mere meters from a hunter, I lurched forward gripping my teeth around the crook of his neck before he had the chance to turn around. The bullets slowly stopped firing as the dying screams of the hunters took their place. I flung this hunter around smashing his body into a tree beside me. He hit the tree hard and the sound of his snapping bones thrilled me.

A sharp pain and a burning sensation grew in my left shoulder. I glanced down and saw my blood spreading through my fur. I looked to where the shot came from and spotted a hunter lining me up for another shot. I growled ferociously and leaped towards him pinning him to the ground. He got off another shot as he fell back, just missing my head. I felt a pain in my ear and warm blood started to run down the side of my head and neck. Infuriated that I let him hit me, not once but twice, I wrapped my teeth around his neck and ripped the flesh from his throat. He spluttered and coughed as his head fell back in the dirt and his blood pooled around him.

You've been hit, Alpha

Felix flashed as he nudged his head into my side.

I'll be fine

Yes Alpha

I looked around at the remaining hunters. They were being taken down, one by one, by the rest of the fighters easily. A sudden wave of energy flew through the trees washing over me. It came from the direction of the pack house. Zelena. The energy was identical to what I felt from her in the cabin when she killed her father. This is bad, Zelena needs help. I went to run for the house but the pain in my shoulder slowed me. Damn fucking bullet. I snapped my head back and changed back into my human form. I looked down at my bloodied shoulder. The skin was torn open and peeled back by seared flesh. It was dark red and still bleeding. It'll be fine, worry about it later. I held my arm in place across my chest. The same large grey wolf came up beside me and held out its hind leg. He growled and huffed, nodding his head to the leg. I hadn't noticed before but there were a pair of shorts tied to his ankle. Smart idea, I'll have to remember that. I grabbed the shorts and pulled them on with one hand. We ran for the pack house side by side, I kept pace with his wolf, no problem. As we neared the tree line, the ringing of gunfire at the house was indisputable.

The grey wolf and I burst through the trees at the edge of the village and I could clearly see the circle of hunters closing in on Zee and Tobias's wolf. The wolf beside me growled angrily and launched forward, charging at the hunters. He was running right towards one of the traps. I ran as hard as I could and tackled him to the side just as the arrows fired. I hissed at the pain in my shoulder as we rolled through the dirt landing behind another cabin, he looked at me growled. I pointed at the arrows now poking out of the ground where we were running just moments ago. He nodded and growled lowly. I put my finger to my lips and glanced around the corner of the cabin.

Zee had her hands out in front of her, waving one of them out and back. A hunter went soaring through the air with one of her movements. Tobias was in front of her, protectively growling and snapping but he didn't attack. I looked closer and noticed the bullets stopping mid-air and falling to the ground at their feet. Zelena had put up her force field. Tobias couldn't get out to attack and the bullets couldn't get in. That's my girl.

To the right of them, I could make out a few bare-chested men on their knees, Tobias's men. Hunters were standing behind them with knives to their throats. Why hadn't they killed them? One older man was standing close to them but facing Zelena, watching her intently. He was in charge, he stood with a cocky authority to his posture. I ducked back behind the cabin and looked at the grey wolf.

"Zelena has a force field up around her and Tobias, we can't get to them and neither can the hunters". The grey wolf tilted his head to the side as I spoke. Not everyone knows the extent of her powers yet, they have only seen the bare minimum. If this wolf is one of Tobias's then he would have no idea how far her powers can go.

"She won't be able to hold it up for too long, or risk becoming to weak. One of the hunters have a few of Tobias's men on their knees in human form, with knives at their necks. It looks like he is using them to bait Zelena into dropping the shield". The wolf's growl rumbled through his body as he started inching forward. That was confirmation enough that he belongs with Tobias. I held him back as I continued.

"You need to free the wolves and then start taking out the hunters. I'll take them out as I go, but I need to get to Zee." The wolf nodded and launched out from behind the cabin, I followed after him running out towards the ring of hunters. I jumped through the air landing on the back of a hunter. I dug my claws into his neck and jerked my hand to the side, the rip of his flesh was evident by the blood that squirted from his neck. He fell forward and I quickly turned and rolled across the dirt to the one next to him. I sliced my claws through the back of his knees, he screamed out and fell to the ground. The sound of his cry alerted the others to my presence. I looked to the next hunter and he was slowly turning his gun to me. I jumped up at him, wrapping my knees around his neck, I twisted my body around and threw my feet back to the ground. The force of my twisting body snapped his neck, a move I learned from a Marvel movie. His body flew through the air and landed behind me with a thud. The new hunter in front of me now had his gun pointed at my face and ready to fire. He suddenly dropped the gun as his face scrunched up in pain, his feet lifted off the ground and his body twisted and contorted in the air. It took just a few seconds, too quick for him to even let out a scream. His broken and mangled body hit the ground and I turned to look at Zelena. She was floating just above the ground and her eyes were glowing a bright yellow.

The growls and howls behind me let me know that the grey wolf has succeeded in freeing the other fighters. A shot zoomed past me, close enough to feel the heat from it. I looked ahead of me and the hunter standing there took a quick step back in fear. I lunged at him grabbing hold of his head with both my hands, I twisted his neck with a loud snap and threw his body at the hunter that was behind him. The next hunter flew back across the clearing slamming hard into a cabin wall. Another two beside him were sent flying up into the air and came crashing back down at incredible speed. Their weak bodies popped like jelly filled balloons at the impact. A wolf zoomed past me tackling another hunter and digging its teeth into his neck.

I took a quick look around, the wolves were effortlessly taking down the last of the hunters. Zelena was sending two more of them flying through the air in the direction of one of Felix's traps. The hunter's bodies bounced along the ground and then disappeared into the hole filled with spikes. I looked back and saw Tobias's wolf standing over a hunter, his large paw was pinning him down. It was the man that was watching Zelena, the one in charge. I quickly ran over to them,

"Tobias Stop!" I screamed. He whipped his head to look at me and growled baring his teeth.

"I want that one alive". Tobias looked back down at the hunter and pressed his claws into his skin, leaning down to his face, Tobias snapped his teeth. He let the hunter go and stepped back to Zelena's side. He growled at two of his wolves to step forward, changing into their human form the two men then grabbed the hunter and lifted him to his feet. The hunter had slashes across his chest but was otherwise fine.

With the situation under control here I took the minute to check in with the others. Not being in my wolf form meant I couldn't flash the commanders.

Cole report

We're good here at the south

Smith report

Clearing out the stragglers in the east

Cole, report on the commanders

Yes Alpha

Dad?

He didn't answer my flash.

Dad, report

Still no answer. My stomach tightened and a panic started to build.

Has anyone got eyes on my father?

There was a moment of silence that seemed to go on forever before an answer came from Cole,

My dad has him, he's wounded pretty badly, but still alive

Get him to the house immediately

Yes Alpha

And the commanders?

They are all clear

With the news of my father's injuries, the rage inside me increased tenfold. I turned to look at the surviving hunter. I stalked towards him slowly, a growl rumbling in the back of my throat made my whole body vibrate.

"Why did you come here?" I snapped at the hunter. He was older, with a short silvering beard and streaks of grey through his dark brown hair.

"You know why" he chuckled. Yeah, I know why. Zelena.

"Why do you want the Triple Goddess?" I roared. The hunter just smirked at me, staying silent. I stepped closer and threw my fist into the side of his face. Growls of excitement came from around me.

"Answer me" I growled. The hunter spat blood from his mouth and looked back at me with a grin. I lowered my head and growled a warning, if he isn't going to answer he isn't going to live.

"Gunner" Zelena's voice came from behind me. I held my hand out to silence her.

"Talk hunter" I warned him, one last time.

"Her power can destroy your filthy kind. Her line can end you all" he snarled, venom dripping from his words. I chuckled at him and he looked at me surprised.

"You don't know her at all" I smirked. These hunters thought that Zelena would turn on us, on were-kind. It was the abuse from one of their own that ensured she would never side with them. Thanks to the years of torture and abuse at the hands of a hunter, Zelena knew them for what they really were. Heartless monsters. I couldn't hold the laugh in any longer, I began to chuckle out loud. They have no idea what she is capable of, and they thought she would do their bidding.

"She is a werewolf, she is our family. You thought you could turn her into one of you, turn her against her own kind?" I leaned forward and laughed hard.

"Babe, are you alright" Zelena called out. I looked back at her, she was confused but almost smiling at my reaction. She quickly brought me back to reality. No, I wasn't alright. They tried to take her from me. My Mate. They wanted to hurt her and use her. My rage exploded inside me, the fire flowed through my arms and legs. I stood up straight and stepped closer to the hunter. I grabbed his head with my hands and forced his face to look at me.

"She will never be your weapon" I snarled. With a quick flick of my hands, I snapped his head to the side and his body fell limp in the arms of the fighters. They let him go and his body slumped to the ground, dead.

I turned to Zee and took three large steps towards her and pulled her into my arms. I sniffed at her hair, taking in her delicious scent, citrus and cherry-blossoms. She wrapped her arms around my waist and buried her face into my chest. The contact of her skin calmed me instantly. With the adrenalin gone, the pain in my arm was staggering. She pulled her head back and looked over my face.

"You're bleeding" she snapped, grabbing my chin and turning my head.

"Your ear, Gunner" she gasped releasing my face.

"I'm okay Zee, don't panic" I told her trying to sound soothing. I failed though and she could tell. She looked over at my shoulder and noticed the blood and bullet hole. Her eyes glowed yellow and her hands on my forearms felt like fire.

"They shot you" she growled. Her body started shaking and her eyes burned into mine. She was pushing her rage onto me and I wanted to give over to it. I could feel her anger coursing through my veins. The urge to kill everything around us pulsed through me. I did the first thing I could think of and smashed my lips against hers, pulling her body into mine and forcing her lips apart. I kissed her hard and fast, tasting her with my tongue. She hesitated but began to kiss me back, moving her lips with mine. The rage gradually died down, and our burning bodies cooled. I pulled my lips away and she sucked in a deep breath.

"I'm okay Zelena, I need you to stay calm" I whispered keeping my forehead pressed against hers.

"I'm sorry" she said softly,

"Don't be sorry my love, just try and keep your cool, okay?".

"Okay" she breathed out.

Chapter Twenty-Seven

Zelena

After cutting the power to the pack house at the switch box, the village was now dark. A small glow from the direction of the driveway told me that the loud bang I heard a few minutes ago was an explosion. I stood in the clearing that Gunner had marked out for me. Tobias stood next to me in his wolf form. Four of his fighters were surrounding us, also in their wolf form. I feel like I should change as well, but I haven't mastered my power as my wolf yet. I don't even know if I can. My best bet is to stay in human form.

A startled yelp escaped my lips when gunfire rang out around us. Shit, here we go. Tobias nudged his head against my shoulder.

I got you little one

I looked up at him wide eyed. He flashed me, how did he flash me?

We can flash?

I assumed as much, being your guardian and all that, we have to be able to communicate

Oh, yeah of course

More gunfire began to echo through the trees and I whipped around and stared off into the forest.

Stay calm, Goddess

I am calm

I can smell you, Zelena

Shut up, I said I'm calm

Okay, you're calm

I most definitely was not calm. I was on the verge of a full blown panic attack. There was so much shooting and it was coming from all directions. Oh god, what if Gunner gets hurt? My head was whipping around in all directions, following the sound of screams and gunfire. I closed my eyes and took a deep breath. I need to chill out a bit. I won't do anyone any good if I end up a nervous wreck lying in the dirt. I sucked in a breath, held it for a minute then blew it out. A warm calmness slowly spread through my blood. Ah, that's better. I felt a vibration in my hand and I snapped my eyes open. Tobias had lowered his head and my fingers were now twisting through his fur, he was purring softly.

Feel better?

I frowned at him but didn't pull away, because I was indeed feeling better.

How do you do that?

Do what?

Make me feel calm and safe

It's my job now, as your guardian

Yes, but how?

I don't know little one, we just have a bond now. Not quite like the bond you have with your Mate, but not completely different either

Are we Mates too?

No, no, no. Not Mates, just bonded

Uh okay, I guess

A growl from one of the fighters pulled my attention. Tobias stood up straight and repositioned himself around me, he was growly viciously and looking off to the trees. The other fighters started growling too. I followed his line of sight and gazed at the tree line. The more I focused the more I could see. Humans slowly started emerging from the tree line and started to spread out. A bark from the fighter behind us had me turn around, more hunters were behind us now too. We were slowly being surrounded. How did they even get passed the wolves at the borders?

"You must be Zelena" a voiced called from the other direction, I spun around again and my eyes landed on a man standing a step in front of the others.

"My how you've grown" he sneered. He wore black combat pants and a long sleeve black shirt with what looked like a utility vest, or maybe a bullet proof vest, over the top. His feet were apart and his hands were on his hips. They were still far away from us, but close enough for me to make out the devilish smile he wore under his smug bearded face. Tobias pressed his body against me, his growl echoed through the clearing.

"How do you know my name?" I called out to him. He chuckled and the sound felt so familiar to me. It sent a cold shiver up my spine.

"Well, I guess I'm your Uncle Trevor" he said sarcastically. Wait, my what now?

"Tell me mutt, where is my dear little brother?"

His brother? Am I meant to know who the fuck he is talking about? Who is this idiot anyway? The man shifted in his position a little and the moonlight hit his face. I know that face, well at least someone that had a very similar face. Oh shit, I almost burst out laughing. The dots all connected in my mind, Uncle Trevor, his little brother. I laughed out loud and it must have caught him off guard. He dropped his arms to the side of his body and tilted his head slightly.

"You mean Hank?" I chuckled. He didn't respond, just stared at me.

"Sorry Uncle Trevor, Daddy can't come out to play" I laughed again. Why the fuck am I laughing right now? I mean it's a little funny that he thinks Hank is still alive, but this is not the time to be cracking jokes and laughing. Especially at a man who has me surrounded with big ass guns pointed at my head.

"Bring. Me. My. Brother" Trevor snarled from across the clearing. My delirium passed and I stopped laughing instantly and glared at the man.

"Don't worry, you'll see him soon" I taunted. He seemed to have caught on at that point. He walked a few steps closer and I could now see his tightly balled fists. The other hunters followed his lead and closed in on us too. Tobias had his teeth bared and hackles raised, he was itching to attack.

"He's dead" he said firmly, not asking me, just confirming the reality of it out loud.

"He got what he deserved" I spat, disgusted at the thought that anyone could love Hank. The all so familiar warmth began to spread through my body as my rage increased.

"You'll pay for that, dog" he snarled. Pure hatred was wrapped around his words. A smile pulled at my lips at the sound of his threat.

"We'll see" I said confidently. The fire in my stomach was ready to be released. I was ready to be released. To unleash a world of pain on him, on all of them.

Trevor waved his hand to his shoulder and the hunters fired at as from all directions. Small canisters landed on the ground close to our feet, purple gas seeped from the cans with a hiss. One of them landed between the legs of one of the fighters. He snarled and wheezed and fell to the ground, changing back to his human form. Tobias growled and stepped towards him, but I quickly lifted my hands, pulling up my force field. Tobias was behind the wall with me, but the other fighters began to attack at the sight of their fallen pack mate. They had moved out of the way before they too were entrapped inside my safety barrier.

One by one the fighters were engulfed in the smoke before they too fell to the ground, back in their human form. I watched on helplessly as the hunters pulled the half-conscious men from the ground and dragged them to a kneeling position in front of me. A small white spark lit up on the wall of the force field. I hadn't noticed that Trevor had come close enough to touch the shield wall. He encircled Tobias and I, running his hand along the invisible wall. His mouth was moving, like he was talking, but I couldn't hear a word from him. Weird. I looked around at Tobias and he was watching Trevor closely.

Can you hear him?

Barely

I can't hear a thing

It must be this wall thing you put up

I felt a jolt of electricity and snapped my head back to Trevor. He was banging his fist against my force field. What an idiot, how weak does he think I am? If Gunner can't get through it, then this dumb hunter stands no chance. I smirked at the man and his face reddened with anger. He took out a handgun from his belt and pointed it at me. Tobias growled and stepped in front of me. I flinched as he fired the weapon. I felt another burst of electricity, but that was all. The bullet didn't penetrate the barrier. I let out a laugh and looked at Trevor. I could almost see the steam coming out of his ears.

It's bulletproof
You didn't know this before?
Tobias snapped his head around to me and glared at me with his piercing black eyes.
I haven't exactly had time to test all my powers
He huffed and turned back to Trevor.
Oh Goddess
Trevor glared at me as he stepped back away from us, I could see the veins in his forehead ready to pop. He gave a crooked smirk and waved his hand to his shoulder again. The wall lit up in little white lights. I could hear a muffled hum sound as my skin was crawling with sparks. I looked around and realised the hunters had unleashed their full firepower on my force field. Not a single bullet broke through, it was impenetrable. I locked my eyes back on Trevor and watched as he slowly stalked along behind his men, stopping in front of the kneeling fighters. Oh god the fighters, they weren't shielded.

The four men sat on their knees, completely naked I might add, each with a hunter pressing a knife to their throats. I growled at the sight, my lips curling back over my teeth. Trevor smirked and his mouth moved, saying something that I still couldn't hear. The lights on the shield and the electric shocks on my skin stopped. Trevor's mouth began to move again, how has this dickhead still not figured out that I can't hear him. I let out a frustrated breath and tilted my head at him.

Tobias, will you ask one of your men to tell this idiot that we can't hear him
Trevor's head spun around to look at the fighter on the far right, he stomped towards him and collided the back of his hand across the fighter's face. Tobias and I both growled angrily.
Max said he wants us to put it down
I glared at Trevor and shook my head, overmouthing the word 'No' to him. He smirked and spoke over his shoulder to one of the hunters. That hunter grabbed the fighter Max by his hair and lifted his head up. He pressed the knife hard against Max's throat, and a small trail of blood trickled down his neck. My anger boiled over and that cold feeling of darkness engulfed me once again. As the icy darkness grasped hold of my heart, I felt a wave of energy flow out of me. I flung my arm out towards the hunter holding Max, sending him flying backward across the

clearing. Trevor watched the hunter hit the ground and turned back to glower at me. He tried to hide the fear from his face, but his eyes gave it away. He waved his hand and the gunfire rained down on the force field once again.

I am going to rip this piece of shit hunter to pieces, and I'll enjoy every second of it.

I threw forward my arm sending another hunter flying through the air. Tobias growled and snapped at the hunters, the heated fury coming from his body was only increasing my own anger. I was about to go for another hunter went I felt a presence in the clearing. A blur of dark grey fur ran into view and headed toward the fighters. Tobias's head lifted and turned to the wolf and his ears pricked up, he knows this wolf. The wolf lunged at a hunter and ripped his head clean off before grabbing hold of the next one. A muffled sound echoed over the humming gunfire and I searched for its source. My eyes landed on a sight that filled me with pride and lust.

Gunner's knees wrapped around the hunter's head as he gracefully threw his body through the air, landing in a crouching position. My eyes snapped to the hunter in front of him, pointing his gun at Gunner's face. I felt my skin burst into flames of rage and my heart exploded inside me, I lifted off the ground ready to unleash hell on these monsters. I reached for the hunter with my power, lifting him into the air. I tensed and turned my fingers, compacting his body in on itself. I let his broken and twisted body fall to the ground in front of Gunner. He turned to look at me and our eyes connected for a moment, his eyes flickered with a silver glow before he turned back to the hunter ahead of him.

The gunfire against the force field died down until it was only misfires or random shots lighting it up. The dark grey wolf I saw attack the hunters had freed the other fighters, drawing the hunter's attention to them now. Tobias barged against the shield wall, hitting it with his shoulder.

Let me out Zelena

Tobias growled angrily through the flash.

I let down the wall and my ears were ravaged by the sounds of dying screams and gunfire. I flinched at the sudden intrusion. Tobias took off and tackled the closest hunter, sinking his teeth deep into the hunter's side. With a vigorous shake of his head, the body of the hunter tore in half. I turned my focus back to Gunner.

He was clearly a skilled and strong fighter, even in his human form. But there were still too many hunters. I flung my arm at the closest one to him, sending the hunter flying back towards the wall of a cabin. The next two I lifted high into the sky and pulled them back down to the ground at impossible speed. I quickly remembered the traps around the village. I sent two hunters flying toward the giant hole filled with spikes. Another one I pushed into the line of fire from a flame thrower. His feet landed on the weight pad, initiating the flames pouring down on him.

"Tobias Stop" I heard Gunner yell. I looked to Tobias who had Trevor pinned beneath him. I brought my feet back to the ground and stepped towards them.

Not him, Tobias, not yet

I want his blood

You'll have it, just not yet

"I want that one alive" Gunner demanded. Tobias leaned down and snapped his teeth at Trevor's face. He lifted his bloody paw off Trevor's chest and came back to stand beside me.

He will die, I assured him.

Agreed

Tobias huffed and growled gesturing to two of his wolves to step forward. They changed into their human form and pulled Trevor to his feet. We waited for a few minutes as Gunner flashed with the rest of the pack. After a moment, Gunner slowly turned to glare at Trevor. An aura of red hot fury ran off him in waves as he stalked forward, releasing a rumbling growl.

"Why did you come here?" Gunner boomed.

"You know why" Trevor replied sarcastically,

"Why do you want the Triple Goddess?" he demanded. Trevor didn't answer, he just smiled arrogantly. Gunner threw back his fist and crashed it into the side of Trevor's face.

"Answer me" he growled. Trevor glanced at me and winked, spitting blood from his mouth. That cocky bastard. He looked back to Gunner and smirked. Gunner leaned forward and growled at him loudly. This isn't going to work, he won't talk.

"Gunner" I called to him, but he held his hand out for me to be quiet. Is he for fucking real right now? Silencing me like that. My anger again began to bubble over. Tobias pressed his body against my shoulder, and I cooled down instantly.

Thank you

He huffed in response.

"Talk hunter" Gunner roared.

"Her power can destroy your filthy kind. Her line can end you all" Trevor revealed with a hatred lacing his tone. Ah shit, Gunner is going to rip his head off now I thought. But instead, he laughed. What the heck?

"You don't know her at all" he chuckled and took a breath.

"She is a werewolf, she is our family. You thought you could turn her into one of you, turn her against her own kind" he bent over laughing hysterically. Oh god, I think he has lost his mind. Maybe he hit his head. I filled with worry, but his laugh was a little contagious, causing me to blurt out a small giggle.

"Babe, are you alright?" I asked trying to stifle my own laugh.

Gunner turned to look at me and his cheerful face dropped. His brows furrowed together, and his lips pursed into a thin line. His eyes flickered silver before he looked back to Trevor and a wave of his anger washed over me. Gunner's anger. He stepped up to Trevor, taking his head in his hands.

"She will never be your weapon" he snarled softly, the venom in his voice was evident. I heard the snap of bone and Trevor's body fell to the ground with a thump. He was dead. Tobias growled lowly, sending shivers down my body. Before I could look away from Trevor's lifeless body, I was pulled into Gunner's arms. I snaked my arms around his back and pressed my face into his chest. He's okay, my Gunner is okay. I lifted my head to gaze at him. He had blood covering the entire left side of his face,

"You're bleeding" I hissed as I forcefully grabbed his chin, turning his head so I could inspect his wounds. My eyes fell on his ear, or what was left of it. The top half of it was now missing, leaving behind a burned and bloody mess.

"Your ear, Gunner" I gasped as I let him go. Oh, my sweet Gunner.

"I'm okay Zee, don't panic" he said softly, his voice sounding like smooth velvet, though there was a tinge of pain behind it. I looked over his chest and abdomen and I noticed more blood on his shoulder. I inspected more closely and found a bloodied hole in his upper arm. A bullet hole. My chest tightened and my skin prickled, they shot my Mate. My body started to ache and the urge to wolf out and kill everything around me was pulling at my bones. I swallowed hard, trying to fight against the change.

"They shot you" I growled in a low husky voice. There was no denying it, the change was happening. My body began to shake as my skin heated up. I am going to hunt down every last remaining hunter and tear them to shreds. I stared into Gunner's eyes and the flicker of bright silver tried to shine through. His eyes glow now? They tried to kill him. Those heinous hunters came here, to MY territory, endangering MY pack members and shot MY mate. I will end every hunter clan there is in this world and the next if it's the last thing I do. Just as I was about to give in and snap my bones, Gunner's lips crashed against mine. He pulled me tighter into his body, hardening his kiss and forcing his tongue into my mouth. Mm, 'my Gunner' I groaned inwardly as I returned his kiss eagerly. I forgot my rage and murderous thoughts, they melted away at the feel of Gunner's delicious lips. After a minute, he pulled away and gazed down at me. I suddenly felt breathless and full of lust. I wanted nothing more than to rip his clothes off and have his throbbing cock buried deep inside me. "I'm okay Zelena, I need you to stay calm" he said smoothly pressing his forehead against mine.

"I'm sorry" I whispered, coming back to myself a little more.

"Don't be sorry my love, just try and keep your cool, okay?".

"Okay" I replied, letting go of my desire and rage, for now at least.

"Is it over?" I asked peering into his eyes.

"It's over" he nodded.

"How many are injured?"

"I don't know yet, we have to wait for a full report from the commanders". I nodded as I looked around us. The sounds of gunshots had all but ended. Random shots sounded every few seconds, slowly becoming less and less. Tobias stayed in his wolf form, pacing closely off to the side. His men were standing together, talking in hushed whispers.

"Dad has been hurt though, he's alive, but it's bad apparently" Gunner said, recapturing my attention. My stomach tightened and I stiffened. Looking away from him, I tried to swallow the lump in my throat. Even though Lupus isn't my father, since we shared that sweet moment at dinner on the night we met, I have come to care for him as my own. He has already done so much for me, more than my pretend father ever did.

"Oh Gunner, I'm so..."

A single shot echoed through the air, slicing the eery quiet of the aftermath. I felt a dull pain in my back and then an intense burning sensation. I gasped but couldn't get a full breath. A searing pain shot through my body and my legs fell out from under me. I fell limp in Gunner's arms. I wanted to scream but I couldn't make a sound. The pain was unlike anything I had ever experienced. I could no longer feel my legs and the sheer agony coursing through my body was constricting my ability to breathe. I looked up to Gunner's face, his mouth was moving in panic, but his words were silent to my ears. His eyes again shone with a magnificent silver glow. My body felt like it was floating on water, completely weightless. Darkness threatened to take my vision as my eyes began to cloud over. I reached up and cupped my hand to Gunner's cheek, if his face was the last thing that I saw, then I would die happy.

A pained howl rang out all around me and I was swallowed by the darkness.

Epilogue

Gunner

It's been three months now since the battle. Three months of helplessness and pain. Everyone is telling me to keep pushing on and to throw my all into leading the pack. But it's hard, and it's getting harder each day. Cole has been great with the pack, helping where he can. I appreciate everything he is doing but it's just not right. I thought that I would have Zee beside me, helping me. I thought we were going to do this together.

We lost thirty-six wolves in total. Two from Blue Moon and one from Crescent Wolf. A group service was arranged to bury our dead and a huge black marble boulder was brought in to hold a memorial placard. Mum and some other she-wolves arrange a garden area and small benches to surround the boulder, making a nice area to sit and mourn. I haven't had the strength to go there yet, but I can see it through the trees from my office window. I find myself often staring at it mindlessly.

Alpha Titus of Crescent Wolf was killed in the attack on their pack village, along with the Beta and two thirds of their pack. Their Alpha-Son is only eight years old and not ready to lead. So, after they buried their dead the remaining pack members came to live with us at Tri-Moon. It was the least that I could do to help them, after all the hunters weren't even after them. The Luna Lucile made sure that I understood their stay would only be temporary. She wants to rebuild their village and start fresh. I admire her strength and resilience, even though anyone can see that she is deeply hurting. I will help them, in every way I can. I have started to take the Alpha-Son Frendrick under my wing and continue his teachings on the ways of an Alpha. He's resistant at times, but he's still dealing with the loss of his father.

Tobias has been hard to get rid of. He basically lives here now, even though he has a pack of his own to run. Much to my dismay, Mum set him up with his own room in the pack house. His brother and Beta, Marius, has been running things for him back at Blue Moon. Turns out that Marius was the dark grey wolf that I fought beside in the battle. He's a great guy, a little full of himself, but really loyal and kind. Even though I've been a disaster to be around, we've actually become good friends since the battle.

Unfortunately, this battle was no small event. The news of the hunter's attack on our pack, the Crescent Wolf pack, and three more packs in the Eastern Canadian regions during their search for Zelena, has begun to travel far and wide. With the news of the hunters, goes the story of the Triple Goddess and her Ture Mate. Although most packs hear the story and think of it as nothing more than a made up or over-exaggerated tale, other packs know differently. The true believers among the were-kind are taking notice, and it can only lead to more dangers.

Sitting at my desk, I realised that I could smell myself, it's been a few days since I last showered. I must do something about that before I head to the hospital. I packed up some paperwork and left my office to head upstairs. Zelena's scent still clung to the air in the bedroom, the bed, and her pillow held it the strongest. I haven't been able to sleep in the bed, I don't want to risk the scent leaving. I walked to the bathroom and pulled off my shirt, discarding it on the floor. I studied my reflection in the mirror, my dead eyes were encircled by large purple bags. My skin is pale and I'm looking a little thinner these days. Everything has been a struggle, not just sleeping but eating and training too.

I washed off quickly and towelled my body dry. After pulling on a pair of jeans and a black t-shirt, I walked to the edge of the bed. I picked up Zelena's pillow and pressed my nose against it, inhaling deeply. Her scent filled my nose and sent tingling through my chest. I placed it back down carefully on the bed and wiped away the tear that had made its way down my cheek.

When I pulled up at the hospital carpark, I spotted a young couple walking to their car carrying a bundle in a small pink blanket. My heart tightened at seeing how happy and full of joy their faces were. A vision of Zelena smiling down at a little baby girl with bright blue eyes and raven black hair, popped into my mind. I smiled to myself picturing how unbearably beautiful our own children could be. I would be tightly wrapped around the finger of my baby girl, giving her everything she could ever want. Our son would be proud and strong and protective of his sister, a spitting image of myself. The possibilities turned to ash in my mouth. I rested my head against my hands and let out a sob. After a few minutes, I wiped the tears away and straightened myself up, time to be strong.

I headed through the hospital doors and took the elevator to the fifth floor. I walked down the hallway to the door of the room. I took a deep breath before twisting the door handle.

"Gunner, Baby" my mum's voice cooed.

"Hi Mum" I answered her.

"You're too thin my boy, have you eaten today?" she fussed, brushing my long hair off my face.

"I'm fine Mum" I told her, pushing her hands away.

"Hey Dad" I smiled walking to the side of the bed.

"How are you, boy? Your mum's right you look terrible" he grunted at me.

"Thanks, Dad" I mumbled, bending over the bed.

"Hello, my little wolf" I whispered, placing a gentle kiss on Zelena's clammy cheek.

"Any news?" I asked standing up again.

"Nothing Baby. Same as yesterday" Mum answered my question. Zelena's wound has completely healed, it healed in just eleven days, but she has remained in a coma since the night of the battle. No one can explain it. No one knows why she hasn't woken up. I'm not giving up hope, I never will. There are hard days and easier days, but I still visit her every day. I talk to her, telling her stories about our history and filling her in on what is going on in the pack.

Tobias comes by just as regularly. I didn't like it at first and we had a few fights over it, my jealousy and protective nature got the best of me. I have come to accept that his feelings for her are strictly platonic, well at least they are now. He did admit that before he found out that we were True Mates, he thought the Goddess may have sent him to her to become her Mate and not just her Guardian. But not anymore, luckily for him.

Dad stood up and gave me his chair by the hospital bed. He was now sporting a scar down the side of his face from a knife wound. He took one hell of a beating during the battle. He took out more than twenty hunters on his own after they cut him off from the other wolves. He was shot three times and had multiple stab wounds, but he still managed to rip those assholes to pieces, and come out of it alive.

"We're just going down to the cafeteria for a coffee, do you want anything?" Mum asked as her and Dad headed for the door.

"No, thanks, I'm good" I answered.

I sat down and took Zelena's hand in mine, gently stroking the back of her hand with my thumb. I blabbered on about Frendrick and his defiant nature, and his sister Freya's crush on Smith. After a while, I rested my head on Zelena's hand and unintentionally drifted off to sleep.

~

Her body collapsed in my arms and her eyes glowed a bright yellow. "Kill that fuck" I shouted, but Tobias had already leaped on top of the crippled hunter, tearing his head from his body. "Zelena, Zelena, you're okay. It'll be okay" I said to her, but my voice broke, and tears welled in my eyes. I pulled my hand out from her back and looked it over, her blood was dripping off my fingers. "Oh, Goddess no. Zee, it's okay. You're going to be okay" I pulled her tighter into my arms and I could feel her warm blood dripping onto my legs. "Someone get Artemis" I shouted. Pain coursed through my body. It was unbearable. I could feel my insides tearing itself apart. Zelena lifted her hand and shakily placed it on my cheek. A weak smile pulled at her lips as her glowing yellow eyes began to flicker. My chest tightened and I couldn't suck in a breath. Her hand dropped from my cheek and her head tipped back. The glow of her eyes faded as her lids slowly closed. I threw my head back and howled an excruciating cry of sorrow.

~

I threw my body up off the bed gasping for air. I snapped my head from side to side, looking around me to try and get my bearings. A frown marred my forehead, I was still in the hospital room. I breathed out heavily and leaned over resting my hands on my knees. Fucking hell. I took slow, deep breaths, attempting to steady my heart rate. Just another nightmare. The same one I have had every day for the last three months. As I listened to my heart rate slow, a sound caught my attention. A sound that shouldn't be in here. A strong and racing heartbeat. I stood up straight and scanned the room, searching for the source. My eyes fell on the bed, on my still Mate. As I raked them over her peaceful body, I halted at her face. I rubbed my eyes and stared at her dumbfounded. Two open golden eyes stared back at me. She's awake.

"Hi handsome" Zelena smiled.

Zelena's story does not end here.

Continue reading for a sneak preview of

Part 2

A Time

Of

Delicate Hope

Lunaya

I flew upright, panting heavily, I clutched my chest and looked around the dark space. My eyes slowly adjusted, and the realisation gradually came back to me, it was just a dream. My tired eyes scanned around the dimly lit cave, the fire just barely alive with a few slow burning embers. Alyse was still asleep in her sleeping bag, curled up into a ball, close to the fire. The entrance of the cave was dark with only the pale glow of the moonlight shining on the ground. I begrudgingly got up out of my sleeping bag and traipsed over to the opening of the cave. I looked out over the trees in front of me, scanning for any signs of life or danger. The ground was splattered with patches of white snow. We will need to find a proper shelter soon, or we will freeze to death in this cave. I shivered as an icy wind brushed against my cheeks. The weather is turning fast. I tiptoed back to the fire and placed two more logs over the embers. Stoking the fire with a stick, the flames started to engulf the new wood, and my cold skin eagerly welcomed the heat.

I lay back down, tucking myself into my worn-out sleeping bag and rested my head on my arm. I stared blankly at the flames licking at the logs, as my mind began to replay the dream again.

Red stained the snow covered ground. The space before me was littered with the bodies of my pack. The air was filled with the stench of blood and gunpowder. The dying howl of my Alpha ripped into my already aching heart. Dead, all of them. My entire pack, slaughtered. And it was all my fault. A tear escaped my eye, and I winced as I could once again feel the pain that day had brought me. There was only one thing that the Goddess entrusted me with, and I failed the task. I failed her, I failed myself. Above all, I failed that sweet little girl. I wanted so much to die along with my pack, it was the least that I deserved. I would have gotten my wish if it weren't for Alyse.

Ahh, Alyse, my only companion. We've been together now for near on seventeen years. I still don't know if she saved me from death, or, subjected me to a lifetime of guilt and suffering at the hands of the never-ending replay of my torturous memories. Either way, I am still thankful to have her. She found my broken and bloodied body in the aftermath of the massacre and for some reason took pity on me, nursing me back to health. She says that if it weren't for the snow slowing my heart, I would have bled to death before she found me. I still don't know what compelled her to save my life, she may never tell me. I felt my body start to drift back off to sleep and I prayed to the Goddess to spare me the pain from my nightmares.

"Lunaya, wake up".

I felt my body being rocked back and forth, shaking me awake.

"Come on, you need to get up now".

I forced opened my eyes and found Alyse's green eyes looking down at me. Her chocolate brown hair was tied in a messy bun on top of her head. Her skin was spotted with dirt and grime, and she had a smudge of ash from the fire across her cheek. Living the way we do, we go for long periods of time without luxuries like showers and mirrors. We have become accustomed to it over the years and have learned ways to live on the bare necessities.

I grumbled and pushed her hands off me, sitting up and rubbing my tired eyes.

"You couldn't give me five more minutes?" I moaned.

"The sun has already been up for a while, you never sleep this late" she snapped back, she paused and looked over my face.

"Are you okay?" she asked her voice softening slightly.

"Yeah, just another sleepless night" I said stretching my arms out above my head.

"More nightmares?"

"Yep"

"The same one?"

"As always"

"Hmm" she hummed as she watched me crawl out of my sleeping bag and begin to roll it up.

"They've been coming more and more often these past few months" she said softly.

"Yeah, I know"

"Is there something bothering you?"

"Nothing new, come on we have to get moving" I said brushing of her question, I don't want to talk about it. Simple as that. Alyse already covered up the fire and had her small, tattered backpack packed and ready to go. She turned her head over her shoulder slowly and huffed heavily.

"We don't have to leave just yet you know, we still have a few more days until the snow settles" she said sheepishly, looking over at me. I groaned internally. we have already had this argument a bunch of times. I puffed out a frustrated breath,

"I've already told you, I don't want to wait until the snow sticks. We have to find the Luna Eclipse pack before we freeze to death" I grumbled.

"Ugh whatever, how do you even know they're out here" she groaned standing up and flinging her bag over her shoulder.

It's true, I have only ever heard stories of Luna Eclipse, the only all-female pack in the entire world. But the legends have been told for generations. The stories of their triumphs over their enemies and their great battles and victories, they are known worldwide. Because of their female only law, they were seen as weak by many other packs. But those of them that tried to attack Luna Eclipse were wiped out. They may be all she-wolves, but they are highly skilled and trained warriors and could stand up against any male warrior. Throughout the centuries the stories of Luna Eclipse became just that, stories. Many forgot about them and they began to believe them to be nothing more than a myth, a scary story to tell your pups at night. But I knew better, as did my ancestors.

"Will you just trust me. Have I ever led you astray?" I huffed, placing my hands on my hips and glaring at her with a raised eyebrow.

"Weeellll..." she dragged out the word with a teasing tone. I threw my rolled up sleeping bag at her head and she caught it with a giggle.

"I trust you" she chuckled, tossing it back to me.

~

The weather turned in a blink of an eye, catching us unprepared in the middle of a snowstorm. We definitely picked a bad time of year to go hiking in the Southern Alps of New Zealand. It's the middle of winter here and this part of the mountain takes a beating. I knew we wouldn't cross paths with anybody, the tourist trails don't go up this mountain. And besides, the storm would cover over any of our tracks anyway.

We huddled together and continued to stomp through the freezing snow. The storm has been raging for maybe an hour now, the snow was already knee deep and getting deeper the further we went up the mountain. My boots were soaked through, and I could feel the icy moisture in my socks. I hope we find them soon or else my toes may fall off. The wind howled past my ears, biting at my cheeks. The sound of Alyse's teeth chattering together was almost louder than the wind.

"How f-f-far did you s-s-say" she stuttered,

"It should be here" I told her, squinting into the distance. I looked around at the trees poking out of the snow, searching for the marker. I forced my eyes to open in the cutting wind and tried hard to focus. I followed the old directions perfectly. We are near the top of the mountain, on the southern side. It has to be here. I zoned in on a peculiarly shaped tree ahead of us. After a few quick blinks I could see clearer. That's not a tree. That's it, the stone marker, we've made it.

"There it..." I was cut off by the unmistakable sound a wolfs howl. I turned towards the sound but couldn't see the source through the blizzard. Another howl came from behind us, and then another, and another, until we were surrounded. I saw movement come from behind the large stone, capturing my attention. A pure white wolf slowly came into view as it stalked towards us. Like a predator stalking its prey. The wolf bared its teeth and growled, closing the distance between us. The wolf stood tall and proud, the power emanating off it was dizzying. When it snarled viciously through its exposed fangs, my body erupted with frightful nerves. We may have just made a huge mistake.

www.ingramcontent.com/pod-product-compliance
Lightning Source LLC
Chambersburg PA
CBHW051317190726
48290CB00001B/192